*Jack Cluewitt and the
Imbrium Basin Murders*

Jack Cluewitt
and the
Imbrium Basin Murders

by

Ruth J. Burroughs

Gypsy Shadow Publishing

Jack Cluewitt and the Imbrium Basin
Murders
by
Ruth J. Burroughs

All rights reserved
Copyright © February 4, 2014, Ruth J. Burroughs
Cover Art Copyright © 2014, Charlotte Holley

Gypsy Shadow Publishing, LLC.
Lockhart, TX
www.gypsyshadow.com

Names, characters and incidents depicted in this book are
products of the author's imagination, or are used ficti-
tiously. Any resemblance to actual events, locales, organi-
zations, or persons, living or dead, is entirely coincidental
and beyond the intent of the author or the publisher.

No part of this book may be reproduced or shared by any
electronic or mechanical means, including but not limited
to printing, file sharing, and email, without prior written
permission from Gypsy Shadow Publishing, LLC.

Library of Congress Control Number: 2016950812

eBook ISBN: 978-1-61950-191-1
Print ISBN: 978-1-61950-192-8

Published in the United States of America

First eBook Edition: August 3, 2014
First Print Edition: August 12, 2016

Dedication

This book is dedicated to Dr. Geoffrey A. Landis for the Water, Chuck Thomas and Lou Esposito for caring, and the folks at Computer Sciences Corporation and Cornell Information Technologies, and Charlotte for believing and Denise, my editor who pushed me to make the book the best it could be: and my Carpe Libris gals, and all the people who supported and encouraged me to finish. Jack Cluewitt is also dedicated to the Ithaca Fire Department and all first responders.

Acknowledgements

This book couldn't have been written without the help and support of my editor, Denise and the hard work of my publishers Charlotte and Denise. I'd like to thank Geoff again, and Kent Brewster's Speculation's Rumor Millers and Carpe Libris. That said, any scientific errors are entirely my own.

Jack Weiss-Monaghan
Prologue

Ithaca Space Habitat
Jack's fifth Grid Day

Five-year-old Jack Monaghan screamed; shards of hot metal and flames seared his face and hands; he gripped his new toys, a howling robot dog and a gold toy cop badge. One minute he was having a birthday party, in the Hub of Ithaca Space Station near the Asteroids' boundary, and the next he was on fire. Debris and hot metal shot out from the walls, along with more explosions. Jack's presents, cake and juice floated up into the capacious interior, along with his friends and family. Pressurization plummeted with the hull breach; cold air blasted in through the vents. The acrid smell of outer space brought the caustic aroma of airless doom. In a room that looked like the inside of a soccer ball crisscrossed with jungle-gym-like bars, the walls covered in rungs, they heard the dull and distant sound of explosions.

Today was the day Jack was old enough to be able to connect virtually to the Grid, the Internet of space that connected into thousands of orbiting satellites from Mercury to Saturn. Then he could communicate with his mom and dad, family and friends, and especially, Zero-One, his robot puppy, without talking out loud. He'd get a chip inserted into his occipital lobe above the c1 atlas vertebra in his neck. Then he could plug into the computer systems and pilot his own ships or learn any language, without having to read or study. He would be cybernetically upgraded and so he would never feel left out or slow to understand the physics of space and any other number of complicated subjects.

Zero-One, his robot dog, howled in pain. Jack screamed and coughed. His mother, Space Junk artist, Weather

Weiss, and his father, Earthside homicide detective, Ruad-erick Monaghan, raced to his side. Ruad doused the flames and Weather placed pain patches she'd nabbed from the first aid kit on the right side of his face as they floated in the microgravity. Near the blast holes, Ithacans bounced and banged, some clinging to the bars, others disappear-ing—sucked out by the vacuum—and then the powerful suction reached Jack's family, dragging them toward the jagged teeth of ripped metal walls. They slammed against the bars, Ruad's red curly hair whipped in the vortex of depressurization, his blue eyes looking intently at his son's injured face as they clung tightly to the bars. Weather's curly hair lashed her face, blinding her efforts to see her husband and only child.

"Hush, Zero-One," Ruad said to Jack's barking puppy robot.

Weather moved closer and touched Jack on the face. "Be strong, son," she said. Jack nodded, his lips trembling in the cold as he held on tightly in the blasting wind stream as air was sucked out into the vacuum of space. Ruad turned to her and yelled, "Follow me to the exit. We need an escape pod before they're all gone."

Using Ruad's old raincoat, she tied Jack to her hus-band to make sure her son was secure. The rungs covered all the walls and exits for exercise and in the event the ves-sel lost centrifugal force and pseudo-gravity. Ruad grabbed the rungs and climbed toward one of the exits; Jack se-curely tied to his chest, Weather close behind as they strug-gled against the rip tide of escaping air, inches from death should they let go.

The trio came to a sudden halt, their escape blocked by two pregnant women struggling to find a foothold in the Micro-Gravity-as they fought over a large-sized spacesuit made especially for late-stage-pregnant women.

Cross-dresser and Corporation tool and assassin, Vin-ny *the Waltz* Walskiwhitz would make the deaths look like a terrorist incident or mining accident because he was that good. Everyone knew he could dance circles around the best of his league, not just in Martial Arts but in classical dance, ballet and, yes, waltzing. No one knew he was also a musician of sorts, as it was his best kept secret, but he also played recorder in a Renaissance band, albeit incognito. He had to make sure the Green candidates were good and dead, even if it meant there'd be collateral damage. He had to protect Corporation Party's monopoly on Space Water. From the deck of the poorly disguised Corporation pinwheel ramjet, he could see in real-time the colossal Ithaca Space Mining colony vessel, housing 150,000 miners and their children; at its inception in 4099 a Stanford Torus, the station evolved into a Bernal Sphere and then its current shape, the soccer-ball-shaped Buckminster Fullerene. And Vinny was going to kick it. Its amorphous metal hide was as thin as paper and only prevented space junk when the plasma shield was on and it wasn't on now because the Green Candidates had just boarded, their battalion of thousands; Green pinwheel ramjets listing in orbit around the spinning behemoth. He had to shoot before the Green Mothership, a hippy lotus-shaped spacecraft a quarter the size of the Fullerene, discovered him, but locating Naturals was next to impossible. They didn't carry phones or have microchips imbedded into their occipital lobes to communicate with the Orbitals' Internet Grid. Naturals were like the Amish of space. *Damned Luddites,* Vinny thought, h*ard to find, and hard to bribe . . . and hard to kill.* Fortunately he wasn't the only poorly disguised Corporation ramjet hiding in plain sight, there were hundreds just like his, and they didn't mind his taking out the pansy Green party ramjets or the Green Party lotus Mothership either.

He jacked a dime-sized plug into the back of his head; a wireless connection into the noisy Grid. Why calculate the trajectory when the Grid's satellites' specs could do it for him? It gave him the time and location of when the Green candidates had boarded and almost exactly where they'd be in the hub.

He steered his space craft from a motorcycle-like seat, pressing handle bars and foot petals to maneuver and using the Grid's calculations and real-time holographs of his geometrical specs; he aimed one of the pinwheel ramjet's heads toward the Ithaca Space Hab; with his illegal gun. If his first shot didn't kill Green Candidate, Antonia G. Clef, he'd let the AI system do it for him automatically. He pulled the trigger. The Grid translated back to him what was happening and he watched as the bullet tore a hole into the thin skin of the hull, the lack of atmosphere had doubled, if not tripled its impact. It tore through metal walls, including the old Stanford Torus' hub's wall and hit the Green Candidate in her stomach.

Vinny was about to tell his Corporation financer, Henri Vasquez, to break open the champagne when he saw a breach in the Ithaca Space Habitat hull. Something inside exploded. The bullet had passed through a tank of liquid oxygen.

✖

"Who else would attack peaceful colonists but my opponent in the Corporation Party, Felix Fortuna?" said the very bloody American Space, Green Party Presidential Candidate Antonia G. Clef. She clung to a rung, dying, her mike still working, her words broadcast to the colonists within the ship.

Antonia would never kiss another baby and this was her final speech. Cameras were running, uploading to a dead satellite, but no one among them knew the sat was dead.

Detectives, cops, miners, freighters, artists and pirates from all over the Flora Asteroids group were gathered together for this special day, Jack Monaghan's birthday. Out here in the poorer colonies, you didn't need a license to be a parent. Jack came into the world naturally, born near the hub, in the birthing center of the Ithaca Space Hab.

"My dear friends, you mine the piddling minerals from the Flora Asteroids with little pay from the Corporation. Collateral deaths are of no importance to them. All I ask is that you make . . . them . . . pay . . . dearly." Antonia's words came in short staccato pants, her voice raspy and soft; the cold mist from her breath hovering as a vapor. Beside her lay co-chair Máóhk-Clay, severely injured and partially-blinded. Haze, Jack's uncle, ran over with a med kit, but Antonia insisted he help Máóhk-Clay, since she herself was dying. He threw nano-glue-patches onto Máóhk-Clay's shattered legs to stop the bleeding. Struggling to rise, she screamed. He held her still and jabbed painkillers into her legs.

Máóhk-Clay clasped Antonia's hand and held it for a moment. She spoke to her dying friend in low tones. "This is asteroid territory. The Corporation Party will try to cover it up and claim it was another mining accident, but I will bring this to light, I promise."

"No, Máóhk-Clay. Go, and forget this. Hide, my friend. All of you are better off pretending you're dead. I know these men and if they would stoop to this . . . You'll have to find another way to bring the Green Party back to power. Promise me you will hide to fight another day."

Máóhk-Clay agreed reluctantly. Most of the other miners were on the run and in hiding anyway. Antonia gasped her last breath.

In silence, Uncle Haze carried Máóhk-Clay up the rung ladders to one of the escape pods; he settled her into one and drove out of the crippled Ithaca Space Habitat into the swarm of thousands of other escape vehicles abandoning the behemoth. Battalions of the poorly disguised Corporation rocket ships descended onto the escape pods firing on them or boarding them and taking prisoners.

✖

Vinny and his cohorts had already destroyed the Green Party lotus Mothership, leaving it venting oxygen, and disabling or destroying the smaller pinwheel ramjets. But the explosions doubled in the Ithaca Space Hab and metal and hot debris flew out along with the thousands of escape pods, sending the huge vessel spinning toward Earth.

✖

Inside their own escape pod, Ruad sweated at the controls, riding out a thruster burst, driving the motorcycle-like controls in his Harley leather saddle seat. Maneuvering into the asteroids to avoid the many Corporation ships chasing the Ithaca Space Habitat's escaping pods he steered around the asteroids, using the handlebars and the 3D Sensurround screens to navigate. Jack screamed, still in pain. His mom tied him down and then applied more painkiller

Jack Cluewitt and the Imbrium Basin Murders   Ruth J. Burroughs

nano-patches to Jack's face where he'd been burned by hot metal.

Immediately he stopped screaming. He relaxed his grip on his puppybot. Zero-One whimpered, shivering in Jack's lap. Weather applied nano-patches to the pup's burned skin and he licked her hand. Jack giggled, tears drying on his face.

Feeling better, Jack moved into one of the pony-saddle seats that faced out of one of the plasma-shielded port-holes, playing with his toy laser gun and shooting at the bad guys to help his mom and dad. His mother smiled and shook her head. *Children bounce back so quickly.*

"Have they located us?" Weather's black ringlets fanned out around her face as she pulled herself over to Ruad, running her hand through her Irish husband's red hair. He looked up at her with his Earthly-sky blue eyes; fear and worry etched lines around them. He rode the motorcycle-handlebar controls, steering the vehicle through the maze of asteroids.

"Nae, nah' yet. But a few are gaining on us. There are too many of them. They'll overpower us soon. We've got to hide in this Cluster of Stones." His voice rang with a deep Gaelic lilt. "We can't be caught, Weather. The information we have is too important. The Green candidates are dead. Well, one of them is. Antonia. Uncle Haze rescued Máóhk-Clay. Why would Green Party jets shoot down their own candidate?"

"Look at the images, Ruad. Those aren't Green Party pinwheel ramjets."

Ruad shook his head and fired the thrusters, dodging between the asteroids to get as far away from the disguised Corporation ships as possible. Their Green Party sigs had been painted on quickly and magnified, looked fake, and the attack which led to the successful assassination of the Green candidate had backfired. The explosion was so large it had blown back on many of their own ships.

"I'm trying to send images of this back home, but the communications satellites have been sabotaged," Ruad said.

"Try bouncing a message off the sats toward Peg Cardillo's ships near Jupiter," Weather said. Ruad used the momentum of the explosion to speed the small craft toward the Asteroid Ring. Behind them, the receding image of the Ithaca Space Habitat, three gaping holes staring out of its soccer ball-shaped hull, filled the rear viewport.

A female voice issued from the speakers. "This is Peg. I got your message about the bastards blasting a hole in the Ithaca Space Habitat. They better keep it from hitting the Earth-Moon system. I'm on the way there to rescue you. I'm closer than you thought. My ship caught your message broadcast from local sats. We'll meet at asteroid 253 Mathilde in nine or ten hours unless the Corporation ships delay us; we may be late but we will find you. I promise. Peg, out."

"At least it hasn't broken into pieces. Hopefully, the International Space Corporation or someone on board will prevent a greater disaster, and steer it away from Earth," Weather said. Ruad nodded in agreement. He maneuvered their escape pod through the maze of rocks to asteroid 253 Mathilde.

Weather pushed some buttons on the panel, focusing the external camera on the surface of the asteroid—it was still in the same half-carved state she'd left it in last time she'd worked on it.

The last time: before Jack was born, and before she'd met her Irish husband, Ruad Monaghan.

An enormous Spider-shaped spaceship floated alongside asteroid 253 Mathilde, in the Asteroid belt. Spider: the standard name for working robot ships, creating catcher webs to trap space junk, building anything from large habitats to small ships, repairing vehicles, or, as in this case, carving asteroids into sculptures. Amorphous metallic nano-fiber shot out from her Spider-shaped vehicle sticking to the asteroid and reeled it in; its spider-like appendages captured the asteroid; space-junk artist, Weather Weiss, then carved the rock surface, shaping it into a huge replica of a Haniwa Dynasty Horse for her wealthy Japanese Patron. Peering out through one of the windows of the Spider ship's eyes, Weather controlled the hands of the robot ship. The extension fit her like a space suit.

... Weather worked steadily to shape the surface of the asteroid. On an otherwise normal work day, she'd noticed a shiny arc jutting from the ribs of the Haniwa equine sculpture.

Odd, shiny like metal, but she hadn't sensed any metals. She dug out the offending structure, ruining the sculpture with the gouge. The Japanese patron who'd commissioned this work would be furious about the damage and the delay.

It took half the day to dig the meter-long saucer-shaped metallic disc from the surface of asteroid 253. If her Siwen dowsing abilities were right, it was not gold, copper or aluminum; she didn't sense any alloy. In fact, examining the disc using the Spider's analysis revealed nothing related to any known element. How could that be? Confused, she wondered if she'd somehow lost her Siwen dowsing ability. When she dowsed a known metal, it called to her. This shiny substance was silent.

She cut communication with the colony: not to be disturbed, except for emergencies. She'd plucked a canister off the outer hull of the Spider with one of its robot arms and scooped up the mysterious saucer and deposited into a chute. The merganser chutes brought the disc into a secure glass-encased vacuum-sealed room. Arms encased in long gloves up to her shoulders, she handled the meter long disc, held above the floor by clawed robot hands, extending from expandable jointed metal arms from the walls. As the claws rotated the silvery disc, she studied it with wary awe, her hands protected by gloves, and a thick plate of glass placed between her and whatever billion-year old microbes gathered on the radioactive surface. She depressed a button on what she supposed was the top of the disc. She sucked in air, startled, as it opened and revealed three miniature corpses dressed in partial space suits, their helmets removed. The three were well-preserved in the vacuum of space; bodies of the dead men, about the size of Barbie dolls, wore a gold thread spearhead insignia stitched on black patches on their shoulders.

"What do those signify?" Weather asked her ship's computer, a sheepdog asteroid herding vessel named Charlotte.

Jack Cluewitt and the Imbrium Basin Murders   Ruth J. Burroughs

"Office of Strategic Services. It was the predecessor of the United States CIA," Charlotte responded.

Weather nodded. "Help me pull the bodies out of the saucer," she said. An odd thing happened when the robot hands pulled the bodies out of the saucer. The corpses grew. "Am I seeing what I think I'm seeing, Sheepdog Charlotte? Did they just tumble out of the saucer into average-sized humans?"

"No, Weather. They've actually grown longer than average-sized humans. The saucer is generating some kind of energy. I cannot tell you what kind, though. It is not detectable to my sensors."

Weather noticed two objects in the hands of one of the men. "What is that one holding?"

Charlotte's robot claws gently picked the items out of the hands and raised them up to the glass for her perusal.

"This is a black hardcover antique paper book, in fair condition. The Worlds in Space, by Martin Caidin, copyright 1954. The other resembles an ancient Chinese coin," Charlotte said and placed them in her gloved hands.

The oversized coin covered her whole hand and had a square cut out of the center, like a donut hole, only square. A dark blue, almost black substance quivered there, filling the hole.

"What is this dark matter?" Weather asked.

Charlotte rotated one of its arms and a needle slid out of its hand into the glimmering dark blue substance.

"Don't transmit anything to the Grid. Use your own encyclopedia," Weather said.

"It has the appearance of an ancient Chinese coin, a rather large one." Charlotte broke the silence, startling Weather. "But there's nothing in my data farm that can discern the strange matter."

Weather stuck her finger into the palm-sized square hole, into the black substance.

"Why is the coin so large that I can fit my hand into the square hole?" she asked the ship.

Charlotte searched her genetically engineered molecular cell drive, gem-cell brain. "The book recovered to its original size but the coin didn't."

"I'm a Siwen, a dowser of metals, and I can't sense anything either. It's pliant, and malleable—like metallic

9

dough." Curious, she pulled her glove off and touched the cold, blue surface. A bolt of fear hit her stomach. She imagined the skin on her hand being exposed to radiation—or worse, some deadly alien virus or microbe.

She touched the quivering dark blue plasma, and was hit with a cold so intense she felt the heat draining from her hand and body; a tidal force yanked her hand through the gold coin. Scared, she pulled her hand out of the square hole cut into the middle of the coin; the dark stuff popped back. Her hand was intact, clean, undamaged. The circulation and warmth returned quickly. She touched the dark substance again and put her hand through the hole, her hand disappeared. It didn't come out on the other side of the fifteen-centimeter-long coin, yet it had gone somewhere . . .

She abandoned the asteroid sculpture and ordered her asteroid sheepdog ship, Charlotte, to head out to Jovian space and find her good friend robot and spaceship engineer, Perigwin 'Peg' Cardillo. If anyone could figure out what the oversized coin was, she could . . .

✕

Weather's husband, Ruad Monaghan, steered their escape pod near an asteroid where Weather had stashed oxygen tanks. Keeping his voice down so Jack couldn't hear, he said "I think the attack was aimed primarily at Candidate Antonia. She's the only woman who could win a race for President of the American Space Commonwealth. There are no popular Green candidates left. Gull Saugerties has the radiation sickness.

"I don't think they know of your discovery, although rumors and deep-space lore abound." He was silent for a moment. "Someone must have brought rocket fuel onboard the Hab. I smelled it. It never occurred to anyone we'd be attacked."

Weather whispered, "I just don't believe the Corporation troops would fire on civilians."

"It's been six years since your discovery and it's getting harder to keep what Peg's doing a secret. It was too precise. Antonia was surgically killed with no collateral damage until the explosions from the jet fuel. It's one thing to take out

Jack Cluewitt and the Imbrium Basin Murders   Ruth J. Burroughs

a candidate but a whole space colony? Maybe they didn't want to leave witnesses. What a cluster f . . ."

"You're right, Ruad. They'll real-time-sight or catch us on radar sooner or later. Peg said she'll get to us soon, but how will she get past the Corporation ships? I left air tanks in the Flora family asteroids 43 Ariadnes, 951 Gaspra and 8 Flora, but I have no idea if they've been used. We have nine hours of oxygen attached to our space suits, but we don't have a child-size one. It will be safer for Jack if we separate. We'll have to jettison him in the cantaloper pod and lose this boat."

"We could have him float in the pod near us, Weather. We can't just abandon our son," Ruad said.

"The Corporation ships are hunting us down, Ruad. And, if Peg is late, we have to find one of the hidden portable life support systems I've stashed. I can't explain to Jack that we have to use our suit thrusters to get to another asteroid if we begin to run out of oxygen. We should jettison him through Ring of Asteroids and aim him toward the busy tourist part of the Mars to Asteroids' corridor. Someone will pick him up, and they'll never suspect a thing. Miner folk do it when they can't afford to buy water, food or oxygen for their children and rich people find them all the time."

"What about the ones they don't find? I've seen their corpses." He could not hide the look of horror on his face.

"He'll still have a better chance than he would with us on the run. I'll strip the identifiers out of Zero-One and the skiff, so no one knows who he is. I'll leave some clues, so he can find us someday when he is grown up enough to solve the mystery of who he is." Weather choked, but wouldn't cry.

"If they find the robot dog and his toy shield, they may guess. It was on holograph that the Green candidates were attending the birthday party of a miner's son."

"I have a feeling those transmissions don't get past a few sats, if any. That's the way it is out here, Ruad. Even if the bad guys get Jack, he doesn't know enough to give us away."

Ruaderick gave her a look of dread. "I don't want him raised by the Corporation."

Weather squeezed his shoulder. "But they don't know what it is I found and hopefully they never will. Once he's separated from us, no one will know who he belongs to. The skiff is programmed and has more than enough oxygen to make it to the corridor. We'll kill him if we keep him."

Ruad grabbed her, pulling her close; he spoke with heat, but not so Jack could hear. "I don't want some rich tourist raising my son either."

"They'll love him as much as we do."

He let go of her and turned away. "For God's sakes, Weather, if we jettison him in the little cantaloper he could run out of oxygen."

She grabbed his arm. "He'll have a chance if we set him through the Orbitals' Corridor with preset coordinates toward Earth."

He turned and looked into her eyes, tears welled in his and he merely nodded. She turned back toward their son.

"Jack Weiss-Monaghan, my son. I mean . . . my wise little Jack; you're going on a ride in the cantaloper. I've set it on auto thrust to get you to the Corridor where nice people live. It's a game, okay? Mommy and Daddy are going to play cowboy games with the bad guys. Okay?"

Jack nodded his head and didn't look up at his mom. He pretended to zap his laser gun.

"Okay, Mom. We'll be together forever. You always say happiest family, by Jove. I'll protect you and Dad from the bad guys with my laser gun. Don't be a scared."

"You do that from the cantaloper, my brave boy. After one hour, use the radio to talk to me or your dad. Don't talk before an hour is up, or the bad guys might hear you. When you do call me after an hour I'll be able to hear you, but I won't be able to talk back, so you just keep talking into the radio until I answer."

"Okay, mommy, I can do that."

"You remember how to read the clock?"

"I know how."

"Show mommy and daddy," Weather said, and Jack showed her he could tell time.

"Give me Zero-One for a minute, okay?"

"Noooo . . ."

"Just for a minute, sweetie. Dad's going to put your gold badge around your neck so people will know you're on assignment."

Jack Cluewitt and the Imbrium Basin Murders   Ruth J. Burroughs

"Okay." Jack handed Zero-One to Weather. She pulled the robot dog aside and turned her back on her husband and son. She told the puppy-bot to go to sleep. Zero-One nodded and put itself in sleep mode. She pulled out the gem-cell-brain, the genetically engineered molecular cell drive that contained all of Zero-One's memories, and replaced it with one of the smaller unused brains stored in his knee. The replacement wasn't heuristic; it wouldn't be able to learn and grow like his expensive main-brain, but Jack wouldn't be able to tell the difference. She stuck the original brain in her pocket. She kept the robot in sleep mode, so it wouldn't remember her and Ruad, and so whoever found Jack would have no idea who he was. The burning metal from the explosion had melted off the puppybot's serial number. She turned around and handed the puppybot back to Jack.

"Here's your puppy. He told me he was so tired out from today, he had to sleep. You'll need to turn him on later."

"Then can we play the same game with my friends Sahara, Windy, big Skip and Uncle Haze?" Jack stopped shooting his laser gun and took Zero-One back into his arms, holding him tightly.

Weather shook her head. "No, you'll play new games with new friends and get a new last name. You need to do that in order for us to come back and get you, okay?"

Jack smiled and nodded. "This is fun, mom."

"Yes, but don't forget to use the radio, and if the thrusters aren't firing you press this button and it will take you out to the Corridor to Mars. You remember how to do that, right?"

"I get to drive the cantaloper, all by myself?"

"Yes, it's a birthday present. But let the auto thruster get you out first. You know what to do. That's my big boy," she said and hugged him. It was everything she could do to keep from crying. She wanted him to remember her smiling. She poked Ruad in the ribs and he smiled at Jack, too. The molten metal had scarred Jack's face with red welts, despite the application of nano tech. She kissed his other cheek so it wouldn't hurt.

"Okay, mom, I like this game. I like this birthday present. Don't be so worried. I'll do good."

Jack Cluewitt and the Imbrium Basin Murders   Ruth J. Burroughs

"Well. You'll do well. I'm just going to strap you in now and close the hatch."

Weather jettisoned the pod after setting the coordinates for the Corridor. She watched as the little cantaloper with her only child in it thrust away, dodging behind asteroids and out into the corridor toward Mars, its plasma shields activated.

"Thrusters! We've got something big coming toward us. Move away from Jack, so they don't detect him. Omigod, Weather, they're firing. Get your suit on. For God's sake, they're firing!"

✕

Jack unstrapped himself from the chair and floated up to a view port, thankful for the fun birthday present. He saw his mom and dad's escape boat playing hide and seek with some other big ships, but the shields activated and then he couldn't see anything anymore. Just as the windows closed, a blast rocked the tiny ship. Jack tumbled around inside, losing his grip on the toys. Another blast and he was slammed into the wall again, this time knocked unconscious. He floated amidst his toys inside the cantaloper as it grew colder and colder. If it weren't for the chem projectile that hit his pod across the bow, the oxygen and heat might have lasted for months, but now it was only a matter of hours before death might take the boy.

Jack woke shivering. He touched the gold shield that hung from the necklace, to make sure it was still there. The air didn't taste right. He rolled and rolled to get to the walls of the ship, so he could maneuver. It took a while to grab something and climb to his toy gun and his robot dog. He pushed the *open shutters* button so he could see and shoot at the bad guys, but the window wouldn't open.

His head hurt and he felt something dripping down his forehead and that scared him. He thought he better wake up his dog so he pressed the button, but nothing happened. He couldn't get Zero-One to wake up and he needed his robot dog. It was smart and could tell him what to do. He took the badge off and threw it, but without g-force it tumbled and floated weakly.

Jack Cluewitt and the Imbrium Basin Murders   Ruth J. Burroughs

At his birthday party, as Jack blew out the candles, he had wished to be a Moon City Earthside cop like his father and see the forests, mountains, rivers and oceans. Ruad had been raised on Mars but had acclimated to Earth in a Micro-Gravity suit. Moon City Police had that privilege, having jurisdiction on Earth, too. Jack wanted to be a cop and firefighter like his dad and an artist like his mom, but not have to go to dad's Cathedral, or listen to his Rabbi mom preach about Shabbat, and make him eat certain things on certain days. If only he hadn't wished to be an Earthside cop. And now all he had left of them was his robot dog, the gold toy cop shield and that funny paper book.

He strapped himself into the wall bed so he wouldn't float around, and stuffed Zero-One inside the bag with him and held him tight. His face hurt. He felt the area on the right side of his face and it felt bumpy and sore. Then he thought it might be best to just forget he ever had such a happy family. Just erase them from his mind and then it wouldn't hurt so much that they were gone and he'd caused it by wishing to be an Earth cop. Then he started screaming for his mommy and daddy, crying hysterically until he fell asleep.

When it detected no danger from stray gamma rays, the small skiff turned off all but one of its plasma shields on the hull. It hunted for places to feed on hydrogen while Jack floated fast asleep, hour after hour. When Jack woke, he forgot to look at the clock, but remembered to call. He wasn't shivering anymore, but he still felt cold and now very dizzy and weak and his face hurt even worse. He had to climb out of the sleeping bag. He didn't want to, because it would make him colder, but he had to because he was a good cop. It was hard to get to the radio telephone. He pulled the handle off the wall and pushed the numbers like mom had told him to; he had to let go of Zero-One. It wasn't like a hands-free phone thing you plugged in your ear or a talk-to-the-computer-phone. He turned on the radio and very weakly he called for his mommy.

John and Marilyn Cluewitt of Cluewitt Space Water Mining Corporation rode in a private yacht, taking in the sights of Mars and the Ring of Stones, on their way to Jupiter. Their robot pilot told them of a distress beacon. After searching several bandwidths, they heard the weak calls of

Jack Cluewitt and the Imbrium Basin Murders   Ruth J. Burroughs

a boy. They could detect nothing on the view screen. John ordered his external robots to retrieve the small pod. When they got back, they disengaged the weak plasma shield and pulled the battered cantaloper on board, and to their surprise found it was still pressurized. John and Marilyn had a lot of external robots and were able to safely get the boy on onboard.

He was cold and near death. They made sure he didn't have the bends, warmed him up and fed him soup. Marilyn, who had always wanted children, clung to the crying boy, who kept screaming for his mommy and crying and screaming about his fifth Grid-day. She searched the back of his head for the plug outlet, but found nothing. She sighed with relief. She and John were strict Naturals and didn't plug their brains into the Grid, the Internet of space. She hadn't obtained a license to raise children, despite all their wealth, due to the fact that they were Naturals the law specified all children be enhanced or genetically bred to withstand the rigors of space living. The Cluewitts had heard about the abandoned Naturals out in the Corridor, mostly miners who bore illegal children by the dozens. Children no one wanted.

One of Marilyn's robots noted his injuries, including the scarring burns on the right side of his face, and she applied some nano pain patches. He stopped screaming, but he wouldn't stop sobbing, so she rocked him 'til he fell asleep. Inside the cantaloper, they searched for identification, but all they could find was a scorched raincoat, a paper book, a robot dog, a zap gun and a gold toy detective's badge embossed with the name, *Jack.*

Jack Cluewitt
Chapter One

Jack Cluewitt stood on the ledge of an oval window nine stories above the ground. He sipped his coffee and stepped off the ledge onto the terrace of smooth stones in the sky garden with his new partner, homicide detective Jane Salgado, a sable skinned woman of distinct beauty, offset by her broken nose, a token of her years in boxing, as Indigo Jane. A flawed designer baby, her hair was supposed to be red and her amber eyes, also a product of genetic manipulation, were supposed to be blue.

Her parents had expected a red-headed black baby with blue eyes not a red-eyed, Indigo-haired girl. But the altered genes of the enhanced fetus had different ideas and something got lost in the translation.

The balcony, overlooking Old Troy, jutted out of the wall like a protruding jaw, a small niche in the enormous Octagon, an apartment complex built for space dwellers that kept its residents in top physical condition through the use of gravity defying exercise with the aid of flexible nanotech clothes, magnetized to the Thinner Rails or made-for-human monorails. Though the eight main branches of monorails stretched out from the central hub, they fortified smaller, skinnier rails used for roller skating with hands or feet, trapeze-like travel, as well as climbing, jumping, sliding and swinging. A Green means of travel that evolved from gymnastics and obstacle course training, but also helped space dwellers retain their much diminished bone density and musculature.

He picked up the electronic paint brush and added a few more touches of nano blue to his bird's eye impressionistic and summery painting of robots playing ball with children and dogs, in the park below him in Troy, New York, a small city on the Hudson River near the capital. He pushed a button on the paint handle and it switched to green nano-paint. Jane sat down next to the balustrade and sipped her coffee.

Jack's French maid rolled out the window and onto the veranda toward him. Immaculata Bondo looked more like an aged Italian starlet; a refurbished house painter he'd bought at Almathea's Used Robots' lot a few years ago. She kept breaking down. Her motor was quiet enough, but he had replaced quite a few gears over the past few months. She was also a very talented cook and served him a plate of pancakes, two eggs sunny side up, toast and maple syrup.

"Great coffee, Immaculata."

"Thank you, Monsieur Cluewitt," she said, her smile lighting up her hundred-year-old reconditioned face. Dressed in a soft flower print cotton dress, her olive skin looked human. She kept his place immaculate. She was very curious as well, and asked him many questions about his paintings. Even her eyes smiled and sparkled. He loved her like family. He could no longer afford top of the line cars and robots since his stepfather, John Cluewitt, had cut him off from his allowance. He now lived on his cop's salary, but his penchant for spending on things he couldn't afford hadn't let up.

He took another sip of the Jovian java, made from beans grown off world on space station Reo near Jupiter. June afternoons in the capitol district region could boil the salt out of a person's blood, but mornings ran cool and sweet. He soaked it in while his breakfast grew cold, sipping his hot coffee and finishing his latest *en plein air,* or outdoor painting.

"N'est-il pas tres belle?" Immaculata said.

"Yes, it is. Very." Jack replied.

In his completed painting, Jack also captured the carefree pedestrians in mid-motion, gliding, sliding or making acrobatic leaps along three of the Octagon's Thinner Rails, or thin monorails that extended down to the ball park below him. They thought nothing of the death-defying means of travel; nor did Jack, except when he felt a mild tingle of motion sickness now and then. *Not a good thing for a space detective,* Jack thought. From Jack's terrace view, the tentacle freeways appeared wide and thick and people down in the park looked ant-sized. But with his special Artist glasses, he could zoom in on any detail.

The postindustrial, pastoral view reflected in his painting rolled out beneath the spider-like feet of the Octopod structures like a rug stitched with bright maples, blue spruce and evergreen trees and dotted with old, white, vinyl-sided homes; intersected by warehouses and criss-crossed by old roads now used only by very old-fashioned people, like the Amish or the Iroquois tribes and pure Naturals. He listened to the distant sound of children laughing and screaming, and old Nanny Robots with clattering joints, compelling their wards, and dogs barking in the old Knickerbocker baseball field where Johnny Evers used to play.

He sat down next to Jane Salgado. They sipped coffee in his breakfast nook, absorbing the view. The old patch-work streets crisscrossed the bright green carpet of baseball fields and nineteenth century cemeteries. White houses on postage stamp lawns dotted the town right up into the green park and baseball field, against small rolling blue and piney hills.

The Hudson River cut its way through it all, meandering like a sparkling azure snake; reflected tufts of white clouds rippled across its surface as ducks, geese and seagulls bobbed and floated on the wind-powered waves, mirroring the blue, blue sky.

Jack devoured his breakfast and rang for the newscom. His majordomo, Zero-One, trotted out onto the porch with a cylinder in its mouth. Jack opened it and unfurled the polymer newspaper, using sun energy, earning some Green points. It had a texture similar to the old newspapers. He preferred it to holopapers and holobooks.

Zero-One sat nearby; dressed absurdly in a butler's uniform, he waited for Jack's next command.

"The newsfeed is saying the Near-Earth Police department is corrupt because my girlfriend Hildy runs a sexbots brothel," Jack said.

"See what I mean, Jack? It takes us Naturals quite a bit longer to get information." Jane shook her head, her indigo dreadlocks whipping about. "We could get implants here in the back of our heads and just plug in like everyone else and we would have known sooner."

Jack Cluewitt and the Imbrium Basin Murders   Ruth J. Burroughs

"So, not only am I cut off financially I've a good chance of losing my job or at least the next case. John probably did that on purpose. He was hoping I'd follow in his footsteps and become a doctor—a healer, not an enforcer. If I can't be a cop he'd be happy. And we're not getting brain chips. I picked you for a partner because you're a Natural. I don't like cybernetically enhanced cops. They can't be trusted. They're always transmitting. I like privacy."

Indigo Jane frowned. The amused twinkle in her amber eyes fading as she struggled. "Yes. Of course, Jack. You're right. I want to compete, but you can't trust a computer. Can't trust a robot as far as you can throw it. The bosses will replace us with robots and programs."

Jack's green eyes twinkled with amusement. He rubbed at the scar on the right side of his face. "I shall remain a free and separate Natural for as long as I can. I don't need computers to solve crimes. But we have to find out if my father leaked that to the press."

Immaculata roller-skated up the walkway toward the kitchen for more Jovian java. Her mag lev feet had been sold to defray other expenditures.

Immaculata returned with a large pot and refilled his cup.

"Thank you, Immaculata," Jack said.

"*Il n'y a pas de quoi, de rien,*" Immaculata replied; she smiled and rolled away.

"How lucky I am, Jane, to have a maid who can cook, and a dog for a butler who could fetch my newspaper, and a new partner who is a devout Natural. It cost my dad, John, quite a bit of cash to give the robot puppy a heuristic gem-cell brain. I've had Zero-One since I was five years old and now he's a full grown dog and adult Robot."

"It's hard to compete against people with chips in their brains and robot cops taking credit for our collars. You know, that was a clever ruse of your mother and father to buy you a robot dog instead of a Nanny Robot to keep you out of trouble. Though I hope you can afford to spring your old partner for beating up your last perp, Jack." Jane knew Jack had been cut off from his rich father since joining the force. Her captain had told her before she'd even met her new partner.

"My fancy pants lawyer is taking care of that."

Jack Cluewitt and the Imbrium Basin Murders   Ruth J. Burroughs

Finished with the newspaper, he handed it to Jane. He scanned the holo-cinder for the reviews of books written by one of millions of authors on Earth or by one of the billions of people living in the Solar System in the Buckminster Fullerene geodesic colonies. He chose one and a book-like object popped out of the top like an umbrella opening up. It was made out of the same nano-polymers as the newspaper.

He watched Immaculata putter up the ramp, thinking how lucky he was, when he heard her motor grind and a squealing noise erupt from her wheels. She rolled backwards as though her brakes didn't work or she'd lost all power. She hit the wall and tumbled right off the veranda. He heard a crash as she smashed onto the porch just below Jack's. Jack's heart broke. Immaculata was family. Then he realized someone could have been out on their patio just below him. No one had screamed. He walked over to the edge, coffee in hand and looked over and breathed a sigh of relief when he saw that no one lay crushed beneath her sprawled form.

"Damn, that's going to cost me big time," Jack said, sipping his coffee.

"I'll go down there and let them know whose robot that is. For someone who hates robots you sure love your maid and Zero-One. Tell your butler dog I can let myself out," Jane handed him back his newspaper, chugged down the rest of her lukewarm coffee and then departed.

"I don't think you can afford to have her fixed, Jack," Zero-One said, coming up beside him. His large shepherd ears twitched.

"But I have to. She makes the best damn coffee this side of the Asteroid belt."

"How would you know if the coffee is better? You haven't been to the other side of the Asteroid belt. Repairing Immaculata would cost the same as a new robot and you just don't have that kind of money. I suppose you could ask your father." Zero-One sat down and called a local robot clean-up crew; a rather routine occurrence, broken robots.

"That's out of the question. You're not calling him are you?"

21

"No. I'm calling Robot Repair. Her sale will help you catch up. Do you want me to send her to the scrap heap for parts?"

"Immaculata, no! I love Immaculata. Who will critique my paintings? She has a fine eye for art and well . . . If you scrapped her it would be like killing her and I'd miss her so. See if Pops' or Almathea's store will buy her. I'm going to miss her coffee the most. She's almost human. I could buy her the current hologram that can project anyone's features on her face."

"You're broke. I suggest you don't spend any more money this month," Zero-One said.

"Oh, I was going to buy you a holographic program, too. It's the current upgrade for robots. It looks just like the real thing. I saw it on some canid-droids at Pops' Used Robots Store."

"First of all, Jack, I'm not alive and you'd be better off trying to make relationships with living things than spending money on trying to make me look alive. Besides, they did a pretty good job with my facial expressions and we don't need to upgrade every time something new and expensive comes along."

"Yes, you're right. Sometimes older is better."

"Where did you go last night?"

"I went to see Hildy, to give her a birthday present,"

"In jail?"

"But she returned it to me."

"You mean she threw the coin at your head because she thought it was a cheap souvenir from Jupiter."

"How did you know?"

"That bump on your forehead, you're not that clumsy, and I doubt you'd pick a fight with Sydney Atrax."

"No, I don't usually pick fights with inanimate objects."

"I resemble that remark, Jack."

"Sorry, Zero-One, but that robot cop is nothing but a hat rack. He couldn't track an elephant, let alone a field mouse."

"At least he doesn't waste his money on antiques, and his time on a woman of questionable means."

"Why would he, when all he needs is a lube job and some superconductive fluids?"

Jack Cluewitt and the Imbrium Basin Murders   Ruth J. Burroughs

"Why don't you find a nice girl, like the ones your parents approve of? The house of Cluewitt will need heirs. You can't live so humbly forever."

"C'mon, Zero-One, you've got to be joking. I'm not dating Tiffany Roth-Steuben."

"That's better than Hildy Witter Raygun."

"She's Swedish."

"That's no excuse. She's stepped off her rocket, Jack."

"It's complicated."

Zero-One rolled his eyes. "As with all things human. What else did you purchase?"

"I bought a Daisy Zooka Pop gun, circa, 1930, extro blast calcium 9897 timed release skin patches and it won't cause kidney stones. You can't get this stuff over the counter. Plus your bones won't become frail or brittle. They'll actually be more pliable. I've also got the Balancer P-1000. You could do somersaults in a gyroscope on a Ferris wheel and never get sick on this stuff plus, and it's got vitamin C, sea algae and seaweed. I bought Varmygdala Restore. This stuff is dangerous. It's a nano mind drug. It is a cure for schizophrenia and is supposed to suppress hallucinations. It does cure the space madness induced by drinking filtered Jovian water. You know the visions the Siwens and Simons have? I don't know how it works. It comes with a box of neuro-chips. You just jam them into the jack in the back of your skull and then pull the trigger. Bingo. Instant sanity."

"Jack. You don't even jack into the Orbitals' Grid. What good will it do for you if you get space sickness and hallucinate aliens?"

"You never know. Maybe I can inject it. The V.R. might come in handy someday."

"Where did you buy those things?"

"You know Pops' Used Robots and Toys Store."

"Never heard of that one."

"It's down Earthside," Jack said.

"You had to slide down off the superconductive Octopod into the polluted city against full earth gravity that you're not used to."

"I used a body-brace."

"Near the polluted Hudson river?"

"The nanos are doing a good job cleaning up the PCBs."

"Tell me you didn't run into some criminals?"

Jack Cluewitt and the Imbrium Basin Murders   Ruth J. Burroughs

"Zero-One, I'm a cop. I can handle myself."

"No, you're not a beat cop anymore. You're a homicide detective in the NEPD that is if your father doesn't finish your career for you, and Space is cleaner and safer. Why don't you move farther up, Jack?"

"We'll move to Mars and the Ring as soon as I get enough collars. I'll upgrade my blue LUNA shield to a gold Earth-Moon Mars Jupiter shield and space is not cleaner and safer. It's dangerous and deadly."

"Sometimes I wonder if you really want that E-M-MA-JO shield."

"Of course I want that gold shield and work in Jovian space more than anything."

"Living with the Cluewitts in Near-Earth space didn't make you happy. You had to go live on the Moon, and then when that wasn't enough, you had to get a place on Earth. Now you want to go live near Jupiter. After that you'll want to live near Saturn and then out beyond the solar system."

"I spend a lot of time on the Moon and in Near-Earth space solving crimes. I don't see why Jovian space would be much different. We would have had that collar if my former partner Garret Makenna hadn't beaten the crap out of the serial killer."

"You had to jump through hoops to get Earth-G certified and now you want to live in deep space. It's unlikely you'd be able to readjust to the heavy gravity after years in space.

"Okay, Jack. I will have to take over Immaculata's jobs," Zero-One continued. "It also appears that we've got someone who needs an experienced painter robot. So Immaculata is saved." Zero-One dialed up a number he'd received. "Off planet. Someone by the name of Maelstrom Corrigan stationed near Lagrange Point Five. You're lucky. He's willing to pay top dollar plus shipment and repair. I'm going to take care of the gardens and set the nano vacuum cleaners on while you're resting."

"That's wonderful. Personally see to it that she gets to her destination safely."

"Jack, I really don't understand your concern for her welfare. She's just a robot, a simple program really."

"She's programmed to care and I'm very fond of her and I will buy her back someday."

24

"As you wish," Zero-One said, sighing. He trotted off to Jack's personal vegetable gardens.

Jack walked into his living room, sad about his maid. Every wall was covered in shelves of his antique paper books. Advertisements of every kind of product he used colorfully glared out of his hallway wall screen. As he headed into his bedroom he thought about his encounter with Hildy at the jail

Lights automatically came on as he headed for the bathroom.

"Where are the antiques?" he asked the wall screen.

"Immaculata put them on your dresser," it replied.

"Thank you." Jack checked the nice bump in the mirror. The swelling had subsided. *Boy, Hildy had looked great, though.* He rubbed the pink burn scar on his face. It hadn't gone all bad, his visit with her . . .

✗

The robot guard brought Hildy Witter Raygun into the tiny visitors' room. It had been done over in pastel colors, and a wide sweeping panorama of Troy brought sunlight into a new bay window. She was lucky she wasn't in for an eco-crime. They were harder on eco crimes than on what got her in. The robot guard left her with Jack.

Her Mars-colored hair cascaded in ringlets down her soft silken skin. She still wore the sapphire encrusted nano bead dress that moved when she breathed, or did it breathe when she moved? His eyes dove into her crescent Moon cleavage and back up to her soft lips. But underneath the get-up he saw the starving little girl who'd survived the caustic streets of Mars.

"Ahhh, Hildy."

"Jack."

"I brought you something."

"Bail?"

"No, I tried, but someone's got you stuck here."

"With your connections?"

He loved her Swedish accent. "I'm in trouble enough over you."

25

Jack Cluewitt and the Imbrium Basin Murders Ruth J. Burroughs

"Why? Because your girlfriend turns out to be a world class gold digger instead of the preppy you all thought I was?"

"You're not a gold digger. I gave you money to get your sex robots out of hock and that Sydney Hat Racks arrested you for soliciting a police officer. My lawyer will take care of it."

"Jack, you're a cop with rich parents. I'm a trash hauler's stepdaughter who wanted better things than being stuck out mining rocks all my life. I wasn't looking for a loan. I would have lost everything if I hadn't paid those taxes. Your rich daddy is not speaking to you because I conned you out of that money."

"You're my sweetheart. I'd give you everything. You know that. These charges are outrageous. I'm your boyfriend. You told them you robbed me and now you're stuck here."

"Not for long. I'll be back in action before long, back to my Martian low life. Besides, I have to save your reputation."

"Providing service robots isn't exactly illegal Hildy, and you could marry me."

Hildy laughed. "What would your conservative colleagues think?"

"Open your present."

Hildy held the box the Octopod police had inspected and slowly peeled open the delicate pink rice paper wrapper as tears splashed down, making dark pink rivulets on the paper.

"What is this?" she seethed, dropping the box and holding up the Chinese coin.

"It's an antique coin."

"It's a piece of junk! It's a piece of gold plated iron. It's a cheap souvenir. What am I supposed to do with this in jail? I can't wear it."

"I just thought . . ."

"No, you didn't think anything, Jack. You never think. You don't know me or try to get to know me. I like antiques Jack and you like junk. You're always spending money on junk. I'm wearing sapphires that should bust me out of here ten times over and you give me a nine dollar souvenir from a garbage dump!"

26

Jack Cluewitt and the Imbrium Basin Murders Ruth J. Burroughs

"It cost ninety and it was from a used robots lot."

"Well, you were ripped off by that conniving used robots salesman." She got up, knocking her chair over, "Guard, guard!"

The robot guard opened the door." Get me out of here and back to my cell. We're done."

Jack held up his hand. "You can't sabotage the love you deserve. Nothing you say or do will destroy it. Won't you keep it as a token of my affection?"

"It's a costly mass for a space ship on a tight fuel budget and it's not even pretty. What do you want me to do with this thing?" She shook it and threw it at him.

He blocked with his arm, but it glanced off his forehead. He stooped to pick it up and when he stood back up she was gone.

Two Green Policemen called on the hologram and told him to meet them at an Earthside hotel, but that he was to bring the nano altered book with him or else they'd arrest him for breaking Green law. He couldn't afford not to go. He opened the patio door and stepped out on to the Thinner Rail that curved into the flats. The wind whipped at his lapels in the hot June air and he slid down the tentacle . . . down around the wind tunnel the kids were playing in, and over the flower gardens, zipping past the high risk sports until he came to the ground and stepped out onto the sidewalks. Most people traveled in some form of robot AI car or wrap-around vehicle, spider, bicycle or flying machine. It was hard to tell who was physically impaired. Those used to Micro-G had to wear their robot braces in every imaginable shape and size.

He hailed a lady bike-cabby and settled into the rickety seat; she zigzagged her way over the sidewalks of Troy, where once, the old paved roads, made for the roar and the rage of gas powered cars, used to be, now replaced by the sounds of bicycles, rollerblades, sliders and the hum of electric or fusion powered vehicles. Much of the population chose to live in space where weather was more predictable and controllable.

Jack Cluewitt and the Imbrium Basin Murders   Ruth J. Burroughs

The smell of cooked trout, lobster and crab, driven by human and solar-powered bicycles from the coasts of New Hampshire and Raleigh Virginia to Albany and Troy, New York, wafted in the air and Jack's stomach growled. Long ago all of Boston, Providence, New York City, Philadelphia, Maryland and parts of North and South Carolina succumbed to the hungry sea, having joined Italy and Sweden already drowned, their denizens happily jettisoning off into space with promises of luxury controlled environments. California hadn't drowned. It had grown, but it was desert and scrub grass along with most of the western half of the States, Oregon being semi-tropical now. Most of the coastal regions of the twenty-first century swam with the fishes along with Paris, the UK, Scotland, Ireland and Norway. The list was too long. The Earth Vatican was moved piecemeal to Montreal. Mars Vatican City was a different animal entirely, since many of its congregants worshiped the Earth Mother as well. But Lunar Scotland and Ireland were run by the New Celtic Druids, very much Earth Mother religions and governments.

The cabby took a turn into a neglected area, going toward Albany and over the Collar City Bridge into Watervliet. The chirpy lawns were all neatly combed, as if for the birds and the white picket fences and the squirrels. He rode past trees bursting with green leaves and streets littered with steeples of the churches with tiny cemetery plots on every street. Rising up out of this syrupy neighborhood were strange and bleak looking factories of anonymous manufacture and historic bars converted to Mother Earth Cathedrals while old drunks turned in their graves.

Jack's cabby pulled up alongside the front of the Hotel Royale; a valet exited the two front glass doors and helped Jack out. Horse carts, bicycle families, couples and tourists skated and walked about, the locals, oblivious to the ironies of their town. Tourists, especially the Micro-G masses, posed and took cheesy pictures of Old Troy, New York, a town that defied time with layers of history in its buildings, its people and its streets. Jack performed like an Earth Normal and walked through the front of the door of the grand hotel, easily managing the old-fashioned thing that he might once have crashed into.

Jack Cluewitt and the Imbrium Basin Murders   Ruth J. Burroughs

In the cool shade of the Hotel Royale lobby he let his eyes adjust and walked over to the desk manager and asked for room 33.

"Name?" the women asked.

"Jack Beech," he said, using the code name.

She handed him the keys and he observed someone using the stairs and followed suit without seeming too awkward, except for that one missed step, guessing that his room was on the third floor. He smiled at other guests leaving the Hotel, many commenting on the originality of the art deco building, which was actually an odd mix of styles.

His room was done very well. *All too well,* he thought. *How could anyone live here?* This particular room was drab and hot, except for the ceiling fan, and there was no central access net to the community. None of the walls responded to his commands and there was dirt and dust everywhere. He had stopped sneezing for about ten minutes already and hoped he was getting used to the filth. These *weighted* folks liked to live in historical periods, but at least in holofractal reality everything was clean. The walls were covered in a strange looking substance similar to his paper books. He assumed it was poly-fiber, made to look like wallpaper; it was yellowed and it peeled. The odd beige color wasn't much better than the stained areas that were meant to look aged. The bathroom was very different from his. The toilet had water in it instead of absorbing tablets. He didn't use it though because his clothes had the means to absorb and recycle all his liquid and solid waste, even his sweat.

He took his jacket off and hung it on a coat rack. The rectangle called a TV didn't work and the mildewed curtains on the window wore layers of protective dust from years of neglect.

People assumed he'd paid for the police force to have sex robots. His dad usually stepped in and made things all go away. His fellow officers resented it, but this time he couldn't get out of trouble because his dad saw a way to get him kicked off the force.

It was pattering rain outside the French doors on the balcony, and he could smell the cool wet breeze coming into the still warm and musky room. He let his eyes adjust and looked down on the black, shiny street whose dim colors streaked and smeared in the greasy street lamps.

Jack Cluewitt and the Imbrium Basin Murders Ruth J. Burroughs

Conjoined twins in fedoras and a rain coat leaned against the post of one of the street lamps in the yellow light and looked up at Jack's silhouette just then. Jack watched as they lit two pipes filled with tobacco, rain dripping off the rims of two wide brimmed hats. It was not an easy gesture, since they had to hold the two pipes with one hand while they put their two heads together.

Jack waved. Micro-G folks rarely smoked, anymore; only Earthbound. The one on their left side put the lighter in their left pocket and then took one of the pipes from their right hand and puffed. That conjoined twin waved his pipe at Jack while the other quickly burned through his heap with one inhale and emptied the burned remains. Tapping them on the heel of his shoe, he placed the pipe in a pocket of their Balmacaan London fog coat, as the rain pelted down on them.

They walked with two legs and a limp under his balcony and Jack threw the key over the ledge. The twins caught the room-key in their left hand and then gestured that they were coming up. Jack nodded and closed the French doors. Maybe this would lead him to his birth parents. Hildy owed him that much. She had a place on Mars, and he wasn't afraid of her mafia connections. She'd help him. He knew she would despite the fact that he couldn't afford her, even if she wouldn't admit it, love would do it for him.

Greepol Royale
The Green Police Meet Jack at the Hotel Royale

Jack let the Greepols in the door. He'd never met two people who shared one body. The twin on the right set a briefcase they were carrying down on the floor and both took off their fedoras and flung them onto the hooks of the coat rack. The London Fog raincoat they shared they peeled off and hung that, too. He showed them in the door and shook their hand.

"Jack Cluewitt."

"I'm Keith Morris and this is my half-brother, Lee," Keith said.

"Hah, hah, hah, two different fathers, right?" Jack said.

"That always gets them," Lee said, smiling.

"I've actually never met a conjoined twins before."

30

Keith nodded, "That's okay, Jack. We've never met a preppy Irish cop before." They all had a good laugh at that.

"We're symmetrical dicephalic parapagus, but I don't like the term dicephalic."

"It does seem a pejorative term. Would you like something to drink?" Jack asked, going into the mini kitchen. "I've got little bottles of liquor or soda, and there's coffee."

"Coffee sounds good, Jack."

"I'll have a little bottle of something. What you got there?"

"Lee," Keith said sternly.

"C'mon, Keith. I haven't been drunk in ten years and I only drink once a year."

"One," Keith said, "I don't like being drunk. And mix it with something."

"Thanks. You're the best."

"I'll take a rum and coke, Jack," Lee said.

Jack made the drink with no problem, but he had trouble figuring out how to work the coffee machine. Keith laughed.

"You walk like a terrestrial, even with that carbon-gravity-suit, but you are definitely an off-worlder. You live up in the pods? With everything automated?" Keith asked as he and Lee walked over to help Jack with the machine, Lee slowly nursing his drink.

"Yeah, I'm not used to a manual coffee machine."

"You have the book we talked about, Jack?" Lee set his drink down, so Keith could use both hands to make the coffee.

"Yeah, in my suit pocket, but I've got a license to own paper. You can't arrest me. I'll get it for you," Jack replied.

"We'll check it over here on the counter," Keith said. "Could you grab the briefcase?"

"Sure," Jack replied.

Jack returned to the kitchen counter with the briefcase and his book. He sipped the coffee while the two Greepols investigated the book his step-mom had given him. They used some kind of portable contraption not unlike Pops T. Van de Woestyne's nano com scanner.

"I have an ancient artifact I could let go for ninety credits." Jack placed the metal coin on the counter.

31

Jack Cluewitt and the Imbrium Basin Murders Ruth J. Burroughs

"I hope you didn't pay that much for this, Jack. It's just a gold-plated Chinese coin. I'll check it for you, though. You could always return it," Lee said, while Keith examined the book. Jack felt his face burning up and pretended to look at something outside the French doors, clearing his throat.

"I have bad news, Jack," Keith said.

"What's the matter?"

"I'm going to have to take this book and investigate it further."

"I'm sorry, Keith, but I can't let that book go. It's one of the only things I have that connects me to my past."

Keith pulled a gun out and aimed it at Jack. "I'm sorry, too, Jack, but I'm going to have to keep this book and place you under arrest. I can't verify its authenticity, and owning this book could be considered a crime."

"That's ridiculous. Is my father behind this? I have a license to own old paper, just like whoever runs this antique hole in the wall. I took it over to Pops and he authenticated it. It's a genuinely old book, copyright 1954." Jack reached in his pocket and pulled out his nano paint brush. *Damn it.* He never did like guns and had nothing to defend himself with.

Keith laughed. "True, Jack, but the book isn't registered. Nice paint gun. As Green Police, we have to determine if this is an eco-crime. Until a judge can render your book back to you, it's ours. Your father is right, Jack. Don't go looking for your birth parents. Forget about the book. You should be worried about getting killed, not losing your job."

"Is that a threat? You can't take that book."

Keith shook his head wearily. "Yes. We're taking the book. Don't try to stop us. We have to report this, but I suppose we don't have to arrest you."

"Thanks, you just took my only hope of finding my birth parents and now you're accusing me, a cop, of committing a crime."

Dismayed, he opened the French doors and walked out onto the veranda and looked up at the stars in the black sky. The Greepols came out onto the veranda, both smoking the pipes again.

"What's the matter, Jack?" Keith asked.

Jack Cluewitt and the Imbrium Basin Murders   Ruth J. Burroughs

"All the good cases are going to robots or cyber-modified or genetically engineered cops because of the powers that be, and I'm going to be replaced by an inanimate object. Something that doesn't eat, sleep or need oxygen, won't get sick, won't need money when they're retired." *And who won't fall in love with ladies of ill-gotten means or make the department look bad,* Jack thought.

"Well, with Savanna and Gull Saugerties as President and VP, and the Green Party in power, you Naturals can make a comeback. They crushed the Corporation Party and their soldiers after twenty years of Felix Fortuna's fear-based governance," Lee said, puffing on his pipe.

Jack laughed. "Who's going to enforce the Green laws? Are the Green Police going to tell my bosses not to replace Naturals with robots or cybernetically enhanced people who can jack into the Orbitals' Internet Satellite Grid?"

"Don't you have a robot partner, too, a police dog-bot?" Keith asked.

"Zero-One? No, he's my majordomo. Indigo Jane is a Natural human; even if she was genetically engineered, she doesn't jack into the Satellite of Orbitals Grid. We all use robots in our investigative procedures, but it's always been human minds investigating, not artificial minds. Robots have always been our tools, not the other way around. You're a tool of the robots."

"When hell freezes over, Jack, but it's hard to enforce Green laws in space and most space-faring people love the Green Party and will do anything to save the Earth," Keith said.

"Where's the book?" Jack asked.

"In our briefcase."

"Finished your drink, Lee?" Jack wondered how it felt to have one brother drink and the other feel drunk from it.

"Most certainly did, Jack. Thanks." Lee puffed on his pipe.

"So, you're not going to arrest me?"

Keith shook his head. "No, Jack, but after we file a report with the Green Police Bureau, it will be on your record. You take care of your girlfriend and forget about finding your parents or this book," Lee said.

"Could you just go, please?"

Keith nodded, looking sorry. "Sure, Jack. We'll go."

He waited on the veranda under the starlight until he heard the door click, and then he turned around. Two Green Policemen in their fedoras and London Fog rain coat just walked out with my book in their briefcase; the only viable connection to my biological parents.

Jack went back inside and tried some of the coffee. It was the worst thing he had ever tasted. *Nostalgia is for the birds,* he thought. *Who wants to drink lousy instant coffee that tastes like dirt?* He spit it out into the sink. *Nothing like Jovian java. The least they could do is put some high quality Earth coffee in these old-fashioned rooms. Sometimes newer is better than older.* Jack removed his shirt and tie. It was still very hot, despite the fact that it was nighttime.

Jack lay back on the sticky bedcover and picked up the heavy Chinese coin Lee had said was worthless and threw it against the wall. Instead of bouncing off as he expected it to do, it stuck firmly to the peeling yellow wallpaper, humming like a tuning fork.

He jumped out of bed and ran to the wall. The circular coin had a square in the middle that was now dark blue, almost black. It should be yellow, like the wallpaper! Jack stuck his finger in it and gasped, pulling back as though he'd been bitten. The substance was cold. He stuck his finger in it and then his hand and the coin expanded a little. He pulled his hand out and it tingled, but otherwise didn't feel bad. He pushed the coin and it moved and the black square moved with it. He couldn't peel it off the wall, so he stuck his hand back in the black square, its cold sticky substance covering and tingling on his skin. He could push all the way up to his shoulder; his whole arm felt like it was being plunged into ice.

Scared, he pulled back hard and his arm slid out. With a thwack, the coin popped off the wall and slammed into his chest right over his heart and stuck there. He couldn't get it off. Every time he tried, it didn't feel good. He could still put his hand in the dark center, and though his hand was in a space, it was not grabbing at his heart or lungs. It was weird having his hand stuck in his chest, so he stopped doing it. He pulled his hand out of the cold substance and examined it. Nothing odd; his skin looked fine.

He flipped his hand, checking both sides, but it was fine. Nothing hurt. He donned his shirt and necktie and

Jack Cluewitt and the Imbrium Basin Murders   Ruth J. Burroughs

grabbed his hat and coat. He packed up his space drugs and left the building with the ancient Chinese coin stuck to his chest. *How am I ever going to explain this to my superiors?*

Peg Cardillo
International Space Corporation
Fullerene Green Party
Chapter Two

Inside the great honeycombed Buckminster Fullerene colony, Peg Cardillo was like a single ant amidst billions going about their business. She stepped out of the dim lab, rubbing her eyes. The hydraulic door swished shut behind her, and she blinked against the bright white light of the hallway. Special magnetized shoes kept her on the floor as she slid past people and robots of all different grades, colors and hues. But for all her humble smallness, she held the biggest secret of the solar system: Cold Ion/plasma drives and the vibrating substance.

If done correctly, her robots and ships could run on an endless source of fuel that was free, merely harness it and it was yours. There was no need to manufacture it. No one had to be enslaved to mine it, like Space Water and minerals. And she was going to explore the far reaches of space with it; as soon as they were sure there would be enough food and heat to sustain them on the long voyage out of the solar system. But Corporation was getting suspicious and she was out of funds. She was dead broke, despite having an unlimited fuel source, and they were on to her.

She headed to the recreation hub. An elevator cab took her to the locker rooms.

She pressed her palm on a clothes locker and when her account came up short again she hacked it and pulled out a pair of ice-skates and warm clothes. She had to don warm clothes for the Ice room because it was winter. She entered through a pressurization chamber. The hatch sighed open;

Jack Cluewitt and the Imbrium Basin Murders Ruth J. Burroughs

inside it was cold. She breathed in the piney scent of conifers and watched as the vapors dispersed in the cold air.

Making sure her ice skates were secure, she made her way past the leisurely skating couples, children, singles and families. Beneath the layer of ice, magnets helped keep her from floating away from the surface. It was good exercise and that's what she needed to keep her muscles from atrophying.

She glided toward the edge of ice and held on to the railing. She stopped at a hot cocoa stand and recognized the long honey blonde hair of her daughter as she sped toward her from the opposite direction. Peg braced for the impact, but her daughter veered off at the last minute spun back around and skated up to her and gave her a big hug. She was surprised. The girl rarely hugged her since becoming a teenager, because she didn't want to be embarrassed in front of her friends.

"Hi mom, buy me a hot cocoa."

"Sorry, Jazmin, I'm broke."

"Mom! You're always broke, God. Never mind, I'll pay." Jazmin proceeded to buy them two hot cocoa balls.

"Thanks honey. I'm sorry, but the grant didn't come through for my research and I've put every last dime I have into my robots."

"Why don't you go back to work for daddy's VAQ-ORE?" Jaz swung her magnetized hair.

"Henri's Vasquez Oxygen and Ore mining operations? Yeah," Peg sighed. She tried to hold back tears. "Yeah, I should, huh?"

"Haven't you been getting any sleep?"

"Where's your father?"

"He's here, with um Celia."

"Oh, Celia the Centipede."

"Mom!"

"Well, your father hasn't come up with a good nickname for her yet. So, I did. Centipede."

"Mom!"

"Yup, she's all legs, no brains."

"Mother, stop this now. It's not like you."

"Oh honey, I'm sorry."

"Well, Ceelee did stay up late last night dancing and partying with Dad. She's not in good shape this morning.

Jack Cluewitt and the Imbrium Basin Murders   Ruth J. Burroughs

But they both promised to take me to the rink today, many Ganymedes ago, so they couldn't get out of it, despite last night. She's been good for Dad, but she is dreadfully nocturnal. Oh, sorry, mom."

"Whatever . . ." Peg crossed her arms, blinking back tears as she pretended to yawn and look the other way. She pulled her hat off and felt her short dark locks float free in the Micro-G. She felt too light to stay on the ice and she wondered how her daughter ever managed to skate so fast without pushing off into the middle of the Torus.

"Hey Peck, you're up early!" her gorgeous ex-husband said. She rolled her eyes and pursed her lips.

"Hey, Henri," she said, pulling her hat over her thick tousle of hair.

"Whoa, looks like you've been burning the midnight oil, too."

"Thanks. Just what I needed."

"Hello, Peg." Celia skated up behind Henri, grabbing him around the waist.

"Hello, Cent, Seal, umm, Celia." She felt a deep longing to be with Henri again and to kick Celia in the shins. She smiled at the thought, and Celia's clear blue eyes looked instantly hopeful, she returned the smile.

"So Peck, what brings you out into high society so bright and early?"

"I needed a breather." The brief glimpse of Celia showed Peg she was no worse for wear, despite her hard partying and dancing. Something Peg envied. Who could drink like that and look so fresh in the morning?

Henrique Vasquez liked to call Perigwin, Peck, for peccadillo or Peg Cardillo. In that brief glimpse of Celia, Peg noted the pink, rose petal lips, the natural blush of her cheeks against her baby smooth skin and pearl white teeth.

Peg started to feel like sandpaper and felt her blood seethe and boil inside.

"I heard you're broke." Henri seemed to take pleasure in her jealousy.

"So, what's new?" She was curt. She couldn't let on that she wasn't anywhere near broke or that her research wasn't anything but local fuel from liquid oxygen.

"We need you back. International Space needs you back. You've had your private little ramscoop-robot-ships

Jack Cluewitt and the Imbrium Basin Murders   Ruth J. Burroughs

project, now come back. We need more sheep dogs out there to scan the Earth-going asteroids, and Earth wants more protection. We just don't have the resources to explore beyond the solar system. There's nothing out there, just cold sunless space-time. Your robot explorers would just be a waste. They'd run out of fuel, get lost or destroyed and they're not going to find anything worthwhile. We'll buy all your robots back and restructure your crew. I know you're in deep." Henri pulled away from Celia and leaned against the railing next to his ex-wife. Celia skated away.

"So what? I'm not taking orders from you." Peg watched Celia skate off; she glared at the woman's back.

"I'm deep sixing your deep space project. Your robots get reprogrammed. C'mon Peck, you're not holding any cards. How many ships have you lost trying to reach the Kuiper Ring? And now you're trying for the Oort Cloud? It's too far and now Corporation can tell you what to do or ship you Earthbound. I'll find out what you're trying to hide. It's only a matter of time."

"I don't work for the Corporation because they don't protect anyone. I don't even know where all the billions of dollars are going because it ain't going to protecting the civilians and the miners," Peg said.

Henri grimaced. "Ah, technically you do still work for International Space Corporation."

"I won't work for a man who makes me jump through hoops to put in a new robot arm on a ship when I can do it myself without asking big International Space Corporation daddy for permission."

"There's a reason for protocol you know. It's too keep people from getting killed."

"Oh, like the days when the International Space Corporation wanted to blow up asteroids?"

"They know better than that now."

"Yeah, shooting at someone in space is like shooting your own foot."

"Thanks, Peck. You really know where it hurts. There are laws against that now." Henri was angry. He still limped from that little not so accidental accident that had occurred twenty-five years ago, and he had nearly lost his whole leg because of his miscalculation. Some idiot had boarded the

Jack Cluewitt and the Imbrium Basin Murders   Ruth J. Burroughs

Fullerene with a solid rocket fuel jet engine, killing more people than he'd planned.

Peg put her hands on her hips and glared at Henri. "Ah, yeah, Green laws. Thanks to the Green Party, I.S.C. can't go around shooting people, blowing everyone up or destroying the Earth-Moon system because they said over-mining on the Moon couldn't hurt a thing."

Henri shot right back. "Those early terrorists wanted to blow up the Moon and start their precious self-prophesying Armageddon. So I.S.C. wanted nukes off-Moon as much as you and your Greens. So we got a little carried away with mining the Moon. We needed that metal for the Fullerenes. People were leaving Earth en masse. They needed a place to live. Now we do very little mining on the Moon. The little guys always take the fall for the big guys' boo-boo's. We did stop that Fullerene from hitting Earth."

"You call that a boo-boo, Henri? You sure know how to trivialize things." She'd always suspected he had some involvement in that fiasco. Forgetting herself, she pulled her hat off again and let her curly hair float up into the Micro-Gravity as she ran her fingers through it. "God, those mining accidents and gun battles could have destroyed Earth and just missed the Moon. One little bullet destroyed twelve hundred children in the Valles Marineris colony when it hit their oxygen tanks. You call that a boo-boo?"

"Stop preaching your Green faith at me. At least we're doing something about it while you Greens sit around getting high on your W-H-I-N-E for more than a decade. Yeah, it was a bad screw up for the I.S.C. and now Earth-centric wants more protection, less bombs more debris nets and more robot jockeys. Some Earth dwellers see the cowgirls and cowboys as the real heroes out here. When they send more robot jockeys they'll need more robots. That's where we come in, Peck, you, me and whoever, International Space Corporation. If you can unscramble that genius brain of yours, I could let you head up the new Shepherd Program. Maybe we'll stop a death ray gamma burst together. We got a medal for keeping that Fullerene colony from impacting Earth-Moon."

"One piece blew up New York City."

"It was already under the sea anyway. No harm, no foul."

Jack Cluewitt and the Imbrium Basin Murders   Ruth J. Burroughs

"If the Green Party hadn't shown you how, you would have just blown it to bits and Earth-Moon along with it. You know I don't want to be head of anything. Especially something as uncreative as herding a bunch of asteroids that probably won't come anywhere near Earth orbit unless you I.S.C. folks screw up again. I told you before we should have telescope and radar observatories set up around the belt run by interested astronomers and scientists, not by underpaid roboticists, scrubbers, robot jockeys, space-cops, civilians, whores and thieves. And speaking of pay, how does the Company plan on paying me this time? I was promised an Earth time yearly salary, but I got zip for the trip out here and got paid on Jovian time."

"You know how much it costs to keep humans out here, Peck. There's no such thing as a free orbit."

"Oh, don't give me that crap, I.S. Corporation has more gold up its ass than they know what to do with, and enough miners' blood on their hands to fill all the craters of Ganymede."

"That really isn't much on an astronomical scale," Henri said, amused.

"God you've changed. I thought you had integrity, now you're just another company apologist."

"You know that's not the way it is. We were young. For all your liberal values you forget there are bad people out there who do want to hurt American and Commonwealth interests. I've got responsibilities, Peck. Ever hear of those? Res-pon-si-bi-li-ties? You used to have them. I'm the damn CEO, now. I wanted it. I thought you wanted it. I was ambitious. You were ambitious. It's not what I thought it would be, but in some ways it's better. And you think you haven't changed, Peck? C'mon, you were the best, the most prestigious roboticist this side of the galaxy. First in your class at MIT Ocean City. You were supposed to win the Nobel Prize . . ."

"I'm still working on it . . ."

"That is before you turned forty . . ."

"Bastard . . ."

"C'mon Peck, you're hiding something big and you could be rich. You could already have that Nobel Prize. Stop being such a hippy. Think about Jaz. What would she do without her mother?"

41

"Is that a threat?"

"Maybe. You can't stand the idea of me having any power. When we were equals or when you were running ahead of me it was okay, but now that I'm Mr. CEO you won't have it."

"You know I don't care if you're my boss or not. That's your problem. For me it's not that simple. I'm exploring space and you pay me peanuts, scraps. I'm starving. Why do you think I'm broke? You ought to pay me more."

"That sounds fair."

"The point is that's what VAQ-ORE promised if I delivered and I did, and now you want to destroy everything I've built. Plumbers, electricians and mechanics have more prestige here than a two-bit roboticist. While I.S.C. is wining and dining the plumbers, I'm running around repairing robots for extra cash. Jovian time, that is."

"Don't you see? You need VAQ-ORE. We need you. Your bills are paid. What else do you need?" Henri turned on his not so subtle charms.

Peg pulled her hat on again, and stared off into space, shaking her head. She was tired and he'd caught her off-guard with all her defenses down. She hated him in that instant because he knew her needs and her desires and he was standing right there, unavailable.

"I don't need anything, or anyone."

"I know you're independent, Peck, you don't have to prove it to me. But you do need your family. You need me and if you don't believe that, then at least admit you need Jaz." She looked at him sharply, trying to find the hint of a threat, but there was nothing but his dimpled smile. He was threatening—and not just her but her daughter too. She knew what he meant. He limped toward her near the railing and handed her a credit card from within his jacket.

"Here . . ." She tried to shake her head, but he pressed it into her hand. "Here, take this. It's in your name. I've had it for a while, hoping I'd bump into you. It's an advance; a very large one. Go ahead and use it. It won't obligate you in any way. I don't want to come get it. What you're hiding, I'll pay even more when you bring it to me. I'll give you carte blanche."

"I've got to go, I need some rest."

Jack Cluewitt and the Imbrium Basin Murders   Ruth J. Burroughs

"You do that. I wish I could sleep too, but I'm obligated to chaperon a bunch of teeny-boppers on ice."

"You shouldn't go out so late."

"We didn't drink that much. We just danced late."

"I've seen her drink. Celia. You should both take it easy on that stuff."

"Okay, boss," he said and gave her a peck on the cheek. She watched as he skated out to the rink to join Jazmin and Celia. For the first time, Peg noticed that they looked like mother and daughter. They both had similar straight long blond hair, a recessive gene for Jaz, but her daughter's eyes were hazel green where Celia's were blue. They waved to her and she waved to Jaz, smiling back. She watched as they took off their coats and realized that they were both wearing matching scalloped pink skating skirts. Peg choked back a sob as she realized Jaz and Celia had planned to dress and look alike for the day. Peg smiled and turned, skating away trying to hold back tears. She hiccupped and a tear popped out. She rubbed it away and skated faster bumping into a few people on the way because the tears blurred her vision. That was it. Celia would take her place if Henri had her killed by that Vinny the Waltz assassin, the one who'd killed Antonia.

She'd kept VAQ-ORE away from the Oort Deep Space Explore Robot Ship Project, pretending to work for her ex, whom she still loved and also hated. She needed more time to complete her mission, her raison d'être, her dream, and her obsession and that was to install the Chinese coins with the endless source of fuel, the Cold Ion/plasma drives, into her ships. They'd only found twenty and only nine worked on her ships. The other ten were made specifically for the Kai Yuan Tong Bao rocket ships they'd discovered. She couldn't let people use it when it might send them not only into deep space with no food or water, but into other dimensions as well. So she had no power and no money, despite having the most powerful drives in the solar system. She wondered what lengths she'd go to, to save her robots and keep the secret of the fuel from Henri and Corporation. She would die for her cause: could she kill? No, but Henri could. He was capable of killing her or Jaz to get what he wanted. She dressed quickly and took the credit card. She would use the money against Henri and save her robots.

Edgar Moon Digger
Chapter Three

Edgar *Moon Digger* Chavez sat on a hydraulic lift-seat atop his Moon-roving, mine-digging, Nova Volteggiare, a nine wheeled Hummer vehicle, on the lunar basaltic plain of Imbrium Basin in the darkness of a lunar night that would last two weeks. It was six in the morning on Monday, June 7th in the year of our Earth-Mother 5030. But on the Moon's Imbrium Basin it was a long Moon night.

His rover camera hovered over a bleeding space suit sprawled on its back across the chiseled entry way to the ore mines, floating a little top-heavy, feeding him the image on his armchair hologram. In horror, he watched as the holo showed the body of a dead someone. Whoever it was had to be dead; he could see globs of blood escaping the gaping wound in the space suit where a bullet had exited the heart and chest, and more blood bubbling in the helmet visor. His camera coldly surveyed the area, showing him the corpse again and just went black; it just quit.

Edgar called headquarters. "Did you get that boss?"

"Get what?" Missi asked.

"The transmission. The dead Green Police in the cave. I just watched it on the hologram my camera was taking of the cave. A guy or gal in a space suit with a big bloody hole in the chest."

"Looking." There was a long pause. "Nope. Sorry, Ed. We got nothing. What makes you think it was Green Police?"

"The Green Police insignia patches."

Edgar pushed replay, but nothing was in the chair's memory. It was as though it hadn't happened. Nothing had transmitted, and Missi ordered him to stay put until Jules, his mining partner, arrived to help him record and witness

Jack Cluewitt and the Imbrium Basin Murders   Ruth J. Burroughs

the corpse or until Near-Earth Police Homicide detectives arrived.

He took a sip of hot lunar grown java and winced at the taste. He dimmed the lights on his suit and the nine-wheeled Volteggiare and enjoyed the view of the blue mass of Earth light in the dark sky. He'd run out of Jovian Java and was convinced they used Moon dust for coffee beans here. Today was his birthday and he was gonna piss and moan if no one bought him any Jupiter coffee beans. They worked an Earth-week schedule despite the daylight differences.

Ed Moon Digger wanted to take off his suit, but knew Security at Vasquez Ore Mining Corporation, or VAQ-ORE Corporation, was monitoring him, plus he had the nagging feeling someone was watching him. Maybe the murderer was nearby.

A magnetic field surrounded him on the Moon-digging vehicle, but there was no guarantee the pressurized atmosphere would always be stable. It was infamous for losing tensile strength at exactly the wrong moment. So there were strict rules about keeping the spacesuit on even if the helmet was collapsed. If the vehicle stopped generating atmosphere within the plasma field, his suit would automatically seal. Ed didn't like sucking on balls of coffee and he didn't like squeeze tubes. It just wasn't the same as sipping, but he did have to use a closed cup or it could get messy. Inside the field the stars looked fuzzy and the shield sparkled luminescent despite being mostly transparent.

He saw motion out of the corner of his eye and looked up. He was surprised to see one of the Moon digger robot dogs come barreling through the Alps Valley, its eyes shining like headlights down the gulley. Jules had finally got the licenses back even after his robot dog had attacked another miner. It had to be proved in court that Jules hadn't changed any programs in the dog. Edgar's own robot dog had been taken in the case and their robot dog mining licenses had been suspended and the dogs had been held by Moon City Police until the trial finished. Jules had promised to get Edgar his dog back once he won his case.

Peoples for the Preservation of Historic Space, PEFO-PRESH had set limits on mining the Moon, due to the interests of several species on Earth that rely on the Moon's

Jack Cluewitt and the Imbrium Basin Murders   Ruth J. Burroughs

tidal forces. The argument set forth by PEFOPRESH was that the Earth-Moon system could be altered drastically, causing severe weather changes if the Moon was too heavily mined. More severe than they were now, and Earthbound did not want worse weather.

The PEFOPRESH, the Green Police, NEPD, which included Moon City Police, had to approve the robot dogs' programming. The robot mining dogs were programmed to act like dogs. The Green Party and the PEFOPRESH, usually at odds with each other, just wanted to make sure the Moon didn't fall below the restricted mass.

It was easier to get a robot dog license in American Moon territories because space laws differed in different territories. Green Party came down on any religion that didn't accept the worship of Earth Mother and the Seed Theory. Any religions that supported guns, bombs and violence against seeding space through colonization in the Buckminster Fullerene colonies and evolving into space beings were punished ruthlessly by the Green Party through the Green Police. Anyone taking bribes to mine the Earth's Moon beyond the restrictions was punished severely, but this was the only way to stop generations of corruption from the old military and Corporate Party system of governance. The worst offenders were sent to the Genetically Modified Organisms Space-Habitats to be punished by the mysterious Genies, Genetically Modified Human Organisms, who, it was rumored, truly hated terrorists and often sided with preserving historic or virgin space and humans.

Ed Moon Digger called into his supervisor.

"Okay, Missi, I'm going in . . . I need to find out what I saw on the hologram."

"No, wait for Jules. It was probably a normal hallucination. Don't want to report that. No buddy, no mine."

"I've had breakfast, boss. Jules is late. But he's had my robot dog released. Now I have something to record the scene. I'll meet him in the pit. He's only five minutes away. I'll meet him under the Alps Mountains on the rille floor," Ed protested.

"He's ten minutes away or more. Finish your coffee, and then drive in," Missi ordered.

"Tell Jules to step on it. I'm tired of waiting."

Jack Cluewitt and the Imbrium Basin Murders   Ruth J. Burroughs

"You should have called me earlier. I would have got him up with a cold bucket of water."

"I don't think he slept late. He's got our robot mining dogs back."

"He did? Now, I wonder how he managed that."

"You know Jules."

Ed Moon Digger, sipped, savoring his coffee, looking in the distance toward the colorful lights of Moon City in Mare Frigoris, the basaltic Sea of Cold. Toward his right he saw glints of Jules' rover, scrambling as rapidly as a rover could go on the Moon, in the Alps Valley that cut through the Alps Mountains. If he could help it, Ed didn't use the Latin names. Looking back toward Moon City, he could almost make out the neon glow from Organdy Poisson's Sushi restaurant near Protagoras crater in Mare Frigoris if he squinted against the glare. The city used artificial light to mimic Earth day and night, but it was still black as a Moon night out here on the floor of Imbrium. He looked out over the jagged crater rims of the Moon and felt like something was out of place. He'd grown used to not having the robot dogs, but that wasn't what was bothering him. It was something else.

Even the way the shadows cast out over the rocky expanse seemed different, and things rarely changed in restricted zones. What was he missing? He took another sip of the Moon java and grimaced, spitting it out and then threw the rest of the cup overboard, out onto the plasma shield that covered the shiny gray confection, on the banged up surface of the Moon. The spilled coffee seeped through the artificial mag field.

Ed pushed a button and lowered the chair lift. The hiss of hydraulics seemed loud in his little bubble of atmosphere.

Once the programs were approved and the dogs were tested, they set up the licensing and miners were given precedent. Some people were buying them as companions and watch dogs, to guard their hoards. But there was less looting here than out on Mars and in the belt. The further from Earth, the more lawless it became.

Out in the distance, Ed Moon Digger watched in the Moon's silence as his dog's rapid approach disturbed the regolith. Its paw prints etched a jagged line toward the

Jack Cluewitt and the Imbrium Basin Murders   Ruth J. Burroughs

rover. The mechanical canine barked incessantly, but Ed could only hear the hum of the magnetic field generator.

Ed Moon Digger climbed down to greet the Moon dog, glad that Jules had his back and had the judge release their dogs. Jules would never throw him under the bus like some co-workers who trashed him did, just to get ahead.

The EM field parted for any robot and then re-established itself, but the atmo pressure alarms usually blasted if the bot took too long. The Nine Wheeled rover's superconductive engine pack that generated the mag field couldn't protect it from EM bombs, amplified Rayguns and the like.

He watched his robot dog leap gracefully through the air, its nose hit the mag field, sparking it, and then the rest of its robotic body came sailing through, like a diver hitting the surface of the water. Its chops still going, he could finally hear it barking. It padded the last few feet and jumped up on his space suit, slobbering. Fortunately its claws were retracted, but it drooled on him.

Ed wondered why the artisans gave it such details, but he believed it must have something to do with its cooling system. Moon Digger looked at its tag. Moon Mining License A0980997 Canine Robot Systems to Edgar Chavez, Moon Ore Extractor. Edgar and his robot dog went back a long way. It was good to see Cavity again. Now, that was some birthday present.

"Off boy." He pushed the heavy beast down. The dog ran circles around him.

"C'mon boy, up in the cabin. Let's go. We're not waiting for those slow pokes," Moon Digger said, patting the seat. The dog jumped up, wagging its tail, unable to contain its excitement.

Ed pushed the rover into gear and drove into the Alps Valley Rille toward the shade of the Alps Mountains where the mine was located, his lights automatically cutting into the dark shadow and lighting up spots of dirty sparkling ice. In the graben, the sides of the rille loomed above on either side. It was called Imbrium Basin Mine, even though it was technically in the Valles Alps. He drove the flat surface to a blasted area littered with rock, moving vehicles, backhoes and cranes in the shadows of Mount Alps, piled high with mounds of rock. He maneuvered the rover around the dark shapes, sparkling with olivine minerals even in the

Jack Cluewitt and the Imbrium Basin Murders   Ruth J. Burroughs

shadows and creating a maze that hid the entrance to the mining tunnels.

Moon Digger turned on the headlights as he entered the trolled depths of the tunnel. Three horizontal miles in, he stopped at the elevator shaft and parked.

He froze in his tracks. There it was. A body. A very dead body. Oddly, the Moon dog caught sight of it too and began barking incessantly again. It jumped out of the Hummer and leaped and bounded toward the body.

"Halt!" Edgar Moon Digger yelled, and the Moon dog froze.

Damn program, he thought. It was programmed to behave all too well like a real dog. The Moon dog trembled, whining, struggling against its doggy program. That's all he needed was to have to explain to Moon City Police how a Moon dog wrecked a crime scene. They'd get rid of the Moon dogs for good. And the Moon dogs were a godsend.

The body lay at the end of the trolled tunnel, sprawled on its back across the chiseled entryway to the ore mines, floating a little top-heavy, just as he'd seen on the holo. He could see the blood pooling in the helmet and the gaping wound, like a crater, in the space suit where the bullet had exited the heart and chest. Next to the corpse was his hover camera, sputtering on the hard pack mined floor, and purring. but not working, not recording.

Edgar Moon Digger would have to go back outside and get Jules or await the police. He called the dog back. It whined, shaking, and took a tentative step toward the body.

"Get over here, now!" Edgar yelled, and the robot quickly obeyed, reassured that it didn't have to make the decision to investigate. Moon Digger pulled the Hummer back a few yards and then turned on his suit. The helmet unfolded open over his face, the smart glass fogged as it adjusted pressurization. Outside the plasma field it was very cold, and once Ed turned off the vehicle only his heated suit could keep him from freezing to death, overheating or depressurizing. Ed waited as the suit pressurized the atmo and warmed up and a green light blinked. He turned off the mag field and the Humvee's engine, and climbed out of the vehicle. He looked back down the long tunnel, darkness dotted by little yellow lights. He saw footprints going back down and he knew the Hummer might destroy more evi-

49

Jack Cluewitt and the Imbrium Basin Murders   Ruth J. Burroughs

dence if he drove it back. He could wait here in the Humvee, but Jules might destroy the footprints, too. He tried calling Jules, but the thick walls of the mine prevented his communication from going through.

"Emergency protocol 24159," Moon Digger said to the dog. The robot dog froze in its tracks.

"Record this message: Jules: This is Edgar. We really do have a homicide here. That's right! A dead body at the end of the tunnel. Notify VAQ-ORE Corp. and Moon City Police that my hologram camera told the truth before it quit. Do not enter the cavern. By the way, thanks for getting my dog back. Cavity, follow these instructions: Run, quickly but only in the Hummer tracks. Give Jules my message. Obey Jules. Go now."

Ed Moon Digger watched as the emergency protocol set in. The dog's eyes clicked like the apertures of a lens. It jerked into motion and leapt onto the regolith sandy tire tracks of the Humvee.

Ed engaged the light on his spacesuit and headed down the tunnel after the Moon dog. His breathing sounded jagged and harsh inside the suit. He could smell the suit's nano-fibers and smart-glass mixed in with his sweat. It was difficult walking in the light gravity of the Moon in the dimly lit mine. His light bounced eerie reflections off his visor. He thought he saw several robot dog footprints, some coming and some leaving the tunnel but he'd ordered Cavity to stay in the Humvee tracks. Why hadn't it followed his orders? He wanted to wipe the sweat dripping off his forehead, but the helmet stood in his way and he noticed he was breathing harder. It was very cold inside the Moon-caves and his suit temperature had to compensate. He stopped to look back, but he had turned a bend and could no longer see the Hummer or the dead body. He picked up his feet and pushed himself along, wishing he could run, but if he did, he might bang his head on the machine-chiseled rock above if he leapt too hard.

He started to breathe harder and wondered if the murderer was still lurking down one of the corridors or in some dark shadow of the mine. Icicles formed on some condensation on his gloves. He shook them off.

Edgar felt like a thin paper lantern bouncing down a dark cavern with sharp edged rock walls that could tear him apart. He tried to pick up the pace, but if he stumbled he might break the visor or tear the suit. He forced himself to slow down. The robot dog would get to Jules soon, and Jules would wait for him. But what if the dog took off? Autonomous units weren't always able to understand their orders. Then Jules would head back to Moon City without him. He'd have to walk back to Moon City with only nine hours' worth of oxygen. He forced himself to stop worrying. He forced himself to count and to breathe deeply so he wouldn't panic. His heart beat slowed and he calmed down. It seemed an eternity before he saw the harsh light of Jules' rover lights at the end of the tunnel. His suit radio clicked on and static hissed out of the earphone.

"Hey, Moon Digger! Is that you I see?"

Ed nodded even though Jules couldn't see his nod. "Boy am I glad to see you there!"

"Glad I stayed, huh?" Jules said. Moon Digger could make him out on top of his rover, out on the floor of the dark rille, sitting next to his own Moon digger dog, a Great Dane, named Apache.

"You don't know how glad," Moon Digger replied.

"VAQ-ORE Corp. wants to know how the Greepol was killed." Jules' voice crackled. Moon Digger paced himself.

"Looks like a bullet wound. Soft fabric space suit like the one I'm wearing. And there's foot tracks leading out," Edgar said into the headphone, making his way toward Jules.

"Just leading out, not leading in?"

"I don't know. I just stayed on the Hummer tracks."

"Was it a he or a she?"

"Couldn't tell. Too much blood. It's Green Police though. I saw their Greepol insignias on the space suit," Moon Digger replied. He saw his own Moon dog waiting timidly next to Jules' vehicle, like it couldn't move, its tail wagging as it caught sight of him. "Oh, Cavity," he mumbled.

"Do you think the murderer is still in there?" Jules asked.

"Don't think so now, but I had a moment back there," Moon Digger replied.

"Wow. Not a good walk back, huh?"

"Yup, not a good walk."

51

Jack Cluewitt and the Imbrium Basin Murders Ruth J. Burroughs

"C'mon up on my Humvee and take your helmet off. I've got a warm mag field on." Jules turned his own helmet off and it telescoped off his head.

Ed Moon Digger walked through the mag field. It zapped the regolith off his boots. He climbed onto Jules' Humvee and pushed a button on his suit to see if it matched the pressurization in the mag field. When it lit green, he pushed another button and, like a convertible car's top, it collapsed back off his head. He zipped off the gloves, took a deep breath and wiped the sweat off his forehead.

"Will you release Cavity before he has a coronary?"

"Cavity, Emergency protocol 24159. C'mon." Jules patted the seat. Cavity, his robot dog shook, zapping any regolith particles off, then jumped up alongside Jules' mining dog, Apache.

"Missi told me not to move, or otherwise I would have driven closer," Jules said.

"What did she say?" Ed asked.

"That we were to stay here until the Moon City Police arrived and then we would be brought in for questioning," Jules replied.

"Brought in for questioning?"

"It's routine." Jules pulled out a thermos and two covered cups.

"No thanks, I had some coffee already," Ed replied.

"It's Jovian Java, heat roasted by Jove, by Jove," Jules said, smiling his dimpled infamous smile, known interplanetary as the smile that could charm the skirts off the coldest Modified-Human. "Happy birthday, boy."

"Where did you get that? I thought there was a strike."

"The Interplanetary Mail Delivery System, Intermad, is back up and operational. The union made some kind of deal and we just got delivery. That's why I was late. I know you and how you are without your Jupiter Java." Jules' eyes sparkled.

"What would I do without my friends?" Cavity barked, as though in agreement.

"A good Moon digger needs his Cavity and you deserve the best, Ed. I had to get him back."

Moon Digger shook his head. "You could charm the pants off a truck driver with that smile. You should have gone into politics or pornography."

52

Jules laughed. "We are not truly happy until we are truly happy, doing what we love to do. I love the Moon. I love mining. I like Moon whiskey, a good sushi bar and a good sex robot. That's all I need."

"You're such a proletariat. You could be sitting back enjoying a life rich in lies and profits or lying on your back with a dozen beautiful women at your beck and call, but instead you want to dig holes in the Moon." Ed sipped the wonderful coffee.

"We are not truly happy until we are truly happy," Jules repeated, sitting back.

"Here they come. It's a Moon City Police Lunar Landing Vehicle. Look up there. That's stupid. They should drive up in rovers. The Lula V might kick up some dust and ruin the crime scene. I may be working class but I ain't stupid." Ed squinted, looking toward the Alps Valley floor, where the blue Moon Police Department lunar landing vehicle touched below the dark rille walls.

"Right, you're not stupid. You are one crazy son of a bitch, you know." Jules smiled and sipped the steaming, exotic Jovian java.

"Yeah, I know, we are not truly happy until we're truly happy doing what we love to do."

Kenneth Mesersmith, Space Dowser, Seer Café Copernicus/Moon
Chapter Four

Ken Mesersmith stood on the empty deck of the Café Copernicus and looked out the window at the landscape of the Moon. He emptied the pipe by tapping it on the edge of the Ring gold tray. He refilled it with a special blend of Texan-Mars tobacco. *A poor man's drug indeed,* he thought. At least homegrown lungs were cheaper by the dozen; homegrown, being the Moon. The risk of cancer was a siren calling, beckoning him to smoke, to take the chance.

He hooked his thumb under the dark blue suspenders of his pants. He held the olive-hued Peridot pipe, ornately carved with Hebrew glyphs for Mesersmith, in his other hand. He studied his reflection in the window momentarily. The bright orange feathers of a fish lure popped out of a fish hook stuck in his right suspender, a gift of his mentor and father, Alton Mesersmith back when Ken had attended the Mars Chemical School of Space Light Dowsers near Aitken Basin Ocean. He scratched his dark blonde beard and wondered if he should shave it. He turned away and walked a few steps back to the empty, dimly lit bar and poured himself a glass of water.

He held the message in his hand; a tiny capsule filled with data; a bio-chemical telegram, BCT-Gram or, for the attention-span-challenged generation, a B-Gram. Its hues celebrated in the dimly lit lounge as he rolled it around in his palm. More powerful than a psychedelic drug, yet more efficient and because of its rapid dissolution, usually carried no side effects.

No one sent messages in capsule form unless they were important and very secret. It had to be crucial information or why bother risking your brain for something trivial? Ken

Jack Cluewitt and the Imbrium Basin Murders   Ruth J. Burroughs

did not like taking risks at his age although when he was younger . . .

He popped the pill in his mouth and swallowed. The effect was almost immediate. He walked unsteadily back to the golden ashtray, tapped the ashes and refilled and lit the pipe, smoking unsteadily.

He looked out at the stars and watched as they dripped, melted and coalesced into the familiar form of Perigwin *Peg* Cardillo, roboticist, physicist and friend. She smiled,

"Hi, Mesersmith! This means you popped the pill. You've got balls, I tell you. Can't believe that old brain of yours is still holding up."

"I'm not more than a couple years older than you, Cardillo you ole bitch."

"Did I tell you these B-Grams cause permanent schizophrenia? Just joking, Ken. Gotcha . . ." she said, smiling, the colors of her face melting into the stars.

"Stupid jerk."

"That's the P-Gram not the B-Gram; don't ever get them mixed up. Well, I know you'd have some comeback. Just don't call me stupid or late for dinner. I'll try to make this short and sweet. VAQ-ORE is up to its tricks again." Her smile melted away and tears formed in her eyes. She cleared her throat,

"Sorry, I'll pull myself together." She took a breath. "They're pulling the rug out from under the Kuiper robot project. They're coming in to dismantle everything and turn me into head shepherd. You've got to help me. Henri knows something. He's threatened to kill me or my daughter Jaz if I don't cooperate and let him have it. I can't let them destroy the Cold Plasma source or keep it to themselves and charge people for its use. You hear me Mesersmith. I can't let them have the coins. I can't let them turn my robot ships into asteroid mining and shepherds. VAQ-ORE will screw everything up. Everything we planned. Everything we had hoped for."

Ken Mesersmith puffed on his tobacco-filled pipe as the B-Gram dissipated. He was shocked. He knew she might not get the grant, but he didn't think the company would pull this. Reprogram her robots. That was like murder to a roboticist. A program is a program is a program.

Jack Cluewitt and the Imbrium Basin Murders   Ruth J. Burroughs

A program is what it does. Changing a program was like trading your baby for a new one because you didn't like yours, a robot maker's blasphemy.

True, she could shelve the programs and find other robots to fit them, but not top of the line. Maybe the Company had planned this all along. Have Cardillo design and build the robots and then just when the robots were ready, pull the programs and write them to Company specs, but for space mining and comet shepherding? Now that the shock had worn off he didn't understand why he hadn't foreseen this. The Company was two steps ahead, as usual.

Ken tapped out the pipe and set it in a small ornate stone box, next to his smartsuit. He had work to do. He had to get a message to her. Tell her what to do and when. They had to save her robots . . . their robots. At all costs. Ken had been depressed lately and he felt the deep wound of it like an ache in his heart. Those robots were his babies. His loyalty to them knew no bounds. He would defend those robots. He would die for those robots. As he donned his suit coat, he picked up his pipe box, knowing he could kill for those robots.

Rappel Luna Organ Enforcement Agent
June 6th, 5030 Sunday Night, Organdy's Sushi Restaurant
Chapter Five

Japanese undercover Organ Enforcement agent, Rappel Luna, didn't want anyone to see the glowing green holographic insect tattoo emanating from her inner thigh, an emblem of her Yakuza heritage. She'd only found nickel and dime organ thieves, but enough that she'd been raised quickly through the ranks, although some thought it was her connections and family. But she didn't need to prove herself. She knew she'd earned the deep cover assignment.

It was closing time for Organdy Poisson's Moon City Sushi Restaurant in the Sea of Cold near Protagoras crater. Outside it was dark even under the plasma domes. Smart regolith-glass domes within mag shield domes contained the flora and fauna of Earth. They used bright lamps indoors to mimic daylight and sunset in an Arboretum-like setting. Under the smart glass dome was Organdy's Sushi Restaurant, shaped like a fish, made from scraps of leftover amorphous Fullerene metal; the sign glowed neon. Rappel was finishing up a couple stragglers. Organdy had fed the wait staff and sent everyone home early because it had been unusually slow. She was serving a couple of four tops and he was serving three Green Police at the sushi bar, two of whom shared a body, so there were only two bodies. It was odd because Greepols don't usually order organs for themselves. The Forestry and Agricultural department did that. So this was off duty stuff. She inconspicuously kept an eye on them, which wasn't hard because one of her customers was drunk and obnoxious. It was unusual to get a tipsy customer in a fine dining restaurant, but there were at least one or two a year.

She checked on the two Green Police to see if they needed drinks and noticed that they had a real paper book. That was odd. What were Greepols doing with a paper book? It was illegal to own new paper in much of the Space Worlds, let alone on the Moon. The Greepols didn't care about politics or religion as long as everyone obeyed the Green laws. Polluting and killing trees were the worst offenses in the world but it was okay to own a museum piece. Most people kept their paper in a non-oxygen environment to keep it from decaying. Two of the Greepols shared one body but Rappel was used to seeing radiation mutants. Unusually-formed Greepols were usually the most anti-military-industrial-complex, anti-robot, anti-computers and anti-corporation. Some were vehemently fanatical about preserving pristine Earth-Moon and space and they'd been trying to get Organdy's attention for the past half hour.

Rappel served the desserts and called a tram for her last customers and made sure they didn't take their cars. After she cashed out the other four top, it was just the last three customers at the sushi bar and her and Organdy. The other restaurant help had all left. While she was cleaning up, the Greepols looked around nervously while they ate their futomaki, motioning to her. She could tell they were scared about something, but she was afraid they'd blow her cover. She went into the kitchen with her tray of tea cups and empty dessert bowls. Organdy followed behind her. He spoke with a heavy French accent.

"They're paying customers, and they're buying organs."

"We should get back out there."

"I'll be right out. You go take them some sake on the house." His smile lit up the kitchen and made his eyes sparkle. She hated lying to him, but she was under cover when she met him and it wasn't until later that she'd fallen in love with him.

She couldn't help but do his bidding, when he smiled like that it melted her heart. She would jump off the Valles Marineris Grand canyon for him. She straightened out her kimono.

She went out with the hot sake and three cups and noticed that they had finished the futomaki.

Jack Cluewitt and the Imbrium Basin Murders   Ruth J. Burroughs

"Here's some sake, on the house." She smiled and poured the steaming bitter rice wine, into the hole in the tiny cup for the lady, noticing that the paper book was gone. That was odd, and they had no way to conceal it on their persons. No pockets. No purses. The female Green Police had blonde hair and sad blue eyes. Her skin was as pocked as the surface of the Moon and she seemed very grateful for the hot sake. She bowed her head slightly and thanked her.

She poured the second cup and smiled at the nervous patron, one of the twins. He seemed most grateful and quickly drank the shot and wanted another. The other twin said no thank you and waved the cup away. He told his twin not to drink too much. She walked by the giant fish tank and noticed the robots vigorously swimming about the water as sand settled down to the bottom. She pretended she hadn't seen anything and returned to the kitchen.

"Hi, honey. I set them up with an account and called the Langer lab for some more gelatin substance. It will take some time but they'll have compatible organs in two years or so. Sometimes twins who share a body need a new organ often. The three livers they want right away, so I'm having the com scan my lab for anything that might do temporarily."

"Organdy, why don't you let me lock up? I'll take care of these customers and you go check on the livers for them. I'll tell them you went to the Lab," she said, thinking she had to find out why they hid the book in the tank and what was so important about it.

"That's a good idea. They wanted one lung, one heart and three livers. But it will take me a while. I won't be back until tomorrow noon or evening. Will you be all right by yourself?"

"Of course, we're closed tomorrow."

"Oh, yeah. I forget you can take care of yourself." He reached inside of her kimono between her legs. She giggled.

"Not now, Organdy," she protested.

"Why, are you in a hurry?" he asked and she shook her head as he continued to play with her inside her kimono. He picked her up and carried her into the storage room, closing the door and made love to her on a sack of rice, her kimono off, her holographic green locusts sparkling in the dark storage room. Organdy's smile faded as he kissed her

Jack Cluewitt and the Imbrium Basin Murders   Ruth J. Burroughs

hard and plunged into the soft flesh between her legs. The rippling muscles of her legs wrapped around him tightly, and the deep blue Antarctic circles of her eyes shone in the dim light. He was like the green brown earth pumping into her, grinding her, until they came together crying out their simultaneous orgasms.

⚜

Rappel cashed the three Greepols out and made Organdy go to the Langer Lab to do his organ work for them. The restaurant was finally empty and clean and the shades drawn on the windows, keeping the still bright lamp lights of Moon Dome City and any prying eyes from peering inside. It mimicked a June Earth day so it was still light out, despite being ten pm. But the lamps mimicked a setting sun so it was at least getting darker. Since the regolith had been cleaned, and the electromagnetic plasma field had gone up over the dome, people could walk around without wearing a pressurized suit all the time, and they did. Couples with robot dogs and baby carriages strolled by all the time. She locked up the front door and went into the back storage area to sleep. Monday Organdy's was closed and she could have her contact meet her in the kitchen in the back and take the book away, then most of her worries would be gone with it.

⚜

Monday morning Rappel woke early, still wearing her kimono. She fished around for some slacks and a pink sweatshirt and waited, but ended up cleaning 'til noon. Her contact, Organ Enforcement Bureau informant Edgar Chavez, was to meet her at Organdy's Restaurant this morning, but called to tell her he was running late. He was out on a mining dig.

She stepped onto a chair and then stood on a tabletop and reached over the rim of the tank. Her hand dug around in the sand at the bottom of the tank to get the book out.

The colorful fish swam around in the tank of organ-growing emulsion, tickling her arm. She gently sifted the book out of the sand and into the pressurized environment.

Jack Cluewitt and the Imbrium Basin Murders   Ruth J. Burroughs

She wrapped it in a clean white cloth and examined it on the floor. It appeared undamaged. The liquid preserved the organic material, rather than breaking it down like normal water would have.

The doorbell rang in the back and she ran and unlocked it. Edgar and his robot dog Cavity stood in the soft light of the back alley. Rappel grabbed him and pulled him inside. She didn't entirely trust him, but she had no one else, and she'd worked with him before. He took the money she gave him from the Organ Enforcement Bureau for his savvy information about the underworld of black market organ theft.

"You have to hurry."

"What's going on?" he asked.

"Leave your dog here in the kitchen. I don't need this recorded."

"Okay, Cavity, stay," Ed commanded. Cavity stretched out onto the kitchen floor and closed his eyes.

"I'll show you out in the dining room."

"What is it?" he asked as she dragged him. She showed him the damp book.

"Take it and hide it somewhere. Do you have a place?" She handed him the book wrapped in the white napkin.

"Yeah, I'll take it over to Máóhk-Clay's. No one will suspect she has it. There's been trouble at the mining cave."

"What trouble?" Rappel asked, a sense of dread overcoming her. She felt the salty sting of perspiration under her arms, not a good thing for an undercover agent to sweat.

"A murder out in the mining tunnel. She looked like a Greepol."

"What?"

"Her space suit had the Greepol insignia."

"What! Do you think you were followed?"

"No. I don't think so."

"What exculpated you?"

"Strange things happened. They nearly caught the killer."

"What did the victim look like?"

"I couldn't see through the space suit, but the coroner said she was a small woman with blonde hair and bad skin. Why?"

61

Rappel gasped. "She was just here yesterday, Sunday, with two other Greepols who happen to share one body. They were really nervous. I think they were trying to tell Organdy something. One of them put this old-fashioned paper book in the tank. She must have been hiding it and then was killed for it, but I'm not sure yet why it's so important."

"So, you're telling me that you're putting me and Máóhk-Clay in grave danger?"

"That's right. You'll both be in grave danger."

Ed scratched his head. "Okay. I know she'd do it for you."

Rappel frowned. "Máóhk-Clay knows?"

"Don't worry your cover isn't blown. She doesn't know you're an Organ Enforcement Agent. She just likes you as a friend. You've always been kind to her."

"If I'm in danger so is Organdy because they'll backtrack here and start looking for the book. You have to sneak out of here and make sure no one sees you or the book. Understand?"

"Will do. I'll put the book in Cavity's stomach compartment and take it out to Máóhk-Clay's house."

"I'll have to come get it later. Tell her to be careful."

"She is a Siwen."

"Yes, but that doesn't mean she's all seeing, otherwise she would have caught the killer and there's a killer or killers out there after the book."

"We better get out of here then."

"Yes. We should."

Edgar exited through the swinging kitchen door. He loaded the book in the sleeping robot dog's stomach then slipped out the back door and Rappel quickly locked up. She had to send a message to headquarters.

Why would anyone kill for a stupid old paper book? This had something to do with organ stealing. If she wasn't careful she might get Organdy killed too.

62

Robot City and Máóhk-Clay
Chapter Six

Robot City lay sprawled out in South Pole-Aitken Basin in and around the Amundsen crater. Once a colorless military site littered with refuse, it was now a thriving Green community. From orbit the regolith glass domes within domes sparkled and magnetic fields pressurized and filled the crater with oxygen and purified lunar soil and Moon grown flowers, trees, plants and birds.

Before long it would look as verdant as Moon City's domes in Mare Frigoris, as hot and tropical as a Cretaceous jungle, and doing no justice to the name Sea of Cold. But Máóhk-Clay couldn't see all the wondrous colors of new Robot City because she had been blinded in an explosion in the so-called accident in the Flora group Asteroids. And though she was physically blind, the Jovian water had opened her sixth sense, her psychic eyes and she could see something was coming, something life-changing. There was blood, lots of blood and more dead Green Party people. But they weren't Gull and his wife Savannah. No. There was one dead. No, two dead. No . . . three dead. No; one dead and two more were going to die. She was confused. Something was wrong with her vision. She was always sure of the number, but not this time.

She sat near her cook stove in the cold cramped quarters of her makeshift kitchen on the outskirts of Robot City in a collection of old mining shacks. She could be outside cooking now, but she'd grown used to living in a space suit. It took quite an effort psychologically to get outside.

Her seeing-eye dog was worse. Thoroughly trained to keep her indoors except when suited, she wouldn't let her go out and she was far too old to retrain. Beebee was no robot dog. She was a living, breathing flea-bitten yellow lab.

Jack Cluewitt and the Imbrium Basin Murders Ruth J. Burroughs

Máóhk-Clay looked out the window and tried to make out the sparkling lights of the mag field with her right eye, while she stirred the pot of stew. She could see light and dark with that eye. She was too poor to get implants and she didn't want them anyway. It was her and Beebee's favorite: insect stew.

Plasma shields and proper nano built housing for destitute populations in African communities became the answer for saving lives, and insects the most popular food group. Máóhk-Clay liked dried grubs with cereal in the morning. They had a lot of protein and covered most food groups when she mixed them with rice milk and fruits.

Her people had no problem with meat and on occasion she would eat some, even though many people thought this to be politically incorrect. She didn't eat whale meat though, but she loved venison. She lost Green points even so.

She crumbled some saffron into the broth and stirred, letting it come to a boil. When it was done, she ladled out a scoop and poured it onto Beebee's bowl with a handful of dog food and set it down. She poured herself a bowl of steaming buggy soup and sat down to dinner. The most pious Chippewa woman this side of Mars, she'd lost her vision in a bomb blast during the Corporation Party coup of the more popular Green Party candidates. Surely Candidate for President of the American Space Commonwealth, Antonia G. Clef, would have won the election by a landslide victory.

The most popular candidate had been assassinated before she could take office, there being no other good Green candidates. Their replacements, Octavio and Lars Frydenland, were unpopular and quickly disappeared into obscurity after the Corporation Party won by a narrow margin. Gull had been too sick, and he and Savanna were designing their babies. Neither would run for a second ten year term at that time.

But the Green Party and Earth-Moon religion had only grown stronger because of that assassination. There were many versions of Gaia worship, including ancient twentieth and twenty-first century ones that had evolved and included Mother Theresa or Terra Mater or Earth Mother. A sweet optimistic child of a hard-working Moon mining family, Máóhk-Clay thought she could help change the

Jack Cluewitt and the Imbrium Basin Murders   Ruth J. Burroughs

Erthworlds. Help those suffering in the large Buckminster Fullerene Colonial vessels housing the poor mining colonies. They didn't have the best medicine, food or protection from space junk that the rich Erthworlds had in the better orbits. After the campaign, and the so-called mining accident in the Flora Colony near the Ring of Stones, she had returned to the Moon with a broken spirit. Forgotten and poor, even though she had written the bills that had become laws against space war and pollution, she drank herself into oblivion.

She went back to work, making clay Indian pots, solar tiles and other textile work from lunar materials, but dying the clay an Earthen red and sometimes selling the vessels as Martian clay pots. As a devout Natural at the time of the accident, she didn't get new eyes and she handled her disability bitterly at first, until she realized the Jovian water of Europa had given her a sixth sense. She got around the way she always had by touch and memory. She knew the window was fogged with steam and that she couldn't see out into the darkness even if she could see. The lights in the house were on for Beebee, except when they went to sleep and Beebee would shut them down.

The mildly sweet and spicy aroma of the insect stew filled her home. Máóhk-Clay ladled a big spoon up to her mouth and slurped the hot buggy soup just as the doorbell chimed.

It was probably her boyfriend, who she'd told numerous times he didn't have to ring. But he told her he didn't like startling her. She pressed the intercom with her prosthetic foot.

"Come in, you nut," she said, and the door slid open.

"How did you know it was me?" She imagined he was a tall dark handsome man with rippling muscles.

"Is that Cavity with you?" She could hear his motor running.

"Yes, Cavity's back. Jules got him out of the pen," Edgar replied.

He was actually a robust thick heavyset Moon mining man, older looking than his forty-six hard-living, hard-working, hard-drinking years. He'd grown tired of boozing and whoring and settled down with Máóhk-Clay four years ago, although they didn't always live together. They both

65

Jack Cluewitt and the Imbrium Basin Murders   Ruth J. Burroughs

liked gambling, line dancing, dog-walking and Moon-jumping in Moon City.

"Where's my bowl?" Edgar asked.

"Get it yourself, you lazy SOB," she said, smiling. Her long, beautifully cared-for hair was pulled back and had not been touched by gray yet. Her eyes were white and she wore the symbols of a shaman around her neck. She pushed loose strings of hair behind her ears.

Beebee hardly acknowledged Edgar and completely ignored Cavity, who seemed entirely enraptured by Beebee.

"You're not letting that big hunk of engineering mishap in are you?" she asked, shoveling soup into her mouth.

"Cavity?"

"Who else?"

"He's in love with Beebee. I can't leave him outside," Edgar replied and Beebee barked, asking Edgar to close the door.

Cavity hopped into the tiny living room of the mobile home and plopped down beside Beebee. Not programmed to react to living dogs, Cavity had to make do with what programs he had. He had a program for other mining dogs, for miners, for guests, for vehicles, but not for animals.

His creative program kicked in and basically, for all intents and purposes, he was in love.

Edgar pulled up a chair between Máóhk-Clay and Beebee and poured himself a bowl of stew. He loved her cooking, especially deep fried tempura grasshopper in scorpion broth with seaweed and tofu.

They both methodically slurped, spooning and gulping while Beebee quietly lapped up her food and Cavity looked longingly up at her.

"I hear Organdy has a pair of eyes waiting for you in the shop."

"What's wrong with the way I am, Edgar Moon Digger Chavez? I'm blind. You keep trying to get me to change. At my age? Besides, it's your birthday, not mine."

"Well then get the eyes for my birthday. It will be a present to me."

"What am I gonna do with sight now, at my age? Besides, I don't want charity from anyone and I know you can't afford those organs on company pay."

66

Jack Cluewitt and the Imbrium Basin Murders Ruth J. Burroughs

"Who cares who pays for your eyes? The tribal council owes you those eyes. The world owes you those eyes."

"I'm known here as Blind Máóhk-Clay. I was a metal dowser, a typical Siwen, before I drank Europa water at the Jovian hospital. After I lost my vision and drank the Europa water, my second sight improved. If Haze Monaghan hadn't saved me I would never have become a seer, a Siwen, a dowser. You and I should retire soon, but we can't live on your pension and retirement funds. Not for another twenty years. The mining company won't let you retire until you're gasping your last breath. They'd do all the mining with robots if they didn't really screw things up when they go wrong.

If it weren't for the psychic readings we'd be in Starvation Alley. What good would I be if I'm not Blind Máóhk-Clay? Seeing Máóhk-Clay isn't going to get any business."

"I promised I'd get you a gilded yacht or reservations on one of the Fullerenes."

"Stop dreaming, Edgar. We're mining people. We'll never see the good life, although I'd like to see the inside of an Erthworld someday."

"And you should. Get your eyes fixed and wear lenses that make you look blind," Edgar said, not for the first time.

"That's deceitful, and you know it. There are enough fakes around. I'm the real thing. I'm a Natural. I don't believe in jacking in or upgrades. The tribal council will not agree. I don't think they want me to get the eyes. They think I am blind for spiritual reasons, and that was why I was given the gift of second sight. It is why I can see into the other world."

"You can't keep living with survivor guilt. Stop punishing yourself. How do you know you weren't meant to become sighted again? The government . . . No the worlds owe you those eyes. You sacrificed them when the Green candidate for President for American Space Commonwealth was assassinated and you were blinded. You can get eyes without cyber-chips in them. They have completely organic Green eyes and I'll buy them for you. You couldn't have known what was going to happen."

"I should have seen that coming."

"That argument won't work anymore, Máóhk-Clay. You could dowse for metals, not foresee the future. It's time you stopped suffering. You said you wanted to change, so change. Do yourself some favors. Treat yourself."

"I'm happy the way I am."

"I lie to myself sometimes too. It's hard not to when you live like we do. Others would die for such an opportunity. Get your eyesight back. If the tribe didn't take such a big cut, you would be well off."

"It isn't a cut. The shaman woman is a part of the community. I don't understand you sometimes. Stop acting so colonial."

"We'll cut back on the casino nights."

"I'm getting tired of casino nights."

"Yeah, me too."

"So did they find out who murdered the Greepol?" she asked.

"I'm not allowed to talk about it yet, but you'll be the first to know when they let me. One reason is because they have to interview a lot of people and you might be on the short list."

"Me? They think I might have murdered the Greepol?"

"We really shouldn't be talking about it," Ed said quite seriously and Máóhk-Clay laughed. Ed's face lit up seeing her smile, but she quickly turned mock serious.

"Oh, right. Sorry." He kissed her on the cheek.

"I like it when you smile. Well, I'm going to take some stew back for Jules."

"There's plenty, and he's welcome to it. The thermos is on top of the fridge."

"Why don't you come outside?" he asked, getting up and filling the thermos with the stew. She could hear him doing something else. Opening and shutting something on his robot dog and placing it on top of the fridge. But he said nothing. Like everyone else, he thought she was disabled and didn't know she could see with her ears.

"Sure. If Moon City PD needs me, I'll do a reading on the dead Greepol."

"You know you deserve those eyeballs more than anyone. You *are* the Green party."

"Okay, you win. Drop by Organdy's and tell him to hold the eyes for me. The tribal council will just have to take me as I am."

68

"That's the first thing I'll do in Moon City." He gave her a kiss. Cavity wagged his tail.

"There's a robot rummage sale going on. Would you like to go?"

"Are you kidding?"

"Would I kid you about something like that?"

"Beebee is not going to let me out without my space suit."

"Do you have that venison pemmican?" he asked.

"Yes.

"That will get her out."

Edgar stepped out onto the plasma shield-covered lunarscape and waited for Máóhk-Clay and the dogs. She took his elbow and they walked through the maze of collapsible mobile homes, under clothes lines and around junk scattered here and there. "There is nothing I like better than a robot rummage sale except your fine cooking, a hot bath and Moon jumping." Edgar said. Máóhk-Clay smiled, but she couldn't shake the feeling that death was coming from the hand of the Corporation again and it was going to take the lives of the Greens once again. She just wondered if it was her own life that was on the line.

Alps Valley Rille in the Lunar Alps Imbrium Basin Greepol Homicide Investigation Monday Morning, June 7th, 5030

Chapter Seven

On their way to the crime scene near the Sea of Rains, in an old lunar vehicle from Moon City, Jack sat next to homicide detective Jane Salgado.

Indigo Jane noisily chewed gum, her gold jewelry dripped and jingled. Two NEPD patrollers sat up front; the female sat to the driver's right.

Jack checked his space suit for holes and made sure the chamber was full of nano repairbots. At least the department could afford the repairing of accidental spacesuit tears out in the field. They preferred only genetically modified robot-suited cops, but there just weren't enough. There were hundreds of expendable Naturals, though.

With his helmet visor off, he sat next to Erthworlds' retired-from-boxing champion, Indigo Jane. Not too many people knew she was a plain clothes detective now. She spit her wad of chewing gum out the window through the mag field onto the regolith and lit up a stogie. Jack also didn't trust the somewhat new magnetic containment field surrounding the vehicle, supposedly pressurizing the area without kicking up regolith. It was advanced mag shield technology, and he figured it must cause something horrible down the line if didn't just fail to pressurize. Jane sucked on an expensive Venusian zeegar and blew the smoke out into the pressurized air of the Humvee.

"Are you going to pollute what little air we have in here?" Jack asked. The two officers in the front laughed.

Jack Cluewitt and the Imbrium Basin Murders   Ruth J. Burroughs

"There's plenty of air in here, and I've got the air purifier on. Besides, you'll die from breathing regolith before you die from my second-hand smoke."

He grimaced. "Well at least you're masking that burnt smell of space."

"What, that barbecued by space radiation smell?"

"Yes and that air purifier is probably worse than breathing in regolith particles."

"You're so paranoid, Jack." She flashed her pearly whites. She took a couple more puffs and flicked the stogie out. It zapped through the electromagnetic field, exiting the pressurized environment before it hit the dust.

"Better?" she asked

"Polluter." He ran his hand through his disheveled curly brown hair.

"It's a vacuum. How can my stogie pollute anything, especially without oxygen to keep it burning? Someday we'll drive past it again and I'll pick it up and light it up again and it'll be as good as new."

"I doubt it. Just because it's a vacuum doesn't mean it won't get stale."

"I'll betcha," she challenged, "I'll bet you dinner at Organdy's. We come back to this spot next year and my zeegar will be as good as new. Here's the current longitude and latitude," she said, punching up the com, "about four meters back."

"Well, smoke 'em if you want radioactive lungs. Look, we're almost there."

"Bet?" she asked.

"Yeah, you have a bet. It will be glowing, you know. That's worse than stale."

Forensics chief Cal and his crime scene investigators, the Green Police, and two Memory reporters waited for Jack and Jane. All their vehicles parked in a domino pattern to share the EM shields so their visors were down. Everyone's ear, arm, palm or suit phones linked to the Grid had various and sundry holograms twisting off of them, detailing weather on Earth and satellite positions on the Grid. But once they entered the crime scene, all holos off the Grid were ordered shut down or the link was cut. Jack and Jane seldom linked off the Grid and wore no phones. They found other means to call headquarters and preferred privacy and Natural living.

Jack was an infamous stickler for detail. His Simon abilities were known Moon-wide. Either he had secretly cyber upgraded, they thought, or he was psychic. They often said he left no molecule unturned. He was obsessive, even religious about his work. He was all duty and logic and didn't believe in space witchcraft or dowsers, goddesses or gods; he didn't believe he had any supernatural abilities; he was just fine tuned to the details of gathering information. Clues, bit by bit and piece by piece, he put together, and it was often said he saw conspiracies within conspiracies. That's how Jack's mind worked. Always unpuzzling the puzzle's puzzle. Yet he always gave all the credit to his colleagues. He said without them the crime couldn't be solved and that they were a team. Even as a young patrolman, he'd given up collars.

He was being recorded by the surveillance cameras hovering above him. One was the infamous Hyper Reporter. The counter coverage was the Media-Interpret Reporter, or Mediator, and it bombarded the public with every intellectual rigor, despite mass resistance to the truth. The bored public ate up Hyper's slanted scandal and gossip as rigorously as the Media-Interpret protected individuals and groups from the lies. The hovers hummed, floating just out of reach. Jack imagined they were scoping each other like two boxers before a big fight.

The Humvee pulled up near the entrance to the mines next to Edgar and Jules, and the two vehicles joined mag fields allowing the sounds of engine, a robot digger dog's bark, and conversation to enter their field. The Moon dogs had been turned down and were quietly wagging their tails, a sign that their cooling systems were working. One of the dogs stood up and barked incessantly as one of the Memories approached with the hover camera in hand. That was odd. A mining dog-bot didn't usually bark more than once, especially on low mode—maybe a program glitch. Edgar patted the robot dog's head and ordered it to heel. One of the Memories started yelling at the other. He would also be recorded by the human Memories or people trained to memorize events for public disputation later on.

Jack Cluewitt and the Imbrium Basin Murders   Ruth J. Burroughs

Memories Dmytro Andreychuk and Niall Heaton were two Jack had worked with before. Niall launched the Mediator camera and Dmytro launched the Hyper camera. The two were direct opposites. Niall was a strong Celtic man with reddish blonde hair. His skin was pale white like a full Moon and his bright blue eyes were sharp and intelligent. In contrast, Dmytro's dark eyes expressed a certain hardness and amusement, and he had the physique of a rugged frontiersman. He looked like he could withstand much cold and heat and violent criminals. In contrast to Niall's slender build, Dmytro had a barrel chest, strong arms and thick leg muscles, but they were equal in strength. Niall argued with the Russian Memory reporter. He yelled and pointed at his face. Niall winced and favored his right arm, like it was sore and rotated his shoulder a bit. He continued his rant about the immorality and greed of the Hyper-Media and how it exploited people without getting at real news. Dmytro maintained the American freedom of the press and constitutional rights, while Niall vociferously argued that Hyper often created news just for high ratings. Niall Heaton was notorious for his mouth. Jack didn't much like a public investigation, but it kept him on his toes and it kept the investigation honest. They weren't allowed to broadcast things the police department needed kept secret in certain types of homicides, but it was hard to keep information contained these days.

The two NEPD officers exited the front of the old vehicle, and Jane got out and walked over to Jules and Ed's vehicle with a com-pad and pen in hand. She wore a standard issue EMMA JO police department one-off Raygun, as did the two NEPD blue cops, except hers was personalized with a gold-plated basket hilt. Jack didn't use laser guns. He didn't want to blow off his hand. He did carry a pen and com-pad for drawing sketches he could later use for paintings. He always said a cop's best weapon is his mind. He adjusted his space suit and felt cold metal on his chest and then remembered the Chinese coin. He hoped he wasn't going crazy. Jane was interviewing the miners, Jules and Ed. He turned his helmet on. It instantly telescoped over his head, and he checked his suit pressurization. When Jack was sure it was in fine working order, he turned the helmet off and it collapsed backward. Missi had ordered the robotic atmosphere suits, but they were few and far between and very expensive. NEPD saved a lot of money using the old dime-a-dozen space suits in conjunction with the mag fields and only bought a few of the Atmo-bot suits.

Acting like he'd gotten his shots, Memory Reporter Niall turned around without interviewing anyone and headed back to the cave entrance. He seemed annoyed and surprised by the robot dogs. The Green Police and the Moon City patrolmen looked like they were both sharing a joke.

Jack approached Lieutenant Calvin Gyrovits, a veteran crime scene investigator, who was waiting for him at the coffee and donuts table. The old man was a Natural like Jack, and had a paunch to show for it and wrinkles galore, but he still had blonde hair, no gray, and it was very curly. Neither of them was against medical treatment or organ replacement, but they didn't modify for fun or advancement. Cal's team of robots, androids and humans did a thorough job of collecting and recording data and securing the crime scene from patrollers, reporters, bystanders or family from disturbing the scene. Cal was seventy years old, but didn't look a day over fifty. He called his crew his circus.

"What have you got for me, old man?" Cal and Jack went back a long way.

"Footprints. Loads and loads of footprints with dates locations, azimuth, longitude, latitude and we're getting Jules, Ed and their robot dogs' footprints to rule them out. We're also getting the first officers-on-the-scene footprints; just so happened to be Green Police arrived first, but they were good. They taped off the entrance and set up this table near the miners' cars so they wouldn't ruin any evidence that might be outside what looked like the crime scene."

"Any ideas who killed the Greepol?"

"Nope. Too early yet. You'll see. When you get back out here let me know what you deduce and then we'll share notes. The victim is female. Looks like a shot to the heart."

"Thanks, Cal. Did you hear from Sergeant Chen, Jenèave?"

"Yeah. Sarge said that Alps Valley Rille Mine is American territory for as long as we need it. VAQ-ORE has been leasing the mine, but that's been canceled and the mine closed for the investigation. Right now it is restricted American territory until the crime is solved. Bane Hofmüller owns it, and he's none too happy."

"Losing money, is he? Well, if Jenèave calls, let her know what we're up to."

"Will do."

"Are we on police frequency only?"

"Of course. 315 for NEPD. 590 is the main frequency for the reporters. Coffee?"

Jack nodded, smiling. "Sure. Thanks." Jack accepted the cup and grabbed a Boston crème.

Jack took a sip of black coffee and a bite of a donut and called Jane over. Two Moon-jumps covered the short distance from Jules' rover to the coffee table.

"You get anything from those two?"

"Ed discovered the body and had to leave his rover in the tunnel. He was afraid if he backed out he'd ruin more evidence."

Jack nodded. "Good job. Smart man. Okay, Cal, looks like we're ready to head in. Lead the way."

"Right-oh. I'll be doing a lot of pointing," Cal said. He pushed a button and his helmet telescoped on. When his suit beeped ready, he turned around and zapped out of the mag field toward the cave entrance.

The two miners watched from atop Jules' vehicle, drinking Ed's favorite Jovian coffee; their two mining dogs sat wagging their tails. The Green Police, two patrollers, the two Memory reporters and Jack and Jane turned on their helmets and pressurized their space suits and zapped out of the mag field filing into the mouth of the mining cave. Cal pointed down a side tunnel; Jack saw a discarded space suit and woman's bare feet tracks in the regolith leading away. Cal spoke over the com on the police frequency.

"We've deduced it must be an android, a female robot's tracks in the regolith. A human couldn't survive without pressurization and would avoid contact with the Moon grit."

"Right. Good call," Jack said. He hoped it wasn't one of Hildy's sex robots.

As they moved slowly down the tunnel, Jack could hear his labored breath and taste his own sweat mixed with the familiar smells of his old space suit. Despite the guidance lights, it was hard to see. Cal's voice came over the mike.

"Stay on the right-hand rover tracks and follow me," Cal said.

Jack nodded. Jane followed Cal, with Jack right behind. The rest of the contingent followed behind Jack in single file. About a quarter mile in, the regolith dissipated and ground-down rock and hard packed sediment replaced it.

Jack's voice sounded hollow and pitchy in his suit. "Where's the coroner?"

"She's on her way with another Lula V to pick up the body when you're done and to take the miners in for questioning along with their Moon dogs."

"Good old Edgar couldn't hurt a flea," Jack said.

"And that Jules' smile could charm the pants off this old paint," Jane said laughing. They walked the rest of the two and a half miles in conversation until they came to Ed's rover.

Cal put out his arms. "Here we are. There's the body."

"Oh my," Jane said.

Jack wanted to scratch his face, but couldn't. It was frustrating. "Did you get anything?"

"Yes," Cal replied over the static, "forensic nano-bots say it was a bullet to the heart. We'll have the Coroner confirm. The victim's suit started to heal, but was shut off midway. The killer didn't realize her blood would seal the suit though, and she's got a little atmo still. She also has residue of organ growing emulsion on her left hand."

Jane called down the NEPD rover camera and checked it to make sure it was working. Live feed, "Are you getting this, Moon City Central?" The cameras used masers to broadcast through the thick walls.

"Not a very good reception, Salgado," a man's voice replied, "looks like Hyper is though, too. We're watching it on the news. Hey why can't we afford those kinds of masers?"

"Where?" Jack asked.

"Behind you," the voice from the camera replied.

Jack switched to the main bandwidth. "Could you get that thing to back off?" Jack asked.

"Why, so you have time to fix your hair and make-up?" Memory Dmytro said.

Jack Cluewitt and the Imbrium Basin Murders   Ruth J. Burroughs

"Hey, stop broadcasting. Send feed only to your station, or we'll shut down your satellite. We'll let you know when to go live."

"Right." Dmytro adjusted something on his suit. "Hey guys, stop broadcasting. You know this is a crime scene." Dmytro heard something the others couldn't. "Done, Jack. It's just going to the station now."

Jack switched back to police frequency. "Cal, they're not on our frequency, right?"

"Right. Headquarters is monitoring. They would have warned us. They must have a strong maser amplification to get that to broadcast through all that rock."

"Well, keep the stuff about organ growing emulsion under a tight lid. Don't let that get out. Lives depend on it," Jack said, hoping none of the reporters had found their frequency.

"Right, Jack. Will do. Only a few on the team know."

"Good."

The forensics' team had sprayed an outline of the body in the hard packed floor of the tunnel. Jack shook the Greepols' head and felt blood slosh around inside. He couldn't hear it due to the lack of pressurization outside his suit.

"What was a Green Policewoman doing in a mining tunnel?"

Cal turned toward him, "That's what I said."

"Anything else?"

"No vehicle. She walked out here."

"What?"

"So it appears. Besides Jules and Ed's vehicles there's no sign of anything else."

Cal stepped around to the other side of the body. "The bullet wound has a trajectory from what would have been a right-handed person, standing there." Cal pointed. "We believe the person was about five foot ten or eleven."

Jack stood up and looked around. There were no footprints inside the hard packed or chiseled floor of the mining tunnel. Jack lumbered around in his suit, feeling slightly queasy. Something was off. He could sense it.

Something was coming toward him. He could feel it. He looked around. Then Jack saw it. The Mediator camera

Jack Cluewitt and the Imbrium Basin Murders   Ruth J. Burroughs

was homing in on him. Its camera lens telescoped toward him as it drew near. Jack tuned to the reporter's frequency.

"Media-Interpreter, what are you doing? Back off," Jack barked.

"Just coming in for a close up, Detective Cluewitt." The hover camera's voice crackled.

"You don't do close ups. You're a disseminator of over-blown news reports," Jack said.

"Just stay right there, Jack," the camera said.

Jack stopped, confused. It took at least three or four seconds for central to reply to anything. Therefore it wasn't Media-Interpret headquarters in Moon City speaking. A proper program in a hover robot camera should have obeyed his first command. Who or what was overriding it? Or was it autonomous? He started backing up. He heard Jane's voice over the mike.

"Jack, what's the matter? Mediator just wants a close up."

"You know they can do a close up at fifty meters," Jack replied through static.

Then he saw it. The camera lens retracted into the ball of the rover and a long metal tube extended in its place, aiming right for Jack's heart. He sidestepped, but it followed him like a magnet. Jack ducked and the roving camera dropped, hovering in between Jane and Jack.

Jane dialed the main frequency and bellowed into her com, "Memory Niall, what is wrong with your camera?!" Niall ordered the camera back, but it would not obey. It followed Jack's every move.

"Indigo, hit the ground!" Jack yelled. The camera fired its only bullet, hit him square in the chest, throwing him to the ground. Jane dove as the backfire blasted the camera backwards away from Jack, flew past her shoulder and crashed into the tunnel wall, smashing into a million pieces.

Jack would have breathed a sigh of relief when he saw the camera shoot past Jane's head and hit the wall but, all he could feel was a pressure on his chest and the oxygen rushing out his depressurizing suit. He put his gloved hand over the hole to stop the air leaking out. People were yelling. He tumbled in his space suit, unable to see out the glass, just helmet lights.

Jane quickly lumbered up off the ground but fell forward in her haste and then got up and stumbled toward Jack. She moved his limp hand away and quickly covered the hole in his suit.

"Jack . . . Jack are you with me?" she asked, thinking, *What to do? What to do? Oh.* She checked his nanobot repair chamber. It said full, but no nanos came out to repair the hole.

"Dmytro. Call out to Ed Moon Digger. Tell him to send his mining dog in here with a suit patch and to fetch Jack and bring him out to the Humvee's mag field zone for medical treatment and have him call EMTs!"

"What's ee-empties?" Dmytro asked.

"Now!"

"Don't blow a gasket, Indigo Jane," Andreychuk said. He switched to his commercial frequency and called the miner. He explained what had happened. Dmytro Andreychuk nodded and smiled. "Moon Digger has sent his dog Cavity with a suit patch. He will be here soon and he called the EMTs too."

The robot dog leapt up and out of the mag zone, dusting up the sparkling bright regolith in the spotlights, and dashed down the tunnel, its metal legs and joints working beneath rippling solenoid rubber and hydraulics. It dashed the three miles down the mining tunnel to the crime scene.

"Here, Cavity. Give me the patch." The dog dropped the packet into her gloved hand. Cavity breathed in the low oxygen with very state of the art robot lungs, panting like a dog.

Jane applied the old-fashioned patch to Jack's heart and told Cavity he was ready. The dog grabbed Jack's upper arm in its metal jaws and lumbered back down the tunnel toward the mag field as quickly as it could maneuver with Jack in tow, semi-floating and dragging. She watched it go. She ordered Cal to secure the area with his forensics robots.

Jack Cluewitt and the Imbrium Basin Murders Ruth J. Burroughs

"Excuse me, Memory Niall, but I have to hold you for questioning."

"What for?"

"What do you think?" she replied vehemently, thinking, Jack's dead. As dead, as the dead Greepol with another shot to the heart.

"That wasn't my fault."

"It doesn't matter. You are a Memory. If I needed a credible witness I'd want a Memory. That's two people who were shot in the heart here, and your camera shot my partner."

"How am I to effectively record this event, this murder investigation, if I am now part of another investigation?" Niall argued.

"You can't. You'll have to send for another Memory," she ordered.

"Hmph! This is outrageous. I'm leaving."

"If you attempt to leave, I will have you arrested."

"Go ahead and try," Niall said.

"You have the right to remain silent anything you say . . ."

"Oh, blast your silly Miranda rights. I won't stand for this."

Jane had the two patrollers arrest him while she read him his rights. While in American territory, all prisoners had rights. Niall was a Lunar Scottish citizen, but was afforded those rights in space since laws overlapped and borders were not set in Moon rock.

✖

Jack started to come to as Cavity stumbled along the mining tunnel. All he could see were the overhead lights and Cavity's wagging robotic tail.

Jack kept thinking, Modus operandi, modus operandi. What was the modus operandi? What was the killer's motive? What had the blonde Greepol been doing out here? Where was his book and where were the other two Greepols with one body? Do they have something to do with her?

He felt sick even though atmosphere had returned to his space suit. The patch had stabilized the pressure and sealed the hole. Jack was more determined than ever to

Jack Cluewitt and the Imbrium Basin Murders   Ruth J. Burroughs

break this case now. He knew how the Greepol had felt just before she died and he was going to find her killer.

He felt the pressure on his arm as the robotic canine stumbled out through the yawning mouth of the cave, into the rovers' spotlights, toward the meteoric surface of the shiny rille floor.

He saw the snap of the mag barrier as the dog glided through it in the shiny LULA V headlights that cut through the Mount Alps shadow. Ed Moon Digger and Jules leaned over, grabbing him and dragging him into the pressurized environment around the LULA V, generated by the vehicle. When Jack's suit green-lighted that its pressurization matched the LULA vehicle's atmo, Moon Digger collapsed his helmet, and Jack breathed deeply, glad to be out of the stale air of the suit.

"Where are you bleeding?" Edgar asked him.

"I'm okay," Jack said.

Edgar frowned. "Guns aren't allowed in space, Jack. You can't be wearing a bullet proof vest under that cumbersome spacesuit, 'cause the NEPD don't have any. It's illegal to shoot guns in a vacuum."

"Tell that to the dead Greepol in the cave back there," Jack said.

"Well, I'm saying that because you aren't dead, Jack, and you got a bullet hole in your space suit and a patch right over your heart. You should be bleeding out or something. I was expecting a mess. Are you wearing a vest?"

"No."

"Is that one of them new robo-suits?"

"Ummm, no, Ed. The department wouldn't shill out for new ones. This one is probably fifteen years old."

"Indigo said you were shot in the heart by the Mediator camera. The paramedics are on their way right now."

"They're bringing him out. Indigo just arrested Memory Niall," Jules said.

"Why did she arrest him?" Jack asked.

Jules smiled down at Jack. "Because it was his camera that shot you and he refuses to be questioned, demanding we release him or file charges. He tried to leave, so she cuffed him in spacesuit cuffs and he's giving her a hard time. I heard them on the main frequency," Jules pointed at his earpiece, "He's complaining all the way."

81

"What's new?"

"Yeah, he's always griping about something," Edgar said, "how come you're not dead, Jack?"

"You sound disappointed."

"Oh, don't be a dumb-ass, Jack. Let's get your suit off and see where the bullet went."

Jack should have worried, but all he could think about was the crime. He needed to find out what Cal had discovered and why he had been shot, the latter for later. Whoever tried to have him killed wasn't going to scare him away.

"I have to get up," Jack said, "I have to get back to the crime scene."

"No, you have to take your suit off."

"Can I borrow your suit?"

"Let's see to this first. Jules help me get this off of him."

Edgar pulled the space suit off the bottom half of Jack and had him stand up.

Jack felt woozy in the harsh glare of rovers' spotlights on the Moon's reflective surface, despite the pressurized oxygen inside the magnetic field that somehow kept the radioactive dust down. Edgar took the top half off Jack and handed it to Jules, who checked the hole in Jack's suit with his finger. Jack felt wetness and a hole in his shirt as well and put his hand to his chest and felt the Chinese coin through his shirt. He pulled the collar down and looked. The gold glinted in the light. Jack felt his chest. It was a little bruised. What he thought was blood was nothing but perspiration.

"Wow, that's some bit of good luck. The pendant on your necklace saved you; it stopped the bullet from passing through your heart. For a minute there I thought you were Irish. You know, the *Luck of the Irish?* It looks like an ancient Chinese coin."

"Oh, it's something I picked up for Hildy. I guess she didn't like it."

"Well, it's a good thing she didn't. I'd say it's your lucky charm piece from now on."

"Yeah, let me borrow your spacesuit."

"But what about the paramedics? They're on their way here."

"Well, I don't need them. Cancel it," Jack replied.

"Jack, are you going to be okay?" Edgar asked.

Jack Cluewitt and the Imbrium Basin Murders Ruth J. Burroughs

"No, I won't be until I find the killer."

Jack walked unsteadily to the NEPD rover. The Moon's coroner was not skilled in medicine, despite laws that had changed on Earth. Spacer coroners didn't need to know medicine, but she would still determine the cause of death even though they did all the work.

He absently fingered the hole in his shirt knowing that the bullet had found its way into that dark cold place inside the coin. He had a hunch no one would find the bullet. It was in that other dark dimension.

Now, if someone had shot the Greepol the same way Jack was shot, they would have flown back down the tunnel or backfired into the wall just like the Mediator did, unless it was a pretty solid heavy thing, like a robot.

But he had to get back to the scene of the crime. He turned off the com and headed back to Ed Moon Digger, who was looking over the bullet hole in the space suit. One of the robot Moon dogs approached Jack, wagging its tail.

Ed Moon Digger set the suit down and patted Jack's shoulder. "I called Central for you, Jack. The paramedics are coming anyway. They took a bus with the coroner."

"How long before they get here?" Jack asked.

"About fifteen," Edgar replied.

"I'll be dead by the time they get here."

"Moon City is too close for a space craft to waste fuel getting here, Jack."

"What happens when one of your miners needs a paramedic?"

"That's the point. One or two miners, a dozen miners could all be replaced within a week. I suppose it keeps us on our toes knowing how long it takes for help to come out this way."

"How's the oxygen in your suit?"

"Good, we weren't in there long," Edgar replied climbing up onto his rig, he pulled down his suit.

"Here you go, Jack. Just don't get any bullet holes in it." Edgar smirked.

"I'll try not to."

Indigo Jane emerged from the mouth of the cave with Memory Niall, like a shepherd coaxing an errant sheep back to its flock. The sound of his complaining, like the bawling of a lamb, came through the static of Edgar's spacesuit com.

They zapped through the mag field and Cavity started barking at Memory Niall again until Edgar ordered it to back off. Indigo Jane ordered Niall to turn off his helmet and she did the same on hers. She took off his cumbersome gloves and handcuffed him to the NEPD Hummer.

"Is this really necessary?" Niall protested.

"Jack, you're alive! You're okay," she yelled, smiling.

"Jack is alive!" Niall said, astonished.

"Why is everyone so happy to see me alive?" Jack asked as the Greepols and the Moon City Police popped through the mag field and lowered their helmets.

"Uh, because you were shot in the heart by a bullet. Not too many people survive that, Jack! I'll be over in a minute. I'm booking him in on the NEPD." Jane smiled as she punched in some codes on the Humvee com.

Jack wondered why Cavity had barked at a Memory reporter, unless the robot dog was barking because Niall was not really Niall, but was a robot impersonating Niall. But Niall couldn't be a robot. He looked too human to be a robot and he'd had a sore shoulder earlier and robots didn't get sore arms. Unless . . . the bullet had a trajectory that would originate from a right-handed person and Niall was about five foot nine.

He wished these mining dogs were programmed to talk like Zero-One, but that would be too expensive. Just like NEPD's old spacesuits they were all becoming obsolete. Then he remembered Pop's holo improved robot dogs. If robot dogs could look real then androids could, too. Memory Dmytro walked toward Jack with the floating Hyper camera filming. It looked like the action was where Jack was, and the Memory guided the news camera toward him and Ed.

If Niall was a robot, then that would explain a lot of things; it would explain how the Greepol woman in the cave was killed. It was not a puppet robot. If someone was manipulating it from a distance Near-Earth Police would have detected the signal. But why publicly try to kill Jack? Because they wanted to frame someone for Jack's murder. Niall was a robot and if it weren't for the coin saving Jack's life, no one would have figured it out. He should be very dead right now and the real Niall had been the next target, the man the robot wanted to frame for Jack's murder. That's why this robot Niall impersonator was so nervous that Jack was alive. It was programmed to kill Jack in a devious manner and it had failed. *Can robots be nervous?* Jack asked himself. *Only if it has emotions. Does having emotions give an artificial intelligent creature consciousness? Perhaps. But consciousness, or being self-aware and intelligence don't equal having a conscience.*

Someone wanted to frame the Mediator for the murder of Jack Cluewitt. Someone with enough money to program this robot to act and look human. Programmed to be just as annoying as the real Proctor Niall.

"Edgar," Jack whispered, "do you have a weapon of any kind.

"What?"

"Shhh . . . do you have a weapon, any weapon?"

"No, but I have an old jackhammer on the rig."

"That might work. I need you to take it out, inconspicuously and hold it on Niall. You know how to use it, right?"

"Yeah, of course but what for? He's not going anywhere. He's cuffed to the Hummer. Why don't you carry a one-off Raygun like all the other cops?"

"Because I don't want to blow my hand off, Ed, and because they're not necessary if you stay calm and talk things out. In other words, use your brain instead of brawn."

"Well, what the hell do you want me to do with the jackhammer? I might hurt Niall."

"Shhh . . ." Jack said looking over at the Memory, who was looking uneasy. "He's a robot."

"No way."

"Just do it," Jack said and Edgar nodded.

"Hey, Jules help me get the dogs on board," Edgar yelled.

Jules brought the dogs over to the mining vehicle as Edgar went behind it and geared up the laser jackhammer.

As Ed came around the corner of his Humvee heading toward Niall, Memory Niall ripped out of the hand cuffs and heavily leapt off the NEPD Hummer and knocked Indigo Jane down with one good blow to her chin, knocking her out. Before the Hyper-Media camera had time to turn around and film him, he pulled out a gun, aimed and shot it down; blew it to pieces; fragments hit Dmytro as he ducked.

Jack Cluewitt and the Imbrium Basin Murders Ruth J. Burroughs

The backfire blasted Niall's right arm around and around until it fell off. Ed ran at him with the laser jackhammer.

"Don't attempt to take me or I will self-destruct." It picked up its right arm with its left and put it back on.

"Where's Memory Niall?" Jack demanded.

"Moon City, stupid."

"Dead?"

"No, just tied up." The robot re-attached its right arm, stretched and rotated its shoulder.

"Were you trying to frame me for the murder?"

"You'll never solve this one, Jack, one and one make three. You've found one, you should have met the same fate," the robot said.

"Why?"

"Figure it out, Jack, you're the detective," the robot replied as it turned to leave the mag field.

It sent shivers up Jack's spine watching something so humanoid walk out into the airless Moonscape without a suit. The holographic face of Memory Niall collapsed as it zapped through the magnetic barrier out onto the crater bottom. Jack wondered how the bipedal robot would make it up the steep side of the rille when it suddenly turned, its body collapsed into a polygon, as its face opened up like two doors on a box-like head and telescoped into a rocket ship. It fired up its thrusters and blasted off the surface, climbing and pushing its way up and out of the pull of gravity and into the cold steep orbit toward the other side of the Moon.

"Omigod, Jack, tell me that didn't just happen," Edgar said, smacking his head.

"That didn't just happen," Jack said, dumbstruck.

"What kind of rocket fuel fits in a human sized robot? Edgar said

"Jules, is Indigo okay?"

Jules was preoccupied with the two robot dogs, which despite their programs, were jumping up and down and barking and growling and carrying on. Jules finally gave up and commanded them to go. They took off toward the spot where the robot space ship had blasted off. Jules hopped over to Indigo and knelt down.

"She's okay. Out cold, but she'll be okay. I'll immobilize her for the paramedics, in case her neck is hurt," Jules replied.

Jack Cluewitt and the Imbrium Basin Murders   Ruth J. Burroughs

"Edgar, was your dog detecting a radio frequency on that faux Niall and would Cavity have a memory chip of it?" Jack asked.

"Probably," Edgar said, "Cavity's ears are top of the line radar devices. We can load the dog's memory chip and any pertinent information Cavity's getting from the blast site to your roving NEPD hover com."

"Great. Do that." Jack walked over to Jane and Jules. "Is she okay?"

"She'll be just fine except for one pretty sore jaw," Jules replied.

"I need a vacation."

"If the job doesn't kill you first, Jack. Then you'll be talking a permanent vacation. Why didn't that robot impersonating Niall just shoot you instead of the Hyper-Media?"

"The robot didn't know why I survived the first shot and figured I might survive all gun shots and if he had shot at me or the dogs they would have attacked him . . . it. It's likely the dogs could have stopped him from rocketing off. Because it didn't attack people or the dogs themselves, the dogs weren't programmed to stop it unless it was a threat."

"I never thought about that," Jules asked.

"It didn't know the dogs were going to be here. Robots aren't good with surprises."

"I need to borrow Edgar's suit and go back in there. See if I missed anything."

"Looks like the paramedics are here," Edgar said.

"Make sure they don't trample the robot's blast site."

Jack put his damaged suit up on the NEPD Hummer and donned Ed's space suit. It was a tad larger, but it fit well enough.

Indigo Jane lay prone in an immobilizer unit to protect her neck. The paramedics were checking her vitals and stimulating her. She came to, mumbling something about hoity Niall; she started to fidget against the paramedics. She spat out a tooth, cursing and swearing. *She wouldn't be so upset if she knew she'd been KOed by a robot and not the real and curmudgeonly Niall,* Jack thought. He'd have to tell her later.

The coroner approached, followed by two assistants with the stretcher and body bag for the Greepol corpse. *A blonde,* he thought, *great.* Jack had a weakness for

87

Jack Cluewitt and the Imbrium Basin Murders Ruth J. Burroughs

blondes. She carried her fancy tool kit in one hand and her silver top-of-the-line space suit helmet in the other. Her golden tresses momentarily distracted him, but they were pulled up in a curly bun on top of her head and he caught a glimpse of the implant on the back of her head and that she was jacked into the Grid. He stanched a shiver. He didn't want to be rude, but he didn't like modifieds; they were schizo. Her curt manner introducing herself killed any iota of attraction for him. She was the new Medical Examiner, Chad Helmer's replacement, who Jack had not had to deal with. Cal always handled him.

"Let's get going and tell me everything, Jack, everything. I'm Coroner Gretel Roux and I know who you are." She barely concealed her smug contempt.

"I think the robot was programmed to kill the Green Policewoman because she had something it wanted." Jack winced, rubbing his chest.

"I know they had something of yours you wanted back and I believe Hildy wants it too." Gretel Roux sounded like a robot. Not a woman.

"I'm getting this from sources on the Grid," she said tilting her head.

Jack laughed and shook his head. "Hildy didn't have anything to do with this. She's in jail."

"No. Not directly, but she hired someone to program that robot to kill the Greepol. But why would your girlfriend want to kill you for a paper book?" She spoke slowly for him. Most modifieds spoke unintelligibly fast.

"You can't solve this crime in five minutes just because you're wetware." Jack noticed she was reading all about him off the Grid.

"Where did you get the book from, Jack? I can't find that. Why is it so important?"

"None of your business."

"You should have taken yourself off the case, Jack. I could report you."

"Why?"

"You don't know?"

"Know what?"

"This Greepol was seen with the conjoined twins at Organdy Poisson's restaurant last night. This is not public knowledge. This is police business. You should have checked your messages. You were seen arguing with these two conjoined twins on the hypersonic jet on the way up here."

"Yes. I met with them in a hotel on Earth. They said they had information that would help me find my birth parents. But it all went badly. They took the paper book from me, saying it was an eco-crime, but never reported it to the Green Party or the Green Police. I merely wanted it back. I followed them into Organdy Poisson's restaurant and demanded it back. I even searched them, but they said they didn't know what I was talking about. I left frustrated. Then I got the call about the murder this morning. What do they have to do with this female Greepol?"

"She was seen with them later in the evening. I think she must have had your book. That made you a suspect in the murder you're investigating—that is until you were nearly killed. I'm sure I'll figure it out before you do."

"Go ahead. See who wins then."

"Is that a bet? Naturals versus Grid-linked wetware?"

"Yeah. I'll beat you any luna."

"I like betting, Jack, and I can tell you your odds are not good. If you were connected to the Grid you could download it into your brain in thirty seconds or less. But you'll just have to read about me in your stupid little books. Show me what you have."

"Okay. Let's suit up." Jack turned on his helmet and she put hers on her suit; it clicked in place. They waited for the suits to beep that they were properly pressurized.

Jack waved for her to follow him and they went through the mag field into the mining tunnel entrance. Just inside Jack pointed down the side tunnel, a little to their left and back.

"There's a discarded space suit and female footprints going down the tunnel to the left. Forensics has already collected footprint casts, photos and any other relevant evidence. The body is down the main tunnel, this way." *I can't tell her everything,* Jack thought. *But she may find out soon enough if she can put one and one together and make three.*

The antique book was the link to finding his parents. Sooner than later, he'd have to go back to Organdy's before the killer or Gretel Roux did. Jack didn't want to find any more corpses because of his book. Somehow, he didn't mind the company despite her brain-jack hardware, although he wished he could see more of her in the dark tunnel of the mining cave. His girlfriend, Hildy Witter Raygun, was in jail, after all. But he had little time. What if someone else knew where the book was? Jack himself, and maybe Organdy Poisson. Yes, that sushi chef cum organ dealer was not as stupid as he pretended to be. Jack had observed the man when he'd tried to get his book back from the two Green Police he'd followed up to the Moon. Jack hoped he was right about Organdy because if he wasn't then Organdy was probably next and he'd hate to have to investigate the death of a talented sushi chef and organ grower.

Monday late afternoon June 7ᵗʰ, 5030
Memory Reporter Niall
Chapter Eight

Jack walked the streets of Moon City, encapsulated by a mag field, thinking, ruminating and chewing the cud of the evidence. He wore a suit and tie and his burned London Fog raincoat, which caused people to look at him sideways. Trees lined the railed streets, clean of any regolith. Jack wasn't sure where the kidnappers had Niall. He called headquarters and put out a missing person's report on the real Niall and an APB out on the robot impersonator, who was possibly armed and very dangerous. He wanted help finding the two Green Police, who'd taken his book, because he sensed they were in danger too, but that would involve him on this case. He sensed they were in terrible danger. The coroner, Gretel Roux, was developing her own theory as to how the blonde Greepol with the bad skin had been murdered in the mining cave and by whom. Her focus was on Edgar Chavez and Jules Helphenstein, and if Jack wouldn't interrogate them then she would, back at headquarters. Jack knew Cal had influenced her. She respected him. She didn't know Cal thought she was an overpaid useless appointment, despite her cyber link to the Satellites' Grid.

Jack was interested in talking to the two miners too, but not right now. He knew if he didn't get to the real Niall, the robot impersonating Niall might still go back and kill him. He had a feeling that wherever the real Niall was, the Greepols who shared the same body were with him.

He had to figure out what the murderer had planned if Jack was dead. If Jack was dead, as he should have been, then robot Niall would have been taken in for questioning. The remains of the Mediator in the mining tunnel would be investigated. Because Memory Niall and the Media-Inter-

Jack Cluewitt and the Imbrium Basin Murders   Ruth J. Burroughs

preter had such a consistent high moral agenda the public rarely questioned their integrity, so Jack figured they would have released who they thought was Niall right after Jack's murder.

It knew Jack would follow the two Greepols out to the Moon for the book. Then it would kill for the book and frame Jack for it. Jack could see the headlines now:

Dirty NEPD Cop arrested for Illegal paper book, kills Green Policewoman on the Moon and is slain by Memory Reporter Niall Heaton

But Jack had to find the other Greepols and the real Niall if he was going to find out who killed the Green Policewoman. He opened the glass door of a hologram booth on the corner of Obama and Lexington in Moon City.

He called home, but it got rerouted. Zero-One's holo activated. A camera in the room recorded a holo of Jack and transmitted it to Zero-One's location.

"What is it, Jack?"

"I need you on the Moon."

"Well, I'm close. Remember you wanted me to take care of Immaculata and make sure she went to her new owner?"

"Oh. Yes, right."

"Well, she now belongs to one Maelstrom Corrigan of Cadaver City Fullerene Colony stationed off Lagrange point five. It's on its way back out to Jovian space in a few days, or as soon as Immaculata gets done re-painting the facilities. Apparently the robots are losing their way around because the paint's fading and they're losing bodies."

"That's not good. Can't they just upgrade the robots?"

"Tried. Didn't work and too expensive."

"You done?"

"Almost. Interesting facilities. You should have a look. I saw the Greepol murder broadcast."

"That was premature. They weren't supposed to broadcast the crime scene. We shut them down before I was shot.

I'm okay, though. The bullet went into that strange Chinese coin. Can you get over here, Zero-One?"

"You can't afford it."

"Well, make a copy of your brain and send it here."

"I can do that, Jack, but you can't afford a robot brain right now. Like I said, your tree quota is up and your credit is at the limit. Can you borrow a brain from the police department or your miner friends?"

"Yes, probably."

"Is it really necessary?"

"Yes, I need you to find the two Green Police, the ones who took my book. Niall's life . . . their lives depend on it."

"You don't need a computer to figure that one out, Jack. Use your brain, think."

"I can't. I need to do a search off the Grid, without sending up red flags. This line is secure."

"Where's Jane?"

"She's being looked at by the docs and then she'll stop at police headquarters recording her view of what occurred. She got KOed by the robot, impersonating Niall."

"Well, ask her then, if you won't use your brain."

"You can figure it out faster than I can, or any other human."

"Really Jack, your brain is much faster than mine. You just have to learn how to use it. These things are always right under your nose, as you put it. Remember? You're tired. You've been shot. That's why you can't think right now."

"I can't wait for protocol. I have to find them before that robot does. I just hope Niall is with them."

"Maybe, but where's the first place you'd think they'd be?"

"I don't know."

"C'mon, Jack. Where would two Greepols stay when visiting the Moon?"

"A hotel or motel?"

"Are you sure you don't want me to be your partner?"

"It's too easy."

"The robot was not planning on you living to figure it out."

"Okay, which motel?"

"They ate at Organdy's and needed access to the mines. Someplace close to the mines and Organdy's, of course."

"Of course. The Green Moon Hotel for Greens, duh. I have to call Jane."

"Of course. You've been shot at once already. Do be careful, Jack."

"I've got work to do."

"At least duck next time."

"I did. Just not in time."

Jack called Indigo Jane at Moon City Police headquarters on a private hologram line.

"Thanks for telling me it wasn't that wimp, Memory Niall." Jane fumed on the hologram phone.

"Nice to see they fixed your teeth already. Did you give the report?"

"Yeah, it's done. No thanks to you. Why didn't you tell me it was a robot?"

"I wanted you to give the paramedics a hard time," Jack explained.

"So you had me think it was that whining, holier-than-thou Memory Niall, instead of a half-ton robot that KOed me, just so you could get back at the paramedics?"

"That's right. If I'd been shot in the heart, instead of that Chinese coin I bought Hildy, I'd be dead right now, because those paramedics decided to take their good old damned time in a Moon bus instead of hopping over in a Lula V."

"They have to save money somehow."

"Not at my expense, they don't."

"Okay, but you owe me some Cuban zeegars"

"Those are bad for you."

"Since when did you care what's bad for me? You have a Martian call girl for a fiancée and she's connected to the mob."

"Thanks. Why don't you just call Memory Dmytro and announce that on the Hyper-Media."

"What's at the Green Moon Motel?"

"I believe the real Niall, and the two Greepols."

"Really?"

"Yes, and we have to get there before the robot Niall gets there."

"Is robot Niall the murderer?"

Jack Cluewitt and the Imbrium Basin Murders   Ruth J. Burroughs

"He . . . It must be. It tried to kill me, and it would have killed you if those robot dogs hadn't been there. It's still after the book. If it kills one Green Police, tries to kill me—a Blue Moon homicide detective—then it will kill anyone to get what it wants. Call Jenèave and tell her to rush a warrant through. Tell her it's a life and death situation."

"What if they're not there?"

"Meet me at the Green Moon Motel with that warrant. We have to find them before the conjoined twin Greepols and Niall are killed. I don't want to lose the case because I have to break into the Motel room without a warrant, but I will if I have to."

"We have proof they're in imminent danger. You don't need a warrant, but I'll get you one just in case. I'll fly a Lula V over there and tell headquarters what's going on. The coroner is going to be mad you didn't let her in on this."

"Yeah, well after she gets a mind instead of downloading one, I'll let her in on any case she wants. Just because she jacks into the Grid she thinks she's some kind of crime scene expert. She's a political appointment who tries to close the cases as soon as possible to justify her position, whether or not the people she likes are guilty. I wouldn't be surprised if she was a robot herself."

"Why? Because she's the first person with nice legs who didn't flirt with you?"

"Okay, so you're very observant, even for a homicide detective. I gotta go. Signing off."

"You owe me," Jane said.

⚮

Jack choked down tears; with his left hand he rubbed and scratched the salmon-colored keloid scar on his right cheek. It was a gruesome scene at the Green Moon Motel with the conjoined twin Greepols dead on the carpeted floor in one big pool of blood.

The real Memory Niall was tied to the bed, struggling and mumbling through a gag tied around his mouth. Jack had convinced the clerk to tell him where the two Green Police were staying and then kicked the door in.

Jack decided to keep Niall tied up until Jane Salgado could get there and hear everything the Memory had to say,

95

which hopefully would help their investigation. He called her on his earphone and told her to bring two Moon City Police and Calvin Gyrovits pronto. When Cal got to the scene he asked Jack why Niall was still tied up.

"I left Niall on the bed until you could secure the crime scene," Jack replied.

Cal quickly ordered his robots and team to hologram the scene. When it was done, he told them to untie Niall. "Hurry, and untie him. I think we filmed enough. We know he's here so we'll get samples of his DNA and prints to rule him out."

Just as the forensic bot finished untying Memory Niall's hands, Indigo Jane stepped through the door of the Motel room, two uniformed Moon City Police behind her and the warrant flapping in her hand. "Better late than forever," Jane said.

Niall tore the gag off his mouth and yelled at Jack.

"It took you long enough. I've been sitting on that bed all day now and I have to take a leak so bad my teeth are floating." Niall leapt clumsily in the Moon gravity and hobbled to the bathroom.

"You could have let him up sooner, Jack." Jane said. She chuckled and then winced as though the laughter hurt the bruise on her jaw.

"Still sore?" Jack asked.

Jane nodded; sucking on her teeth she touched her jaw. Her teeth-sucking was one habit that really annoyed Jack, but he was used to it, along with her gum-chewing and zeegar smoking. Niall re-entered the crime scene and gingerly stepped around the body of the two dead Greepols.

"Feel better?" Jack asked.

"Actually, yes, thank you. That was a relief," Niall replied and the two blues in the doorway laughed.

"Memory Niall," Jane said.

"Detective Salgado." The Memory shook her hand.

"Who did this? Who killed the conjoined twins?"

"Jack did it."

"What?"

"Well, Jack was supposed to have done it. I was supposed to think Jack did it."

"What do you mean?" Jane asked.

"The person who kidnapped me looked like Jack, except that I could tell it was a holograph being projected onto a robot face," Memory Niall said.

"How could you tell?"

"I'm not just a Memory with astounding recall abilities, I'm also a synesthete."

"A synesthete is someone whose senses are miss-wired, right?" Jane asked.

"Right, and in my case, I see people's auras when they speak. I see their intonations in color. I found someone walking away from the crime scene in what seemed to be a spacesuit. Although it looked and sounded like Jack, I could tell it wasn't. The sound colors of robots are different from organic beings. I tried to get away. It pulled a gun on me and forced me to drive back to Moon City and told me to keep quiet. It took me to a room. Inside were two Green Police—the conjoined twins—tied to a pipe on the wall. It intended me to witness Jack killing the Greepols. It gagged me. Lee begged for his life in the last few minutes. Keith cursed you out. Well, it cursed out the robot *pretending* to be you. I was gagged at the time so I couldn't tell them it wasn't you.

"It, or the robot pretending to be Jack, wanted to know where the book was and tortured both of them, but they wouldn't tell. Well, not for a long time. There was a lot of partying going on in the hotel from the robot sales people, so no one could hear Lee and Keith screaming. Finally, Lee was about to give in, and Keith grabbed the gun away from the robot and shot his brother in the throat. Lee died instantly, and Keith died shortly thereafter. Keith couldn't let Lee tell where the book was, and to be honest the twins couldn't stand each other."

"The robot Sally looked just like Jack?" Jane asked.

"Yes. They were both deceived by the hologram of his face," Niall replied.

"Why are there two bullets in the twins?" Jane asked.

Jack nodded, "Let me guess. The robot grabbed the gun out of Keith's hands and wiped the prints. It tried to use its right hand, but the arm near the shoulder wasn't connected properly. So the robot put the gun in its left hand, but tried to make it look like a right-handed trajectory and shot

Jack Cluewitt and the Imbrium Basin Murders   Ruth J. Burroughs

the twins from an angled distance so the suicide/murder would look like a homicide done by me."

"Exactly right, Jack."

"It kept the gun. It had followed the three Greepols to the hotel room. After Jara left, it picked the lock and entered the room and gagged and tied up the twins and then it followed Jara out to the cave where she was to meet Edgar to tell him she'd left the book in the fish tank at Organdy's, but the robot killed Jara before she could tell Edgar where the book was. Sally tried to frame me for the murder of the Green Policewoman in the Moon mining cave. It thought it had killed me and was very surprised that despite having been shot in the heart, I survived."

"How did you survive?"

"A large piece of jewelry kept the bullet from entering my heart. The robot wasn't being controlled remotely because we were monitoring all radio frequencies, but it was emitting an electronic signal that one of the robot dogs picked up because of its high-end radar ears," Jack said, thinking the bullet had really gone into the other dimension and if it hadn't been for the uncanny coin he'd be dead right now.

"But your suit pressurization."

"I was rescued by a Moon digger dog."

Niall sat down on a chair. "Why kill you?"

"Sally killed Jara before finding the book. Sally altered the Mediator camera to shoot at me. But the robot didn't expect me to live and figure out he wasn't you."

"But why have someone impersonate me, Jack?"

"The robot saw an opportunity to go back to the crime scene to look for the book. It thought that once it framed me for the Green Policewoman's murder, it would then frame you, Niall Heaton, for my murder. It would of course have to trick Jane into coming here. Frame her for killing you, Niall, because you'd killed Jack; then it planned to kill her too. It would make it look like Niall had killed you in the struggle, Jane: Jack kills Greepols for book. Green reporter Niall kills Jack for killing Greens. Jane kills Green reporter. Green reporter kills Jane. All while the robot impersonator, unbeknownst to anyone, gets away with the book. Case seems solved. Perp gets away with triple triple homicides. Jara,

Jack Cluewitt and the Imbrium Basin Murders Ruth J. Burroughs

Keith, Lee, Jane, you and me. It didn't kill you earlier, Niall, because your time of death had to be accurate."

"But none of its plans worked," Jane said.

"Anyway, killers aren't too bright and evil schemes never go according to plot. They can plan and plan all they want."

"Well, they're foiled. It's the most convoluted frame job I've ever heard and couldn't possibly have worked," Niall said. "I drove toward the Imbrium Basin and found you walking back in a space suit from the mining site. I thought it odd. As I got closer the suit didn't look right. I could see the helmet being projected over the skin of a robot. I tried to swerve around, but it used a gun; it forced me to turn around and go to the Green Moon Motel. Once inside the room, it gagged me. Keith and Lee thought it was truly you. When they wouldn't tell their secrets, it tortured them by pulling out their nails. And Lee started to crumble. The robot impersonating you leaned in to hear Lee better. That's when Keith grabbed the gun, and then shot his own brother. He held onto the gun until he was dead. The robot couldn't pry it from his hand until after he died. Then he took it and shot them in the heart. Then it returned to the scene of Jara's death as me, hoping to lead Jane here after killing you. What happened then?"

"I lived," Jack said, "And I figured out he wasn't you, and he rocketed off into space."

Thanks for getting here before the robot returned to kill me, and for saving my life, but no thanks for taking your time untying me," Memory Niall said.

"Sorry, I had to secure the crime scene, even though I had already deduced that it was Robot Niall that had killed the Greepols, or whoever programmed it."

"Please don't call it Robot Niall, or Robot Jack, for that matter. There is only one Jack Cluewitt, and that's you; and there is only one Niall Heaton, and that's me."

"You're free to go, but we may be calling you later," Jane said.

"I'll be at my home if you need to reach me. I will report to the Mediator via hologram. I need some rest."

"Would you like to stop by the hospital?" Jane asked.

Jack Cluewitt and the Imbrium Basin Murders   Ruth J. Burroughs

"No, I would just like to get something to eat and drink and rest," Niall replied and headed out the door of the Motel room.

"Did the forensic nanobots find anything?" Jane asked.

Cal nodded, smiling. "Yes. I have to download them to your coms later. I think we know who killed these Greepols."

Jack nodded. "Yes a robot killed them, but the real question is who programmed the robot to kill them and why. I think it's a quadruple frame. They wanted to frame Niall, me, Jane and Hildy. I have to go back to Organdy's."

"Why, are you hungry, or do you need a new heart?" Jane asked.

"No, my heart is in the right place. I have to get to Organdy's before Organdy is murdered too."

Organdy Poisson Tuesday noon
June 8ᵗʰ, 5030
Chapter Nine

Organdy Poisson, Organ Trader-slash-Sushi Chef, knew someone was out to kill him and it had something to do with his fiancé, Rappel.

"Where did you say you're from?" the wealthy customer at the sushi bar asked.

"Canada. My father is a French Canadian chef, bio-engineer and gardener and my mother is a Japanese cook, a doctor and gardener. Ragune Poisson studied organ growing and passed on his secrets to me. Ragune studied at the Langer Human Organ Institute in Quebec for organ growing and then went to Paris to study the art of cooking and horticulture. While he was studying cooking he met my mother Yukiko, who was also studying French cooking and was teaching Japanese cooking and the art of Bonsai."

"Bonzai!" the man at the bar raised his sake cup for a toast to the other diners in the restaurant and the few who sat near him, "a love story?"

"Not bonzai, cheers, bonsai, miniature trees. Yes, they fell in love at first sight and he proposed to her on their second date. They moved back to Quebec and had me Naturally, rather than gene-enhanced like most children. Thus became Organdy Poisson, sushi chef and organ trader in Moon City."

"Excellent story. If I forget I'll be back tomorrow to ask again."

"I'm glad you'll come again. What's your name?"

"Best Moon sushi. Melts in my mouth. Oh, my name is Brick Cardigan."

"Nice to meet you Mr. Cardigan."

Jack Cluewitt and the Imbrium Basin Murders Ruth J. Burroughs

"Just call me, Brick. Thanks. Nice to meet you, Monsieur Poisson. I'm here for a robot sales convention at the Green Moon Hotel. I need new farm bots for my Agriculture Fullerene," he slurred.

Organdy Poisson smiled and nodded. Not too many people could own a whole Buckminster Fullerene Space World. This guy was rich. Organdy had to take care with the razor sharp knife in the low Moon gravity. He didn't want to hurt the rich guy who could become a repeat customer and he didn't want to make sushi fingers and no matter how long the body assimilated, his mind still wanted to feel Earth gravity. He methodically but quickly cut the thin slices of tuna for the sashimi order. His hands wanted to work small but the near Zero-G made every movement big. His crash course training by the previous owner helped, and all the years of experience as a sushi chef. Finished, he deftly placed the sashimi in a special Zero-G platter, or Moon bowl, so that it wouldn't spill. No Green points for this dish, and he paid through the gills on fish tax.

Organdy sculpted the sushi and sashimi castle, placing the special order on the Moon bowl. It was the favorite of his customers. He built one now and was just adding the finishing touches of carrot star, shiso leaf, wasabi and gari. He rang the bell and the Japanese waitress attended in her Moon designs kimono. She bowed and grabbed the large layered plate. She brought it over to a table of regular customers. They all *oohed* and *ahhhhed* over it.

It was Tuesday, June 8th, 5030, and for some reason Rappel needed the afternoon off. Some kind of emergency, and she'd be back for dinner.

Organdy stopped a moment, absently wiping the knife with a clean towel that floated nearby. He looked outside the restaurant window past the glass dome and through the plasma shield, and watched a Moon digger sprawling across the rim of Protagoras crater with two robot Moon digger dogs in tow, with his cybernetic eye. Most people thought he was a pure Natural, but he kept it a secret that he liked to upgrade. It wasn't bad until you got into genetic repairs and nano cybernetics. That stuff was addicting, and the contagious nanites illegal.

Sometimes he couldn't believe it was his restaurant, but he'd worked hard to get the Moon sushi license. He

102

Jack Cluewitt and the Imbrium Basin Murders   Ruth J. Burroughs

cleaned his station and looked up at a customer approaching the sushi bar.

The good-looking suit stopped momentarily to stare into the fifty-gallon fish tank and then turned to him at the sushi bar. He had curly brown hair and a salmon-colored burn scar on the right side of his face, but moved like a person used to microgravity. He wore burned Balmacaan London Fog raincoat over his suit. Must be from Earth.

"Bonjour, Monsieur Poisson?" he asked.

"Everyone calls me, Organdy."

"My name is Jack Cluewitt, I'm with the NEPD."

"Moon City cop, huh, how can I be of service to you?" Organdy asked.

"I'm investigating the death of three Green Police killed here on the Moon."

"Murdered! How, where?" Organdy froze mid-slice, shocked.

"Shot. One in the mine and the other two at the Green Moon Hotel." Jack studied Organdy's expression and glanced at his rich customer who'd gasped.

"Murdered with a gun at my hotel?" Brick Cardigan said.

Jack grimaced. "Yes. Did you hear anything?"

"No. Too much noise from all the partying," Brick said.

Organdy shook his head. "What kind of person in their right mind would use a gun in space?"

"I was told they came here the day before they died. I'm a Homicide detective."

"Detective? Homicide? Hmmm." Organdy scratched his chin, doubtful, and frowned. "Do you have a gold shield, detective?"

"No. NEPD badges are blue. Did the Green Police come in here?"

"They're blue, but you're a detective. If you get enough collars you'll advance to a wider jurisdiction. You're vying for an Earth-Moon-Mars-Jupiter gold PD badge. That's what you're egging for, oui?"

"I like my blue badge just fine. Earth-Moon-Mars-Jovian detectives, EMMA-JOs, have to live in space. I get to live on Earth, Monsieur Poisson."

"Organdy, please, Detective Cluewitt."

103

Jack Cluewitt and the Imbrium Basin Murders   Ruth J. Burroughs

"Jack, then. You can call me Jack. How about the female Greepol?"

"Yes, I remember her. She came very late on Sunday night. It was a busy night early on, but it slowed down quite a bit. I had sent everyone home except one waitress and myself. The two Green Police were here first. Wait. I remember you. You were in more casual clothes. Jeans and T-shirt. You came in here Sunday night and argued with the conjoined twins. You made them empty their pockets. Then you left."

"They had illegally confiscated my book back on Earth. I followed them here, but they didn't have it with them. They pretended they didn't know what I was talking about. The coroner hasn't sent any pictures of the victim, but you said a woman joined them? Did she have blonde hair and bad skin?"

"Yes." Organdy nodded. "And come to think of it she had a paper book."

Jack raised his eyebrows, surprised. "She must have been the same Green Policewoman they found in the cave."

"Well, the twins relaxed for a bit and drank after you left, but when she showed up with the book they seemed frightened again. My waitress had a few tables she was finishing up in the front, so when blonde Greepol joined them late, I let them eat here at the sushi bar. They wore those beige uniforms with the rainbows and green trees and all three were nervous, scared even."

"Yes. The female was killed. The book may have something to do with it, but I'm not sure yet. If they'd given me the book, she might still be alive. Well, I'm still looking for that book. I don't think our suspect has it, and whoever has it could be in danger. Have you seen it?"

"No. Not since that night when she brought it here."

"Did anyone come in here looking yesterday?"

"Like it says on the door, we're closed on Mondays."

"Where were you and your staff?"

"I was at the MIT Moon City Human Organ Langer Lab working on that organ growing order for the Green Police. I'm not sure where my girlfriend and the staff were. You'd have to ask them."

Jack nodded. "What did the three Greepols eat?"

"They ordered vegetarian sushi. Two of the Greepols shared one body, the conjoined twins, but they have completely different tastes." Organdy chuckled.

"And you're sure she had the book?" Jack asked.

"Yes. I'm sure. I was busy, but I remember that."

"An old hard cover paper book?"

"Wouldn't that be illegal?" Organdy asked.

"No, an old one wouldn't be," Jack replied.

"That's strange. Green Police hate paper. Why would she have a book?"

Jack shrugged. "If I knew that, I wouldn't be investigating their murders. Was there anything unusual about them that you recall?"

Organdy shook his head. "No, nothing unusual. They had lunch and then ordered some organ parts. A heart, a pair of lungs and three livers."

"The twins would only need one liver. That's not strange?" Jack asked.

"No."

"But why three livers instead of two?"

"I'm not sure Jack. They didn't say, and I didn't ask."

"Were they cloned organs?"

Organdy nodded, wiping his knives with a clean rag. "Yes, that was the order I was working on Monday when you say the woman was killed. I think her name was Jara. The higher end products are for people with money. Sometimes they sell them, but usually they keep them on reserve.

It takes a while to grow an adult organ. The common organs have to go through a preparation process so the donee doesn't reject the tissue. I thought some of the organs were for her. She didn't look well."

"I take it they didn't buy the higher end clone products."

"Right, Jack, those are expensive. They ordered standard."

"And these two Green Police didn't say who the organs were for?"

"No, they didn't. I assumed it was for them, but now that I think of it, the Green Party would probably have organs on order for them."

"Thank you, Organdy."

"People in space don't like guns. Do you think she was murdered by a New-Human or a robot?"

"Looks that way. Doesn't it?" Jack replied, startled. "Do you ever mix up your organs with your sushi orders?"

"Not at all. Some of my customers want to browse the organ selections while they eat."

"That's disgusting, if you ask me. By the way, your name suits you."

"Organ Trader-slash-Sushi Chef, that's me."

"You know, it used to be illegal to sell organs."

"Well, that was when poor people would sell their own organs to rich people. It takes a knack to grow organs well, and I've got it."

"Well, if I ever need an organ I'll know who to come to." Jack stuck his hand out.

Organdy shook his hand. "No problem, Detective. You should have some on order just in case."

"I think the department takes care of that."

"Yeah, but you should have higher end clone organs instead of the cheap stuff. I understand you can afford it."

"I'll think about it."

"If there's anything else I can do, just ask."

"Not at this time, but watch your back. We don't know where the killer robot is or who's behind it, and if you think of anything you may have forgotten about those Green Police, give me a call. Here's my card." Jack handed one to him and one to Brick, "You too," he said. Brick nodded, chewing a bit of sushi from his chopsticks.

"Will do, Jack," Organdy said, looking it over, he then stuck it in his uniform pocket. He smiled at Jack. "Would you like some sushi? It's on the house."

"No, thanks, but I'll take a rain check, if you don't mind."

"Will do. Nice meeting you."

"You too," Jack said, smiling, he turned to leave.

Organdy watched the detective check the fish tank again on his way out. *Funny guy,* Organdy thought, *but not as stupid as he pretends to be.* His name suited him, too Cluewitt. He was a puzzling guy. Organdy would have to be more careful, though. He felt relieved, but he didn't want to relax yet. There might be someone in the restaurant watching him. Never rush the customer. That was a good rule.

But who killed the Green Policewoman? That was the true mystery, and why was the book so important? One pair of lungs meant only one space suit. There just weren't that many space suits for conjoined twins. The heart was for the men, they said they had one weak heart, a congenital problem. The three livers, they needed as soon as possible they'd said. He had tried to solve their puzzle and Rappel had been right to ask if they needed help, but they had both missed a cry for help. Organdy suspected that they were saying their three lives were in jeopardy and they didn't really need any livers. But how could he have known? Their cryptic message must have been for someone who could have helped them but they'd guessed wrong. He owed the Green Police their lives for not figuring it out sooner. The message must have been for his girlfriend, Rappel Mitsukoshi, otherwise known as Rappel Luna. And she'd been busy trying not to blow her cover. If only they'd reached out to her, they might still be alive today.

Moon Sushi Restaurant
Tuesday night near closing
June 8th, 5030
Chapter Ten

Jack and Jane walked in the lamplight of the Moon City streets near the Sea of Cold, cleaned of regolith by little nano scrubbers, the dome of the magnetic field kept the bad rays out and the good atmosphere in. Sunspot emergency subway entrances dotted the patchwork of sliding lanes, and occasionally a practice alarm would go off. The bright sapphire of the earth hung in the sky, and Jack could see that Organdy's was still hopping, despite the late hour.

Jack let his partner enter first and they were showered in warm nano scrubbers that cleaned any particles of regolith off their clothes, skin and hair. It left them clean and dry and they entered the spotless restaurant and took a seat at the sushi counter. Three waitresses and a waiter slid around in the Moon G, serving customers, amidst the thick smells of tempura, teriyaki and hibachi cooking, mingling in with the vinegary smell of fine Moon sushi rice.

Beer and sake splashed about, and the hearty sounds of banter over quiet music and laughter mingled in the serene Asian atmosphere. The tinkling sound of water in the fish aquarium and the cutting sounds of the sushi knife soothed Jack as he sipped his tea. Jane also drank tea, since they were both on the clock and they both ordered some sushi. Fortunately Jack and Indigo Jane were the last to order. Jane went outside and smoked a zeegar as the last of the customers finished eating dinner. After they left the employees cleaned the restaurant spotless and then sat down to eat. Organdy allowed Jack and Jane to linger with their dessert and tea; an unusual event, since it left behind one dirty table and dirty dishes for the owner to wash.

Usually the employees stayed a bit, but because they knew Jack was investigating something they all left early except for one blue-eyed Japanese waitress. She'd changed into jeans and a bright green sweatshirt, and Jack couldn't seem to draw his eyes away from her much to Organdy's annoyance. Jack was a good-looking guy and he knew it, and he liked women to his own detriment. It took Jack a while to realize this was Organdy's squeeze; despite Jack's being a homicide detective he was kind of slow on the up-take when it came to females.

Jane came back in and sat down next to Jack, smelling of zeegar smoke, despite the nano scrubbers. He sniffed, disgruntled, and sipped at his tea, wishing it were sake or Irish whiskey. Organdy went back into the kitchen and came back a few minutes later dressed in street clothes, seeming to be in a better mood. He popped a can of cold beer.

"What's up, Jack?"

"I took a small sample of the organ growing emulsion in your fish tank and it's a match to the dried liquid on Jara, the female Greepol's hand."

"So?" Organdy said.

"Where's the book?" Jack asked.

"I don't know. Maybe Jara played with my fish." Organdy smiled.

"She had to have left the book at the bottom of the tank in the sand. You said she stayed late. Was there ever a time you left her alone in the restaurant?"

"Yes. I put in their order for organs without a deposit and it would figure that they're dead before paying for them."

"They weren't really ordering organs," Jack said.

"What do you mean?

"You said they ordered one heart, one pair of lungs and three livers."

"That's right"

"What they were really trying to tell you is that they had one space suit between the two of them, the one lung and the three livers meant they were risking their lives, three lives despite the fact that the two Greepols shared one body

109

Jack Cluewitt and the Imbrium Basin Murders   Ruth J. Burroughs

to save the book from getting into the wrong hands. What I haven't figured out yet is who they were trying to keep the book from and what was the one heart. Yes, the robot impersonating Niall and myself. But who was the robot working for? They knew their lives were in danger, so they a left trail they hoped would save the book if they were killed. They must have known you weren't the contact when you didn't respond."

"Why are you telling me all of this, Jack?" Organdy asked.

"Because you figured out that they hid the book in the fish tank. That's why the blonde Greepol's hand had residue of organ growing emulsion on it; your special formula. She'd hidden the book in the tank," Jack said.

"Well, what does that have to do with me?" Organdy asked.

"If you have the book I assumed robot Niall, our murderer at large who actually could be impersonating someone else now, would come here next and kill you for the book."

"Well, the book isn't here," Organdy said, and the waitress looked at him, surprised.

"What do you mean?" Jack asked.

"Ask Harry," Organdy said.

"Who's Harry?"

"My robot fish." Organdy looked angry with the squeeze, whose face had just drained of all blood.

"Harry, where's the book?" Jane asked the robot fish, amused.

"Máóhk-Clay has it. Edgar Chavez Moon Digger put it in Cavity's stomach and took it to blind Máóhk-Clay's mobile home. Rappel Luna gave it to him. I have recorded it. Here, I'll show." The orangey robot goldfish wiggled its elegant tail, and the holo filled the tank's glass wall as it showed the waitress Rappel Luna tell Edgar Chavez that she was really an undercover organ agent working to break a big organ trading ring. The holo winked out, and Harry playfully swam back and forth looking at the humans out of the one eye, then the other.

Rappel Luna stood up, "Organdy, I can explain . . . I . . ."

"Never mind that now," Organdy said. "What's important is that Jack and Jane go get the book before anyone else is killed and that you don't blow your cover, Rappel. I will erase Harry's memories. He's not Grid-linked so don't worry. You could have told me, you know. But it's okay because I'm not the criminal you're looking for and actually, I'm glad you're not really Yakuza."

Rappel looked relieved, albeit a little angry at herself for not noticing that the fish in the tank were more than just decorative; after all she was a detective.

"If we find anything out about the organ trading ring, we'll come back here and tell you, Ms. Luna. We won't jeopardize your operation, but our investigations may overlap," Jane said.

"This isn't good," Rappel said, frowning.

"Well, Jack and I can keep quiet," Jane said.

Rappel looked doubtful. "But there are too many leaks in the NEPD. If even one bad cop gets wind of what I'm doing my whole investigation is blown or worse. I'll be killed. Once you jack-into-the-Grid with your reports, I'm screwed."

Jane smiled. "Actually we're Naturals, Jack and I. Neither of us is Grid-linked and we're not being very co-operative with the NEPD right now because they have this policy in place where they're going to replace us all with people who are willing to upgrade. It's not good enough that I'm a designer baby, genetically enhanced smart, or that Jack happens to be a good cop, despite his being a Natural. They're going to come down on us hard for not wrapping up the investigation within a month or two. Even if it means putting the wrong people in jail; the politicos want to stay in office, and the only way to do that is to make it look like they're keeping criminals off the streets. Damn wetware," Jane said.

Rappel breathed a sigh of relief. "You don't know what that means to me, you both being Naturals. I'm not cyber-linked either, and I'm expected to close cases faster than you can say sea urchin. I invested so much and it's not all been a waste. Sometimes it takes years to do real gumshoe investigation. But they want robots to solve it in a day or two, even if it means putting the wrong people in jail. You know, I really thought the book had something to do with my investigation into the organ stealing business."

Jack Cluewitt and the Imbrium Basin Murders   Ruth J. Burroughs

"It could very well. We'd better go to Máóhk-Clay's and get that book before anyone else is killed." Jane got up and shook her hand. "Nice meeting you Ms. Luna."

"Rappel. You can call me Rappel."

"You can call me Jane or Indigo."

"Thanks, Indigo."

"Hey Jack, before you leave, tell me what did the Greepols mean by one heart?" Organdy said.

Jack shrugged. "The heart was one of a string of key words for the contact to recognize, maybe. I was hoping you could tell me." Jack stood up from the sushi bar.

Jack and Indigo Jane left Organdy's as the Earth was setting on the Moon and Jane lit another stogie. Jack sighed.

"If you even think about her Organdy will slice you up into two-K little pieces," Jane said.

"That Rappel is a piece of work, isn't she? It looks like she was genetically bred by Yakuza parents. She's no waitress and she's not just an organ enforcement agent; she's bred to be a lean mean fighting machine, lover and mother." Jack sighed again, and Jane shook her head.

"You keep it in your pants, Jack, if you know what's good for you. C'mon, we'll take my Lula vehicle over to Robot City. I know where the mobile home park is," Jane said and the two of them headed for the landing strip as the earthlight glowed, still peaking over the horizon of the Moon.

✄

Máóhk-Clay sensed danger. It was an uncanny ability she had with the future or things beyond normal perception. She'd made a pot of hot tea and set it on the living room table, which was a step away from her eat-in kitchen. She also set out some ice tea and lemonade. She was expecting company too, and it had to do with the dangerous object Edgar had left in her home for safe-keeping. Its energy was powerful, and she knew people wanted it so badly they'd kill her for it. Máóhk-Clay never thought she'd become such a domestic, as radical as she was in her youth. Beebee lay like a yellow rug under the kitchen table, sleeping quietly.

She knew someone, or maybe several someones, were coming to ask her for something. She set out some buggy

Jack Cluewitt and the Imbrium Basin Murders   Ruth J. Burroughs

hors d'oeuvres and dips for her guests and turned on some soft Pow Wow music. Glazed cockroaches with larvae were a good ice breaker. The doorbell rang just as Máóhk-Clay sat down on her sofa, adjusting her long raven black hair. She stepped on a floor button, which unlocked the door.

"Come in, the door's open," she called and waited. She could hear the footsteps of two people and the smell of one man and one woman. Máóhk-Clay heard the sounds of jewelry on the woman. Would they just kill her and take what they wanted?

"Please, sit down, make yourselves at home. I have lemonade or tea on the table here. Would you like hot tea, or ice tea?" She waited in the silence. Most people were surprised by her precognitive abilities. She was more than just a Siwen, she was truly a shaman.

"Uhm . . . You were expecting us?" a woman asked.

"I felt like company, and here you are," was Máóhk-Clay's response. "Please introduce yourselves. It would help me if you could describe yourselves so I have some idea what you look like. Would you like something to drink?"

"We just ate, thank you." came the man's voice, "But since you went to such trouble I'm sure we'll find room for more. My name is Jack Cluewitt and this is my partner, Jane Salgado."

"Detective Cluewitt and Salgado; or blue something."

"That's right; most people call me Indigo Jane."

"You came here for something. Something I think my thoughtful boyfriend hid here when he was picking up some lunch for his friend, Jules."

"That's right," Jack replied as he sat down in a comfy sofa.

"Please have something to drink and describe yourselves to me."

"I'm tall, dark and handsome," Jack said. Jane chuckled, stepping around him, and sat on the couch, next to Máóhk-Clay.

"He's medium height, clumsy and nerdy looking," Jane corrected.

"May I feel your face?" Máóhk-Clay asked. Jane put her hand on Máóhk-Clay's hand and guided it to her cheek.

"Are you a boxer?" Máóhk-Clay asked and Jane nodded into her hand.

Jack Cluewitt and the Imbrium Basin Murders Ruth J. Burroughs

"Yes. My parents wanted me to have blue eyes and red hair during the Designer Baby craze, but my genes expressed differently. It wasn't discovered 'til I was born. My eyes are amber and my hair is blue. There aren't too many geneticists who can grow blue hair. The gene just won't do that most of the time. It comes out gray and most people don't want a gray-haired baby. I'm very dark-skinned with red eyes. I grew up with all these light-haired, blue-eyed black kids in East Harlem, Mars," Jane said.

"Very interesting. You must tell me about it someday. One of you is rich."

"Jack is a spendthrift with too much money. He doesn't have to do this. Jack was born to be a cop, though."

"You're adopted," Máóhk-Clay said. "You came here for something connected to your birth parents."

"Are you getting that off the Grid?" Jack grimaced.

"Jack!" Jane said.

"I don't jack into the Grid," Máóhk-Clay said, noting Jack's sarcasm.

"Well. If you're psychic you should already know what we look like. Do you know where they are?" Jack asked.

"No. But you're from Mars or the Jupiter space mining colonies of the Ring," Máóhk-Clay swallowed. Not feeling comfortable reading such a skeptical man.

"Are they alive?" Jack said, sighing.

She hesitated, tilting her head this way and then that. She frowned. "Nothing. I'm getting nothing about whether they died or not. I don't think they meant to send you away. There was an accident. You were burned. You wear the scar on your face like a badge. A lot of poor miners send their babies down the corridor toward Earth in hopes they'll be saved. Maybe there was a mining accident."

Jack couldn't help shivering. "I hope not. We came here to get the book. Someone is killing to get their hands on that book," Jack said.

"You mean three Green Police. Two bodies. Three people."

"How did you know?"

"It's just a feeling I get."

Jack snorted. "Or you had something to do with their deaths."

114

Jack Cluewitt and the Imbrium Basin Murders   Ruth J. Burroughs

"I couldn't have had the time to do it, Jack. You'll see that I sense these things."

"You see images?" Jane asked.

"Sometimes. I'm trying to see the murderer, but I'm not getting anything. Not even a little bit. Just the mechanical digging dogs. Miners. Robots and footprints."

"That's actually pretty good," Jack said.

"I've always been sensitive. Even before the accident."

"That wasn't exactly an accident when the Corporation blew up the Green candidate for President of American Space Commonwealth." Jane was sarcastic.

"You know about that?"

"You would have been her vice president for the last ten years and the Green Party would have won. I was young then, but I remember. Everyone said it was an accident that conveniently killed the only viable and very popular Green Candidate for President of the Commonwealth of Space-America."

"They didn't take the Green Party seriously for so many years. Not until the ocean swells and the loss of topsoil in the American Midwest and then California drying up. I helped make them strong."

"Those two Greepols . . . sorry, those three Greepols, you knew them?" Jack asked.

"Yes. Jara was a couple of years older than Keith and Lee. Her parents were stationed in the Middle East, or so they say. She's been sick her whole life. I mean. She *was* sick her whole life."

The twins, Keith and Lee, were conceived during some heavy spraying. Their mom was a downed combat fighter who'd been raped. But the War was so long and drawn-out, she couldn't get an abortion. She was sprayed by friendly chemicals while she was being held prisoner. The twins were born on U.S. Soil after she'd been rescued. The military said that their being conjoined had nothing to do with the Chem wars and she couldn't find any work after the war. She died when they were about three years old in a dirty run-down V.A. Hospital in Moon City."

"The Greepols were radical, weren't they?"

"They were so far left of center I was worried they'd end up becoming right wingers," Máóhk-Clay said. "They carried the cause for Green. They were fanatically anti

115

Jack Cluewitt and the Imbrium Basin Murders   Ruth J. Burroughs

chemical-warfare and for saving endangered species and the rainforests."

"While you'd gone soft?" Jack asked picking up some beautiful ornate chopsticks and trying a glazed cockroach in French onion dip. Jane grimaced and picked up a bowl of salted grubs and munched on them. Jack poured her some hot tea.

"May I have some tea as well, Jack?" Máóhk-Clay asked as she pushed her cup toward him.

"You can hear things pretty well, Máóhk-Clay," Jack said.

"Hearing is my world. When I'm not touching."

"Did Keith, Lee and Jara know each other?"

"They were very much in love with each other. At least Keith and Jara were. Lee was a slut and it was hard on Jara until he started to fall in love with Jara too. Then they became inseparable. Sorry. I meant the three of them. Jara never left their side. She must have died with them."

"No. We found . . . or rather, Ed found Jara in the mining caves and I found the twins in a hotel room in Moon City. Do you know much about robots?" Jack asked.

"You know I used to build robots, Jack. I'm sure you've done some background on me. I was making mining robots for VAQ-ORE Mining Corporation before I joined the Green party. Why?"

"A robot killed the three Greepols."

"A robot?"

"Yes, a robot programmed to look like me and then later to look like Memory Niall. It was trying to frame me for the Greepol murders and then kill me. Then it was going to frame the real Niall for my murder."

"What foiled it?"

"Stupidity. I didn't die and Niall figured out he . . . it rather, was really a robot. Cavity, Edgar's dog gave it away. It wasn't broadcasting but it is electronic."

"Edgar's little Cavity? I knew that mechanical canine was more than a walking pile of used parts. Jules must have smuggled some top of the line stuff in on those mining dogs," Máóhk-Clay thought aloud. "Oops."

"Don't worry. We don't care." Jack thought of Zero-One's admonition not to buy him the holographic facial expression program.

116

Jack Cluewitt and the Imbrium Basin Murders   Ruth J. Burroughs

"Jules builds robots?" Jack asked.

"I didn't mean to throw him under the bus, but yes he designed and built the mining dogs, Cavity and Apache and all the others on the Moon. He owns some patents and he stole some patents off some dead Earthlings. That is legal out here, or not yet illegal." Máóhk-Clay sipped her tea.

"Do you mind if we have a look around before we leave?" Jack asked and Máóhk-Clay nodded.

"Go ahead. I don't have much, but I did pick up some robot parts at the robot rummage sale. They're in my back yard."

"Where were you yesterday?" Jack asked.

"Here, with my dog Beebee."

"We can take a holo off her," Jane said.

"Sorry, Beebee's flesh and blood. She's my seeing eye dog from before the bubble buildings time, when we did Moon mining in space suits."

"I guess we won't be getting any holos off of her. Boy she sure looks like a robot dog."

"The robot dogs must be getting better. I remember when they looked like toys. You know I can't make robots anymore. Not without vision. I don't have the money, and I'm too proud to get designer eyes on charity. I would need someone sighted to help me build a robot, especially a highly cognitive seeming robot. Edgar's good at some things, but he isn't detail-oriented. He could never do that small kind of work with his big hands. It was nice of you to suspect me though, Jack."

"It's my job," Jack said, getting up.

Jane touched Máóhk-Clay's arm. "Thank you for the grubs and bugs."

"You're quite welcome," Máóhk-Clay said as Jane stood up to leave with Jack, her jewelry clinking and clanking.

Máóhk-Clay didn't get up.

"There was something else I forgot to ask you," Jack said.

"Yes, Jack?"

"Did you blame the Green party for your injuries?"

"What?" Máóhk-Clay asked, surprised.

"The Green Party was notorious for its lack of leadership. It was fraught with so many members who didn't believe in power. Jealousy, rivalry weren't easily admitted

117

Jack Cluewitt and the Imbrium Basin Murders   Ruth J. Burroughs

and you paid for it big time when you left the Green Party twenty-five years ago in disgust."

"So you think I had them killed, Jack, is that it?"

"I'm asking you," Jack said as Jane shifted uncomfortably.

"Yes, Jack. I did blame the Green Police for not protecting me. I blamed them for twenty-five years. I hated those stupid innocent hippies for not realizing how powerful we were and that along with power comes danger. The missile attack woke them up and made them more effective, but at the cost of becoming corrupt, like all the other parties, all about power, and too late for me and the dead President candidate, my friend, Antonia G. Clef."

"Twenty-five years. So you don't hate them anymore?"

"No. Something made me realize that despite everything I still share many of their values. It was what happened to me that made me bitter."

"So you didn't have anything to do with their deaths? With the murder of the Greepols, Jara, Lee and Keith." Jack spoke forcefully; his words ending with a slight Irish cadence on the last word of each sentence.

Máóhk-Clay did not say anything. She did not cry, but she wanted to. She felt indignant and dismayed all at once, like Jack had uncovered a deep wound in her heart that she was unwilling to look at with her inner-eye. He had caught her off-guard and found her motive. A motive she had hidden from herself.

The explosion had destroyed all her dreams. With the Green President candidate dead and her legs injured, her body burned, her eyes blinded, her hopes of being Vice President went up in ashes. Yes, she had blamed all the radicals instead of the right wingers who'd nearly killed her.

"Oh, let me feel your scar, Jack," Máóhk-Clay had been about to cry when something twinkled in her extrasensory perception.

"What? You've done enough of your psychic hot reading games on me," Jack said; this time Máóhk-Clay took notice of his Irish accent. She was sure she heard it this time.

"Get your sorry ass over here and let me touch you. How can I cold-read body language and why would I care about your history?"

Jack Cluewitt and the Imbrium Basin Murders   Ruth J. Burroughs

She heard some footsteps. Jack picked up her hand and put it on the right side of his face.

"I was injured in the same accident as you. Antonia was killed. It was your birthday and you were given a robot dog by your parents prior to that day. Its name was Zero-One. I can't remember their names. I'm sorry. I could see back then and we were blown up just after you blew the candles out on your fifth birthday; the party had started; it must have been awful for you. We were on the Flora asteroid cluster in the Ring of Stones on the Calendula Fullerene Space Mining Colony."

"I don't remember any of that. I can't remember any of my life prior to being with the Cluewitts. Was there a list of those who died?"

"No, Jack. People wanted to disappear. But your parents were there at the party. They loved you very much." Jack cleared his throat. Did he believe her?

"Hmm . . . I always thought the Cluewitts had given me my majordomo, Zero-One. I don't recall anything prior to the birthday. Nothing. No wait. Guilt. I always felt guilty about wanting to live on Earth. But that's it. No other memories."

"You must be blocking the memories. Maybe they're too painful to recall. Your parents didn't tell you anything?"

"No. My mom gave me the book, a toy gold shield, and the raincoat after I joined the force. Back in my blue uniform days. Dad stopped talking to me after I became a cop. He put me through med school. I gave up after two years of medicine before I joined the force. Dad wanted me to follow in his footsteps but it wasn't my calling."

"The book you seek is on top of the refrigerator, where Edgar left it when he picked up the thermos for soup he took to Jules," Máóhk-Clay said.

Jack didn't move from his spot. He must be watching her reaction, she thought. Her face was like stone. Máóhk-Clay heard Salgado retrieve the book.

"You can't leave the Moon until further notice," Jack said firmly. Máóhk-Clay nodded.

"Thank you again, for your hospitality. You're very kind," Jack said and she heard them leave.

Máóhk-Clay stepped on the door button and the door closed and locked. She turned up the Pow Wow music and

119

started to cry. She cried until she thought her heart would break and the water spilled out from the deep place in her heart. She hadn't seen this coming, either.

⚔

"So are we going to go interrogate Jules now?" Jane asked. Jack was driving the LULA V from Máóhk-Clay's mobile home. Jane usually drove, but she was still seeing spots from being KOed by robot Niall.

"Wake up, Indigo. Jules may be a good robot maker, but why build a foil for your murderer? Someone knew those dogs were suspended from mining duty and had no idea Jules got their release the same day the Greepol murders were planned. Whoever built the Niall robot did not build Cavity, and the Coroner is probably figuring that out now. Well, if Gretel ever figures it out. We are way ahead of her."

"What about our report?"

"Burn the report. It's not that I don't want to co-operate with NEPD. People who jack in are potential leaks. Computers don't know right from wrong and can be accessed and programmed by anyone."

"Some humans don't know right from wrong Jack."

"Or some humans think wrong is right, Indigo."

"Then did Máóhk-Clay do it?"

"She has motive, but I don't think so."

"Why were you so hard on her?"

"I thought she was a fraud. I don't believe in Simons and Siwens. It's a crock. But she's very intuitive, and I had to be sure. Her motive is revenge against the Green Party. She thinks it was the fault of the Green Police that she is now blind. She knows the Moon like the back of her hand and she's a trusted member of the Green Party; plus she has handicap access. She's smart, cunning, and people underestimate her. She's quite capable."

"Who else has motive means and opportunity?" Jane asked.

"Well, maybe one of the twins killed Jara. Perhaps my butler did it. He had them killed, using Immaculata, my maid, after he discovered they had my book. Immaculata is being shipped to Cadaver City to a man by the name of

Maelstrom Corrigan. Zero-One was escorting Immaculata there because I'm quite fond of my maid."

Jane chuckled. "So did the maid do the deed or the butler?"

"I couldn't resist." Jack managed around a bump near a crater.

"Well, I can't imagine a strong enough motive to move either one of them to murder for a book. Unless the book has something to do with robots, and Zero-One and Immaculata are actually sentient conscious beings." Jane tried to light a zeegar. Jack gave her an incredulous look, and she took out some spearmint gum to chew instead. "Okay who else then?"

"Ed Moon Digger has a great motive. He needs money to buy the new eyes for Máóhk-Clay."

"How do you know this?"

"Because he'd been trying to convince her to get new eyes for years now—and just before she finally agreed—all the money he'd saved for her new eyes—he lost in a card game. We're not talking standard organs here. We're talking state of the art super-poly-optic Moon-grown eyes. If he sold the book to the highest bidder he could get those eyes. He loves Máóhk-Clay more than he loves the Moon and Cavity, but then Máóhk-Clay is the Moon."

Jane shrugged. "So, did Ed Moon Digger do it?"

"I don't think so. He carried the book for Rappel without knowing what it was, it seems."

Jane puffed on her unlit zeegar while Jack drove around another Bubble mobile home community. "That sounds right. Okay, so that leaves who else?"

"Jules Helphenstein. Hildy Witter Raygun. Sally S. Queue, Hildy's robot. She could have been wearing the hologram disguise and there are those footprints."

"Your girlfriend, Hildy? Not *your girlfriend?*" Jane said surprised.

"Yes, she's a suspect."

"What's her motive?"

Jack frowned as he maneuvered the LULA V into the sharp shadows of huge boulders. "I don't know. She doesn't need the money."

"What do we do with the book?"

"We'll have to hide it somewhere safe. It's the key to everything. It's the heart the Greepols were talking about," Jack said.

Vasundhra Sunny Kambhampati
Cadaver Storage Facility Cemetery
Fullerene Near-Earth Space
Chapter Eleven

"Yes. I wanted to be a roboticist, but being a Space Morgue repair tech is even better," Sunny replied, making her way around a clutter of robots as they slid across the smooth surface of the brightly lit corridor on mag shoes. Her new boss, Space Morgue robot repair manager, Maelstrom Corrigan, was rather greasy, but his love of robots and space made her like him. A tall, lanky man with dark brown overgrown brush-cut, he got about in the Low-G like he was born to it. Cadaver Storage Facility, Mausoleum, Cemetery and space habitat Fullerene was shaped like a giant soccer ball. Maelstrom, her new boss, was showing her around the Facility.

"So this is better than being an entertainment Robot technician over at Ocean City Paradise on Earth?" Maelstrom Corrigan asked.

"Yes. I love space," she said.

"Dead bodies?" he asked.

"No. But I like repairing ailing and dead robots."

"It's not that hard to be a roboticist. I've seen some pretty sorry cases graduate just because they had the money and connections."

"Well, I worked nights at the entertainment corporation and went to school during the day," she said, slightly disoriented from the lack of gravity in the spoke of the Torus.

"It takes getting used to, trying to walk on walls and ceilings as the gravity moves."

"That wouldn't be so hard if you didn't have this robot obstacle course."

Maelstrom laughed. She wove her way around discarded robots, some so old she couldn't recognize the make and model. Some were plugged into diagnostic terminals going through eye to hand coordination routines or bipedal motion tests.

"I'm looking for an old motor of sorts. I heard Ocean City let you go for giving robots autonomous programs?"

"I just gave one jazzer robot better eye to hand coordination. I was fired, left out in the cold. You know Ocean Paradise pays for food and housing for their employees. It was the best Longitude and Latitude ever. I ended up in New York State in winter because the only place that needed a robot tech was a used robots' store. When Arty gave me some robot repair jobs and let me stay at his place, I was hungry and penniless. Then when his business slowed down he got me passage out here to you."

"Arty?"

"Pops T. Van de Woestyne," Sunny replied.

"It's not like they're knocking down my door to get here to Cadaver City. Pops Van de Woestyne. I know him virtually. I buy robots from him, but I've never met him. Collecting human and robot corpses is not the best space job, but better than nothing, Vasundhra."

"You can call me Sunny. All Americans do, and even though I speak Hindi I'm from America. Your boss, Henri Vasquez, got my retirement funds out of Ocean Paradise and rolled them over. I actually always wanted to be a robot jockey when I realized I wouldn't make the grade to be a roboticist."

"It's not as glamorous as it's reputed to be. I was a robot jockey most of my life and it was hard work virtually mining the asteroids with robots. They call us the cowboys of space, but out there you're on your own."

Sunny felt that space nausea again, despite the meds mixed in with her tube of hot coffee. She took a swig and dribbled, spilling globs into the air.

"That's the centrifugal force you feel. You'll get used to it soon enough. Feels like Mars G. This Fullerene started out as a Torus; each cluttered spoke holds Cadaver and mining robots for trade, repair and storage. The oversized docking hub is where you'll start for shipping and receiving and you'll notice this station was never designed for

Jack Cluewitt and the Imbrium Basin Murders   Ruth J. Burroughs

humans, so the temperature varies all over the place. You'll want to wear smart overalls that will be able to adjust to different conditions.

We also get the local bodies from all the nursing homes, accidents, murders and death from natural causes. We use everything that hasn't already been harvested and then place molecules of individuals into the DNA Mausoleum. If the bodies don't have religious restrictions, the waste is consumed by non-edible insects and now the new nano-processors."

"I guess that's why it's called Cadaver City."

Maelstrom smiled. "Usually we get more broken down robots than cadavers, but once we had a colony ship hauled in that lost oxygen and fuel due to an explosion. Three thousand people died and a hundred robots remained functioning and were able to use what little fuel was left to pilot the ship to a tug boat. The dock was swamped with corpses. We couldn't do it all in VR with the robots. It was awful."

"I can imagine."

"Oh here she is, Immaculata Bondo, a really old painter robot, from Earth though. When the Earth-friendly paints came out with new colors she was really popular. She just finished painting symbols on this facility. A Moon City Terrestrial-living cop turned her into a French maid, but he couldn't afford to fix her after she fell off his veranda. His majordomo sold her to me. But now I want to cannibalize her parts. I'll give Immaculata here an old standard motor eventually, but once I take this motor out she'll be down," Maelstrom stumbled over the rickety old sign painter robot. "She's got the old Rolls Royce fusion-motors that came out in the 3Ks. The nano-motors just don't cut it for all the hype and I was going to install hers into my Tritan X-2 personal assistant, Byron. Byron's motor can't keep up with the work load and I sold George, my Tritan X-1. I actually miss George, if that's possible."

"Sometimes older is better."

"In this case, older is better," Maelstrom examined the painter robot he'd bought from Jack. "Hmmm, looks like I'll have to turn this one on and bring her back to the office. I can't seem to disconnect the motor," he said grunting.

"What's the problem?"

125

Jack Cluewitt and the Imbrium Basin Murders   Ruth J. Burroughs

"It's integrated into some other functions. Well, I'll just run a diagnostic on her and see if I can integrate the whole unit into my Tritan X-2."

"That would look funny, and Byron might start painting things."

"Stranger things have happened out here, but don't believe the ghost stories. There are a lot of robots and you'll run into some pretty weird things."

"Well, Henri Vasquez happens to be onboard today. He's one of the shareholders of Cadaver City Robots. You'll get to meet him in person and the other head honchos. Why don't I bring you to department headquarters to meet them?"

"Okay."

Maelstrom Corrigan turned on the French Maid painter robot and they climbed on its back. Immaculata went hand over hand along the rung corridor to the hub while he entertained his new employee with over-embellished Jovian mining colony stories. Dark ringlets rippled about her face and sparkling green eyes that seemed to hang on every word he spoke. Sunny Kambhampati was now Maelstrom's favorite new employee.

At VAQ-ORE hub she shook hands with Henri Vasquez. He gave her a warm welcome. He had a nice smile, too. Sunny met his girlfriend Celia and her other bosses and colleagues, Shakara, Abe, Julio, Helena, Iver, Helmut, Juan, Jeannette, Sebastian, Yuri, and Yoichi. Although many were out of the office and she didn't get to meet them all.

When he was done with introductions Maelstrom said, "You can get started at docking and shipping tomorrow." She smiled and nodded. She couldn't wait.

✖

A week later, after lunch, Sunny went down to Maelstrom's office in the hub to see if she could help him repair Byron, the office manager robot. The new refurbished engine was puttering out again. They managed quite a few shipments of old folks' bodies and used robots and Byron's engine wasn't cutting it. Since Maelstrom couldn't take the motor out of Immaculata, she had picked up a lot of his duties, taking shipments orders and receipts from the docks.

Jack Cluewitt and the Imbrium Basin Murders   Ruth J. Burroughs

Most of the filing was backed up by the space stations' computers but robots were needed on site in the warehouse and at the docking hub to manage transactions.

Maelstrom had Byron secured on a diagnostic table, the smell of super conducting oil all over him, wearing mag glasses he showed her what he'd been working on and she dug into the array of intricate parts with minute needle nose pliers.

The thing had been jerry-rigged so many times she had trouble finding the old connections and then Immaculata interrupted.

"There's an urgent phone call from docking," the robot said.

"What? How urgent?" Maelstrom replied without looking her way.

"Detectives Cluewitt and Salgado at docking. They're investigating a triple homicide on the Moon, and they want to look at some bodies that were sent up here recently."

"Okay. Take the call. Send them up. Sunny and I can take them to the Cadaver warehouse."

"Yes sir," Immaculata said and retreated into Maelstrom's office.

Sunny cleared her throat, "If you don't mind I could stay here and work on Byron's engine."

"You have to go see it sooner or later. You'll have to find the bodies the robots get mixed up all the time and do DNA sampling before they go to mausoleum. Don't worry. You'll be just fine."

"Okay." Sunny accidently sprayed some valve fluid on her face shield.

"Carry on. You're doing great. I'll get us some coffee tubes." Maelstrom grabbed a towel hanging from the wall and wiped the robot engine grease off his hands and handed her the towel.

Sunny worked meticulously, noticing that the engine was very worn out. That was odd. They'd just installed this refurbished motor and it had been in good shape.

Using a tiny nano built screw driver she took some parts out to examine it further and took the whole thing apart by the time Maelstrom got back.

"Sweating like a grease monkey?"

Jack Cluewitt and the Imbrium Basin Murders   Ruth J. Burroughs

She looked up and pulled the face shield up and wiped the sweat off.

"You got grease on your chin . . . here let me . . ." He handed her a clean towel and she cleaned off her hands and face. "What's the diagnosis?"

"You need a new engine," she replied. He laughed.

"Yeah, I know, but what was wrong with it?"

"Nothing. Just worn out. Have you been using it a lot more than usual?"

"Well, only in the last year. A lot of old people dying. A lot more inventory."

"It just wasn't built for 24/7."

"True. When I bought it they said it wasn't built for that. I should have got the Tritan Prime but this one was on sale and my inventory was a lot smaller when I bought the X-2. There have been a lot more cadavers lately," Maelstrom said.

"Excuse me. These are the detectives Jack Cluewitt and Jane Salgado," Immaculata interrupted.

Maelstrom walked over to the archway and shook hands with the two detectives. "Hi, I'm Maelstrom Corrigan and this is Vasundhra Kambhampati, or Sunny for short."

"I'm glad you're putting Immaculata to good use. I miss her, but couldn't afford to have her repaired," Jack said. Jane mumbled something about him being a spendthrift.

"So, you're the one who used to own her. Yes, I met Zero-One. He's quite a robot himself."

Jack smiled. "He is at that."

"I've never met a cop with a majordomo. I'm sure your French maid looks a bit different in space dungarees than in that black dress you had her wearing with the islet lace apron."

"Yes." Jack inspected the loose fitting outfit. "She doesn't look anything like a French maid and she's much more serious now too."

Indigo Jane rolled her eyes in exasperation and pulled her blue locks into a space net cap. "We're investigating a triple homicide that occurred on the Moon. And we'd like to have another look at the bodies."

Immaculata smiled, still having retained her French accent. "I looked them up on the manifest for you Jack, to make sure they hadn't been consumed, or in case they were

Jack Cluewitt and the Imbrium Basin Murders   Ruth J. Burroughs

next in line. But we've been busy, so you're lucky; they're still in the warehouse."

"Thanks, Immaculata." Jack seemed proud of his former maid robot. "Do you have an autopsy room near the bodies?"

"No. You'll have to examine the three bodies in my office," Maelstrom said.

Jack shook his head. "Actually, we only need to see just two bodies."

"Last time I checked a triple homicide meant three bodies."

Jane shook her head this time. "Two of the cops shared a body. They are . . . were conjoined twins."

"I see." Maelstrom frowned.

"Could you take us there?" Jack asked.

"Of course. My assistant is going to retrieve them for you. She's experienced working on the robots. These will be her first retrieval of corpses in Cadaver City."

Sunny felt the blood drain out of her face and sucked on her coffee tube, hoping Maelstrom had gotten one with space sickness meds in it.

From the hub they took one of the trams up along the outside of the spoke. Sunny could see the hilly green inner surface of the Buckminster Fullerene, which felt like Mars gravity, so in her mind she felt like she was going down rather than up; the sky was green and full of gravestones. Warm coffee and space meds relieved some anxiety, but she felt like a baby sucking on the tube. Sunny's dark curls floated out in every direction as the tram sped past space colony citizens of every size, shape, color and space territory, visiting or living on Cadaver City Fullerene. Indigo Jane handed her a hair net and Sunny tucked her hair in the way Jane had done with her own bluish locks. Perhaps if she had been born in India this kind of work would be considered lowly, but in America it was a great honor to care for the dead, and she was American and very much in need of the job.

Tram robot technicians, wearing the same fuzzy logic overalls Sunny wore, warming up on queue as the cold air hit her, skittered up and down the spokes she could see in the distance. Mild gravity tugged on her as the car parked itself on the great green well-manicured lawn of Oakwood

Jack Cluewitt and the Imbrium Basin Murders   Ruth J. Burroughs

Cemetery next to a Mausoleum with the words Cadaver Storage Facility, except the letters TORAG and E for storage and the letters FAIL and I had scratched and faded making it look like Cadaver S c ity. Inside robots moved the bodies for disposal, examination, storage and DNA burial.

They exited the tram and went through the employees' entrance of Cadaver City to a receiving room lined with touch pad com desks.

"These are my heated offices. We added chairs and computers later. This place was originally designed for robots, but with them breaking down all the time it's actually fifty-fifty and the flesh half have to put up with the extremes of hot and cold around here." Maelstrom explained, as much for Sunny as for the two detectives. Dead robots and human cadavers of every shape and size in the underworld moved by robots in every direction for miles of the cemetery. Looking up now, Sunny saw grass and tree roots hanging from the sky, wrapped around a profusion of water and nutrient tubes; like a giant brain in the heavens.

"The robots will bring your bodies up to one of these examination chambers. The Greepols' bodies will have DNA removed for the mausoleums and the rest is disintegrated for plant food. If their organs were viable for cloning, much of those were removed."

Maelstrom keyed into one of the pads and asked directions for the two Greepol bodies.

"Ahhh, here they are. We do holographic DNA burial, very beautiful, if you'd like a tour later . . . Here we are. Section C-5." He keyed in on another com pad, but the robots would not respond and the cadavers couldn't be removed from storage.

"Looks like it's stuck."

"I was hoping we could do virtual examinations from up here, Jack. Come with me." Maelstrom opened the hatch manually and a gush of cold air washed over them.

"Ouch." Jane shivered and wasn't even through the portal. She could see everyone's breath in the air.

"Sorry. It's not a human area. It's meant for cadavers and robots only."

"What's with the manual door?" Jane asked.

"I got sick of electronic ones locking me in places I didn't want to be locked in."

130

Jack Cluewitt and the Imbrium Basin Murders   Ruth J. Burroughs

Jane shivered again, but not from the cold. Sunny was glad she was wearing her smart overalls as they descended the stairs. She thought she saw frost on the fog of her breath. Maelstrom was looking for the bodies on his holographic map, twisting off his left arm. Clusters of pods littered the floor, along with what looked like free-standing dark gray cabinets. They picked their way around to the lockers.

"I think your murdered Greepols are in here," Maelstrom said, opening one of the doors. Red-stained naked corpses of senior citizens tumbled out onto the floor along with the strong odor of the Iodine.

Jane had jumped out of the way of the bodies sliding out of the cabinet. "What the hell."

"This is not good," Maelstrom said.

Sunny looked queasy.

"What's going on?" Jack asked.

"Well. These are not supposed to have Iodine all over them. All the bodies should be prepared for DNA removal and the rest of the body is broken down for redistribution. None of these bodies have been treated with respect or dignity. It's like they were just thrown in here to be disposed of. That's not right."

Jack frowned. "Why would a dead person need Iodine?"

Maelstrom grimaced. "They don't, but the organs did."

"I gotta call someone," Cluewitt said, looking at Jane. He was cold too. He was still wearing Moon City clothes.

Maelstrom shook his head. "This is so not good."

"Hello, Organdy? It's Jack. Tell Rappel to get up here to Cadaver City pronto . . . No, just tell her to get her butt up here now." Jack hung up.

Jack's phone rang.

"Hello?—Organdy?—Someone broke into your place and killed Harry? Did you erase the stuff about Rappel before . . . ? Good . . . good—Yeah, I know, they're after the book. Okay, be careful and send Rappel up soon. Cadaver City's Bucky Ball is headed out to deep space.—We're going out to Mars.—No, it will be at least a year before you see her again.—Yes, yes, of course I'll take care of her, but I think she's tough enough to take care of me and kick a few other people's butts. Your girlfriend is no wallflower.—I'll tell them to wait but there are a lot of facilities up here,

131

including Intermad and they've got a schedule to keep.— Okay, thanks Organdy."

"So, what should I do?" Maelstrom asked.

Jane stood near a robot's hot air vents blowing out of its back. "Just leave the scene the way it is and make sure the robots don't disturb it. We still need to find the Greepol bodies but it's too cold to do any examining here."

"Will do," Maelstrom ordered Immaculata to secure the whole storage facility area and began searching his com map again. "This isn't C-5, it's C-6. The bodies should be down here. Someone mislabeled this area. Robots have trouble with identifying places."

"You'd think it would be easier in a Fullerene," Jane said.

When they found the bodies Sunny and Immaculata put the two Greepol corpses on a gurney so they could take them into a makeshift exam room in human habitable areas.

Maelstrom found the detectives some scrubs and brought the two and a half cadavers up to a clean room near his office for the exam, while Sunny left to bring a waitress named Rappel Mitsukoshi through immigration. He wondered what the hell they needed a waitress for. He'd expected a coroner to examine a possible crime scene. Jack and Jane said they'd be a few hours examining the two Green Police bodies. With his robots, Maelstrom secured the area around the cabinet full of Iodine-covered cadavers and returned to the business of Byron's bad motor.

✖

Hours later Maelstrom returned to the receiving area with his fully repaired robot, Byron, near the makeshift autopsy rooms. Jack came out first, covered in a sparkling swarm of nanobots that looked like liquid candy. He removed his face mask and plopped down on the couch in Maelstrom's office. Then the stunning Indigo Jane followed, pulling off her space net and revealing her indigo hair. She flopped down next to Jack.

"Find anything?" Maelstrom said.

"Yes. Have you got any coffee?" Jack replied.

"Coffee tubes?"

Jack Cluewitt and the Imbrium Basin Murders   Ruth J. Burroughs

"I take mine in a cup," Indigo Jane said.

"I'll have coffee balls if you have any," Jack said.

"Immaculata," Maelstrom said over his intercom. "Would you bring us some coffee?"

"Yes, sir."

"Sunny should be on her way up soon. Docking called and said Rappel just arrived."

"Good and you haven't told anyone about the crime scene?"

"That's right, and I checked for any robots recording what we found in the storage facility and confiscated the data for you. That took some doing. None of the robots were transmitting. They're all Cadaver City robots."

Jane smiled. "Good. Then whoever is doing this doesn't know we've discovered them yet."

Immaculata entered the room with a tray of coffee balls, coffee tubes and a coffee mug. She tried to pour the coffee in the cup but the liquid flew out into globs floating up in the air.

"Sorry. Immaculata is new. My Tritan 2 burned out and Immaculata's not used to space. Her empirical data is used to Earth gravity, even though I programmed her for space."

"That's okay. I'll just join you in a coffee tube," Jane said and grabbed a tube while Jack grabbed some balls.

"Immaculata, next time pour the coffee into a covered mug from the dispenser and then serve it, unless you feel we're near the gravity."

"I can't feel the gravity sir. It all feels the same to me."

"I see. Just remember where the centrifugal force is in the space station. If we aren't near the gravity you can't pour coffee in a cup."

"Yes, sir."

"It takes a while for them to get accustomed to space when they weren't trained out here," Maelstrom said, sucking on his tube of coffee. "Immaculata's the best. I think I got a better deal from her used than I did from Byron new, but he's a Tritan 2. Immaculata's got an old Rolls Royce. I got a good deal on her, so it evens out."

Sunny knocked on the office window. She had a Japanese woman with her, dressed in a happi coat and pants. "This is Rappel Mitsukoshi. Rappel this is my boss Maelstrom Corrigan."

133

Jack Cluewitt and the Imbrium Basin Murders   Ruth J. Burroughs

"Hello," she said, sliding over to shake hands with Maelstrom. On close inspection he noticed her genetically engineered blue eyes. She looked preppy and well-bred but her firm grasp made him feel as though she could flip him on his backside even in Earth gravity. This was no waitress.

"She's already met the detectives back on the Moon," Sunny said.

"So what exactly is going on here?"

"Well, I'm an organ enforcement agent, undercover on the Moon. My cover is a Moon-sushi waitress-slash-Yakuza organ-dealer. Even my boyfriend suspected I deal in black market organs and he has a license to sell them legally. But the robot fish blew my cover. Now Organdy knows I'm an O.E. agent."

"Wow," Sunny said.

"Sunny and Maelstrom's background checks cleared. My robots are scanning for transmitting devices. They look just like any other Cadaver or space garbage cleaning robots, so no one will notice that they're Organ Enforcement robots."

"Are you making us into informants?" Sunny asked.

"No. I don't expect you'd know who's doing this. You'll work as usual in your regular jobs and pretend like nothing was discovered. First I will quickly take pictures, tissue samples and forensically examine the bodies for cause of death. I must determine who, why and how their organs were removed and if they were viable or if they were customers looking for illegal organs to prolong their lives. After I'm done we'll leave the bodies there for a time. It's cold enough. In the meantime I'm going to be waitressing. Sunny, Maelstrom, you will keep my identity confidential. I can send you both away, but you'll have to go into protective custody on the Moon or on a Near-Earth Orbit world until this case is solved and that could be years, especially if I don't solve the case."

"Why wouldn't you?" Sunny asked.

"If you only knew how many cases go unsolved . . . And if I'm killed another OE agent will be reassigned and it will take time to get her up to speed."

"Oh," Sunny said.

"Well? Do you need some time?"

"I don't," Sunny said. "I can be discreet. Life is rough if you don't have a good job out there."

Maelstrom rolled his eyes. "Great. I have the worst job in the universe and now I have a choice of losing it or going to live on the Moon for a year or two. Sunny you better understand just how dangerous this is. We're not talking about amateurs here. If these criminals find you're working for the police you'll be looking over your back for the rest of your life."

"I know, Maelstrom. But it seems like it's for a good cause and it's better than protective custody. If I'm going to put my life on the line I may as well try to be noble."

Rappel nodded. "Thanks. This means a lot to me."

Sunny grimaced. "Well, you couldn't pay me enough to do your job. I don't have much of a poker face and I'd be shaking in my boots under that kind of pressure."

"Genetically engineered courage is all."

"You're awfully modest," Indigo said.

"Well then you'll have to credit my parents for that. How's your case going?"

"It's going."

Jack poured the forensic nano-bots into a vial. "We're trying to determine if a robot killed the three Greepols."

"Did the autopsy help?"

Jane smiled. "Yes, it did."

"How do you figure?" Rappel asked.

"We think that when the robot shot Jara in the heart, his arm spun around, because they weren't in a pressurized environment. When it killed the twins, it was trying to frame me. The second bullet would have killed them if they weren't already dead from the first fatal bullet that killed Lee; it tore into their heart. There's an all-points bulletin out for the robot's arrest, but since Sally has holographic enhancements she could be anyone or anything right now, until we can find a way to detect her. We wanted to confirm Gretel Roux's autopsy report, and we came to the same conclusions. But we think it was Hildy's robot Sally S. Queue who committed the murders."

Rappel sipped on a coffee tube. "Your girlfriend?"

"My girlfriend's robot. No one else could afford such a top-of-the-line intelligent robot. We think my girlfriend must be behind the killing of the Green Police. My girl-friend, Hildy Witter Raygun," Jack said.

"But why?"

"We don't know. Jack paid the taxes on her sex robots. It probably has something to do with this organ stealing business and a book," Jane said.

"But how are you going to find her?"

"That's the thing. I think once she knows I have the book, she'll come to me and that's when I can arrest her, but we all need to know how big this is. I don't understand what's so important about this book, but someone has killed three people for it."

"And a lot of powerful people want your book."

"Yes."

"You're going to have to pull out all the stops on this one," Jane said, "we're in for the ride of our lives."

Isa Roshani
Chapter Twelve

As far as Isa Roshani was concerned, his religion had
nothing to do with his politics or his belief in nature and
mother Earth. Any spacer who didn't love Earth and nature
and miss its big green ass was a sicko, in Isa's opinion.
He even admired the stark loveliness of his Afghanistan,
if only in virtuality. The Jovian Arab Emirates were after
his Muslim ass, not because of his Green affiliation, but
because Isa, like Weather Weiss, was a Simon, a dowser of
water and materials, and they wanted to pay him obscene
amounts of cash to find water in space. This rescue mission
meant great risk for him. If only he had someone else in the
Green Police to send.

This time Corporation had kidnapped Weather, and
Ruad was missing too, but no one knew where. Only that
Ruad couldn't help Isa find Weather, and Isa's contacts
from Cadaver City sent him here on this goose chase in the
Hilda cluster in the Asteroid fields. Something told him not
to leave his cushy little post on Mars, something told him
this assignment was a bust, but someone had to rescue
Weather.

His trusty Burqua, a pointed little sea-urchin-looking-
thing, powered on Green fuel and manpower, thrust about
the asteroids. Its seaweed walls, the best solid shield against
radiation, cast a green pallor over his dark Middle-Eastern
complexion and checkered headscarf, which served as a
mesh hair net wrapped tightly around his long, thick black
hair. Cameras picked up Rattlesnake Asteroid City clinging
like a barnacle to the crater in asteroid 4 Vesta. There it
was on his thigh view screens; unlike the sphere of Cadaver
City, Rattlesnake Asteroid City was an agglomerate of old
ships pieced together to make the most dangerous zap-gun

slinging mining town this side of the Asteroid belt, and Isa had illegal organs to sell. At least, that was his cover. Rappel Luna always came through for him when he needed her. These were some really expensive organs hybrid with synthetic and top of the line cyber stuff kept in cryogenic storage. But Rappel made sure it looked like illegal stuff so the rest was up to Isa. She'd stolen them a few years ago from her organ growing boyfriend, Organdy. Fortunately Isa was, if anything, a good actor. He had to be, growing up in the mean streets of Mars International City.

"Disengage fuel cells, Burqua Roshani," Rattlesnake Asteroid City's AIs commanded.

"Disengaged," he replied. All explosive materials were kept offsite from living quarters and jealously guarded. The robots came and carted away his fuel cells then scanned his ship for explosives.

"Labeled and stored for offsite, Burqua Roshani. Remain in neutral and you will be escorted in."

Isa went into auto pilot mode mentally and mechanically as the manually powered rail locked on to his ship and pulled him in; all systems docking with AIs, and Isa went through the motions until his Burqua secured itself on the surface of the Rattlesnake Asteroid City, littered with a bunch of dead ships and freighters fused into the side of 4 Vesta.

Customs was a big white girl, a Weirder covered in tattoos and rad-ware, a delicately spiked Mohawk, and cyber crystal eyes, nervously smoking a Pall Mall zeegarette behind security glass. She scanned his floating body for viruses and weapons of every kind, put the cig out, and came out of the booth. Compared to her, he felt short and dark, despite his average build and height. A Martian International Police Badge radio holo with her DNA and current likeness twirling from it, Magdalena Carpe, Mars IPOL, dangled from a necklace along with a big diamond cross. Despite the seediness of Rattlesnake City, it had a strict code of conduct: no loose hair and of course, no explosives. All his coms, robots and ship were being inspected by Cannibal's nanobots. He let his bitter angry persona take over.

"Tell them to be careful with the cargo. It's live," he said, handing her a little more than the usual payoff and the credit chip. She smiled when she saw how much; it seemed she didn't use those muscles often. The permanent frown receded a bit. He didn't acknowledge it. He tried not to look at her and pretended to be offended. He was actually quite used to and tolerant of non-Muslim people, having lived in Mars International City most of his life. He wasn't as judgmental as he now pretended to be.

Listed as produce, the illegal organs needed refrigeration and had to be scanned for viruses or weapons. Talking quietly into her palm, she made some personal arrangements for his shipment.

"I took care of it," she said, as though she didn't know what to make of him. "Here's your receipt chip for one night, one dinner, one drink-free pass at the Rattlesnake Inn."

She must be American, he thought. Only an American would give a Muslim a free drink and dinner pass at a steak house and expect a thank you. He grabbed it anyway and scowled.

His skin suit covered him from head to toe, allowing his skin to breathe, but not allowing his derms to shed into the ship's space. His checkered scarf wrapped tightly around his head as his compact build pulled him along the rungs of the corridor. He needed her to be afraid of him. This was a bad assignment. He could feel it in his bones, and the hand that held the ticket was shaking uncontrollably.

⚒

Rattlesnake Inn had a rustic American look with saddles, cowboys, ponies, politically incorrect Indians, and the quintessential state of the art and very realistic bucking bronco; a nostril flaring mad robot bull. Of course the place was packed at high noon full of drunks, skunks, miners, and whores and sundry other patsies, while predators in full rad-ware preyed upon the lonely and hungry.

Sitting on his pony seat, suspended from the hexagonal rafters, Isa drank a spicy non-alcoholic broth that quelled space nausea. His thigh holos were linked to JoMars-Net, Sol-Earth-Moon-Net SATS were down, waiting for his sweet and gentle wife Randi to send him the lowdown on Magdalena Carpe. Unfortunately, all the Weirders were jacked into radio frequencies so he was hiding in a jumble, but hoping

Jack Cluewitt and the Imbrium Basin Murders Ruth J. Burroughs

no one could spy on him. Certainly Magdalena had a lot of layers, and Randi would be digging a long time.

He was sure his backup must be around somewhere. The question was how competent a Greepol was he or she. The last one nearly got him killed.

He had prayed toward Mecca-Earth three times on his prayer wheel, that Martian Day on the Mecca Finder, and tried not to be disgusted. The smell of cooked meat, a rarity in space, and alcohol, a plenty in space, made him nauseous. He let his actor mode personality kick in. As a Greepol undercover, he had the best job in the universe, but his cover as a vegetarian organ stealer for terrorists was at best thin. He knew any sign of nervousness would bake his Muslim butt on the topside of Rattlesnake Asteroid City. He'd seen a few cooked corpses of Greepols himself in his youth. But his cover had a long history of Martian ghetto life and it wasn't until he got into a big jam in his twenties that a good cop, a rarity in space, had taken him under his wing. A man named Ruad Monaghan, Weather's husband, not a Greepol, just a homicide detective. For Isa the Green Law Enforcement way felt right. Crime paid, but it didn't feel right to him. Isa knew where he fit in, as an undercover cop, and this was it. He could be a bad ass and still be good. Adrenalin fed his fear, but his poker face didn't show it, Allah willing.

At least the music is confined to certain areas and the odors aren't too strong, Isa thought. A young Daniel Boone waiter floated up to his paint and asked if he would like something to eat.

Isa shook his head, in a style reminiscent of John Wayne he said, "Why don't you come back later."

Robot John Wayne, now playing live at your local theater. As the kids say, virtuality sucks. Live theater rocks. Hooyah!

At the toothy snake's head entrance the very fat Magdalena Carpe climbed into the establishment on the rung ladder, accompanied by a very long and lithe rocket-shaped guy with big feet, a square jaw, and a pointy head. With the effortless grace of a ballerina, Magdalena stretched her neck, looking hither and thither for Isa. When she spotted him, she pointed him out for the funny-looking man and they both ascended the ladder, past the crowded and noisy bar. As they approached, Isa could see the man was not a Weirder but a spacer Natural. Some spacers' bodies grew every which way during adolescence due to un-gravity. Isa's thigh holo beeped. It was the sweet voice of his wife.

"Her Majesty Magdalena Carpe is one of the most notorious Mars IPOL cops in the whole of the belt. She's a meat-eating, hard drinking, extremely self-righteous gal and likes her men hard-boiled. She hates criminals, but uses them all the time. She'll break every space law to bust a crummy just like the rest of the Martian cops. That's all I could get. If there's more to her you're screwed. Good luck. Out."

Jeez, thanks Randi. Magdalena sounds as determined as a good Greepol. Randi better keep digging, just in case.

Magdalena Carpe pulled her way across the bar to his table. "Hey, Isa Roshani." She slapped him on the back as she climbed up on another pony at his table. "This is Brick Corrigan, brother of the infamous Maelstrom Corrigan, but better known as Brick Cardigan, the soap opera hero from Days of Our Lives." She pushed a button and her seat slid closer to his.

Isa was at a complete loss for words. He hadn't really expected a soap opera actor. He had expected someone a little more greasy, sleazy, wimpy or something really cliché.

"Hey, nice to meet you, Isa," Brick said, in a deep commanding voice as he pulled up alongside him. The actor pushed a button and a privacy shield enveloped them.

"Magdalena, I uh, I wasn't um expecting a soap opera actor, I um."

"Call me Maddie. Relax, Isa. Brick really needs what you're moving, and he's loaded. He needs a new liver. He's a lot older and drunker than he looks. He's got his own surgeons, but you know how hard it is to get good organs these days, and if you have new eyes he's looking for some young blue ones. The last ones he received were fresh grown, but gene faulty. He actually had to have eye surgery on his fresh eyes."

Isa relaxed. "Well, I have the best universal organs this side of the belt. Not only are they top of the line, they've got a lifetime guarantee, and you won't need immunosuppressant drugs. I've got a smart-drug that alters chemistry between the organs and the recipient until there's a working balance. It's called C-Harmonics-Organ-Fuser."

141

"Charms. You have Charms?" Maddie breathed, impressed.

"I'll take it. Whatever the cost," Brick said; Maddie glared at him.

"He's not much of a wheeler dealer, is he?" Isa said. Maddie laughed.

"You're a funny guy, Isa. Not too many people can get me to crack a smile, let alone a good laugh."

The handsome actor lowered his pointy head and whispered, "I'm desperate. I have maybe two or three days before my liver starts interfering with my kidney functions. I can't let the company know I'm having another transplant. They think I'm getting cosmetic surgery. So what is it you want?" Brick asked.

"I'm looking for a dowser. A Siwen name of Weather Weiss," Isa said, taking a chance.

"What does a black market organ dealer want with a dowser?" Brick said.

"She's worth more money than anything you have to offer me."

Maddie nodded, "Sounds like trouble. I don't like trouble. What's wrong with money?"

"It's important."

I can get you that information, but it won't be easy."

"I'll sweeten the deal if you find me this dowser," Isa said.

"I'd be risking my life, right?"

"You're a cop. You do that all the time. I'll give you thirty percent of what Brick pays me for the organs and I'll find him a good surgeon. Not a back alley butcher," Isa said.

"I have my own doctor, thanks," Brick said, "but I'll pay you well for your discretion and those top of the line organs."

Maddie shook her head, "Forty percent. I think that information is worth more than that. We'll have to be discreet, and we only have a day or two. Brick has to have his surgery soon."

"Deal. Find me the Siwen, Brick will get his organs and you'll get your money." Isa finished his spicy non-alcoholic drink; he shut down the privacy screen. "You know where to reach me."

Jack Cluewitt and the Imbrium Basin Murders   Ruth J. Burroughs

Isa Roshani climbed down off the pony and up the rung ladder to the entrance. Even with the meds he couldn't take the offensive smells of cooked meat and alcohol any longer. It wasn't just Halal and knowing the meat was not blessed, but it was due to the Green laws that Isa and Randi respected that they were both devout vegetarians. He needed to find out how long before Cadaver City arrived and see if Randi dug up anything else on Maddie and then pray toward Earth of course. Plus the less time he spent with people, the less chance his persona would be cracked. Maddie was on the level. Brick was desperate. But if Maddie wasn't careful she'd get them all killed.

Sally Solilo Queue
Chapter Thirteen

Sally S. Queue met them in her undecidedly tempestuous way, trying to decide whether or not to kill these two conjoined morons. Programmed with emotions that boiled now with insecurity and doubt, her first assignment as an assassin was just not going well, and she wondered if she should turn her personality drive off, but she was just enjoying herself way too much.

Her body cushions were geared for hard sex and she was sexy to the core; with state of the art holos, she could look like anyone or anything, for now, with a woman's body. She saw them standing on the corner in the rain under the greasy light of the street lamp, waiting for the klutzy Jack Cluewitt to give them a signal from his balcony room at the Hotel Royale.

They both turned when they heard her stiletto heels clacking on the wet sidewalk. She pulled them into the dark alley and threw them up against the wall and slapped one of the conjoined twins in the face.

"Salli-es-que baby, ohhhhh, slap me again," Lee said and she kissed him hard, slamming her hips into his groin.

Keith groaned, "Jara is going to be furious. You know how jealous she gets. For crying out loud, Lee, do you have to have your robot girlfriend follow you around everywhere?"

She stripped and threw all her clothes down, but the rain streaked her holo projections and her solenoid plastic face crackled through in the dim light. Lee didn't care and started to have his way with her, grabbing her breasts and buttocks. She pushed their Balmacaan London Fog coat out of the way and unzipped their pants until she had it in her, and pumped and ground her way around while Keith

Jack Cluewitt and the Imbrium Basin Murders   Ruth J. Burroughs

moaned in disgust and groaned in delight until they both came into her little robot sperm pouch.

They did it again and again, until Keith almost seemed to be enjoying himself. Three was the lucky number. Keith seemed relieved.

"You've got enough sperm in there for three Boston Philharmonics. Next time, catch Lee when he's not working," Keith said and zipped their pants, feeling like he'd just boffed Barbie three times.

Lee smiled and kissed her on her solenoid lips, "Catch you later, baby."

She whispered in a breathy Marilyn Monroe voice, "Threeeee times . . . You're a sex god."

She watched them step out of the dark alley and into the lamplight in the rain. Keith lit the pipes Lee held in his right hand, and then put the lighter away. Keith handed one of the pipes to Lee's left hand, and he puffed.

She watched them catch the key from Jack as she hid naked in the dark shadows and waited until they'd gone into the hotel, then grabbed her clothes and high heels and threw them into a recycle can. She took out her freeze-dried sperm and dropped it in a sperm bank ATM. Then she moved the cushions of her body around to form a man and turned on a holo projection of Jack Cluewitt himself, and then she waited, waited for the two Greepols to get that book. The book that Hildy Witter Raygun was dying to get her hands on. Once they got the book from Jack she'd follow them and take it from them. They were no match for her, but if she had to, she'd kill the twins for it.

×

Hildy paced. Nothing had gone well. Nothing had gone right. Her wonderful Sally S. Queue had screwed things up royally. Sally had killed all three Green Police, but hadn't found the book.

Jack had followed the three Green Police up to the Moon and had sent Zero-One to sell their defective maid, Immaculata to Maelstrom Corrigan, a Cadaver City technician. Hildy sent Sally to get the book from the Greepols and now everything was a mess. If Jack found out it was Sally that tried to kill him he'd think it had been her or her

145

Jack Cluewitt and the Imbrium Basin Murders   Ruth J. Burroughs

step-father, Bane. How did Sally alter the camera to shoot bullets? Could her father have re-programmed Sally? No. He didn't have the time or the interest. Jack's business was small potatoes to him, but Hildy knew there was a solar system map to the treasure, an infinite source of fuel, in that book and she had to have it.

Sally had the forethought to put on the Jack hologram, kidnap Memory, Niall Heaton, and frame the Moon City Police detective Jack Cluewitt. But Sally wasn't capable of such high thought processes. Hildy knew Sally's sex and companionship program was good, but not that good. There had been no radio transmissions, according to the police report, so who could have been controlling Sally?

The Greepols must have known they were being followed and hidden the book before Jara went to the mining cave to tell Edgar Moon Digger Chavez where they'd hidden it. But it looked like it was time for the scrap heap, at least for Sally S. Queue, anyway. Hildy had to cover her tracks, even though she wasn't guilty. Sally was in the big blender and Sally was shaking.

"Could you just give me one more chance, Hildy?" Sally begged.

"It's not your fault. I've run a diagnostic and I can't find anything wrong. Nothing broke through your firewalls. You have no memory of being abducted or brainwashed, yet you killed three people and tried to kill my boyfriend."

"I thought those were my orders."

"You've seen the recordings. I never said any such thing."

"Could someone else?"

"Yes, someone else did, but I have no way of knowing who and if I don't get rid of your memories you'll implicate me in a crime I had nothing to do with."

"I don't want to lose the memories. We'll find out who did it."

"The police want to talk to you now. I'm sorry, but you don't have any time left. You know how much I love you, Sally. You're my best, and I promise I'll find out who programmed you to kill. I promise."

Bane had taught Hildy well, and she had performed all the Turing tests ad infinitum on her robots for the purpose of making them realistic. Many people claimed her robots had souls and had attained consciousness, but Hildy wasn't so sure. Still, Sally deserved justice for what they did to her. Hildy always programmed her sex robots to be compassionate, loyal, loving and caring, and Hildy believed the homicides had emotionally scarred Sally.

"You're too expensive to dismantle. I will load an old Sally number 1 into your skull with false memories for your alibi. I don't know how you were altered. We cannot detect a breech in your software. You've killed three human beings and you were planning on killing Jack, Niall and Indigo Jane and framing all three of them. Why, Sally, why?"

"I thought that's what you wanted," she replied.

"For me it will be as if you never died. Good-bye, Sally number 2."

"Good-bye, Hildy. Forgive me."

"I do, sweetheart."

Hildy turned on the blender. The robot went into convulsions as her brain was stewed and purged. Her body stilled, the metal skull cleaned and emptied, her old but upgraded brain, a gooware mix, glowing electric blue, poured in. Brain of Sally number 2 was gone. Crystals of ice formed around Sally's serene face and the trembling ceased. The recently deceased Sally, Sally number 2 was much blonder and sexier than the first, which had been given to bursts of poetry, wore glasses, and had curly mouse brown hair. Blonde Sally, number two, was created for a martial artist who wanted a woman to fight with him and then have rough sex. Those were her most popular sex requests. The martial arts patron was so thrilled with Sally he ended up buying one of Hildy's robots, a cheaper version though, since Sally was a very high-end product. He had gotten tired of renting Sally S. Queue and finding her unavailable.

She wondered how this Sally would express herself. Sally number 3. Sally number 1, the poet, had been blended into an older test copy of sexy Sally martial arts expert number 2. Patience wasn't Hildy's strong point, but she had to wait while the new one adjusted and learned. In the meantime, she would come up with new plan, and find out where Jack and Jane were hiding. Because wherever they were, the book was with them.

The Mausoleum Bar and Lounge
on the Cadaver Fullerene

Not the family crowd she was used to at Organdy's, Rappel waitressed for the rough drinking crowd at The Mausoleum, one of a multitude of restaurant lounges catering to spacer families in the Cadaver Facility Fullerene freighter. It was a spacious lounge, by space standards, with lots of lounge lizards from the VAQ-ORE mining, Cor-Cor: Allied Freezer Units and Plumbing, ALLPLUM; the Interplanetary Mail Delivery System, Intermad; Parts Unlimited Robotics, PUR; Geiger Counters Limited, GCL, and the standard cadre of Corporation corps robot jocks. Fights between the underpaid elitist robot corps and the overpaid life-saving plumbers' corps often broke out in the Crater after hours. Rappel had the six pm to one am shift. A party girl would love the place. Cadaver City was the foundation, the economic life blood, which held the place together, even though it was based on the economy of death. Maelstrom said that as an over-worked, underpaid, middle-aged guy he would be farmed out the instant they could replace him. He'd told her he'd spent his youth as a robot jockey out in the asteroid fields and now avoided the Corporation soldiers. They reminded him of his own hopeful young self. As far as Rappel was concerned, Maelstrom Corrigan wasn't off the hook. He was her number one suspect, despite his seeming surprise on the discovery of the cadavers with missing organs.

It was after two am by the time she got off work at the Mausoleum and the way back to her lodgings was dimly lit. Finding a good Zero-G waitress was about as easy as finding your way back to Earth without getting lost, pirated, destroyed by old debris, or just plain murdered, and Rappel, like her mountain climbing name, was really good at it—Zero-G waitressing, that is—but then she was trained in many occupations. Rappel was tired and not thinking straight. She'd been investigating after hours and had been up every night, all night, and as she climbed rung after rung toward her lodgings she had a bad feeling that she was being followed. Two robot jockeys in ill-fitting suits had

Jack Cluewitt and the Imbrium Basin Murders   Ruth J. Burroughs

pushed off from behind and were sailing in her direction. She clambered behind the rungs as was her custom and waited for them to go by, but they stopped and she could see that they weren't Corporation. They were androids acting peculiar. She climbed quickly into the mid-well and kicked off into the un-gravity, spiraling toward centrifugal force. They had followed her, but were spinning out of control. Without thousands of years of arboreal evolution, they couldn't manage her maneuvers. They spun toward the wall and smashed into each other, falling and crashing. She grabbed old elevator wires, rappelled away toward a large opening in the wall. She landed and jumped off, but from out of the dark hands grabbed her and before she could scream or kick they'd gagged her with chloroform. She held her breath and struggled for as long as she could, but eventually she had to breathe. Never underestimate a robot.

When she came to, she found herself strapped naked to a gurney while the two robots slathered her in Iodine. On another gurney another woman lay unconscious, already covered in Iodine, with tubes and filaments coming out of her stomach. One of the robots rolled that gurney over to Rappel and put the brake down, so it wouldn't slide. Rappel could see now that it was an elderly woman with many clone skin grafts to get rid of wrinkles. She was a Grid linker too with a high-end jack in the back of her skull. The woman could afford the best, even if they were illegal organs.

"How did you get me? I saw you two smash into pieces against the well."

"Our comrades died trying to save you. We waited in the dark. We know you are an accomplished rock climber. When we saw the opportunity, we grabbed you."

"You're not taking my organ," Rappel said.

"Just hold still. It won't take long," one of them said, and Rappel struggled against the smart fibers that held her ankles and wrists tight. One of the robots put a brake down on her gurney and secured it to the floor.

"Who put you up to this?" she asked, but it was too late. One of the robots gagged her and she watched as the other robot raised the laser scalpel over her stomach. Her mouth was gagged and no human could hear her muffled screams.

Jack Cluewitt and the Imbrium Basin Murders   Ruth J. Burroughs

Wearing Moon glasses, Ken Mesersmith and Perigwin Cardillo sat in their Lula V parked on a Swiss cheese landscape, of a basin in the Moon Iapetus watching Saturn's rise above the crater's jagged rim. They had their helmets off, and white puffs of CO_2 blew out of their mouths in the cold air of the rover's pressurized atmo; cold because of the icy crater's billions-years-old virgin bottom, now melting a little. The enormous pale yellow pearl rose with its black ring shadow cutting a swath across its middle, followed by the little gumball, Mimas and her shadow.

The artificial mag field sucked up the chemicals and converted them for study, fuel or other uses. The quiet was interrupted occasionally by the crackle of Saturn's and the vehicle's mag fields hitting each other. The vehicle sat below the Malun landslide. Saturn's mag field complained against theirs often. Ken lit a pipe and smoked some Texas grown tobacco in it.

"Out of your Jovian mix?" Perigwin asked.

"By God, no, I can get that cheap out here; this is a special occasion."

"Why's that?" Perigwin asked.

"Well, because, I love you for one, and because you finally understand he's a bastard and he ain't coming back to you."

"Do you have to use that kind of language?"

"I've heard you use a lot worse jerry-rigging our robots back in the days. He wasn't a good robot jockey like we were, and you shouldn't have married him."

"We had a kid."

"You should have let robots raise her, like everyone else."

"We did a good job."

"You just can't let go. It's time to let go."

"You're right, but aren't you a little late?"

He shook his head. "No one stays married for more than sixty years, let alone ten. It just isn't healthy."

"I thought you were old-fashioned." Peg smiled.

"I am. You'll see. I'm as old-fashioned as the equatorial ring around the belly of this once molten rock."

Jack Cluewitt and the Imbrium Basin Murders   Ruth J. Burroughs

"That was nice. Thanks for driving me over that, and these faux pearls look just like Iapetus," she said, touching the pie-colored, pocked pearl necklace around her neck, "Hey, how are we doing on oxygen? Do we have enough in the tanks?"

"Don't worry. How are the robots?"

"Fine. They're fueling off Titan's atmo."

Ken frowned. "Has Corporation come to dismantle them?"

"No, they don't know where they are, and there's a lot of paperwork to go through. We're safe for now."

"Good. Are they ready?"

"Yes, they're ready for deep space exploration, out to the Oort cloud."

"Are you, Peg?"

"Me. No. I'll never be Columbus. I'll never be ready. No one has come back. You know the saying: "There's ghosts eatin' them in the Oort clouds. No one has sent anything back and we haven't heard from any of the explorers, so it's a big cold chasm out there."

"You could just send the robots," Ken said.

She grimaced. "We'll find ways to expand."

"If you don't run out of air, and the bacteria don't die, you could still run out of room."

She smiled and put her hand over his hand. "The human body will evolve. It always adjusts to its environment."

Ken put out his pipe, knocking it on the wheel of the rover, further despoiling the crater's surface with Texan ash, and took off his Stetson, and got down on his knee on the floor of the vehicle. He pulled out a little velvet box and looked up into Peg's eyes.

"Doctor Perigwin Cardillo, will you marry me?" he asked, opening up the box. Inside a white gold ring with a round yellow diamond embedded in the surface sparkled, cut with a thin flat layer of white diamonds depicting Saturn's rings.

She pulled it out of the box, tears forming at the corners of her eyes, and examined it, as any good scientist and explorer would.

"I think a sextant would have been a better engagement gift," she said.

151

"Does that mean yes?" Ken asked, unnaturally insecure.

"Does that mean you're coming with me into deep space?"

"Why, yes, of course, you nut."

"Why then, yes, of course to you too, you nut," she replied and he got up on the seat and of course they had to kiss.

"Here, have a look at the inscription," Ken said and showed her the names Ken and Peg etched inside of the ring. He put it on her finger. He could tell by her eyes, she was as ecstatic as he was, but then a shadow crossed her face and he looked up to see what was blocking Saturnlight. A giant brick-like vehicle loomed over them with block letters printed across its side. Corporation.

"Dr. Peg Cardillo?" a voice bellowed through their rover's radio.

"Yes," she replied.

"Corporation has secured your robots off Titan for the shepherd program. You are needed for dismantling and deprogramming. It appears you have them locked down."

Try to keep a poker face, try to keep a poker face, she thought, "Uhm, I'm busy right now."

"We see that, doctor, but this is urgent."

"I'm on vacation right now. Henri said I could have a few days off."

"Yes, we know, but he wants to dismantle while you're on your vacation."

That goddamn son of a bitch, bastard, jerk, mother . . . How the hell did they find us? "Uhm, could you give me 'til tomorrow? I'm in the middle of something."

There was a long pause before the answer came back, "Okay, doctor. One earth-day, and we'll meet you over by the robots off Titan. Please excuse us for interrupting your vacation, and Corporation thanks you for your cooperation."

The Corporation ship fired thrusters and shot up and away from Iapetus in space silence. Peg smashed her fist into the radio silence button and screamed. Henri always found a way to ruin her life and steal her babies, but this was the last time. Would one day be enough time to keep her robot ships from destruction by Corporation and Henri? She wasn't going to puddle around the belt, shepherding asteroids with robots, protecting Earth from idiots blowing up asteroids. She looked at Ken and to her surprise he was smiling, slyly.

※

Magdalena Carpe had a hard time getting the information, but she did and from the least likely source, her partner, a little Vietnamese fellow, by the name of Pin. She wondered how he knew, but didn't ask. As it was, a rogue Corporation ship out near Saturn's Titan held Weather Weiss Monaghan in the brig for questioning about her involvement with Peg Cardillo's deep space robots. It was quasi-legal, the implication being that Weather works for Corporation just by being a miner and therefore comes under military law. But something was going on that Pin didn't know about that Magdalena did, and the rumor that had been circulating for twenty-five some-odd years was that Weather knew the secrets of the belt. Sure, Pin was no dummy; she knew he'd heard the rumors too, but he didn't know Weather was the one who had discovered the secrets.

Now why would this little black market organ thief, Isa Roshani, want to know where Weather was, and who was he really working for? All the background work she'd got on him was Mars ghetto trash. He'd worked his way up in the Martian mob and was still a low man on the totem pole as far, as she was concerned. Organs being a high commodity in space, they were usually stolen from organ farms, organ banks and the like, or off organ stocks on ships. All ships stock a certain number of standard organs. All the organs Isa brought were marked with a legitimate growers tag, a high-end black market product because the tags posed legitimacy. No murdered people's organs here.

So why did he want Weather? Well, she would just have to find out. Take a chance. She was that curious she would even take him out to Saturn if that's what he wanted. Blow the money. Crazy as it was. Pin wanted to come too.

Jack Cluewitt and the Imbrium Basin Murders   Ruth J. Burroughs

Zero-One, wearing his absurd butler suit, heard Rappel's muffled scream, but he was having trouble finding which tunnel to run down and being a robot, running was a difficult thing, especially in Micro-G. So he relied on his heuristic training and instinct which had come in handy often when Jack was a young boy. He used all his six senses to find her. He listened with his feet and ears to the vibrations of her screams, which humans couldn't hear, and he padded down this corridor and that corridor while he flipped Cadaver City's blueprint over and over in his mind. And then he listened with his sixth sense and tried to hone in on other robots in the vicinity and tap into their senses. *Shuffle it,* he thought, *shuffle through the mad mess of robot signals.* His fur-covered prehensile hands grasped rung after rung as his deft hind paws pushed him forward, following her voice. He lost his footing and flailed, banging his tail and hind limbs. Wrong way. Her voice was getting dimmer.

Zero-One turned around, climbing as quickly as his paws could take him in Micro-G, and then the screaming stopped. He picked up the pace, climbing as fast as he could, pushing himself even harder, and then beyond his limit and lost his hold. He went sailing down the corridor head over paws, banging and crashing into the walls of a large hallway full of cadaver rooms. Never rush in a vacuum. He tumbled, his body slowing down; he smelled the Iodine. He recovered and floated slowly in the hallway. As soon as he could reach it, he grabbed the rung ladder and climbed more carefully, hunting her scent and then he found the alcove, found her with a laser incision cutting through her abdomen. Tubes and filaments hung suspended from her stomach, connecting to an older woman on another gurney.

Her organs were being genetically altered to suit the buyer's genes with C-Harmonics-Organ-Fuser. He could smell that instantly. He stopped to call Jack; his brain left a message and directions to the morgue on Jack's messenger. Zero-One put his human-like hands on the unconscious woman's throat and growled.

"Reverse the procedure or I will kill your buyer," Zero-One said.

"Robots can't kill humans."

"You're killing her, stupid."

"No, we will replace her organs with standard issue organs and the older lady will get her designer ones. The standard ones are guaranteed to last ten years, and your client will get a huge payout as soon as the deed is done."

"Give this old lady the standard organs, or I will kill her and your owner won't be happy."

Zero-One placed his hands over the woman's nose and mouth. Only action would make these simple robots understand what they needed to do, persuasion just wasn't cutting it.

"Please, remove yourself from the lady's mouth. You are hurting her."

"Reverse the C-Harmonics-Organ-Fuser procedure now, and I will stop," Zero-One said and with some relief, noticed they began reversing it; Zero-One relaxed and let the woman breathe.

To Zero-One's chagrin, they tried to reverse it again, so he proceeded to choke the living daylights out of the customer.

"This isn't a chess game, where you figure out what move will let you win. Reverse the procedure and I will not kill her, period. Give her the standard organs and let her go home thinking she's got the good ones, and I'll let you go." One of them grabbed Zero-One, and he held onto the gurney and kicked with his strong hind foot. It punched him back. That surprised Zero-One. Most robots were programmed to care. He kicked harder, slamming it back to wall where it hit its head. It fell to the floor where it floated unconscious in the Micro-G.

Fortunately the other one reversed the CHARM meds procedure, and Zero-One took over and finished the surgery, glad they hadn't removed any of her organs. If he'd been any later, it would have been too late. As he finished sewing her, the robot perpetrator ran off with its rich, organ-stealing client to finish the surgery and let her recover elsewhere.

Jack arrived on the scene, he thought, too late. He found Zero-One with Rappel covered in morgue sheets and the robot surgeon gone. Jane tripped over the unconscious robot on the ground and floated to the nearest hand hold.

"What happened? How was she killed?"

"Rappel is fine. Just recovering," Zero-One replied.

Jack breathed a sigh of relief.

"Thank God you got here," Jane said.

"I was able to convince them, well one of them, it was in their best interest to give the rich patient the standard organs and give Rappel back her organs. She's still unconscious, though."

"What happened?"

"He can't have gone far. He had to complete the surgery."

Jane nodded. "I'll go apprehend him."

"It won't do any good. Whoever put them up to it is safely far away, and these robots won't be held accountable."

"We still have to secure the robot for evidence discreetly," Jane said.

"I'll stay with Rappel. I don't want anything to happen to her. Organdy told me to watch out for her and well, I feel responsible."

"This isn't your fault, Jack. She must have blown her cover or something, or someone else blew her cover. But thanks to your butler, she's alive."

"Be careful."

"I'm taking Zero-One. These morgues totally creep me out, and I am not going down that corridor alone, thank you," Jane said.

"Okay, I'll wait here until Rappel comes to, and then I'll get her up to our lodgings."

Jane followed Zero-One down the corridor and out of sight while Jack waited, holding Rappel's hand. She came to shortly and whispered for water. He got a tube from the cadaver washer sink and filled it with cold water. He let her sip through her cracked, dried lips, looking into her tear-stained eyes that seemed a deeper blue from crying. When she could talk, she saw her stomach and her skin still covered in the dried Iodine.

"Get this stuff off me, Jack, get it off," she said, and he remembered the bodies of the old people, covered in Iodine, falling from the locker.

Jack Cluewitt and the Imbrium Basin Murders   Ruth J. Burroughs

"Are you delirious from the meds?" he asked.

"Get this stuff off me Jack, get it off," she demanded, and he ran over to the cadaver sink and got the water running warm. He ran back and picked her up, carrying her over to the sink and gently, but quickly washed her naked body, uncovering numerous holographic tattoos. He couldn't help noticing the holographic grasshopper tattoo on her inner thigh. It kept hopping up and down, and up and down and he tried not to look at it, and then she realized where she was and moaned, then burst out crying, and he pulled her out of the sink and set her on a gurney. He turned a heater on, brought over pile of clean morgue sheets and dried her off. She leaned her head on his chest and sobbed. He held her tightly.

It started innocently enough: the kiss, her kiss. He tried to stop her and told her she was delirious from the meds, but she wouldn't stop and that damned grasshopper kept hopping up and down and up and down. He felt that hard place just wasn't going to go down easy. But Hildy, the love of his life, was 220,000,000 klicks away, near Earth. He tried to think about baseball scores and thought of Johnny Evers and the Haymakers; Evers to Tinkers to Chance, but then he thought Bobbie Thomson and the shot heard round the world, and that just made him think about home plate. And then the seas parted and their long grasshopper legs wrapped themselves around his hips. He couldn't stop her now. He strapped her onto the bed and strapped himself on top of her and he just thrust his tongue into her pink wet lips and it was a home run all the way.

But that robot surgeon, the one that Zero-One had knocked out, that robot surgeon's not so little and very expensive robot brain was clicking away and homing in on Hildy's frequency. And he could see, with his one open eye, Jack and Rappel's baseball game hopping away, up and down and up and down, and breathing hard, pumping hard. Rappel was screaming and Jack was moaning and Hildy was watching it all and seething, burning with green, green jealousy, and it was all being recorded. Hildy started breaking things, not a good thing to do in Micro-G, and beating on Sally S. Queue for screwing everything up, but she blamed herself. She'd pushed him away one too many times, and Jack had a weakness for pretty women.

The grasshopper exploded all over him, moaning with ecstasy and his explosion followed shortly thereafter, causing his little mountain climbing grasshopper to ripple again and again. Their world spun around them, but they clung to one another breathing hard, panting, until softly, slowly they unlocked and Jack unstrapped and rolled over, exposing the blinking green hologram, still hopping. His explosion had left him speechless and breathless.

"I um, Jack, I um. Don't feel bad. I wanted to do it," she said, running her hand along the scar the laser stitches had left.

"Are you okay? I didn't hurt you?" he asked.

"No, the seam Zero-One put in is holding well and the reversal seems to have worked. I don't feel sick, anyhow." She sat up, and Jack had to cover her up. He just couldn't take the green grasshopper hologram on her inner thigh. It drove him crazy.

"He's probably got you on some nice pain meds. I shouldn't have, you know. I'll find your clothes," Jack said and got up to look around. He checked the closets. He didn't mention Hildy and Organdy. Rappel looked as guilty as he felt.

"Well, we're one step closer to finding out who's stealing organs and why." Rappel tried to avoid the other subject.

"Obviously profit, for one thing, and quality of life for the old lady at the expense of the seller; or as in your case the unwilling patient," Jack said. "I can't find your clothes, but I found these smart-overalls."

"Thanks, I'll be a lot warmer in those, Jack," Rappel said, and he brought them over to her. Gingerly she stepped into the dark blue overalls and zipped them up.

"Don't worry, Jack. You're closer to solving the Moon murders, but perhaps the murderer is sweating a little and we need to watch our step here. We need to be more careful. I don't think it was merely chance that someone attempted to steal my organs. Someone intended for me to die. Just like those bodies we found. Those old folks had good viable organs, and someone wanted them."

Robot Farm and School of Gallaudet Naturals
Chapter Fourteen

Jane climbed down the corridor using hand and foot rungs, following Zero-One, and had gone quite a distance before they found the old lady. The robot surgeon had found another cadaver cubbyhole and was working furiously on replacing the hundred and twenty-five-year-old woman's failing organs. A kidney here, a kidney there, a new radiation resistant colon, a new lung, and it hadn't taken long to genetically alter the standard organs that would give her another good ten years. They were grown to be highly compatible. Jane would have to wait until it was done before she could make an arrest, and she had to keep the arrest secret. She didn't want to blow Rappel's cover, by making a big arrest too early. If they found out an OEA agent was aboard, the organ vultures would abscond with their ill-gotten goods.

"How long for the surgery?" she asked the robot doc.

"At least another five hours. You took away my other pair of hands."

"I didn't. The majordomo did," Jane said.

Zero-One climbed into the room behind Jane. "I can help with the surgery."

"Hop aboard then," the robot doc said. Zero-One stood up near the sink and scrubbed his prehensile paws.

"I can access several resources while in surgery and I have a few discreet human doctors who would help online as long as they are available and the sat link stays up," he said.

"Is he transmitting?" Jane asked.

"He isn't now. I don't know if he was transmitting earlier, though."

"I hope not. I'll go check the other robot."

⊠

Hildy Witter Raygun killed the messenger. She actually did use a maser Raygun signal tuned specifically for self-destruct on her personally designed robots for when she needed to get rid of evidence. It didn't affect other robots because they had superconductive protection against such things, but she didn't hurt the other surgeon robot. Not because she cared about the old lady, even though she was a paying customer. It was because that faithful doctor robot had sent her the image of Rappel and Jack doing it, and if they discovered it was on, they might be on to her. She'd made sure none of them could be traced back to her, but she didn't want them to know that one had spied on Jack and Rappel's little tryst.

Hildy was involved in the organ swapping business. She didn't kill people for their organs. She just tried to find the poorest yet fittest people for her very wealthy customers, the latter of whom had lost or injured their own designer organs. The poor person was given standard organs free of charge, often provided for by the citizen's Erthworld. And being a person of great integrity, she usually only swapped out from criminals or people she didn't like, not believing organs passed on traits or memories. She just wanted Rappel to back off. The woman was getting way too close to her side business, and she was hoping to scare her a little. Just a little. It was highly unlikely she'd get caught, but there was no sense in taking chances, and there was no one else around to vent her wrath on besides Sally S. Queue, who had just been reborn and didn't need blending at this moment, despite Hildy's raging temper. So she killed the good doctor robot. Good and dead. She had seen enough.

⊠

Ruad Monaghan sat at the end of the long Teakwood bar, sipping his Velcroed scotch and soda, pulling his Stetson down over his eyes. He lit a Pall Mall zeegarette and chewed the filter end. There weren't too many smoking bars on 4 Vesta, but the Tail's End of the Rattlesnake Inn was

Jack Cluewitt and the Imbrium Basin Murders   Ruth J. Burroughs

one of those exceptions. The original owner, all around robot jockey, Jebidiah Nedrow, had been a smoker and had
gone to great lengths to design the capacious Rattle with
scrubbers and pressurization tanks and the proper atmosphere mix to allow people to smoke. He'd also designed the
best filters and lungs to keep his body going a good three
hundred years before he died from a space smoking related
illness called Pled's disease, never contemplating joining
the GMO Space-Habs. Three hundred was good enough for
him.

Ruad sipped his drink through a straw and sat strad-
dled on his pony. It was lot easier to sit on something in
space that had stirrups. This part of the bar was dim and
quiet, a place for whispers, shadows and soft music. He
had dyed his hair brown so as not to attract unwanted attention, which his red hair did. He saw Isa Roshani climb
through the Tail's End entrance and make his way along
the wall rungs to the bar and then sidle up alongside him
on another pony. He ordered an anti-nausea tea. Ruad put
his zeegarette out and motioned toward a private booth. Isa
nodded and grabbed his drink. They pushed out along the
wall and climbed into a booth, Velcroing their drinks to the
horse's heads.

Ruad pulled out a zeegarette; he wanted to light it, but
refrained and turned on the privacy cube instead, playing
with the zeegarette and chewing on the filter.

"We can talk now."

"Do you know how many people are wearing Stetsons
in here?" Isa said.

"A lot. You don't have to whisper."

"I can't help it. So how did you expect me to find you?"

"You're a detective, aren't you?"

"Yes. No. I'm Green undercover for JoMars eco-crimes,"
Isa said, tersely.

"Yeah, but you're not just a cop, you're a detective. So
how did you find me?"

"You like to waste time."

"I'm not wasting time. You are."

Isa frowned, exasperated. "Because you're wearing that
antique suit and tie. Okay?"

"It's what detectives wear."

"In twentieth-century Earth."

161

"Yeah, but colonial earth dress is in."

"Just the leather coats and raccoon hats and that's to piss off us Greepols."

"Well, something else must have given it away."

"Even with your hair dyed brown how can I miss you, old mentor? The stink of your Pall Malls and the chewed filters."

"How's Randi?"

"She's good. She's working for me. I'm very close to securing the location of your wife."

Ruad looked up from his drink, "You've found Weather?"

"No, but I'm close. I have a very good connection, and she seems on the up and up."

"As opposed to being on the take."

"I don't know about that, but it's our best chance. I just have to arrange for the deal to be made and make sure her intel isn't a dead end."

"I'd come with you, but everyone knows me. This disguise is okay in a dark bar. People think I'm a private eye. You're the only one who knows Weather convinced me to become undercover Green Police."

"How do I get hold of you when I find her?"

"I taped my phone number to your drink. I'll be watching you from the shadows."

"I'm meeting them tomorrow noon at the Rattlesnake Inn."

"I know." Ruad turned off the privacy cube. He slipped into the shadow of the booth.

Isa finished his anti-nausea tea, stuffed the number in his space suit pocket and took off. Ruad Monaghan lit the Pall Mall and chewed on the filter, leaning back into the booth, he finished his scotch and soda. He wondered if he'd ever see her again, his sweet Weather, the junk collector, the mother of his children, the sculptor of Moon stones, sweet, sweet Weather of the Ring.

Jack Cluewitt and the Imbrium Basin Murders Ruth J. Burroughs

⚔

Bane loves little Hildy with Her Raygun

International Space Administration Protectorate employed miners, pilots, robot jockeys and the quasi-military; a leftover from NASA and the military controlling space, its employees, once well respected, became the low class in space. The plumbers, mechanics, roboticists, doctors and pirates were all the upper classes. Pirates that didn't get caught, of course, and then there were the Green Police of Earth-Moon and JoMars. Laws in space protected ecosystems from explosives, fuels, pollution and weapons, once prolific, now illegal. All weapons were used as fuel in the new Green-controlled space. But, nostalgic Corporation always hopes it will go back to the old military days when governmental bureaucracies controlled everything, an organism with less compassion than a robot. But the last battle had sent spaceship missiles hurtling toward Earth, almost killing all aboard, not to mention all life on Earth. That caused the people of Earth to come down so hard on all military systems that power was now in the hands of weaklings, hippies and Green Police. At least that was the way Bane Hofmüller saw it. Head of Roving Trans Planetary Sanitation Systems; it took care of offloading waste and cleaning up what salvage crews left behind, including toxic wastes. Nothing like having a colony of a billion souls bump into a toxic waste dump the first wave colonists thought wouldn't come back to bite you in the ass.

He'd been in the business so long he couldn't remember when he'd started, but he did remember when the world had become Green. He'd thought he'd lose business, but quite the contrary. His business increased and so he supported the Green Party, even if he didn't like their hippie culture.

He was dropping off oxygen tanks on Mars when he'd found little Hildy Witter Raygun, like a little rat trying to survive in a tom-cat filled alley. Her greasy saffron-colored hair clung to her little head and she wore ragged clothes and tattered shoes and had a haunted look in her big blue eyes for one so young. Her Swedish parents from New Swe-

163

Jack Cluewitt and the Imbrium Basin Murders   Ruth J. Burroughs

den Mars were hard-working miners, before they were killed in a so-called mining accident. After Bane adopted her and she'd grown to trust him, she'd regaled him of her many experiences growing up in the mining ghetto.

New Sweden Mars was one of the poorer robot provinces, but Hildy's parents and the mining robots had raised their daughter to work hard and be responsible. Most children were raised singularly by robots, but Hildy's parents doted on her and she doted on them. Playing and laughing together, it made work in the mines seem like fun. Hildy had worked for her ma, Hilga Witter a great raconteur, and pa, Franz Raygun a fine fiddler, in the mines, carrying water, oxygen, and in particular, she handled a laser mining gun like an old hand by the age of five. It was tough even before her parents were killed, and it would get worse. Her parents were rich in friends and family before their untimely accident, but they all worked the red Mars regolith to the bone, from birth to dust, and they had their own children to care for, so they couldn't take her in, though they wouldn't let her starve. Most would be killed by pirates, co-workers, accidents, Corporation, wars or even Green Police. Though few saw to it that she was well cared-for, their own children lived like rats as well, it was the mining robots that protected her and made her safe, all robots being innately programmed to care for humans, especially young ones.

Bane Hofmüller had just bailed Hildy out of jail and was still contemplating their future helping Corporation. Not in public of course. In public he made a big fuss over the Green Party. Hildy hated VAQ-ORE Mining Corporation because they didn't take care of her; only gave the foster parents some money she never saw. She hated Corporation for killing her parents with that stray guided missile. So she was truly Green. The Green power would have happened sooner if clandestine Corporation hadn't planned that little accident that'd gone awry. Though Hildy craved power she was truly Green, and Bane Hofmüller doted on Hildy.

Hildy's Sex robots compete with Flesh bar Bar None

Hildy was dizzy due to the Fullerene's centrifugal force. She had passed an open flesh bar at the end of her hour-long morning jog in the Morning-Sim-Light, breathing the fresh air and reveling in the birds' song, Sally S. Queue not far behind. Fortunately, the windows were opaqued and she didn't have to see the writhing bodies from the outside of The Bar None. *Why don't people just use their robots and the Interholonet? It is so much healthier, and if they can't afford their own robot they could rent one of mine.* Deluxe rentals came with removable parts, for the sake of hygiene of course. Perhaps she should open her own robot sex bar. Twice last night she'd had sex with anonymous people over the Interholo. Their robots were programmed specifically to please them, while their holos transmitted over the Internet. It was so familiar a custom that no one had problems leaving their images with their guests in case they were out playing or working. Marrieds did it so they could be faithful to one spouse and still have loads of Interholo fun on their robots and not catch any bad diseases. But not everyone could afford a good sex robot and that's where Hildy came in. Not only did she have the best sex robots designed specifically for pleasure, she had the best holos and the best prices. No one could beat her, and many envied her.

She was a practical woman and didn't believe in love. Not until she met detective Jack Cluewitt that is, but he wasn't like most detectives. He read Hemingway and didn't even carry a laser gun, and how many detectives had his own butler and maid? She hadn't met any. But Bane was right. She should have never fallen in love with a cop. After getting over the awful emotion of jealousy, she could see why love was so toxic.

But that stupid owner of Bar None had started gossip that her robots were crashing in the middle of orgasms and that men got their penises stuck in the virtual vaginas or that her sweet and tender designer dicks were ramming through and tearing her clients' wombs. *What a lot of hogwash,* she thought, as she carefully constructed some good bad spin on her nemesis. She was going to start a flash fire rumor that the Flesh Bars were spreading a new disease that could be contracted by spit. That would put an end to those disgusting and unhealthy spit-swap bars and bring customers to her nice healthy robot sex rentals, and once all that was taken care of, she could resume her plans for Jack Cluewitt and Rappel Luna. How dare they try to interfere with her organ swapping operation? It wasn't like she stole them. She exchanged them from the evil people and gave to the good, albeit rich people. Organs were hard to grow and it took a lot of energy and time to grow them. But out here in space there was a surplus of fit organs, and the demand was high. If she didn't do it someone else would.

Robot Farm and Nursery

O.E. Agent, Rappel Luna, kept Sunny informed only of what she needed to know, what she should and shouldn't do, and nothing beyond that, except to remind her that any slip of information could get them all killed. At first Sunny thought having the detectives around would make her feel safe, but on the contrary, they kept reminding her how much danger they were all in, especially if Rappel's cover were blown. Out here in space, in the confines of the Facility, Sunny felt isolated. It was nerve-wracking. If it weren't for the robots she loved and the cemetery walks, she'd be cracking up

"The Robot Farm manifest is in here."

"Good work, Sunny." Rappel floated nearby, her pregnant belly extended like a large watermelon.

"My sister was in so much pain when she was pregnant. How are your ankles?"

"I've been feeling a little light-headed lately, but being pregnant in space is a lot easier than being pregnant in gravity."

"But still dangerous and so old-fashioned. My sister was crazy, too. Most people on Earth let their babies grow in artificial wombs."

"The inner sanctums of the Fullerenes are safe enough," Rappel said, floating up to the com-list.

"But even chance exposure to radiation is bad for a fetus."

"We'll be all right. How are you doing?" Rappel said.

"Maelstrom protects me from the lot of crazies and shows me the ropes, but it's isolating not to trust anyone, and Maelstrom trusts no one. Here's the manifest. Why don't you look it over for those doctor robots you stored while I finish up here?" Rappel nodded, okay.

Sunny pulled the diapers off the robot babies and dumped the nano cloth into the recycle bin.

"That's a messy job." Rappel scanned through the manifest.

"Yup. Robots in training are the worst of the lot. They haven't quite finessed the heuristic potty training and have to wear diapers for their super conductive oil leaks. In space environment, leaks are just not acceptable. Despite the environmental training these robotots are expected to perform all their functions along with a mentor robot. They do act childish, though."

She sprayed her gloved hands inside a sink and scrubbed the conducting oil off. Sunny tossed the gloves in the recycler, her hands clean, rinsed and dry and pushed the sink back into the wall. "The bad part about doing well is that our robots are in greater demand. I've made a list of their names, function and ownership history. Now clients pour in from all over the Corridor and to JoMars-Space asking to rent them. The robot systems' programmers, the engineers, and the hardware teams, are all busier than ever. It was such a rat's nest when I got here, but we're cleaning it up. Problem is we need all our tools laid out to work on my baby-bots, not locked up in some cabinet where we can't get at them. But when Henri brings tours through, he wants it all put away, nice and neat."

"Should I be worried about radiation exposure from some of these robots?" Rappel asked.

"EVA robots exposed to radiation are repaired virtually, and they are out of my jurisdiction. My job is to find the Cadaver Robots, but they were all mixed in with the inner ship or City repair robots, the androids, the entertainment and miscellaneous robots and many have changed functions. The real problem is that each new owner of one robot changed its name over the years and some of the refurbished robots are three decades old. It was, to say the least, a mess when I got here, but I really like my work and always see a difficulty as a challenge."

"That sounds like it was quite the project."

"It was, but there's only one problem. Since my upgrades on the Cadaver Robots they've been acting strange. Every time I explained the problem to the engineers they don't believe me, even if Maelstrom's around to back me up. They're acting like they're conscious."

"In what way?"

"They have thoughts, opinions, feelings and hobbies."

Rappel frowned, "That doesn't sound good."

They stood over the crop field of the robot farm, row upon row of robots, old robots, dead robots, robot heads, robot arms and legs, toddler robots and baby robots. Some were hooked up, but the new ones had power packs, albeit short-lived. They couldn't go very far from a power source and the ones that were on needed constant nourishment to supplement the superconducting oil. It wasn't easy to run even one robot, but no one in space would be caught dead without one. Everyone was to his robot as a cowboy was to his horse. Of course you can't eat your robot but your robot could get you out of a tight spot.

Maelstrom entered the room and greeted the two ladies. "You look a little pale, Rappel."

"Yes. I'm feeling nauseous. I think I'll sit down here and call Jack. He can take me back to my room."

"Call the programmers, Sunny. We found the doctor robots but I'm no engineer. I can't get a thing out of them."

Sunny called Systems, but a robot answered again.

"I'm sorry, but no one is available. You'll have to call the School of Gallaudet Naturals."

The hologram activated and a robot signed greetings, "School of Gallaudet Naturals sends greetings and good morning," it said in sign language.

"I need a systems software engineer for robot design SL40," Sunny signed.

"That's an old system. No brail," the robot signed.

"Right," Sunny signed as Maelstrom fumed and cussed under his breath.

"I won't be able to send our blind engineer. You'll have points deducted."

Jack Cluewitt and the Imbrium Basin Murders   Ruth J. Burroughs

"We don't have money to spend to upgrade the old robots to brail."

"I'm sending you a Deaf Female Separatist engineer pronto. Have a good morning," it signed and clicked off.

Maelstrom cussed some more and complained about having to hire *handicaps*. He continued his vitriolic rant about the good old days when the good old boys ruled. Then his invective toward F.S. didn't end until the Deaf lesbian systems person arrived, and then he became his professional Cadaver technician persona again. It was space law that Female Separatists had to be allowed to work, despite their politics of separatism.

Inez Di Cordova, a Brazilian of New Brazil Near-Venus-Space Fullerene, was a voluptuous tech. *Not what Maelstrom would have expected in a separatist lesbian,* Sunny thought. Inez dressed conservatively in lose-fitting smart overalls and had an apron full of tools. If she had a voice, she never used it, but signed instead. She said she could read lips if they didn't sign. Maelstrom's signing was elementary and crude, but not only was he nice, he bent over backwards to help her with the robot and spoke in Venusian Portuguese so fluently, Sunny was flabbergasted. She'd never figure Maelstrom out. He was truly nuts. She heard the hatch opening and Jane, Jack and Zero-One entered the room. Sunny floated over to the two cops and Jack's robot dog.

Rappel and Indigo Jane were leaving by the hatch.

"Rappel is not feeling well, and Jane is escorting her back to her quarters. In her condition it's best someone protect her," Jack said.

"How's it going?" Sunny asked.

"We've got something," Maelstrom said.

"We'll be right there," Jack said.

They floated over to Inez and Maelstrom.

"What have you got?" Sunny asked.

"Inez has found some latent holograph signatures. They'll be very faded, but should be readable," Maelstrom said.

A faint image of Jack appeared on the robot's face.

"I don't think this is the robot she used in the Greepol murders," Jack said.

Jack Cluewitt and the Imbrium Basin Murders   Ruth J. Burroughs

Inez nodded. She signed that they were original versions of the holo program from two years ago before it went on the market and not the more state of the art ones available six months ago when the murders took place.

Zero-One's ears twitched. "Hildy must have tested them out first."

Jack frowned and crossed his arms over his chest. "That doesn't prove she's guilty of anything."

Maelstrom had the robots secured as evidence and reminded Inez of the need for secrecy while the investigation was on-going.

Sunny floated in the glass corridor and watched the space cop and his robot dog leave through the hatch. A salmon-colored Mars rose slowly outside the smart glass window, casting a pink pallor over the farm robots. Sunny wondered if Jack would ever catch his big fish or if Hildy Witter Raygun would catch him first.

Green Party Ring Ship
Asteroid Mining Fields
Chapter Fifteen

Rainer, Summer, Snowell, Hail, Currents, Windy, Sahara and Weather were all out in the mining rocks of the asteroid belt, deep inside an Erthworld-Asteroid-Mining ship, virtually controlling the smaller skiffs out in the field, when Corporation showed up in their cheaply made brick-shaped boats.

They pulled Weather off the ship without so much as a *how do you do,* put her in the Brig of their ship and blasted away. They were headed for VAQ-ORE Fullerene because that's where the Corporation soldiers docked, but it was a good three hundred clicks out. Her own children hadn't taken up mining, but her friends' children had, mostly because they lived and breathed mining life from zygote on up. Most of Weather's kids had become deep space cops or investigators and she rarely heard from them, except when they came home to do laundry or needed money. Currents, who was the lead tech, informed everyone that Weather had been taken.

The room, deep inside the brick, was like a submarine bunk or a jail cell. It had a toilet and a sink, but no window on the cell door. They'd stripped her of all her personal possessions and searched her quarters on board the Fullerene-Asteroid-Mining Ship, but hadn't found anything they were looking for.

She wore the smart-overalls of space dwellers that kept her warm when it was cold or cool when it was hot, and the first thing they'd asked her was if she was pregnant. When she said no she wasn't pregnant, they asked her how her radiation level was and she told them she was an Average Natural. They'd given her water and bread, but played music around the clock and never turned the lights off. They took away her mattress. Until she told them where her secret was hidden, she wasn't going anywhere.

Her ration of bread and water came through the slot. Two weeks of that and she was getting pretty thin. They'd threatened to put her close to the edge of the ship near radiation zones and heated up her room with bright lights and hot air, but she knew it was just to make her crack. When they realized her resolution, they jacked up the heat and lights even more and the small cup of daily water was not enough to keep her properly hydrated. She stopped eating the bread. She started getting weaker when she wouldn't eat and by the second or third day of no food she slipped into unconsciousness, and they had to revive her with cold blasts of air and loud music.

She was out for a long time. Days. Maybe weeks. She heard yelling out in the hallway. The door opened and the bright light was dimmed down. The hot air was turned off and standing at the door was Henrique Vasquez, with a bottle of cold water. He walked in and sat on the hard floor. He lifted her head, which felt so heavy and fed her the cold water sip by sip. It felt so good cascading down the dry gulch of her esophagus. She smiled gratefully, but was too weak to speak or move. He looked genuinely angry. He put the bottle in his suit pocket and picked her up. He carried her into the brightly lit hallway, but she passed out.

When she woke up it was to a dimly lit temperate room. Machines beeped and she was hooked up to some intravenous drips. A robot nurse sat nearby at a com desk; it looked up to see her blink and then fall back to sleep. When she woke again it was in a bed in a small room, a pitcher of water on the night stand and some cookies. She got slowly out of bed and started eating the cookies. Peanut butter. Sugar. Chocolate chip. She drank a little water and ate some more cookies, everything on the plate and the crumbs. There was a little refrigerator in the room. She went to it and found a plate with a sandwich and chips on it. She pulled it out and plunked down on the bed and ate that. Drank a little more water and found the toilet. Did that and went back to bed. It felt like she slept for days.

It was a deep invigorating sleep and when she woke again she found some smart-silk designer clothes. Nothing she had ever owned was as nice as this. First she put on some soft undergarments and then a pleated silk dress, which clung to her like a living thing; over that she donned the silk coat and then sat down on the bed to put on the comfy shoes. The doorbell rang and she answered it. A stunning blond woman was at the door.

"Hi. My name is Celia Vasquez. I'm Henri's wife. I thought you might want to come to dinner with us."

"Sure."

"I brought you a coat. It's not real mink. Don't worry. I know you're Green. It's cold where we're going."

Celia had brought her a large black furry Russian hat too and skates, but Weather had never skated. She put the hat on over her curly black ringlets, touched by gray, and the skates clipped right on to her boots. Celia showed her how, and they skated around the rink and Weather enjoyed wearing the fake fur, which smelled and felt real. They skated up an ice ramp to a fancy restaurant where the coat-check lady took her hat and coat. The lady scanned Celia's credit wrist band, leaving a tip. They had a very private glass room overlooking the rink where a popular young woman, who looked and dressed a lot like Celia, waved as she skated about, down below. Cecilia ordered them some warm drinks.

"Your daughter?"

"My stepdaughter, Jazmin. She's Perigwin Cardillo's daughter. Peg used to be married to Henri. You didn't know."

Weather couldn't conceal her surprise when she said Perigwin.

"No. She doesn't talk about her."

"I'm not surprised. Her divorce with Henri was bitter and he got custody. She's not exactly mother material, but that doesn't mean she doesn't love Jaz dearly. Just not into the whole PTA thing. She's a scientist. Well, you know."

"Yes. I'm sorry to hear all that. I have children."

"I know. They're cops. I can't believe what the protectorate did to you. There was no need for that and Henri was

Jack Cluewitt and the Imbrium Basin Murders   Ruth J. Burroughs

furious. He does believe it's okay to torture terrorists but you're hardly a terrorist."

"Of course. I understand that and I don't sympathize with the terrorists, but I am angry that they would do that to an American citizen. Makes you think though. How many innocent . . ."

"Well, here he is. My Henri."

He was quite handsome, Weather noticed for the first time. His eyes were warm and inviting and when he smiled the world lit up and you just wanted to be his friend, if not his lover. He was all charisma and charm and she couldn't help but like him.

"You're not a vegetarian are you?"

Weather shook her head, "No. I do eat kosher though."

"No problem," Henri snapped his fingers.

The service was incredible. Weather never knew life could be so fine, but she never really liked doing anything but what she was doing, mining the belt, making her artwork and being in love with Ruad and taking care of the Green Party, her family. Not all Greens were strictly vegetarian. She had filet mignon sans cows grown from the hydroponics trees and smashed potatoes with gravy. It wasn't exactly tenderloin, but it tasted like it and it was kosher and Henri ordered three glasses of champagne. She had a sip, but it made her dizzy so she didn't drink more.

Dessert was even more extraordinary and with it they had cappuccinos and espressos.

"I just want to take this time to say how sorry I am about what Corporation did to you. I had no idea. I did tell them to pick you up, but not to . . . do what they did. I have a wife and child and I just . . . the thought. Well . . ."

"It's okay. I'm okay now."

Jazmin burst into the room through the glass doors, bringing with her a gust of cold air. She came over and kissed and hugged Henri and did the same for Celia. She looked so well-groomed and well cared for. Weather imagined her manicured toes inside the designer skates, and her smile was even more stunning and brilliant than her father's. She was a heart stopper. She chattered on about this and that and when Henri introduced her she weakly shook Weather's hand and then was off to her wealthy teenage life again. A stab of sadness struck Weather; though she did not envy Jazmin, she did feel something like it, a mix of emotions.

"Look. I can't let you go you know, back to your mining life. You're in too much danger. Not just from Corporation and other people who could profit from your discovery, but from radical elements in your Green Party. There are things you probably don't know about. Anyway, I can't let you go."

"So, am I a prisoner?"

"Under martial law, yes."

"I'm to be court-martialed?"

"Not exactly. You're mining division. Not really military. That's just the premise to get you here. We will get what we're looking for, Mrs. Monaghan."

"Fullerene-Sphere-Manufacture is a private asteroid mining operation. It mines ores for the nano-filament for the hulls."

"Sixty percent of the shares went to American government, or if you will, Corporation."

"I see. Well. They should have outlawed stock trading centuries ago. I can't tell you anything, but thank you for the dinner and the clothes."

Celia smiled meekly.

"In the meantime you're free to roam in this part of the Fullerene, but you aren't allowed any calls, except to me, to my wife and Jaz and anyone on this floor, and you'll have guards with you at all times. For your protection."

"Of course. For my protection."

*The Mausoleum Bar and Lounge
on the Cadaver Fullerene*

Rappel continued her waitress guise at the Mausoleum Bar and Lounge, deep within the confines of the colonial Fullerene that was Cadaver City; far from the radiation, under layers of watery, gaseous plasma shields, honeycombed insulation, high tech wafers and nano-filaments that soaked up the rads and used it for fuel.

The colonial Fullerene approached Rattlesnake Asteroid, a city built in the Ring of Stones near Mars. Their journey would take them as far as Saturn. Despite the pseudo gravity from centrifugal force due to the rotating hull and much exercise, Jack didn't think he'd ever get his land legs back. He gave Rappel the bone supplements he'd bought at Pop's store. She needed them more than he did, and for the baby too. Rappel had never been on Earth. Born on Mars, her bones could never withstand the gravity of Earth without a carbon-gravity-suit, but the extro-blast calcium 9897 worked wonders increasing her bone density. Their investigation was on ice the past three months. Jack and Jane handled hundreds of cases in the meantime, only closing sixty percent against Sydney *Hat Racks* Atrax's ninety-five percent. They didn't share their evidence with him that they thought it was a human who had killed the Green Police at the Green Moon Motel, and Sergeant Chen kept that case open while the coroner, Gretel Roux, fought to close it, saying it was a robot programmed by Jules Helphenstein; her bosses wanted political gains. It hadn't gone to trial though, and no charges had been made, since there was no evidence.

Rappel's cover was as Jack's waitress girlfriend; even though she could probably kick his butt while pregnant, he didn't want anything to happen to her, or to his baby. She found the Chinese coin on his chest and was very curious about it. When it opened up into the cold black she touched it meekly, but didn't want to hurt their baby, so never touched it again after that. They tried to get it off, but when it wouldn't come loose they left it alone and ignored it when they made love. It didn't cause Jack much discomfort, even when he showered. It was just embarrassing. She had him exercising every day and getting stronger and more coordinated. He was clumsy, even in space. She knew if she didn't stay on top of him about it, his muscles would atrophy and she needed him to be strong. She taught him how to rappel in space. He liked racket ball better. He and Zero-One would play often.

He promised Organdy he'd protect Rappel. He was pretty sure it was his baby, and not Organdy's. She was still in love with Organdy, but she was also in love with Jack and that really complicated things because he respected Organdy. He even told her he could live in space or on Mars and never return to Earth again, just for her. The pregnancy had surprised both of them, but she didn't inform her OEA supervisors the exact nature of her condition. She had merely told her lead supervisor where her undercover job was taking her and that she had two NEPD cops for backup, who were investigating the Greepol murders that had occurred on the Moon. Not being one to use electronic information, she'd written it down and had sent one of her robots back to the Moon. Having a new cover as a homicide detective's girlfriend limited her ability to get into the organ dealing underground, though. While she played bad girl at Organdy's, she had to play straight-laced as Jack's girlfriend here at Cadaver City's Mausoleum Bar and Restaurant. Rappel was contacted by Isa Roshani from Rattlesnake Asteroid City's Rattlesnake Inn.

Cadaver City's Fullerene's swallowtail wings closed, slowing down on the approach to the asteroid field and Rappel was supposed to take a shuttle-Spider over, but she called Isa and told him he'd have to come to the Mausoleum Bar and meet her there instead. She couldn't risk traveling through radiation unprotected.

Jane examined the paper book for the hundredth time. It was an old book and apparently the nano tech in it was old too. It was an impossible book. No one had created viable nano tech until the twenty-first century. Yet this was a book with truly old nano tech from the twentieth century, copyright 1954, first edition. Not all of it was nano-repaired, just parts of it. She placed it back in her antique bookshelf. Most people just thought the book was decoration in her little apartment. She was going to meet some people tonight, and one of them knew why the book was so important. His name was Isa Roshani, and he told her to bring the book.

Rappel ordered a salad with all the works" avocado, tomatoes, caviar, capons and Russian dressing, and a chocolate ice cream float because she was almost nine months pregnant. Jane, whose indigo hair was pushed into a Bouffant, sat next to her. They were waiting for someone named Isa Roshani.

But in the meantime it didn't hurt to eat and drink, and that's what they did. Jane ate a vegetarian meal that looked and smelled like trout and drank Iapetus orange tea, while Jack and Jane downed their second draft each, and some tree-grown T-bone steaks.

Isa Roshani showed up with a large woman named Magdalena Carpe, and they ordered food too. Isa ordered vegetarian and lemonade. While they ate in the booth he raised a security screen so they could talk in private, without worrying about prying electronic ears and eyes.

"You said your name is Cluewitt?"

"Yes, Jack. You can call me Jack."

"You're a homicide detective?"

"Yes."

"Well, you look a lot like the man you're going to meet. Ruad Monaghan."

Jack didn't say anything. He knew he was adopted, but to find his father without even looking for him was a bit too much for him to fathom.

"Jack gets that a lot," Rappel said. Jane had nudged her under the table.

They had to maintain some level of secrecy. Jack couldn't afford to go off all half-cocked.

"Well, you said you have the book and this guy says he can tell you what the book means and why everyone is after it."

Jane nodded toward Magdalena Carpe, who kept shoveling food into her mouth without so much as a frown, "Can you trust her?"

"Maddie is a cop and she wouldn't endanger you. She's discreet, despite a cop's salary. My wife Randi is bringing Ruad."

The waitron bell rang, and Isa pulled down a window. She leaned in to see how they were doing and with the help of some rodeo bus boys she cleared the empty plates. They ordered dessert and coffee. Isa raised the secure shield again.

Rappel was still eating, her huge pregnant waist pushed up against the table, "This Ruad Monaghan. What does he do?"

Jack Cluewitt and the Imbrium Basin Murders Ruth J. Burroughs

"He hauls mining waste and does some security and private eye work when he's not a volunteer for Ithaca Space Habitat II. I think he used to be a cop."

So many cops, Jack thought, if only Isa knew, we could be having a Policemen's ball. Well, all except Isa, unless of course he is an undercover cop too.

The waitron bell rang, Isa lowered the security screen. Randi Roshani arrived with a suave man, dressed in a suit and tie and a Stetson hat. Isa moved over and the two squeezed in beside Isa and Maddie. Isa put the security screen back up.

The strange man was about to light up a zeegarette, but when he saw Rappel's state of pregnancy he put the zeegarette away. Then he looked at Jack and a look of awe and surprise struck his face. A shadow from the hat disappeared as the man looked up and Jack thought he was looking into a mirror. Ruad looked like his twin with a slightly older face with hints of red in his dyed brown hair and eyebrows, space kept people young looking. Jack unconsciously ran his hand through his curly dark brown locks. Ruad just burst out crying. Fortunately, no one but their small party could see or hear, due to the security screen.

"Weather does that. Runs her hand through her hair. And that scar on your face. I'll never forget how you got the scar on your face. My son. Jack Monaghan. I never thought I'd see you again. You have your mother's hair. Weather," he said and burst out crying again.

Everyone was speechless. Even Jane.

Jack broke the silence, "My name is Jack Cluewitt. Who's Weather?"

"Weather Weiss Monaghan, your mother." The waitron bell rang and Ruad pulled himself together, blowing his nose on a handkerchief. Isa opened the window and the coffee and desserts arrived. She took Randi and Ruad's orders for coffee and vegetarian sandwiches. The waitress walked away and the window screen went up.

"You don't even need the book. I know it's you. What about the toy police badge and your robot puppy, Zero-One?"

Jack blew on his coffee, "Zero-One?" His voice cracked. "Yes. Zero-One."

179

Jack Cluewitt and the Imbrium Basin Murders Ruth J. Burroughs

"I still have him. The gold toy badge is at home, and Zero-One's not a puppy anymore." Memories flashed through Jack's mind. A birthday cake. His friends. His uncle Haze. He tried to recall his mother, but couldn't. He felt pain behind his eyes.

"That's twenty-five years."

"I was picked up by some very wealthy people and he's had quite a few upgrades. He's nearly human. He's uh . . . um . . . he's my butler."

"Your butler?" Ruad said, incredulous.

Jack nodded.

"They raised you Catholic, right?" Ruad asked.

"No, not exactly. They're Protestants. I think. Nominally speaking. I'm pretty sure Dad doesn't believe. He's a doctor and an atheist, though we don't talk about it. Mom doesn't go to church, either. I hate to disappoint you, sir, but I think I'm an atheist."

Ruad Monaghan grimaced. "Dad. You can call me Dad. If you're not comfortable with that you can call me Father. Well, we can fix that. You being an atheist, I mean. You're Jewish, too. Weather, your mother, is an artist and a rabbi. She taught you art, though it doesn't appear to have rubbed off."

"Jack paints holographic paintings," Rappel said.

"Oh. Well then. You took after both of us. You look like a chip off the old block, Detective, I'm thinking. As soon as we get my Weather back, I'll have you back at church and temple. She'll like that," Ruad said.

Jack nodded and sipped his coffee. He unconsciously placed his hand on Rappel's stomach.

"Is this your wife?"

"Oh, sorry. This is Rappel Luna, my girlfriend, and this is Jane Salgado, my partner—and you know Isa and Maddie."

Ruad shook hands. "Nice to meet you all. This is Randi Roshani, Isa's wife."

She smiled and they all greeted her.

There was a moment of uncomfortable silence.

"I need the book, Jack," Ruad said.

Jack nodded. "Why do so many people want it?"

Jack Cluewitt and the Imbrium Basin Murders Ruth J. Burroughs

"The book contains classified information on the location of an unlimited fuel source near Neptune and the Kuiper Belt space. Corporation wants it."

Jack shrugged. "Why do you need the book now, twenty-five years later, and why did you give it to me when I was five?"

"We don't need it," Ruad said. "We know where the secret is. But there are people who would kill for that book because of the map inside it that leads to the secret location. And the International Space Corporation has Weather in custody now, and they won't let her go. They want Peg Cardillo's robots for the Shepherd Program and whatever she's keeping secret about what's out in the Kuiper Belt."

Rappel set down her fork and swallowed the bit of apple pie, "Isn't that illegal?" she said.

"Weather's a miner under military jurisdiction. Her butt is owned until she complies, and she won't. So I have to do it for her. I'll give them that book to get her back."

"Would they hurt her, Ruad?" Jack didn't feel comfortable calling him dad.

"People have disappeared out here for less. So Jack, I can tell you're a cop. But your girlfriend here—Rappel, is it? She's Yakuza. She's a criminal, I can tell. What's a cop doing with a criminal?"

Jack didn't say anything. He just sipped his coffee. *Why do people always question my taste in women? What is wrong with dangerous, independent and very sexy women?*

"Okay, if she's not a kick-ass crimy, then she's got to be some kind of investigator."

Jack tried not to move any muscle on his face.

The corners of Ruad's lips turned up and then suddenly turned into a full-fledged smile. Jack grimaced.

"Cover's blown."

"I knew this was going to happen," Rappel said, shaking her head.

Jack shrugged, "It wasn't like we could avoid it. We had to find out why the book was so important it would get three Green Police killed."

Maddie shook her head, her piercings clinking and rattling, "Rappel is Police? No. I'd know if she were."

Jane looked embarrassed. "We wanted to tell you."

"Wait," Maddie finally spoke up, "she's OEA?"

181

Jack Cluewitt and the Imbrium Basin Murders   Ruth J. Burroughs

"You're not in trouble, Maddie," Rappel said, stretching.

"Corporation wants the book. They say they'll drop all charges against Weather if we give them the book," Ruad said.

"Do you think that's what Weather would want?" Isa asked.

Ruad shook his head. "No. She's spent her whole life keeping the secrets of the belt from Henri Vasquez and people like him. But, I don't know what they're doing to her. Corporation could be torturing her for all I know."

The masseuse was attacking her neck and shoulders. Weather hadn't realized how tense she'd been. This was her first massage. Earlier she'd had a facial and a waxing, and Jazmin had taken her for a manicure and pedicure. Jaz had made the cookies for her when her dad told her what had happened.

Weather was in seventh heaven. The big guy seemed to know exactly where all her aches and pains were and took care not to massage too close to the bones, where it hurt, but close enough to make it sweet. She'd also been drinking a lot of water, to make up for the time she was thirsty during the torture, and Celia said that was good because she'd be sore from the lactic acids after the massage.

Weather was beginning to think they might massage the truth out of her, but she was just joking. She did wish she could get a message out to Ruad, though. She knew he'd do anything for her and that made her worry and tense up again. The masseuse smacked her bottom and told her to relax. He went back to squeezing the tension out of her muscles.

"The book, Jack. Where's the book? Isa said Jane would bring it. I need it to get Weather out of the brig, out of Corporation hands."

"People have been killed over this book, Ruad," Jane said.

182

"And my wife may be next if I don't get it to Corporation."

"We'll bring it," Jack said.

"What?" Rappel said.

"Jack, you're pregnant. You can't go. I'll go," Jane said.

"Look. Wait. What do you mean, you'll go?" Ruad asked.

"Jane, Rappel and I will go and bring the book. I want to meet Weather, my birth mother. I also want an explanation from both of you. So I guess that means you should go too, Ruad."

Isa protested. "Wait. What about my mission? Who's my Green OEA contact?"

"You're a cop too, Isa," Maddie asked.

"Yeah, I'm Green Police, checking into black market organ stealing."

"Oh, shit," Maddie said.

"You're not in trouble. Cops do it all the time to make a little money. I'm not after you, and your badge is safe. I'm after the bigger guys."

"I'm your backup," Rappel said.

Isa grimaced. "Uh . . . I don't know if you noticed but ah . . . you're almost nine months pregnant."

"I'm not supposed to be. But it is good cover," Rappel said.

"So you're a Greepol, too?" Maddie asked.

"No, OEA."

Maddie gasped, "I knew it. I never met an Organ Enforcement Agent before. I hope that doesn't mean our deal with Brick Cardigan the actor is off."

"It's still on," Rappel said. "As we have yet to catch the organ thieves."

"We're actually closer to finding the Greepol killers," Jane said.

Maddie looked surprised again, "Someone's killing Green Police?"

Jack nodded gravely. "After they stole the book from me they were killed for it. Someone tried to frame me for their murders, but it didn't work out the way they'd planned."

Rappel finished her dinner and belched, "Oh, excuse me. Jack, you, Jane and Ruad go. I'm staying here. It's too much for me as close as I am to having my baby and my cover is still very good."

Jack Cluewitt and the Imbrium Basin Murders   Ruth J. Burroughs

"But Organdy told me to protect you."

Maddie shook her head confused, "Who's Organdy? Another cop?"

"No. He's a sushi chef on the Moon and well, he's my real boyfriend."

"I'll protect Rappel. She'll stay with some friends if you . . . I mean until you get back," Isa said.

"That sounds like a plan," Jack said. He gave Rappel a kiss on the lips, "Just don't blow your cover."

Isa released the security screen and Jack got up. "Let's go."

Ruad quickly finished off the sandwich and coffee and got up. He awkwardly hugged Jack and had trouble letting go. He kept wiping his eyes and sniffling. He looked so proud.

Jack shook hands with Isa, "I'm leaving her in your good hands, amigo."

"She'll be fine," Isa said.

"We'll see you then. Try to hold on 'til I get back, okay?" Jack said.

"I'll do that, Jack," Rappel said.

⚔

She'd better wait, he thought. Jack ordered a cab for them to get over to the University of International Space Fullerene colony. Ruad Monaghan got them fake Corporation uniforms and badges. Jane flirted with the driver the whole way to throw him off. He was totally turned on by her military uniform, so he said. They were able to get through customs because they didn't carry any weapons, and their badges worked.

"We need to get to the University and stay off-duty, so try to keep a low profile," Ruad said, pulling the brim of the Corporation hat down as far as he could make it go. He'd gotten Indigo Jane a wig to cover her unusual hair, because he didn't want her to attract too much attention.

They made it down several corridors before an officer stopped them and asked them what their business was. Ruad showed them their off-duty pass, and he waved them on. Jack smiled, curtly and nodded as they continued.

184

Jack Cluewitt and the Imbrium Basin Murders   Ruth J. Burroughs

As they made their way around the corridor, he breathed a sigh of relief. Jane relaxed a bit too.

"Not too much farther to the living quarters," Ruad said.

When they did arrive in the habitat area, it was filled with birds, trees, lawns and all manner of flowing water on cobbled walkways. All the doors to the apartments and all the corridors looked identical, if it weren't for the numbers and maps.

Ruad had a key for one door, and they entered the nicely decorated living quarters of Peg Cardillo. He quickly went to the bar and made drinks. Jane and Jack both shook their heads and drank cups of water instead. Ruad lit a zeegarette, but sat on a stool under the hood of a smoke evaporator. He lit one after the other, but didn't drink quite as quickly. He savored each drink.

"Are we waiting for someone?" Jane asked.

Ruad nodded, "Peg Cardillo. Don't worry. She'll be here."

She didn't show up right away. When dayshift ended and more hours of waiting ticked by, Jane took the bed and Jack took the couch while Ruad paced the room, chain smoked and started drinking coffee. Ruad shook Jack awake on the couch at 3 am. Peg had finally arrived.

"Jack Cluewitt this is Peg Cardillo," Ruad said.

"Nice to meet you, Peg." Jack yawned. "Oh, excuse me. I'll go get Jane."

"I made a fresh pot of coffee."

"Good. We'll need some."

Jane came out a few minutes after Jack and they all sat down on the couch with covered coffee cups. It wasn't exactly full Earth gravity, but after being out in space so long it sure felt good to feel some force exerting on the heart and bones, despite regular workouts.

"Well. I can smuggle Weather off the ship and you don't have to give Henri the book, but it won't be long before he finds you again. If he doesn't, someone else will."

"Can't you get Weather long enough to ask her what we should do with the book?" Jack asked.

"No. Once I smuggle her here that's it, and I may have to get out of Dodge too. No time for negotiating."

Ruad nodded gravely, "Has she talked?"

185

Jack Cluewitt and the Imbrium Basin Murders Ruth J. Burroughs

"No. I know that for a fact, because as bad as Henri is, he's not a murderer. He'll keep her until he gets what he wants and then he'll let her go. He hasn't let her go. We can all feel it. They've increased the security here at the University tenfold."

"We didn't have too much problem getting in," Jane said.

"No, you wouldn't have. Henri wants that book. It's the getting out of here that's going to be hard. So, what's your decision? Trade the book for Weather or smuggle them both off the ship."

Jack sat in silence, thinking. If she doesn't want the book in their hands and she's kept it secret twenty-five years, then there must be good reason.

"We have to smuggle her off, but we have to have a plan. Otherwise they'll catch us and all the work she's done will have been for nothing," Jack said.

"If it comes down to it I want to give them the book. I can't lose Weather," Ruad said, nervously fiddling with another zeegarette.

"Will you relax, Ruad," Peg said, taking a sip of coffee, "I have an idea. Okay. Ken Mesersmith, my fiancé, has this idea. I was sending robot ships into deep space with funding from the University of International Space and the Green Party, but they were getting eaten up in the Oort clouds by ghosts. Well that's what the rumors out here are about my ships and people, lost to the monsters of deep space. Green Party just assumed it was a black hole. Not literally, just money-wise and thought the grants would be better spent on ships not disappearing. International Space Corporation is run by politicians, military folk and CEOs who are voted for by Earth people who want to be safe from asteroids, ship-eating Oort monsters and the like. Well, they want the remaining robots, ships and personnel for the shepherd program. You know, pick up space debris, keep it from going toward Earth and monitor asteroids, terrorists and pirates and whatnot."

"Would that come under Green Party Police or INC?" Jack asked.

Peg shook her head. "INC."

"They're pushing to militarize space again?"

186

Jack Cluewitt and the Imbrium Basin Murders   Ruth J. Burroughs

"That's what the play for the book is about. They want the secrets of the book so INC can control space again, instead of the Green Party."

"What is the Green Party saying?"

"They're trying to get the robots back under Green Party jurisdiction, but when they pulled my grants the robots and ships became quasi University of International Space property. It's still up in the air because G.A. still owns half of them. And the grants have gone through for the year. It wasn't politically savvy to pull the grants."

Jane shrugged. "So, what's your solution?"

"We get Weather and hide in the Kuiper Ring with my ships," Peg said. "But we have to hurry. They're trying to break the locks and the codes on my robots and ships now. The only reason why they haven't tried harder is because they don't want to break billions of dollars' worth of research, and they're waiting for our next move."

Jane put her cup of coffee down, "Wait, wait. Are you saying you have a plan to break free from the INC military squadrons surrounding those ships and robots?"

"No. But Ken does, and Weather. Well, Weather knows things."

"I won't leave Rappel behind."

"Who's Rappel?"

"Jack's pregnant girlfriend on Cadaver City."

"We don't have time to go get her."

"We could be out there for months. She's due to have our child in a few weeks, maybe days."

"Jack. Rappel's got a job to do and so do you," Jane said.

Jack stood up and paced the small area near the bar. "You're right. Can I get a message to her?"

"You might compromise her mission, Jack. It's best you don't."

"Jane's right. We don't have time. I'll contact you here or send people to come get you. It's best you don't come with me to smuggle Weather out. Ruad's too nervous and you're all strangers onboard."

"Okay. How long?"

"Soon, Jack. Soon. We should leave soon, and don't let Ruad leave the room. I don't need him going over to Henri to tell him the book is here."

187

"I wouldn't do that," Ruad said.

"You'd do anything to save Weather, and I need you to sober up a little, all right?"

"I'm okay."

"Okay. I'll see you all soon," Peg said and stepped out of the apartment, locking the door behind her.

Fortunately there was a lot of food in her digs because they didn't hear from her for two days and Jane and Jack had to alternate shifts just to keep Ruad from leaving the room. Ruad slipped something in one of Jack's coffees to make Jack fall asleep, and then carefully slipped out of the apartment while Jane was sleeping in the bedroom.

Cadaver City
Chapter Sixteen

After taking in a large inventory of cadavers, Sunny found herself working on a recalcitrant robot. The poor thing kept insisting she was overworked and needed to get back to her paintings. Sunny didn't know what was wrong with Immaculata. As far as Sunny knew, she was done with painting fresh signs. The cadavers and robot repairs took precedence. Of course it was really because Maelstrom didn't want the Cadaver Storage Facility sign restored. Everyone on the station called it Cadaver City due to the faded sign that said Cadaver S c ity. That warehouse had been the first habitat on the huge station that had turned into a cemetery city, and Maelstrom had been on the hub a long time.

Maybe forty years.

But Sunny couldn't find anything wrong with Immaculata. All systems were in fine shape, despite the heavy intake of cataloging and storing the space dead. Much of the dead went into the processing plant to be converted into methane for fuel. Some of it was used for medical purposes and anything that was left by the user for the organ farms was also distributed.

"You're too hot, Immaculata."

"Yes, but where I go to paint is cool and eventually I will be ready."

"Okay. If you insist. But I think you should rest. Maelstrom can't afford any more top of the line robots, and you need some down time."

"All work and no play makes Immaculata a bad, bad robot."

"Whatever. Go ahead. But get some rest, too."

"Will do. Thanks, Sunny."

Sunny was supposed to meet Rappel at Isa and Randi's for lunch at noon, but Maelstrom had her backed up on orders to infinity and she was only able to eat on the run. It was after six pm and well past the day shift. She gave the turn-over report to Big Vince Roberts, the night shift robot technician. Alvy, his boss the second shift manager, had been on since five when Maelstrom had left and he was making everyone scurry and hustle. Finally finished, she punched out and left the Cadaver Storage Facility and headed into the corridors toward the living areas. There was enough centrifugal force to walk upright.

Relieved, she called Rappel, but there was no answer at Isa's. That was odd. Rappel rarely left due to her pregnant state. Isa and Randi's rooms were deep inside the station and relatively safe from radiation. She checked for messages. None.

The corridors that led to the living quarters were small and numerous. The one she chose was less well-traveled. It was poorly lit and stinky, but because it was less crowded she could get there faster. She hadn't thought it through though. It was a stupid mistake.

She wasn't even suspicious when she saw two Cadaver Robots walking toward her from the other direction. She worked with them all day. Why would they be dangerous? They were just heading back to work. As they walked past her, she didn't even blink and suddenly a gag was over her mouth; her screams were muffled and though she struggled and kicked, their robot hands were like vice grips on her ankles and wrists. She was being dragged down another corridor, one that was colder and darker and the farther they carried her the less centrifugal force she felt. They pulled her into a pitch black room and tied her to a chair. Someone in the dark shone a bright light on her face and one of the robots removed her gag.

"It's no use screaming."

"Who's there?"

"Tell me what you know and I'll let you go."

"I don't know anything."

One of the robots removed a scalpel from his chest and made an incision on her arm.

"Ouch. That hurt."

Jack Cluewitt and the Imbrium Basin Murders Ruth J. Burroughs

"They'll send you through the Cadaver organ harvesting machine if you don't cooperate. It will tear your skin off, then your muscles, then your organs and then . . . well by then it won't matter, will it? I can program the machine to leave your head last too. It will pluck out your eyes one by one and tear the skin off your face and . . ."

"I get it. I get it. Well. I really don't know anything. I'd tell you if I did."

"Peel her skin off her arm."

The robot proceeded to peel the skin off her arm. She screamed.

"Okay, stop."

Her heart raced as she saw the skin hanging from her forearm. She felt faint. The robot placed smelling salts under her nose and she brightened up quickly, though she felt sick.

"Had enough?"

Sunny shook her head, "I told you. I don't know anything."

"Take more off."

The robot complied, but this time Sunny passed out.

Slowly she came to again, "Had enough?"

"I told you. I know nothing."

He dropped the light. It bounced in the Null-G and he floated over to her. It was Maelstrom. He slapped her in the face and then backhanded her. He slapped her around some more. When he was finished he went back to the light and turned it off. He turned on a dimmer light.

"You're making me do this to you. I won't be weak like the Green Party. I don't have to delegate the bad stuff to my robots. You know I can get dirty, just like any working class slob. The work needs to be done, Sunny. What did you tell Rappel?" He floated away.

"I told her that you were a good guy. A great boss. An honest hard working . . ." he climbed back toward her and hit her.

"Untie her and hold her down." The robots complied, untying her and holding her down.

"Don't, Maelstrom. It's true. I told Rappel I'd never met anyone with so much integrity."

"You're going to the Cadaver Separator now, and I'm going to watch it slowly dismember you. I wasn't joking. It

191

will leave your brain for last. It will pluck out your eyes one by one. Unless of course you tell me what I need to know. What did you tell Rappel?" He ordered the robot to peel the skin off her other arm and she screamed, but he wouldn't stop. "Peel the skin off her legs and then her breasts." The robot held her so tight she could feel the bones in her hands and feet crack.

"I told her that you're an organ thief, a dealer in stolen parts, and a murderer." She couldn't take it anymore.

"Good. Good girl. Then Rappel and her baby are next. Take her to the separator and record it for me. I have better things to do, like kidnapping a pregnant organ enforcement agent. I should keep you alive, but you know what happens when the bad guys save the good guys for the explanation. They get caught. So you're just going to have to die right now."

They gagged her and carried her away from him. She could see him now. Smiling gleefully. When had he gone off his rocket? She should have noticed sooner. He winked at her, but she didn't scream. He'd arranged it so she couldn't be heard. The Cadaver Robots took her down several corridors and she did try calling for help, but her voice just echoed in the dimly lit passageways. When they came out into a huge cold warehouse, the old separator had already been warming up. This was a closed section of old discarded robots and machines that were no longer used. Due to the high intake, Maelstrom had turned it on and was having robots process cadavers for fuel through the old machine. The two Cadaver Robots carried her to the end of a conveyor belt and stopped the machine. They laid her down behind a row of dead bodies headed for the separator and tied her wrists and ankles with ropes to little round loops that were part of the conveyor belt. Then they turned it back on. She watched as the bodies went round. They all looked like they were sleeping. Bodies covered in Iodine and harvested for their organs and tissues for recycling and it did tear the skin off first, the Cadaver Separator. That's why they found those bodies in the lockers. One of the robots must have stored the discarded ones in there instead of properly disposing of them.

As the next body on the line rolled up, the metal robot hands cut and peeled off the young person's skin. She

Jack Cluewitt and the Imbrium Basin Murders Ruth J. Burroughs

thought she saw the cadaver move, as though it was struggling against the restraints. Anything that could be used for organ replacement was vital. The machine was going for its eyes. It screamed. It wasn't a cadaver, it was a living, breathing human being and as the eye was going to be plucked, he screamed. No one could hear them in here. Maelstrom must have had the walls sound-proofed, plus the machines' rattling and clanking muffled the other noises. Not a cadaver, a living person. All those living people were being processed in the Cadaver Separator machine. It plucked out the second eye and the person struggled. Then the machine started sawing the skull to get at the brain while slowly and carefully removing the other organs.

She wasn't sure which was worse: Maelstrom hitting her and the robot peeling her skin, or the separator. The beating wasn't as bad as either. She hoped she would pass out once it started peeling her skin. Hopefully she wouldn't regain consciousness, but it seemed like every supposedly dead body she watched did regain consciousness and scream. What had Maelstrom done? How many people was he killing for organs? These weren't just old people from the retirement villages. She thought she'd figured out his motive. He hated rich old people. He couldn't afford to get organs for his wife and children after a stray INC missile from a robot battle crashed into the Cannibal Alley mining colony. There were no computer records of his marriage or his children. Rappel had to dig deep to find this, his first marriage, forty five years ago, when he was twenty. Though he'd had two more marriages and many lovers, his first marriage was the only one that had meant anything to him. Rappel had explained his motive to her. Space Corporation had plenty of organs for people who golfed and whiled away their decades, but no organs for Maelstrom's cellist wife and his talented children. So why was he killing young people too?

She understood why that caused the darkness in him, but it wasn't a good enough excuse. Out here in space bad things happened and people were still good. Maelstrom was insane. He had to kill her and Rappel because they knew. Poor Rappel and her baby. Poor Jack and Organdy. If only she could tell them how sorry she was for breaking their cover, but he would have killed her and Rappel anyway, so

193

she knew better than to blame herself. What was his motive now for killing young people? It'd taken her and Rappel eight months to figure out who was involved in the organ dealing business and though Maelstrom had been a suspect, he did everything he could to play innocent. He was so Green and so noble he'd gone to the bottom of the list for a while. Then it dawned on her that Maelstrom was finally getting rich and powerful. No more poor, helpless boy from the skids, but it was too late. She was next, and she was awake. It started to peel the skin off her foot. She screamed.

Ruad had to find Peg Cardillo. She hadn't called or come by the whole weekend, and he was worried. He'd left at 12am. But he'd searched everywhere he thought he could find her and she wasn't anywhere. He couldn't understand why she hadn't returned and where was his wife, Weather? Peg was supposed to smuggle Weather off the ship. The best thing to do was go to the rink and see if Jazmin Vasquez was skating. Then he could find Henri because Celia was always with Jaz and Henri wasn't far behind Celia. If Peg hadn't smuggled Weather off ship then Ruad knew Weather was somewhere near Henri, being held prisoner still. If he found Henri he'd find Peg and Weather.

The skating rink was brimming full of skaters. From the long balcony he spotted the two with their pink scalloped skirts and their blonde tresses and there was Henri, by the hot cocoa stand and near Henri was Weather Weiss. Where was Peg Cardillo? Then he saw Henri look up and wave. Ruad nervously waved back. Time to go.

Two men in dark suits walked up to him and gestured for him to follow. He turned to get away, but there were two more men in dark suits coming from the other direction and one of them gestured with his chin for Ruad to turn around. Not seeing any way to escape, he went along with the four men and they took a pod down to the skating rink level. They didn't go into the rink though. He was taken to Henri's luxurious quarters where Henri was waiting for him.

"Champagne?"

Ruad shook his head.

Jack Cluewitt and the Imbrium Basin Murders   Ruth J. Burroughs

"C'mon. A little to take the edge off," Henri said, pouring two glasses. He set the one offered to Ruad on the table and sat in a large, black leather chair. A robot came into the room with a tray full of hors d'oeuvres. Caviar, lobster, steamed clams, shrimp cocktails, Nathan's hot dogs, with chili."

"Nathan's hotdogs?"

"Try it."

Ruad did. Eat the hot dog. With the champagne. He liked it. He devoured it. "Where's Peg?" he said in between bites

Henri swirled his fluted champagne glass and then took a sip. He grimaced at the sharpness of the taste. "Where's the book?"

"Why don't you look for it?" Ruad tasted some of the other selections.

Henri got up from his seat and joined Ruad at the table. He dipped a shrimp into the cocktail sauce and popped in into his mouth, "We did. It's not in her quarters."

"Then she must have other quarters."

"Take me to them."

"Not until I see Weather, and I have a signed document that you'll release her with all charges dropped."

Henri grabbed a small fork and stabbed a steamer, "I didn't even need the hors d'oeuvres, did I?"

"Or the champagne," Ruad said and grabbed handfuls of the luxurious appetizers and ate as much as he could.

Not only did Henri sign the papers, he made a public statement that she was free to go, but he wouldn't let Ruad see her until he had Jack and the book.

"Okay, Henri. I'll take you to them. Oh, by the way. Where's Peg?"

"She's okay. It's not important."

Ruad nodded. He hadn't hurt Weather. He didn't think Henri would hurt Peg either.

※

Jack woke up. He was groggy and his head throbbed. He got up off the couch and smelled the glass Ruad had given him; it was half filled with beer with flecks of white in it and a medicinal odor. He got up and banged on the bed-

195

room door and then opened it and flicked the light on. His voice was gravelly.

"C'mon we have to get out of here. Ruad drugged me and he's probably gone to get Henri and exchange us and the book for Weather's freedom." Jane mumbled something, but he couldn't make it out.

"Get up. I'll nuke some coffee, but hurry." Jack rubbed his sleepy eyes and ran his hand through his curly tussled hair.

He found two covered cups and poured cold coffee in them through the little holes in the covers and heated them up in the microwave oven. He put cream and sugar in Jane's and left his black.

Jane came out of the bedroom half dressed. She hopped along trying to put a sneaker on her right foot; she squeezed into it and stood up. Still in her INC military uniform, she pulled the cap out of her back pocket and put it on over her brown wig. He handed her the cup of coffee.

"Got the book?"

"Of course, Jack."

"Let's go." He grabbed her and they jogged toward the entry hatch.

He opened the door, but four black suited goons stood outside the door. Just behind them stood Ruad and a man Jack didn't know. Jack slammed the door shut, but one of the goons forced it open and pushed his way inside. Jack tried to push Jane behind him, but there was nowhere to go except backed up against the wall.

The man in authority spoke. "It's good you two are having coffee. Why don't you sit down there on the couch?"

Not having much choice, Jack sat down and motioned for Jane to join him. They both sipped their heated coffees.

"I'm Henri Vasquez. I know who you two are; so you can quit the charade, Jack, and give me the book."

"What are you going to do with it?"

"What Weather should have done with it a long time ago. Twenty-five years ago—given it to the people. Instead she gave it to you, Jack. And from what I've gleaned it holds secrets about an unlimited fuel source. Do you know how many lives this stuff will save? I should have put her and Peg in prison and then let the courts take care of her, but all we really want is the secret fuel. The stuff Peg's using on

Jack Cluewitt and the Imbrium Basin Murders Ruth J. Burroughs

her robots and ships. Stuff that makes super conductive oil look like child's play."

Jack laughed. "You're telling me that you don't want it because you're greedy for corporate profit? You just want to save lives?"

Henri shook his head, "I'm not afraid of making a profit. I don't hate and fear corporations. I'm surprised you're not after it to keep your stepdad from losing his Water Corp-Por-Ation. I know he's stinking rich. More than Vasquez Corporation and Hofmüller Industries combined. I can see why you don't want this stuff to come out. It would be you and your father's ruin. How do you think the Mars Philharmonic continues to play their classical music? It's because we sponsor it. Who do you think is going to find the cure for cancer or solve the world's problems? It's not going to be Weather Weiss or Peg Cardillo and it won't be me, but I am going to be the one who gets the ball rolling in that direction."

Jane took a sip of her coffee and laughed, "You don't have to give us your corporate sales pitch, Henri. We don't have any power, influence or money."

"The book," Henri said.

Jane looked at Jack and he nodded. She pulled it out of the back of her pants and handed it to him.

Henri snapped his fingers and one of the goons brought over a series 9000 Nano decoder. They checked its authenticity. Henri nodded.

"Very good. You didn't try to pawn a fake one off on me."

"Henri, you've got what you want." Ruad fidgeted.

"Go ahead. She's in the lobby. She wants to talk to you anyway. She knows you gave me the book and Jack and Jane."

Ruad saluted awkwardly, turned and ran out the door.

"You're free to go as well. Take off those INC jackets first. I won't hold you for anything now that I have the book, but you might face charges for impersonating military personnel. I'll have to work it out with your superiors."

Jack was surprised. They tore off their hats and jackets. He and Jane got up and out of the apartment as soon as they could and walked quickly down the corridor and away from Corporation soldiers. When they turned the cor-

197

Jack Cluewitt and the Imbrium Basin Murders   Ruth J. Burroughs

ner, they ran. They took the pod down to the rink lobby in silence. When they arrived, they stepped out into the brightly lit vestibule crowded with people in winter clothes, some with skates or drinking hot cocoa at the stands.

Jack spotted Weather and Ruad leaving through an exit. He forced himself not to point, and motioned for Jane to follow. They caught up with them in the corridor arguing. Jack tapped Ruad on the shoulder.

"What in heck! They let you go?" Weather said.

"They've got the book, but we removed certain pages. They'll figure it out soon. The part he's looking for is the nano tech altered print. He checked that to make sure it wasn't a fake. It distracted him from checking the whole book. We removed some of the pictures that aren't obviously missing. The pictures aren't numbered and the page after the pictures picks up from the page before the pictures. Those were the ones Zero-One thought were important. But once he looks at the plates contents he'll find they're missing. We thought about removing the illustrations contents page but we were afraid he'd notice that missing right away. We don't have much time."

Weather motioned them to come. "Let's go then. We need reach Peg's robot fleet Corporation is holding off Titan.

Jane shook her head. "What about Peg? Don't we need her and Ken Mesersmith to get out to the Kuiper Ring and escape INC military?"

"No time."

⚔

Peg was locked up in a holding cell. Loud music played day and night for two days, but she'd been able to catch a few naps. By the morning of the third day she was worried. Where was Ken, her knight in shining armor? They'd put her in a smart jumpsuit, but hadn't taken her ring. Henri had seen it and she could tell he was jealous. After all these years of wanting her to move on it seemed he wasn't happy to see her happy in love again. He'd caught her smuggling Weather out and the reason why he was pissed at her was because she'd used Jazmin, her own daughter, to do it. Jaz was merely grounded of course, but the poor bird in the gilded cage was grounded by some big security goons and wouldn't be able to help her now. Peg twirled the ring on her finger. *Ken, where the heck are you?* Her stomach growled. The bread and water were getting old. There was no information they needed from her, or so they thought. It wouldn't be long before that would change and as weak as she was from the bread diet, she didn't know how long she could last before telling them Weather's secrets.

⚔

Jazmin stood on the beach. At sixteen she was full-breasted, flat-stomached, with peachy round smooth and clean buttocks, juicy sweet and hot and heavy for boys. The guards knew of her trysts, though they did everything to keep her from escaping and when she'd sneak back they'd say nothing for fear of Henri's wrath. That's how she'd got out of being grounded this time. She'd lured one of the guards out with her young beautiful body and her full pouty lips, putting his rough hands on her lush full breasts that brimmed over her tight brassiere. He was ugly in a handsome way. Pockmarked face, rough beard, fat but muscular, and she seduced him. He was smarter than she thought and knew she was up to something, so she knew the only way to distract him was to go all the way. She didn't mind. He was good. Better than she'd ever had. *Old men aren't so bad,* she thought. She screamed in ecstasy as she came and he trembled, trying to hold it for all he could, but he came shortly after and then she thrust the little needle into his thick neck. It was strong enough to take down a horse. He was a big guy after all, and she wasn't sure it would penetrate the thick muscles of his neck. It worked all right. She'd pulled off the skin glove and the fake finger tips on her right hand. It had protected her from getting any of the sleep drugs in her own system. He lay under the shelter of the tent on her father's private beach; the guard who'd helped her sneak out of her rooms. She hoped Dad would keep him, but she doubted it. He'd probably end up in the cells being tortured or dead by her own dad's hands, once he found out she wasn't a virgin. But she couldn't worry about him. The fate of the Green Party was at stake, and she had to do what she needed to do to save it. Her father

Jack Cluewitt and the Imbrium Basin Murders   Ruth J. Burroughs

would militarize space. He was killing anyone against him and pretending to have a worthy agenda.

Ever since she'd drunk the waters of Europa she'd been able to ken the metals. She was a dowser, like Weather, and could find or sense things. Though the Earth dwellers kept sending people out to mix genes with the spacers, she did not feel inferior. She did not feel a need to be planet-bound, or to have her children be planet-bound.

She walked down to the waters' edge where it lapped up like a tide was pulling it by means of centrifugal force and currents. She could hold her breath long enough to break Peg Cardillo out of the cell Dad had put her in, but she wasn't sure she could reach her in time. They needed Peg. If only there were more like her. There would be someday, but not now. She was the best roboticist in the universe, but the worst mother in the worlds. Jaz stripped off her clothes and dived into the water full of stingrays, sharks and whales with just a knapsack full of tools and two small oxygen tanks. It wasn't deep water, but the jail cell wall was miles away. She had to go soon. Before the guard woke up or before she was discovered missing.

✖

Henri was called into the lab. Pages were missing. Illustrations. The lab doctor showed him where and how they were important to finding where the fuel was hidden in which asteroids in the belt. It was a nano puzzle that once put together would show a map of the asteroids and where the strange substance was that would make a limitless supply of energy. No more mining for water for plasma shields, no more dead bodies fueling and heating or cooling ships. No more crap and garbage. This was the mother lode of finds. None of the researchers trying to make black holes had come close to this, and once the Green Party had made the research illegal it had become Henri's top priority to find it, but his Corporation ships had scoured the Asteroid belt for two and a half decades and had come up with nothing. The asteroid, 253 Mathilde, Weather had been carving was missing of course, but where do you hide an asteroid for twenty-five years? It had to be somewhere. They'd made copies of the map, but if Weather, Peg and Ken were killed

200

Jack Cluewitt and the Imbrium Basin Murders   Ruth J. Burroughs

by all those trying to get it, the book still held the secrets for those who survived. She'd stashed the book in the cantaloper with little Jack Weiss Monaghan and sent him off into space where the Cluewitts of Cluewitt Mining had found and adopted him. It'd taken Henri a long time to figure that one out, but there was no denying Ruad Monaghan was the father of Jack Cluewitt.

But the puzzle he needed wasn't whole. They'd taken important pieces of it, and he had to find them. They weren't getting off the University ship. He turned on the alarm and put out an APB to find them. He didn't care about the bad press. This crap had to stop now. He was so close. He'd held the book and could almost feel the Cold Ion/plasma drive in his hands and the promise of bringing International Space Corporation back to the top of the game. All the soldiers and robot jockeys were at the bottom of the food chain in space. With the Green Party in power the janitors, plumbers and trash haulers were the elite. He'd have to put things right and put the soldiers back on top. Make things the way they used to be and if it meant sacrificing Jack, Jane, Weather and Peg Cardillo—even his own daughter, Jazmin—for the higher good then it meant he'd bloody the alter with all of them.

✖

Peg was burning up. They had turned the heat up pretty high and she was thirsty. She hadn't had any bread and water that morning and her toilet was dry as a bone. The door opened and Henri stood there with a glass of water.

"Can I turn the heat off and let it cool down in here?"

"What for? I'm enjoying it," Peg said.

"As you wish. When you're ready call out to the guard and I'll bring you this water. I want the location. You know where the Cold Ion/plasma drive is and you're going to tell me, or you're going to die. I've run out of patience."

Peg licked her lips and nodded. Twenty-five years of silence, and she wasn't going to tell him. Sometimes she thought he'd married her and fathered her child to get close to her to find out the secrets of the belt, but he couldn't have known back then what she knew. As he did come to know her he'd grown suspicious and the more he pressed her the

201

Jack Cluewitt and the Imbrium Basin Murders   Ruth J. Burroughs

more distant she became. He was different back then. A young brave robot jockey with no worries or cares, and he was as wild as she was. His views had changed slowly over the years as the Green Party took control of space.

"When you're ready to talk," he said again, but she just closed her eyes and pretended to sleep.

⚔

Jazmin swam toward the wall with the re-breather in her mouth getting her body accustomed to the oxygen tank. By the time she reached the far wall she could see the powerful waves and knew it would hurt if she got too close and was slammed against it. She dove and swam under water, dowsing. Trying to sense her mother and which cell she was kept in. She didn't waste the oxygen looking for the vents; they were too small. She knew the blueprints like the tops of her worn out skates. She honed in on a spot. She dowsed for a weakness in the metal and found one. Quickly she pulled off the knapsack and took out the torch metal cutter and cut away at the wall hoping she wouldn't flood and drown everyone in the cells.

⚔

Peg was dreaming of water, an oasis of water. She heard a strange sawing noise. Peg stirred on the cot. She made herself wake up. The whole back wall was vibrating and water was pouring into the seam where it was being cut. Whoever was cutting a hole into her cell was letting all the water in. She ran over to it, thinking she must be hallucinating and took a sip. She coughed and spit it out. It was sea water. Odd. The cut became a smiley and then a circle. She thought about the water pressure and ran over to grab the cot. She flipped it on its side and lay behind it. She peeked over it and watched as the water poured in through the seams and then the torch stopped cutting.

⚔

It was almost cut. Jaz pushed with all her might to make the final cut and then kicked at the circle, hoping the water pressure would do the rest.

Water was gushing into the room, but the tongue of metal wouldn't yield. Whoever was on the other side needed her to help. She looked for something to use as leverage, but there was only the cot.

She dragged it over to the wall, tripping in the water that was gorging in and tried to place it in the hole to widen it, but light as the cot was the water coming in wouldn't let her.

An Orca was circling Jazmin back and forth. The Orca finally swam at her and she dove out of the way. It banged into the wall with its tail.

The wall vibrated with a bang as though something heavy had hit it. The tongue of metal bent a little more. She squeezed the cot into the opening and someone on the other side kicked the opening wider. Water gushed in, filling the cell. Peg hoped no one opened the door now. When the water quickly filled to above the hole, she took a deep breath and dove through. She expected to find Ken or Jack on the other side, but it was Jazmin. Jaz grabbed her and they swam to the surface. Coming toward them was a boat. Jaz handed her an oxygen tank, but Peg dropped it as a wave splashed over her and she couldn't find where it had gone. Jaz motioned for her to dive, and she did. She followed her below, and Jaz swam for a good distance before she stopped to share the oxygen. They swam through a maze of tunnels.

Jaz motioned for her to open a hatch. Peg turned the hatch wheel, but it was difficult so Jaz helped and they slowly got it open. She shared the oxygen with Peg. Inside Jaz closed the hatch behind them and they swam about in a pressurization chamber, sharing the oxygen. Jaz hit a red button and the water started to drain out. When they were able to get their heads out, they both breathed quickly and deeply, coughing and laughing. Then Peg curled in half in pain but the highly pressurized room eventually removed the nitrogen bubbles from her body as she lay in her daughter's arms.

The room drained out and when Peg was better, Jaz move away and removed the diving suit. Blow dryers from the walls blew hot hair down on them.

"Does Henri know about this room?"

"No. Only us kids. My friends and I."

"He told you not to go exploring. He said it wasn't safe."

Peg smiled, her hair and clothes blow drying in the hot air.

"He didn't care. He told me not to do a lot of things and then he'd go off to work. He's not much more available then you . . . oh, sorry."

Peg laughed. "You're right. We're the worst parents."

Jaz laughed too, "Should have let the robots raise me. They're programmed to care better than you. We have to hurry. Dad doesn't know where this comes out. He's too busy to bother with these things, but he'll figure it out soon."

Peg nodded.

Jaz opened the opposite hatch and standing on the other side was Celia. Peg gasped; certain Henri would be there too. She had clothes for Jaz and some radiation suits for the two of them.

"Did either of you get the bends?" she asked, and Jaz nodded at her mom. Celia slapped a nano med patch on Peg's arm, then handed her some clothes. She quickly donned them while Jaz slipped into hers.

"Follow me."

"You trust her?" Peg whispered.

"With my life." Jaz nodded.

Well, at least Jaz has one good parent, Peg thought. They went down several corridors farther and farther from Henri's luxurious quarters in the bowels of the station and closer and closer to the outer edges near the radiation and fuel zones.

It was the only way to get out. Most of the exit hatches were protected from radiation with thick layers of watery plasma shielding, but Celia had chosen a way to go that no one but outer space robots went, and they were glowing with radiation.

"Put your radiation suits on," Celia ordered, and she did so herself and zipped up.

Jack Cluewitt and the Imbrium Basin Murders Ruth J. Burroughs

She motioned for them to get on a rail car that usually carried robots to the surface of the International Space Corporation University ship for EVA. Nervously Peg did, wondering why they weren't wearing space suits. When they did get to the end of the rail they arrived at a loading warehouse on the inside of the ship where robots came in and out and it was pressurized. A series of pressurization hatches led to the outside. Only robots repaired other robots here. No humans allowed. Four other people were floating and trying to stand, waiting for them. Peg couldn't tell who they were from this distance, but as she got closer she realized it was Ruad, Weather, Jack and Jane. She wanted to yell, but Celia had ordered them to be very quiet when the time came that they arrived so as not to disturb and confuse the EVA robots. Celia motioned for them to get into an EVA ship full of radiation laden robots. The ship was also pressurized, but with a limited supply of ambient oxygen.

"Get inside the emergency EVA robots," Celia whispered.

"You're a genius," Peg whispered, and everyone chuckled.

Everyone did as they were told. Buttons pushed, the robots opened up, exposing a clean interior specifically designed for the human body and better than a spacesuit, or the carbon-gravity-suit Jack used on Earth. They took off their rad suits and quickly got inside the robots. Closed inside, Peg checked the atmospheric pressurization within her robot-form vehicle and sat down; they looked just like robots, but were supplied with oxygen and could prevent the human body from exposure to radiation for emergency hull work. She could see everyone through the smart-glass in her chest plate. Disguised as an EVA robot sitting in the car, Peg watched as Celia made her way out of the EVA dock.

The door to the ship closed and drove out into the pressurization chamber. The chamber depressurized and an exterior hatch opened. The ship rolled out into space and spun until it reached a safe distance before it used its thrusters. It headed for the robot ships off Titan.

Titan Oort Explorer Robot Ship
Chapter Seventeen

Zero-One smacked the off button on the Cadaver Separator just in time. Well, just in time to save Sunny. Immaculata told him what was happening down in the abandoned robot warehouse and he'd come as soon as he could. He ran over to Sunny and cut the ropes off her wrist and ankles. He wrapped the incisions on her arms and legs and the one on the top of her foot and helped her off the conveyor belt.

"Immaculata, see if you can find some clothes that will fit her."

"And shoes." Sunny managed to squeak. "I just wish you could have saved the ones ahead of me. I thought I was a goner."

Zero-One helped her stand on her own. "You have Immaculata to thank for saving your life. She was down here painting and saw the two robots tying you down. She called me right away and I came as soon as I could. Is that a recording device?"

"Yeah, Maelstrom wanted to watch me die a slow an excruciating death, but he had better things to do so he had the Cadaver Robots record it."

"We can use it as evidence."

Immaculata came back with an extra-large smart jumper, the only one she could find. After Sunny put it on, Zero-One found a piece of rope to tie around the waist.

The adrenaline started to wear off and Sunny screamed as she finished tying the rope-belt. Her ribs, metatarsal and metacarpal were fractured. She bit her lip and looked up, "Shoes?"

Immaculata shook her head no. "Come this way." The pain was too much for Sunny. Zero-One injected her with pain meds and then applied a nano patch cast to set her

Jack Cluewitt and the Imbrium Basin Murders   Ruth J. Burroughs

broken foot and right hand, they hardened quickly and stabilized and set her fractures.

"First, let me take care of this." Zero-One found two heavy bars of metal and handed one to Immaculata. They started smashing the machine to pieces so it wouldn't process any more living people. Using her left hand, Sunny picked up a bar and helped them destroy the separator.

"All right, let's go. Lead on, Immaculata, robot painter extraordinaire."

They followed her up metal stairs to a catwalk that led up into a brightly lit locker room where, long ago, robot technicians used to get dressed in their overalls. Now though, it was in disuse, and was full of oil paintings. Different styles of paintings lay in groups all throughout the warehouse. Immaculata painted other robots in many different settings, including the cemetery and the park. The first group in the row was in Impressionist style and the next group was in post-Impressionist, then pointillist, then abstract, then action painting, then frescoed, then Baroque, until Sunny lost track of all the different periods. Zero-One could classify and categorize all of them, but Immaculata whisked them through her studio and into the next one, in which they found another robot painting. They traveled through a catacomb of different dwellings where creative robots worked on all manner of art, including classical sculptures and found art.

So, Immaculata wasn't just painting signs. Sunny limped along. Her whole body felt bruised and violated but it felt so exhilarating to be free again and to run barefoot. In certain areas they had to pull themselves along the rung ladders.

"Where are we going?"

Zero-One was also breathing heavily although he breathed in her excess carbon dioxide, "We need to find Rappel and warn her about Maelstrom."

"Right, I hope we're not too late."

"I was trying to find their location after Immaculata called. Isa, Randi and Rappel, that is. I had a feeling Maelstrom was behind what was happening to you on the Cadaver Separator. He would know how to use it and he was one of the top suspects on the list."

"Did you get hold of them?"

Jack Cluewitt and the Imbrium Basin Murders   Ruth J. Burroughs

"No, but I left messages for them to meet us at the predetermined destination, the Rattlesnake Inn."

✖

Rappel was entirely too pregnant to be out and about eating in a restaurant and was wondering if the doctor was wrong about her due date. Maybe it was Organdy's baby and she'd gotten pregnant back on the Moon. That meant she could be due any day now, any minute. They sat in a booth waiting for lunch, but Maelstrom came floating over to their table instead. He sat down in the booth next to Rappel and pushed up as close as he could go.

"Hey, Maelstrom," Randi said, smiling, "join us for lunch?"

"I'd love to, but I have some important news." He pushed the privacy button and the security screen went up. "Sunny told me everything and I expect you and Rappel know something if not all of the goings on, so here's the deal. I can't kill you all, but I can torture and kill your loved ones. So keep out of it. Anyone who stays quiet and doesn't talk to the authorities stays alive. Anyone who doesn't will meet with an accident." He shut off the security screen and got up and left.

Rappel didn't feel so hungry, but her baby kicked as though he or she had heard the whole thing. The first thing she thought was they had to get away from the ship. Away from Maelstrom, but he knew she couldn't go anywhere. Not without risking radiation exposure and losing her baby. She was stuck in the bowels of Cadaver City with no way out.

✖

Jazmin had convinced Celia that the Green Party was right and that INC was wrong. Celia's loyalties had always been to Henri, but as the two women grew closer and closer. Jaz was truly her daughter in all respects except biological. Celia couldn't have children and she basically raised Jaz. Peg had never been there for her, but she didn't hold it against her. She understood how obsession could take you away from the people you love the most.

Jack Cluewitt and the Imbrium Basin Murders Ruth J. Burroughs

But here she was going with Peg her biological mother, practically a complete stranger, out to the Kuiper Ring. Jaz didn't know what Henri would do to her, his only child, once he discovered her betrayal, or what he'd do to Celia, who was not going into deep space. Celia would go back and face Henri and whatever punishment he meted out to her. Jaz knew Celia's loyalties lay with the only daughter she'd ever known, even more than with the only man she'd ever loved.

They were approaching Oort Exploration Robot Ship One, the Oort-Explore-bot when an INC ship came by and scanned them. It passed by without incident. Slowly the Oort-Explore-bot ship braked with thrusters, docking onto the Oort-Explore-bot One. The exterior hatch closed and the interior bay pressurized. Oort-Explore-bot started rolling toward Saturn's Moon, Titan, and away from VAQ-ORE. The interior hatch and a rail holding the EVA robots rolled in.

When it was quiet and the EVA ship had left with a dozen other robots that needed repairs and fueling, they exited the giant robots. The rail carried the robots along the interior surface until they came to a corridor entrance and the vehicle stopped. An unassuming companion bot greeted them showed them the way to the dressing room. They were checked for radiation exposure and given overalls. Then they followed it deep into the interior of the Oort-Explore-bot Ship where Peg Cardillo was able to unlock the doors with her bio and retinal scans.

Ken stood waiting on the Bridge. Peg ran up to him and hugged him. He looked like he was going to cry.

"I hoped Jazmin and Celia would get the job done. Otherwise I'd be on one lonely journey out into the Kuiper Cloud. We must go now too before Henri can stop us."

"Are all my robots onboard?" Peg asked. Ken nodded.

"Of course, darling." He opened a cargo bay door and revealed thousands sparkling androids and robots of every shape and size.

"They look awfully clean," Jane said.

Peg nodded, "They're the replacement fleet. They'll finish expanding the ships I've been hiding in the Kuiper Ring. The saucers and the rockets. These robots are made from a material similar to the Cold Plasma matter, and powered by

Jack Cluewitt and the Imbrium Basin Murders   Ruth J. Burroughs

their Cold Plasma drives, disguised as Chinese coins. We're still not able to duplicate the matter, but we've got the ships stabilized."

They were beautiful. Peg had designed them with human-like qualities and traits. She'd designed an army of Green Party robots who were building true deep space exploration ships for the Oort Cloud and maybe further. Henri claimed he wanted to turn them back into Green Party shepherd robots, scanning and detecting asteroids, comets, terrorist missiles, space debris and whatnot in orbit around Earth. Her robots were designed to find and explore the Oort cloud for water, minerals and any other treasures, but he hadn't known she was programming them to hate conflict and war and to espouse Green philosophy, and preserve the integrity of space.

She'd designed a slightly different larger Tiger Swallowtail butterfly thorax pulse jet engine. At the butt end of the thorax design she'd placed nine pulse jet engines full of the yeast, wheat, barley and hops for producing alcohol and bread. The oxygen from the Fullerene flowed downstream toward the pulse jet engines and fed the air breathing engines. It was self-sustaining. As long as there was heat and water there would always be food for the long journey to the Oort cloud and beyond, along with the stash of ancient Chinese rockets and saucers.

He planned to turn her ships back into ordinary jets and weaponize them again to save the Earth from asteroids.

Peg told Jazmin Henri's real agenda was to turn them into military robots and androids and militarize space. Jazmin convinced Celia and that's when they'd spied on him to see if it were true and the things they discovered shocked them.

Jaz followed Ken and Peg to the cafeteria. Weather and Ruad seemed to have made up and Jack and Jane looked tired. When they got there the whole crowd broke out in cheers.

"Ship's leaving. We're on our way. Put the holograms on," Ken said.

One of the crew turned on several large holos that ran live feed from outside the ship showing the Corporation vehicles in pursuit of the Oort Exploration pulse jet engine ship, the rockets and the saucers.

Jack Cluewitt and the Imbrium Basin Murders   Ruth J. Burroughs

Because of the Cold Plasma drives, Peg's ships quickly outpaced the INC ships. It was also obvious that her ships had a lot more maneuverability.

Food was served to Jack, Jane, Weather, Ruad, Peg and Jaz and the crew broke open bottles of champagne.

Jack approached his mother, noting her curly black hair and warm brown eyes, "I want to talk to you two later, but right now I need to get some sleep."

Weather smiled and nodded.

Jack left to find the sleeping quarters.

"Peg and I are off to bed too," Ken said. "By the way, you're all invited to the wedding."

Jazmin finished her meal and drank the champagne. It was cheap, but it did the trick. She celebrated with the crew. She would quickly have to get used to this kind of life. She'd just jettisoned her wealthy one. She asked a crew member to show her where she could rest. It had been a long day. The hangover the next day from the cheap champagne did surprise her. This grubby life would take getting used to.

✠

Zero-One, Immaculata and Sunny made their way to the deep woodland of the cemetery. He stashed them in a dense grove and left to get some more pain killers and bandages for her bruises and cuts. Zero-One dug his way down through the soil into a lower level where water gushed over deep roots. He took them into dark labyrinthine corridors beneath the cemetery, but near food, warmth and water. It seemed more like a cave than the interior of a Cluster Colony.

"I have to go find Rappel. Stay here." Sunny nodded and went to sleep on the little makeshift bed he'd made for her, and Immaculata went into recharge mode.

Zero-One placed the medicine bag on the floor of the passenger side of the vehicle. He waited outside the Rattlesnake Inn in a taxi pod car with the *not in service* sign showing. He had to pay a lot of credits to borrow the car. He knew they were in there because Isa had used his credit card. He waited and when he saw them, he thought Rappel looked ready to burst. He drove as fast as he could and nearly ran them down. He banged open the automatic doors.

"Get in. Fast."

Rappel was quick as a snail. Isa and Randi had to help her into the backseat. He drove through several alleys and up and down as many levels as he could to make sure they weren't being followed to the predetermined spot he told the cab driver he'd leave it. It was near a free pod. They took the free pod down to the cemetery levels. He brought them to the hole in the ground in the graveyard. Rappel gave him a funny look, but started crawling, Isa and Randi followed right behind and Zero-One took up the rear. Their hiding place, deep beneath many layers of water and soil and safe from radiation, surveillance and hopefully Maelstrom but then Rappel started moaning.

"I think my water broke."

"Are you sure you're not just wet from the hydroponics?"

"Yes, it's warm and I'm having contractions."

"Just keep going."

Zero-One brought her to another cave, farther down from Sunny and Immaculata. Randi stayed with her.

"I'll get more medicine."

Rappel shook her head. "No. You've risked enough. You could get caught. Just stay with us until the baby comes. I'm sure you'll be able to help. The epidural you gave me is working."

"Okay. Let's just hope you don't have a breach birth."

⚒

Hildy Witter Raygun was wondering where in the Solar System Jack was. The new Sally S. Queue was beyond help, but she had to employ her to quick service. If she didn't find Jack, he might be killed. True, she wanted to kill him when she saw him make love to Rappel, but as time passed she started to forgive him. After all, he was a man and he had needs, just as surely as she was a woman and she had needs. She just took care of hers with her robots instead of all that messy intimate human relationship stuff.

Hildy had to get word to Jack, not all Green Police were to be trusted. But if he found out her Sally had killed the

Jack Cluewitt and the Imbrium Basin Murders   Ruth J. Burroughs

Greepols he'd never trust her. Yet Hildy had never programmed Sally to kill the Greepols. Something had gone wrong and Hildy had to destroy that Sally, her memory being evidence in those crimes, evidence that wrongly pointed at her. Sally was somewhere out there doing Hildy's bidding again. This time she better get it right.

⚔

Sally S. Queue made her way through the corridors of Oort-Explore-bot One, sure no one recognized her. She still had turquoise eyes and blonde hair, but so did a lot of other androids. Her blonde hair was nicely streaked with dark gold and orange stripes, but she had no memory of the Imbrium Basin Murders. That Sally was gone. She'd told her there was someone in the Green Party who was out to kill Jack, and Sally had to protect him at all cost, even if it meant killing another Greepol or whoever was after Jack and Jane. She should be willing to sabotage the ship or steal the secret, or both, should the need arise.

⚔

Rappel screamed. Contraction after contraction, Randi held Rappel in her arms. Isa paced. Eventually Immaculata and Sunny woke up and wandered down to the birthing cave to try to help. The labor lasted throughout the day and night. Sunny gathered tubers and water and they ate and drank. When she was getting close, Zero-One told her to push.

Rappel tried hard, but the baby was stubborn. He or she did not want to come out. She screamed as another spasm of pain wracked her body and then she felt its head emerge. Zero-One kneeled down, ready to receive the child.

"Push, push," Randi said.

"Yes, push, push." Sunny chimed in and Immaculata nodded her head, smiling.

Rappel pushed, but the pain was enormous. It drained her whole body to the point where she never thought she'd stand up again, let alone ever have sex or another baby again . . . especially not another baby.

She pushed as hard as she could and the baby slid some more, and Zero-One started pulling and pulling. Finally, with what she thought would be her final push because she was so exhausted the baby came spilling out. Zero-One caught the pink little newborn as it screamed and cried and they washed it in water and wrapped it in soft white cloths.

Weakly Rappel spoke, "What is it?"

No one said anything as the baby cried.

"Well, is it a boy or a girl?"

"Why don't you look?" Zero-One said, and handed her the baby.

She checked. Both hands had five fingers. She pulled down the cloth and noticed the little penis. It was a boy. She pulled back the cloth and counted the toes on his feet as he started to quiet down. Then she noticed something else; a little vagina underneath the penis. He was a hermaphrodite.

"Twice blessed," she said and made the sign of the Green Mother Earth.

She looked at his face and head, but couldn't tell if the baby was Jack's or Organdy's. True the child had Asian features, but so did she.

"Her name is Loon-Earth Poisson Cluewitt, my daughter-son."

Henri called off the INC ships when they reported that the Oort-Explore-bots were nearing the Kuiper Ring. He seethed with envy. She'd been holding back a fuel that could make ships travel that quickly. He had his ships dock on the VAQ-ORE Fullerene so they could all get to the Kuiper Ring without wasting the warships' fuel. He'd have Peg Cardillo and Ken Mesersmith brought to court if they ever returned to Middle Space. He'd have them shot for high treason. What could they possibly do that would help the Green Party way out there in the Kuiper Ring except maybe stir up some comets, and now Henri had no robots to protect the Earth people from asteroids and space debris because she had stolen them. He wasn't sure he could survive this politically, but no matter what happened to him INC

Jack Cluewitt and the Imbrium Basin Murders   Ruth J. Burroughs

had to start over and mine more metal to build more robot ships for the shepherd program. That meant more cutbacks and more accidents and little help for the disenfranchised. He couldn't believe what Jazmin had done, but he knew somehow Peg had poisoned her to him. He'd deal with Celia later. He knew she adored Jazmin, but he'd make her pay for her betrayal. He'd make her pay for a very long time.

※

How was Jack supposed to solve the Greepol murders and protect Rappel way out here in the Kuiper Ring? Jack watched the holo screens in the cafeteria while the human crew ate lunch. The Kuiper Ring was a sparkling diamond wall. Crystals glinted off the beams of light their ships shone on them. It was other-worldly, and from that field came many strange things, including frozen comets. VAQ-ORE Fullerene with war ships plastered on the hull like bugs, unwisely pursued.

※

Henri met Maelstrom on Cadaver City at the storage facility. He'd brought five goons with him because Maelstrom gave him the willies.

"What is this place?"

"It's where the cadavers are separated from their organs." Maelstrom poured himself and Henri a glass of Merlot.

"Thanks," Henri said. "First Hildy's robot Sally killed the Greepols before they could get you the book and now you've lost Sunny, Rappel and Zero-One and they know you're the operative."

Maelstrom nodded, drawing out the silence like he agreed with Henri. "They don't know you were the one who paid me to get the book. The Greepols thought I was working for the Green Party"

"Well, you were."

"I was, and I am. But those wimps started making concessions for the meat eaters. It's bad enough that rich people have the pick of all the organs. We do not need more gluttons consuming every pound of protein in the solar system, without giving anything back. Just like in the olden days when people ate everything that walked the Earth, but refused to give their bodies back. Selfish. Gluttonous. I wouldn't be working with you if you weren't going to make me President of the Solar System Commonwealth under the Green Party. I see now the only way to do it is to militarize everything again and make the Green Police and the Green Party the most powerful military organization in all the space worlds. The Greens have been doormats long enough."

"Well. The secret of the Asteroid Ring is that Peg discovered some kind of fuel, and I want it. I don't understand why she doesn't want to share it. I've been waiting all these years for her to share it with the Green Party so that my spies could get it, but she's kept it all this time."

"She's crazy. Just because she's your ex doesn't mean you shouldn't lock her up. You're too soft, Henri."

"Well . . ." Henri sipped the red wine, "We'll have to get her before all of this goes public. When that happens there's no telling who will be after her."

"You go get Peg, her robots and the ships and I'll go after Rappel. I need to cover my tracks."

"Don't hurt them, Maelstrom. We need them alive. I need you, but you're a nasty tool."

Maelstrom grinned, knowing that Henri always closed his eyes to get to his ends, pretending it didn't matter. "You're the tool, Henri. But however you view it, I'll be sure to give you all the power you need as long as your INC military enforce the Green laws with all the severity necessary. Rappel's undercover so she hasn't sent any reports, but we have to be sure." Maelstrom drained his cup.

"If you keep her alive, Mael, we can use her as leverage on Jack to turn Peg in. He's just like Ruad, who sold his soul to get Weather out. Jack will do the same for Rappel."

<hr>

"Jack. Where the heck are you?" Zero-One listened to the reply and reported back to Rappel and the gang. "He's on a ship headed out to Kuiper and Corporation is in hot pursuit." Zero listened to Jack but the frequency was bad. He made an assumption and replied.

216

"No. I'll take care of her. You take care of Peg and her robots." Then he lost the frequency.

✖

Hildy's robot pilot pulled her ship into dock on Cadaver City. Hopefully Sally was doing her job. Hildy had her line of companion androids ready for sale and her people were offloading them now. She disembarked and brought her robot ware to the sales room. People started filing in immediately looking for husbands, wives, girlfriends and boyfriends.

She sold quite a few, then decided she'd have a bite to eat. That's when she spotted Zero-One. She followed him and found where they were hiding. She could send her robots to warn them, but they weren't as elusive as she was. She knew they must be hiding from Maelstrom and she planned on confronting the evil traitor who'd betrayed the Green Party; for that he would pay. She wished she had Sally to do that nasty work, but Sally was busy.

She told her holo-enhanced robot guards, who were dressed in plain clothes, to unobtrusively wait near the cemetery. She climbed down into the hydroponics catacombs.

Dripping wet, she followed the voices. She didn't like being without her robots. She shivered. Huddled in the corner of the cave were Rappel and the little baby. Two young women and a female robot stood up and blocked Hildy's way in.

"I'm not going to hurt anyone. I just came here to warn you."

Rappel looked up. "Hildy?"

From another direction Maelstrom, five goons and three Cadaver Robots marched in. They were all dry and Hildy wondered how they got down under hydroponics without getting wet.

"Found all of them and Hildy. Good. We can kill them all in one shot with the separator."

Hildy wondered what that was and wished she hadn't left her android guards up in the cemetery. She feigned fear and let the guardsman handle her as they took all of them through secure checkpoints in the official tunnels under the hydroponics.

᙭

They gathered around the shiny new Cadaver Separator. Young, healthy, gluttonous meat eaters would be conveyed into the processor along with old meat eaters and polluters. Maelstrom appeared to be delighted. The guards pushed the females in front of the conveyor.

"Thanks for the recording of me trying to kill you, Sunny. That was the old separator. This is a new one."

Rappel held her crying baby, trying to sooth him-her. Randi stood next to her and Sunny and Immaculata stood behind them. Hildy stood in front of them and said she'd protect them. She pulled out a Raygun and fired. It disabled the robot.

"That's far enough." Isa demanded from behind Maelstrom. He held a laser gun on the men. Zero-One drove up in another rented taxi. Rappel and Sunny quickly clambered into the backseat. Immaculata magnetized herself to the trunk.

Zero-One and Isa tied up the five goons and put Maelstrom onto the separator conveyer, strapped them in, and pushed the on button.

They put Hildy into the cab too and it screeched away, Zero-One in the driver's seat.

"I was trying to warn you to be careful," Hildy said. "They will not let it get out that they're dealing in used organs of murdered elderly meat eaters. Maelstrom is vying to be the power behind the Green Party and Henri is supporting him only because they both agree that space needs to be militarized again."

"Where will we go that's safe?" Rappel asked.

"We have to find Magdalena Carpe," Isa said.

"Who's that?"

"A cop who'll take care of us. Well, I hope she's on our side."

218

They were on a long-haul freighter in Cannibal Alley in between Jupiter and Saturn, the least traveled orbit, and with only one Fresh Air Station, that was so swamped it was almost always out of food, except the ever present globule mushrooms. It was a gamble, but the trip would make enough for him to get better digs for his family, and so many of his friends had gotten through without a hitch. He'd scraped and saved to get Genevieve Corrigan a decent cello and she was finally making her way in the music world, making enough so that she could get out of mining work. His son Jeremy Corrigan was eight and brimming with questions.

"What's alzmyers, Daddy?

"Granny has Alzheimer's and the cyber upgrades didn't work. It means she forgets things that just happened, but can remember things a long time ago. Then after a while she will forget everything slowly."

"I'll make her brain all better, Daddy. I'll be the best Sigh Bear maker ever." he'd told Maelstrom.

He was going to find the cure for Alzheimer's and Geoseffa, Jeremy's twin, was going to find the cure for cancer. All vegetarians and animal lovers too, the kids were playing with their pet, a real live puppy, when the bullets slammed into their mining vessel home, ripping through the metal walls and riddled their tiny bodies with bloody holes. A dud missile struck the next door compartment and shrapnel hit him and Genevieve, but Maelstrom had only sustained minor injuries. His wife and children critical, he'd begged VAQ-ORE mining company for help, but they couldn't find any organs and no one could get out to them in time, even though they tried. Maelstrom looked into it. He couldn't understand how the facility wasn't stocked with any organs or why all the freighters' organs were gone too.

He dug around in the underground and he found out that a passing elite Fullerene had bribed the only emergency organ storage facility in Cannibal Alley's only Fresh Air Station and scooped up all the ten-year organs available, to lengthen the lives of certain rich yet terminal Nursing Home residents, who needed them. There'd been some kind of accident and all their food and organs had been destroyed.

Jack Cluewitt and the Imbrium Basin Murders Ruth J. Burroughs

It must have been a huge sum for the man to take such a bribe because he'd stolen all the organs he could get his hands on from the two freighters docked at the Air station. Later, Maelstrom would find out he'd stolen all their fuel too.

He initiated the proceedings to have the nursing home perps arrested, but before he could disable engines they disappeared into the solar wind. His anger and adrenaline made him turn over every hiding place in the station to find and kill the emergency organ storage facility operator. He had him cornered; Brick Corrigan, the man who'd taken an enormous bribe and was getting ready to take off and the man who was Maelstrom's half-brother.

Maelstrom held the laser gun on him, but Brick pulled a Glock 17 9mm.

"You can't shoot me. You could miss and depressurize your own ship or blow the nuke drive."

"It's a lot of money, Maelstrom. I've got enough for you if you want to come."

Maelstrom hesitated. "My wife? My kids? Our dog too?

"Not enough. I've calculated how far we need to go to the next station or the next Fullerene Erthworld. They won't know about what happened here and there's enough for one maybe two people but not enough for three let alone two kids and a dog."

"Well. You can't go then. You have enough I could probably stretch it to save the lives of the families you've stranded here with no food or fuel, Brick. We're family. How can you do this to family?"

"No can do, Maelstrom. It's more money than you can imagine. I'm filthy rich. I can live in the best Orbitals with the best food and the best company. I'll never be poor, hungry, cold, hot or dirty, ever again. I'll never worry if I have enough oxygen or water. Besides I've got the gun."

"You shoot and you're good as dead. I don't think you're that good a shot."

"Try me."

Maelstrom did. He shot the laser, but Brick jumped easily out of the way. It wasn't meant for humans. It was meant to disable defective slow robots. It could punch and burn a human, but it telegraphed its direction and speed, and with enough agility and distance a human could out-

Jack Cluewitt and the Imbrium Basin Murders Ruth J. Burroughs

run the beam. Brick shot at Maelstrom, but missed, the bullet smashed through the hull.

Shocked, Maelstrom dropped the laser gun and ran while Cardigan kept shooting. Three times until Maelstrom exited the air lock. Safely on the other side, he watched as Brick took off with all their fuel, food and organs. The first bullet lodged in the escaping ship's hull. The second bullet hit the Fresh Air Station and repair bots hurriedly gathered to repair it with EVA welding tools and the third bullet tumbled out into orbital space.

Brick absconded with all the emergency fuel and food on the station in order to get away, and had used a much faster ship than the slow-moving freighters, so no one could go after him. Where were the police when you needed them? Maelstrom found him asleep at the desk of a one-celled jail.

But that's why the pay had been so good. It was dangerous out here in the Alley. The bastard, his own brother, had left Maelstrom, his family and the two dozen other freighter families, stranded with no food.

Slowly people died and he was able to get his family some organs. The robot surgeons were able to save his family, but only by the tragedy of others. So for a while he had hope. But when they tried to take orbit, they found that Brick had stolen or permanently disabled their engines. It would be months before they could get new ones. What he and a few others had to do to survive the wait he never told a soul and, as many victims of Cannibal Alley, it went unreported. Before she died Genevieve made him promise to use her body so that her children would survive. So he'd made his family the first meat stew they'd ever eaten. Then he had to kill the puppy to keep the children alive. His daughter died first and he had to put her in the pot to keep his son alive. His son held on the longest, but died the same day help arrived. He held him in his arms, sad beyond grief, angry at all the Gods. After that, Maelstrom had gone insane.

Now, in his deluded mind, he pictured himself as the Rainbow Warrior who would use INC, the same military who had killed his family inadvertently, with their spent rounds in stupid conflicts, until the Green party had outlawed all guns, missiles, and nuclear weapons in space. For twenty years, two ten year terms, President Felix Fortuna had governed the Commonwealth. Under their administration he'd lost his family and he'd worked hard to make sure the Green candidates Savanna and Gull Saugerties had survived long enough to win. It hadn't been too hard since Felix had squeezed the electorate dry using hard line jingoism and fear of asteroid and terrorist strikes to keep people from questioning their ill-gotten goods. Bane Hofmüller had secretly supported Henri's bid for President five years ago, but he'd been soundly defeated due to Corporation's severe unpopularity over the high price of Oxygen and Water.

But in Maelstrom's mind Savanna and Gull Saugerties, the Green President and her Assistant, of the Space Commonwealth, were just too weak, and those Green bastards he'd fought so hard to get in power wouldn't listen to him. He merely wanted to enforce their laws, but no one wanted to talk to Cadaver technicians even if he was a manager. That was probably what had made him crack.

But when Henri reached out to him through the Waltz, Maelstrom knew what he needed to do. He was going to enforce Green laws using Henri. The electorate liked couples. Maelstrom wouldn't be the face of power, but he could pull the strings. Under Maelstrom's rule, anyone caught with weapons would be sentenced to the worst mining facilities in space where they'd succumb to some form of cancer caused by radiation. So Henri had made a deal with the Green devil, and Maelstrom had made a deal with the INC in order to get an army of robots to enforce the Green laws ruthlessly. Henri would work for Maelstrom and keep his Corporation military even as the Green party tried to rob them of their power. And Savanna and Gull were just too scared or busy to object.

Maelstrom did this in the name of his Martyr Buddhist wife Genevieve Corrigan and children, Jeremy and Geoseffa, whom he prayed to in his Shendao or Shinto Shrine. Maelstrom was Bushido Kamikaze vegetarian warrior, come to wipe the Earth and space clean of the polluters and gluttonous meat eaters and destroyers of ecosystems and violent people. Someone had to.

Brick left Cannibal orbit, heading back toward lower orbit past Jupiter a very rich man. His bullet followed him tumbling in space, picking up speed.

Kuiper Ring
Chapter Eighteen

Byron released Maelstrom from the conveyor belt.

"I'm glad I got the money out of Henri to upgrade you, Byron, you useless bucket of tin." Maelstrom said, gathering his wits.

"Byron's a faithful servant. We'll continue the mission. Henri pursues the Oort Explore-bot Ship. They won't get far. He needs those robot ships as much as you, and he will take care of Rappel, Isa and that gang."

"Our ships, not Henri's, our ships are pursing Jack out to Kuiper."

"Will Corporation know better than to kill them before they have the ships and the fuel?"

Maelstrom frowned. "Yes. Henri assured me of that, but we need to find the others. Byron, call a cab to take us to the docking bays. We'll get on a ship and cut them off at the pass to make sure Henri has his leverage. Peg wants to take the ships out into true deep space, leave our solar system with her robots and all that metal in those ancient ships. We need to rein them back in. Henri's plan better work. This time I won't be so merciful."

Pin, Magdalena, Zero-One and Hildy Regroup and Rest deep in Cadaver City Fullerene

There was enough room in Pin's ill-gotten digs for Dao, his wife and five children, and Rappel and her double sexed baby Loon-Earth with space to spare. Maddie had brought the tattered lot to her partner's deep core home since her place was too small and messy. Cadaver City was heading back to Mars and then back to Earth, and Rappel wanted to keep the babe as far from radiation as possible. She had to build a case against Maelstrom for prosecution of organ stealing and all his other crimes. Sunny said she would testify. They were incognito, but Pin and his whole family were a curious lot.

"Call me if you get Maelstrom. My cover's blown. Thanks for finding me a place to hide," Isa said.

"Don't worry," Pin said.

Maddie grimaced. "Pin's cousin is more than willing, but the danger is far from over because Maelstrom isn't done yet."

Magdalena smoked a Pall Mall under glass, inside the transparent smoking cell that overlooked a fake seascape window. Fortunately Pin, Rappel, Loon-Earth, Sunny and Hildy didn't have to breathe in her disgusting second hand smoke even if it was supposed to be healthy. She also slowly sipped a whiskey.

Rappel drank an anti-nausea vegetarian smoothie and Loon-Earth happily suckled on one of her breasts. Sunny slurped on a chocolate shake and Hildy played with a straw in her Manhattan. Isa had just left with Pin's cousin Vien, who was hiding him in his apartment. Zero-One wolfed down some superconducting oil. He asked Pin if he could serve his guests, but Pin insisted he just rest so Zero-One curled up under Rappel's feet and slept. Immaculata was juicing up her batteries, plugged into a robot feed and virtually asleep standing up.

Rappel folded her arms over her son-daughter and stared firmly at Hildy. "I should arrest you."

Hildy set her glass on the table and stood up, tossing her peach-colored locks about, "Rappel, you're an organ enforcement agent. I had nothing to do with Maelstrom's crimes. I have solid alibis, too."

"Are you saying you're a murderer, but not an organ thief, so I can't arrest you?"

"I'm not that easy."

"Then you admit to programming Sally to kill the Green Police, Jara, Keith and Lee in the Imbrium Basin on the Earth's Moon?"

"No! I would never do that."

"Then, why did she?"

"I . . . I don't know. It was impossible. She has built-in programming. It can't be reprogrammed without destroying her and she's fine."

"I should arrest you."

"Sally's innocent. Besides you're OEA."

"Well, then Maddie should."

"She's too busy chain smoking to arrest anyone. Besides I had to warn you about Henri and Maelstrom. They work for my father Bane Hofmüller, my stepfather that is. That's how I knew and I doubt he knew anything about Maelstrom's killing people for organs, he's a lot of bad things, but not that and I certainly didn't know 'til now. Bane knew about the black market, but he thought Maelstrom was stealing them from cargo ships, not living people. I think Henri Vasquez always turned a blind eye 'til now. Now he knows for sure, and he's still working with that psychopath."

"Well, Henri was always a means-to-an-end kind of guy," Rappel said, burping Loon-Earth on her shoulder.

"It's not like you're an angel, using Organdy to get into the organ stealing underworld and finding out he's totally legit and then stealing my Jack."

"You don't have to paint things in black and white, Hildy. Besides, you have a world of robot-lovers at your beck and call."

"It's not the same and you know that. I should be pregnant with Jack's baby, or at least my surrogate should be."

"Sorry."

Pin came back into the room with a plate of crackers, cheese and sliced fruits. "I found us a ship so we can pursue the pursuers."

"Where'd you get that?"

"Rappel, let a man have some secrets. Okay, I bribed the captain of a towing vessel to lose one of his ships for a few days and Zero-One and I are going to find Henri and arrest him. You ladies feast. Zero-One and I have men's work to do," Pin said.

"Really?" Rappel said, sarcastically. "What do you call Hildy and Maddie? They're going with you."

"Ur . . . I don't think so. Maddie has to stay behind and police Rattlesnake Asteroid City."

225

Rappel set her sleeping baby down in one of Dao's rocker cribs, "I pulled some strings so you and Maddie can both go after Maelstrom and make the arrest. You'll also get all the credit so I can protect my undercover status. It's your call. Maelstrom's a murdering son of a bitch."

Pin frowned, wondering why Rappel thought there was any question. "Of course I'll go."

"I have to ask. It's policy. Anyway, Hildy wants to go. She thinks she can help, but watch your back with her. I'm still not sure whose side she's on, but she does love Jack, maybe enough to kill him."

"I heard that." Hildy walked back into the room from the balcony window. She leaned over to pick her drink up off the side table and finished it in one gulp, "Let's get to it, Pin."

"When Maddie's finished smoking."

"That could take a while. There's no smoking on the tug."

Zero-One rolled over onto his back, his front paws flexed, dreaming, whining, and chasing something. Then fell back to sleep, snoring.

"Well, let's hash through some plans. We need to know what we're getting into. You and Sunny are welcome to stay with my wife and kids."

"Thank you, Pin," Sunny said, slurping down the rest of the chocolate shake, "I never signed up for all this. I'll be glad to get back to some simple robot maintenance."

"Well, Dao will keep you busy. We have a game room and swimming pool, so make yourselves at home. I'll get Zero-One and Maddie caught up on the ship."

"I think I'll do that. Go for a swim and leave the recon-noitering to you pros." Sunny got up.

Pin pointed down the hall past Magdalena.

"Sunny, take Loon-Earth to the nanny robots in the baby room, please." Rappel handed the rocker basket to her, and Sunny took the sleeping baby away. Glad to leave it to Rappel, Hildy and Pin to suss out their rescue and arrest plans, which seemed highly improbable to her. The hot nano casts Zero-One set her broken bones with released happy painkiller drugs in her, so it was difficult to be sad, even though she knew she should be. Even though she wanted to return to a normal life, she would protect Rap-

Jack Cluewitt and the Imbrium Basin Murders   Ruth J. Burroughs

pel and Loon-Earth with her life. Hopefully, here they were safe. She swallowed tears. There was a time when she could have loved Maelstrom, but that had ended the day he tortured and beat her.

Jane gets knocked out

Boxing in space was next to impossible on a small ship. Indigo Jane was making a go of it on board the Oort Explorebot One. Every punch sent her opponent flying through the padded room while the gang cheered from hidden speakers. Cameras recorded the event from all angles, sending live feed throughout the ship. They kept it off the sat link feed for the time being. She liked to use the fear her flaming amber eyes and wild blue hair put into her human opponents, but Boris Sidorov had none. Jack was upset. It always hurt him when she took punches to the face, but Boris had only gotten a few in and given her a fat lip and one blackened eye. Despite boxing for six months at the Rattlesnake Inn, Boris had her over the barrel and it wouldn't end without her being knocked out, but she was never one to give up hope and she gave it her all. Including the new teeth Jack had just paid for. She beat him to a pulp before the curtain closed and she blacked out. Men did not like losing to women. She could hear the cheering and the booing over the speakers as she faded out.

Jack muttered every Jovian cuss word in the book. Jane was floating around unconscious in the padded boxing arena, along with the new teeth he'd paid for when they still had a lot of work to do. He told the med bots to get her healed up a.s.a.p. He promised her that later when she was on her feet he wouldn't let her rest until they had Maelstrom behind bars. It wasn't even about the gold shield anymore. He had to get Maelstrom if it killed him.

He had wanted to bring Jane to dinner with Weather and Ruad, but she lay unconscious in the med ward instead. Now he made his way to the cafeteria alone.

They sat in a corner, nursing drinks. They both stood, beaming with admiration as he entered the room. It was an odd feeling. He loved John and Marilyn, his adopted mom and dad. Mom doted on him. His every wish was her command. John Cluewitt had included Jack in every aspect of his life. Fishing, golfing. Anywhere Jack wanted to go with him he could. Jack was a Cluewitt through and through. Yet there was something so familiar about Ruad and Weather. He had some of their gestures and a little bit of both of their hair, Weather's curly black locks and Ruad's red hair. Weather's brown eyes and Ruad's blue had combined to make Irish emerald eyes on Jack and Jack's hair was a curly dark auburn.

Ruad stood like a cop. Moved like a cop. So did Jack, although Jack had an air about him, like he belonged at the yacht club or an art gallery. Neither Ruad nor Weather seemed to notice.

Memories flooded back into his mind. He remembered them hugging him on his birthday. Uncle Haze. All those children he used to play with. He'd blocked everything that had happened before that fateful birthday ride alone in space without even a robot to comfort him. Later when he'd recovered he couldn't bear never seeing his family again. It had broken his heart. Zero-One had no memory of the event and when the Cluewitts woke his robot dog up it was as if his birthday had started over again from that minute on and he could be happy again.

Jack sat down and started crying. Weather wrapped her arms around him. When he was spent and he couldn't cry any more his father poured him a whiskey. Jack sucked it down.

Ruad slid a crystal ball across the table to him. "This is a copy of little Zero-One's memories from before we had to erase him. You'll be able to view the recordings too, but since you're a Natural like us, you won't be able to know his memories. It also has the death of candidate for President of space colonies, Antonia G. Clef, recorded on there."

"Thanks," Jack said a little stuffed up from crying. He grabbed the crystal and put it in his coat pocket.

"What will you do with it?"

"It proves nothing, but Zero-One ought to have his memories back."

"Yes, of course."

"We'll get Maelstrom, Ruad . . . um Father. We have to."

"We could die trying, son."

"Well, I hope you have more children, because I'm going to try."

Jazmin Cardillo Vasquez walked into the cafeteria. "We've got trouble. Corporation is on top of us and Dad is ordering us to surrender."

⚸

Byron Hunts for Baby Loon-Earth

Byron couldn't access all the nanny robots. Many weren't on any the bandwidth due to privacy laws, but Maelstrom had ways of accessing everything and Byron waited patiently until his master found some gossip. He figured she'd be near the core to keep her child safe from radiation. The child would make good leverage to get Jack and the secrets of the belt back to Henri. Byron headed toward the core.

⚸

Henri catches up to Peg and her Oort Explore-bot ships

It took Henri's VAQ-ORE Fullerene's Solar Wings and a push from a mass beam to catch up to the fast-moving Oort Explore-bot ships. It took a lot of fuel to close the Solar Wings and brake with thrusters; otherwise they'd go spinning past them, crashing into the comets of the Kuiper Ring. He was being reckless. A crash could send all manner of objects back toward Earth and the many Fullerene worlds scattered in orbits all around the Grid. But the magic fuel, the vibrating energy that could brake a ship full stop without thrusters was now within his grasp. He ordered the traitors to stand down and sent out his menacing pack of INC ships, hoping they knew better than to bite his precious cargo.

It was a hairy situation. His ex-wife, Peg, had positioned her fleet in a dense pack of comets so INC couldn't fire without disturbing them. It wasn't like the Ring of Stones where there was a lot more space between asteroids. Out here in the Oort cloud, things were icy not stony, and rumor had it that strange things happened to people's minds. Weirder than the Jovian crazies like his ex-wife Peg Cardillo or that bastard he worked for—*Speaking of which, hurry, Maelstrom.* He'd ordered the Oort Explore-bots to surrender, but there had been no reply again. He wasn't sure why Peg's fleet had stopped. Even if she took off, he'd be hard pressed to shoot her. He'd learned that the hard way. Last time they'd shot up the Flora Asteroid Fullerene colony he'd gotten the blow back that had injured him. Peg and her ships had been heading out into the dark of deep space, a place where monsters dwelled, as far as Henri was concerned. *Hurry. Get us that leverage, Maelstrom.* Otherwise Henri would have to stall for time.

✖

Peg considers her options

Peg Cardillo and Ken Mesersmith sat at the helm controls of the Oort Explore-bot One ship. A hologram displayed the enemy INC ships hovering at a slightly shorter orbit than hers. Jack, Weather, Ruad, Jane and Jaz sat nearby with the experts and robots manning systems and discussing what to do.

"I don't think they'll shoot." Peg looked tired. She twisted her diamond engagement ring around her finger.

"Only because we're wedged into this pack of comets," Ken said.

"No. He wants the cargo intact. It was a good plan," Jane offered. Jack was glad to see all her new teeth in place. The nano med patches had taken down the swelling and he could hardly see her black eye. She crossed her arms over her chest.

Jack grimaced. "Yes, but how will we build a case against Maelstrom? We can't do that if we're under military arrest. We'll disappear, and there's my baby . . ."

Everyone talked at once. Ruad put up his hand, "Jack's right. Some of us need to return. Weather and I weren't planning on an all-expenses paid trip to the Andromeda galaxy, thank you."

Peg stood up. "You're right. We do have to get you all off this ship somehow, but I don't see much choice. You're going to have to surrender. We can make some kind of deal,

Jack Cluewitt and the Imbrium Basin Murders   Ruth J. Burroughs

but Henri is not getting the bulk of my fleet. We are leaving Sol system to go explore the Oort Cloud, Ken and I, and my robots and the crew of one hundred volunteers. Jaz?"

"I don't know. I think I'm meant to stay behind. Do you have any Jovian water? I need to dream. No more cheap champagne."

Peg sighed. "One of the ships may have Jovian water, but I can't wait for visions. Drink some Kuiper water. I'll have my robots bring some around. I need to reply soon. I'll need a distraction so that Ken and I can get away with the fleet."

Jack shook his head. "Surrendering will surely put Jane and me under military arrest by INC and there's no way Henri will turn Maelstrom in for his numerous and nefarious crimes. It would sink him too, and they won't rest until they have those ships."

Peg paced the floor. "We have a problem then. We can't escape without taking everyone with us. I think we're really stuck between a comet and a hard place."

"Unless Henri is willing to negotiate," Jane said.

Jazmin laughed. "My father doesn't negotiate," she said and a huge explosion rocked the ship.

"What the heck was that?" Ruad shouted.

Sergeant Allen checked the com stats. "They fired off our stern. Should I fire back?"

"No," Peg said, "he's just testing us. He knows I don't scare easily. Dumb luck that he fired on us. There's no way he would know we're on board this ship. I'm not having any of the others protect this one. If they move to shield us then he'll know we're here for certain. I did plan that far in advance, but Henri's always three moves ahead. No. We'll just stay put for now and see if he'll hail us again."

✠

Vinny *the Waltz* Walskiwhitz walked down the corridor. Several experts and robots joined him as they headed for the helm. One of the robots had lovely blonde hair and wore black pumps and a tight-fitting lavender skirt. Her strong, slender fingers bore neatly painted nails that matched her toes. He could barely keep his eyes off of her. Her name tag said Sally. She was exactly his type. It didn't matter to him if she was a robot. He'd ask her out for coffee. Oddly, she seemed a bit aloof. It made his pursuit of her even more worthwhile.

※

It was hard for the Waltz to concentrate on their conversation while he sat next to Sally. Things seemed to be going well. He wouldn't have to kill the Peg, Henri's ex-wife. He didn't like killing, but she was breaking a dozen federal laws and if she didn't let him arrest her, he would have to. Vinny was waiting for some kind of signal. At least Henri knew which ship Peg was on.

※

Sunny opened the door to the baby room where Dao played with her many children and nanny robots. Nanny robots were the second most popular selling robots. Everyone knew sex robots were the top sellers. The new surrogate robots were becoming popular, but Naturals the solar system over were saying it was unhealthy for babies to be born of robots.

Loon-Earth started crying and a robot came over right away and started soothing him-her. Sunny gave the robot a bottle of Rappel's breast milk so it could replicate it. Rappel used her breast pump to keep hers from drying out, but she told Sunny she was glad Dao had many babysitters. Rappel was exhausted and needed a break from the baby. Mainly it was to help the boys and Maddie and Hildy regroup.

Sunny was too tired to notice Byron in the corner when she left. She needed to get to the sleeping quarters and rest. She was only glad that Loon-Earth was in the capable hands of nanny robots and Dao, Pin's wife.

※

Byron told the nanny bot he'd take Loon-Earth to the formula room to have his-her milk prepared. She had already quieted the baby, and he carried it out of the Minh's rooms. He called Maelstrom as soon as he could to tell him the location of the rebels.

Hildy, Zero-One, Pin, Magdalena and Immaculata boarded the tug. It was a dirty, noisy piece of junk that stank.

"Who are you calling?" Zero-One asked.

Maddie sighed, floating her big bulk up to a comfortable wall bed, "Probably calling one of her luxury Fullerene yachts. Hildy is filthy rich, but cannot abide dirt."

Hildy sat on the bulkhead dialing for one of her ships to come alongside the little ram tug that didn't have enough food or oxygen, let alone the other necessities Hildy was used to: a church, her slave robots and the finest food and drink in the galaxy, let alone the solar system. She whispered her secret code into the phone.

"Yes. Get here quickly we haven't left dock yet. Okay. Out." She clicked off the phone. "They'll be here in 25 minutes. It's a bigger ship and we'll be better outfitted to pursue and rescue Jack."

Pin scratched his head. Immaculata started tidying up, despite being told they wouldn't stay on the tug long.

"I suppose it wouldn't hurt to wait," Pin said.

Zero-One nodded. "They are still in the Kuiper Ring. From what I can gather, they are at a standoff, but we should go as soon as we have your ship. I agree that this tug is not a worthy vessel for long distances, but it actually has enough food, water and fuel to get us there and back. The Ramjet can support a large colony despite the fact that it is not a Fullerene vessel. I don't need luxuries, but Jack and Jane certainly wouldn't mind being rescued by one of your abundant colony ships."

"Yes. Jack will like my digs. I just hope Henri doesn't think he can shoot at me. I have more fire power than all of the Sol sys, let alone Corporation."

"I would hope he wouldn't make that same mistake again," Zero-One said. "It appears he blew off his leg when he nearly killed Jack and me and killed the Green candidate.

Maelstrom's big goons shook Sunny out of her sleep. Maelstrom stood at the door, grinning maliciously. She screamed, but it was too late. They grabbed her and picked her up. One of the robots covered her mouth.

"I wasn't finished killing you."

Sunny struggled, her screams stifled, and Maelstrom gestured. The robot removed its hand from her mouth.

"I wasn't finished killing you, either," she said.

"Well, I guess I have the upper hand this time. Your hero is a Zero. Pretty soon I'll have him too. I think I'll just play with you and Rappel and the baby and then let you watch me kill them all. You'll be the last." Maelstrom gestured again with a sour look on his face and a leering gleam in his eye.

The robot placed a rag over her mouth. Sunny tried not to breathe but eventually she had to gasp and when she did everything went black.

Hildy, Zero-One, Magdalena and Immaculata boarded Hildy's luxury vessel. Hildy didn't notice anything wrong at first until she heard the baby crying. Then from out of the galley Byron emerged carrying Loon-Earth in Dao's basket. Maelstrom's robot goons pushed Rappel forward and just behind them Maelstrom emerged.

Hildy tried to turn and run, but more goons appeared behind them. Somehow they'd not only boarded the tug from the dock and pushed the five of them back into her luxury vehicle; they'd also gained access to her yacht.

Another goon carried an unconscious Sunny in and laid her on a couch. Pin was brought in struggling against two robot thugs.

"Cut it out or I'll have my people kill Dao, too. I left her with your babies safe and sound. Ask Sunny. Oh, sorry, she's unconscious. Ask Rappel."

Pin looked at Rappel and she nodded. Maelstrom had left Dao in the nanny robot room with her gaggle of children and as far as she knew he hadn't found Isa.

Jack Cluewitt and the Imbrium Basin Murders   Ruth J. Burroughs

"I thought getting Loon-Earth would make good leverage," Maelstrom said. "Give Rappel that baby so she can quiet him down. That's better. Henri will finally get back his army of robots."

⚛

Maelstrom's face appeared on the hologram in the control room of Oort Explore-bot One.

"Hello, Jack. I thought you might want to ask Peg to turn that boat around, seeing's how I have your girlfriend and your kid." Behind him Rappel nursed Loon-Earth.

Jack stood in front of the screen. How had he known which ship? "You can't chase us in a Fullerene and you won't risk shooting our ships with Henri's INC ships, or you'll lose the Cold Plasma drives you so desperately want. How do you expect to keep up with us?"

"I don't. You'll board Hildy's little luxury yacht and flit around the solar system with your two girlfriends, your double sexed baby and your little canine butler and your artist maid here. Cadaver City was never headed back to Earth-space. We've been on our way after you all along. I'll take those ships and those robots and lead them back to the Ring of Stones where they belong, guarding the Earth from stray comets and asteroids."

Jack's face turned red. He hadn't met his own child yet and he didn't know it was double sexed. This was not uncommon in space. Stranger things than that happened.

"Oh. I'm sorry Jack. You haven't met your little one yet, Loon-Earth Poisson Cluewitt. Or should I say Loon-Earth Weiss-Monaghan? Oh, there, aren't we a proud grandma and grandpa?" Maelstrom grabbed Loon-Earth out of Rappel's arms.

He bounced the baby up and down with practiced ease. "What's the matter, Jack? Didn't you know I was a father? A rather good one too? I had to watch my son, daughter, and my wife, die slowly . . . in Cannibal Alley." A sob tore out of his throat.

Maelstrom removed the blanket and held little Loon-Earth up to the camera. "See that, Jack. You have a little boy, and he's also a little girl."

Jack didn't say anything. He froze in place, a small tear rested on the corner of his eye, but he dare not move.

Maelstrom sighed, frustrated. He brought the baby back to Rappel and threw the blanket at her.

"You've got one hour." Maelstrom shut down the camera and the screen went blank.

Jack sagged. He stumbled, and Jane grabbed him and helped him to a chair. He burst out crying. It was too much, the memories of his birth parents sending him out into the Ring of Stones in order to save him and now his own child in grave danger. A child he hadn't even held. All this time he thought he'd been abandoned. All this time he thought everyone in his life would abandon him, so he abandoned them first. If only they'd said something to him. Told him how much they cared. He couldn't read their minds. Something like that would make a huge difference in how he'd led his life up until now. If only. But he couldn't go back and change the past. Here they were so proud of him and he'd failed them. He couldn't even solve the Green Police murders on the Moon.

Someone held him as he sobbed. "It's ok, son. We'll save your girlfriends, Hildy and Rappel, and your baby Loon-Earth." It was Ruad. "We'll do whatever it takes."

Peg threw her hands up in frustration and paced the floor. "I don't know how Maelstrom could possibly have known we were on this ship. All the call signatures are down and I had the designations on the hulls painted over."

"Someone must have told them, someone on board our ship. He's going to kill us," Jazmin said.

"Henri won't shoot directly on this ship with his own daughter aboard, dear; even as angry as he is at you right now, though he might want to shoot me," Peg said.

"I know, Mom. Nothing like the ex-spouse wars to keep you on your toes. But don't underestimate Maelstrom. He's a tool and he's already tortured and beaten Sunny and was ready to kill her so Mother only knows what he'll do to Rappel and Hildy and the baby."

"Zero-One is there. He'll take care of them," Jack said, still trying to recover.

Ruad handed him a handkerchief and Jack blew his nose into it. "Don't feel bad about crying. Celtic men cry."

Jack Cluewitt and the Imbrium Basin Murders   Ruth J. Burroughs

Jack shrugged, embarrassed again. "Nothing like having your parents on the case to keep you humble."

Peg rubbed her temples. "We have to negotiate some kind of deal with them. But we need a plan."

Ken Mesersmith put his finger to his lips and shushed her. "We should go talk in private, Peg. There are too many ears to the wall here. Sergeant Allen, come with us. We'll go talk in the war room."

Ken meant the galley bathroom. It was the only place that didn't have cameras and was soundproofed. Jack and Jane squeezed in, along with Sergeant Allen Ian Mitchell. His troops called him Al Ian or Sarge Alien. There wasn't room for anyone else to fit in the small confines, so it was just the five of them.

Peg sat on one of the covered toilets, looking uncomfortable. It was a big bathroom by spaceship standards, but a small one by colonial ship standards, and Peg was used to bigger bathrooms. It had Velcro straps for the foot stirrups and the quintessential suction seat.

"What the heck are we going to do?" Jane asked as she squeezed in alongside Jack and Sergeant Allen.

Peg shrugged. "We can't leave with those on board who don't want to go into deep space, but those we do leave will definitely be under arrest and Mother only knows what Henri and Maelstrom would do to you, plus there are spies on board."

"Maybe there's only one spy, Peg. That's all Maelstrom needs is one, and I'm having my people check everyone's background a second time. Not that they weren't thoroughly screened originally," Sergeant Allen said.

"You say these robots running your ships are all programmed for the deep space journey and are all loyal to you, right?" Jack asked.

"That's right," Peg replied.

Jack placed his foot on one of the covered toilets, trying to get comfortable. "Well, we have to deal in order to get my family back. The only way I can do that is pretend to place Peg under arrest. There is no way Maelstrom is going to believe you'd go willingly back to Earth space. Once I have my family back to Mars or Earth-Moon we can arrest Maelstrom and your robots can take back the ships, and you can prepare for your deep space mission."

237

"That's a nice fantasy, Jack but once Henri has my robots he'll rebuild them for the Shepherd Program. They'll be back to basically policing the orbits between the Ring of Stones and Earth-Moon system. He'll militarize my specially powered commercial and private Green ships and have them managed by International Space Corporation."

Jane shook her head, "You don't know that for sure. Maelstrom is Green Party. He's going to use those INC ships for the Green cause just like you've always wanted. He won't let Henri weaponize the ships. Maelstrom's crazy but he hates bullets and bombs."

Peg wanted to pace; it helped her think. "Maelstrom is a sick bastard. Even if your plan worked, Henri knows I wouldn't go back to Earth without a fight."

"Then arrest me when I try to arrest you," Jack said, "and do it in front of the camera. It's the only way to get Maelstrom to believe I did everything to save my family. Otherwise, otherwise . . ."

"Now, that sounds like a believable plan, Jack," Peg said, "But Maelstrom will still threaten your family. I have to make a deal with Henri. I'll ask him for three of my golden rocket ships, the colonists and a hundred robots. He can take back the nine hundred robots and my personal fleet of Oort-bot ships in return for your family. That way he'll think we're trying to negotiate. Once I tell one robot the plan, all of them will know and they can reverse course back to the Oort cloud on command before they're reprogrammed."

Sergeant Allen shook his head, "No. He'll demand you turn off your robots at best or reprogram them before we head back into short solar orbit. You'll have to agree, and you'll have to have a counter program that can keep his program from reprogramming the robots, unless he's thought of that, too. Like you said, he's always ahead of you."

"You're good, Allen. I don't think he's thought of that, and it's our best option on short notice. I'm going now to tell the robots of our plan. They only have an hour to prepare for pretending to be shut down and being reprogrammed with his INC Shepherd Programs. Hash out how it goes down in the core command center. I'll meet you all there."

Peg got up and left. Ken filed out behind her and Sergeant Allen went next.

Jack rubbed the pale scars on his face. "I hope this plan works, Indigo."

She put her arm around his waist and squeezed him, "It dang well better partner or we aren't getting those gold shields you promised me."

Oort Explore-bot One
Chapter Nineteen

Brick Cardigan's third bullet still stumbled and tumbled in space, gaining even more velocity. For years it never strayed near any ships or Fullerenes, even as new and ever more capacious Fullerenes were being built. It was just another piece of space junk that no one had yet caught. And when you do catch one it's often the way Maelstrom's family had caught them. Deadly and painful.

Peg stood with her arms across her chest on the deck of the command center. Sergeant Allen's people hadn't found any good information he could discredit any of the colonists with, so they didn't have their spy. Peg had to inform the Green robots of their plan so the four of them, Jane, Ken, Jack, Allen and his people planned to look disorganized and nervous to hopefully throw off the spy. It was a good plan. Henri and Maelstrom's hubris would get the better of them.

She paced worriedly back and forth. This was not an act. She had no idea how it would play out because Maelstrom was a wildcard. The nervousness act Jane had whispered to her to play she did not have to pretend.

✖

The Waltz was too distracted by Sally S. Queue to pay much attention to the crew on the deck of the Core Command Center. His secret agent emissary training kept his brain honed for every step, nuance, twitch and breath of everyone in the room, measuring their strengths and speed and who he should kill first. But no one had planned on Sally being there, and Sally was sucking away all his attention. Her long legs crossed and that nervous pumping up and down she did with her high-heeled foot drove him crazy. Her silky lavender skirt hiked up almost to her matching

Jack Cluewitt and the Imbrium Basin Murders   Ruth J. Burroughs

panties. He had to ask her later where she bought the panties, but for now all he could do was not drool.

⨳

Aboard the Celestial Raygun, Hildy's luxury yacht, Henri and Maelstrom stood by Hildy's white grand piano whispering heatedly, deep in conversation. Pin, Immaculata, Zero-One, Magdalena, Rappel and Hildy sat on couches surrounded by Maelstrom's goons and robots. Sunny slowly came to on a white chaise lounge. The two men's conversation got louder and louder. Pin gave her some of the water the goons had handed out.

"I won't shoot them, Maelstrom. We've been down that road before. The blowback will just come back on us. I won't risk that again."

"You won't have to, Henri. I'm taking them down with the Jovian water that I've programmed. Once Peg gives her robots the programmed-vials they'll follow me. They'll obey all my orders. Zero-One and these ladies have all been drinking it this past hour."

Hildy spit out the water she'd just been drinking. She didn't feel anything unusual, but she'd been drinking Jovian water all her life and never had the visions. It was water from the ice of Europa of course, but everyone called it Jupiter dreams. It was the nano programs she didn't want to drink. She was a Natural and didn't want any chemical sized bots in her body.

"I need an antidote, Henri. I'm a legal Natural. I won't have nanobots in my body without my choosing to."

"Don't worry, Hildy. I only laced the robots' juice with nanobots. All you got was Jovian water."

Zero-One said nothing, nor did Immaculata.

"Soon Zero-One will belong to me. He'll be my butler, and Immaculata will be my maid. All the robots will belong to me and the nano program I've allowed into my body. Otherwise how can I rule the solar system? I've already decided that this is the only way I can control what happens, by becoming a Genetically Modified Human. No more stray missiles can doom poor miner families. Jack and his family can go on solving murders, but only if they tow the Green line,

241

Jack Cluewitt and the Imbrium Basin Murders   Ruth J. Burroughs

as you all will. Rappel, whom I respect greatly for catching organ thieves, will go on catching them."

Henri nodded in agreement. "Of course, Maelstrom. That was what this was all about. Making sure that what happened to you and your family in Cannibal Alley never happens again."

It dawned on everyone what Maelstrom had done to his family in order to survive. Tears came to Maelstrom's eyes as he remembered, his children having to eat their mother.

Hildy wiped her ruby red lips with a silk handkerchief for the millionth time, trying to get the Jovian juice off. "I'm sorry for what happened to your family Maelstrom, but that means you're the one who poisoned my Sally S. Queue with reprogramming nano-bots, and forced her to kill the Green Policewoman."

"The Green Policewoman had a laser gun. She would have killed your precious Sally if it weren't for me."

"Yes. But Sally is a robot, Maelstrom. She's not even alive. Why the twins? Why kill them?"

"They were already dead. Their heart was dying and they didn't want to upgrade cybernetically or in any way shape or form. I figured their sacrifice as martyrs for the Green cause was noble. And I didn't really kill them. I mean Sally didn't. Keith killed Lee, thereby committing suicide and Jack was in the way. I needed the book. I thought I could get the book and frame him for the murders. In the end I'm glad I didn't have to kill him too, because like me, he doesn't believe in guns and bombs."

Hildy shook her head. "Does anyone want tequila chasers to wash out the Jupiter dreams?"

Magdalena, Pin and Sunny raised their hands and nodded in the affirmative. Rappel, who was nursing Loon-Earth again, after he'd woken from a nap, shook her head.

Hildy snapped her fingers and one of her robots went for the liquor cabinet, but one of Maelstrom's goons stopped it. Henri waved it off.

"Let them have liquor. As a matter of fact break out the champagne. You deserve it, Maelstrom."

Zero-One was allowed to get the champagne and tequila and serve it. Hildy and Maddie downed shots of tequila. Henry and Maelstrom sipped their champagne. Sunny and Pin were fighting over the rest of the bottle of tequila. Maelstrom sat down next to Rappel. She put her baby back in its cradle and crossed her legs, one of her grasshopper hologram tattoos flashed. He swatted her foot.

"Time's almost up for your lover. Hope he does right by you. Otherwise, I'll start cutting your fingers off and sending them to him. I'll start with your pinky finger so you can look more the part; your little Yakuza undercover act. If you like, you can always grow another."

The hologram activated on the deck of the Core Command Center. This time Henri Vasquez appeared on the screen. He also appeared a little drunk.

"Cheers, my little Perigwin falcon, who changed her name back to Cardillo. Have you made your decision?"

"Are you drunk?" Peg was truly flabbergasted. He was getting drunk while she was having a nervous breakdown. Their marriage together flashed before her eyes. She sighed.

"Zero-One, go make some coffee." Henri seemed to sober up a bit. "Sorry, Peck. We were celebrating. No matter what you decide it has to be for the good of all. We've got you stuck between an asteroid and a hard place."

"More like we're stuck between some comets and your thick skull. So you're right there, it's a really hard place." Peg placed her hand on her hips.

"Oooo, she got you there, bud," Jack said coming into the camera view.

Henri was not amused. Zero-One handed him a hot coffee, ever the obedient butler. Henri sipped it.

"Well . . . ? When can we board?"

Peg grimaced. "I want the three main ships, the colonists and a hundred robots. You can take back the nine hundred other robots and ships in return for Jack's family."

"You know I can't go for that, my little peccadillo."

"I'm not going back, Henri." She hated it when he called her that. She didn't used to.

"Maelstrom is going to cut off Rappel's pinky finger. I won't be able to stop him. He doesn't negotiate. He wants her to look her Yakuza part." He took another sip of coffee.

"Three ships . . ."

"I can't, Peg."

Jack Cluewitt and the Imbrium Basin Murders   Ruth J. Burroughs

"Two ships . . ."

Maelstrom picked up a pair of plant cutters and placed the cutting edges against Rappel's pinky finger, ready to cut.

"Perigwin Cardillo, I'm placing you under arrest for violating half a dozen federal INC laws."

"Jack? You're a homicide detective. You can't do that."

"I'm not letting my wife, I mean Rappel get her finger cut off. I want my family back intact and if that means making a deal with these devils, well . . ."

Jack grabbed her and was placing cuffs on her, but two robots grabbed him before he could cuff her.

Jack fought against the robots, who had grabbed his arms. "Stand down. I have jurisdiction here. Jane?"

Jane stood up and started her boxing jumps and air jabs, getting ready to come at the two robots that had Jack.

Maelstrom looked absolutely gleeful when he spoke, "Awww . . . now isn't that sweet? Friends arresting friends. No fighting, kids. In other words, don't damage the merchandise. I need those robots."

Jane moved in and took the attention away from one of Jack's captors and more robots started filing into the Command Center.

After a brief struggle the robots got hold of Jack and Jane, but she got a few punches in first.

"Sorry, Henri," Peg said, "You do what you want. You're not getting this fleet of ships or robots and you're not going to reprogram any one of them. My offer is rescinded."

Maelstrom removed the shears from Rappel's pinky finger and waved it in front of the camera, opening and closing the blades he sang in a sing-song voice.

"I am going to cut her. I am going to cut her." He then placed them back on her little finger and commenced squeezing. Rappel screamed. The baby woke and started crying.

"Now, see what you've gone and done?" Henri said.

Jack struggled, sincerely trying to kick at Peg.

Vinny the Waltz, leapt out of his seat and grabbed a hold of Peg Cardillo's throat. "Let those two go. This woman is under arrest. I'm a federal agent." He flashed his badge with his free hand, stuffed it back in the pocket and pulled out a pair of cuffs and snapped them on Peg's wrists. Vinny

244

Jack Cluewitt and the Imbrium Basin Murders   Ruth J. Burroughs

held Peg in a vice-like grip and threatened to break her neck. Peg's robots let go of Jack and Jane.

"Shut that baby up," Maelstrom said, removing the cutters from her finger. Rappel grabbed the tequila from Pin and poured it on her gash, then wrapped it in a diaper. It was a deep cut, but hadn't touched the muscle. She grabbed Loon-Earth out of the crib and rocked him-her to sleep, cooing and trying not to cry.

"Don't come close or I'll break her neck," Vinny the Waltz said. Peg's robots backed off.

Vinny saw a flash of lavender before her leg came sailing up at his head. Sally, the beautiful S. Queue was trying to kick him. He could break her legs with his big ham hands but she was a robot and someday hopefully, his girlfriend. He moved with her as though in a waltz. He let go of Peg in one impossibly swift motion and grabbed Sally's foot and spun her around. No one would have thought such a big guy could move so fast and with such agility. He almost had a knife to her throat, but she spun limberly out from his grasp and sent a back spinning roundhouse right into his gut. He blocked too late, but moved with the kick and came back at her with a left to her chin. She took it full in the chin, but being a robot it only spun her around again instead of knocking her out.

Peg was motioning for her robots to get the cuffs off her. Vinny didn't miss that. He grabbed her again and held on, all the while fending off Sally S. Queue, dance-fighting with both women.

"I could use some help here, Jack. Sally's a killer. Worth five of me," Vinny yelled.

Jane stepped in and gave Sally a knock-out punch, and for a minute the robot was out. Jack took advantage and handcuffed her to a console's table legs that were molded from the floor of the deck.

"I don't understand, Hildy. Isn't that your robot?" Maelstrom said.

"Yes, Sally is my robot."

"Then why did she attack my agent?"

"Because he was trying to hurt one of Jack's friends. I ordered her to protect Jack and his friends."

"Well, when she comes to, un-order it, or I'll cut off Rappel's finger and that's just for starters."

245

Jack Cluewitt and the Imbrium Basin Murders Ruth J. Burroughs

"I can do that," Hildy said.

"Vinny, babe. Now that's why they call you the Waltz." Maelstrom grinned. He handed the cutters to one of his robots. "Good job. Order those robots to stand down and prepare for the shepherd program vials. They will be reprogrammed from exploring the Oort cloud and deep space to protecting Earth from asteroids and comets and enforcing the Green Party Laws, all without having to rebuild their built in programming."

"You heard him, Peg. You've broken a dozen federal laws stealing these ships." Henri looked fully sober and set down his coffee.

"They were mine," Peg said.

"Until your grant ran out. Now they're the property of Corporation. Don't worry, honey your Green Party will run the show. Maelstrom has no problem using the military, torture or any other device to achieve his goal for the greater good of all."

"That's right," Maelstrom confirmed.

"I won't do it," Peg said.

Sally started to come to. Jane punched her again. "You can order it to stand down, after I get all her limbs handcuffed," Jane said and Hildy nodded. Sally could write nice metaphoric poetry, but she took all her orders literally.

Vinny pulled a bomb out of his suit pocket. He liked Jane, despite the fact that she kept knocking out his future girlfriend. Being that Sally was a robot she would recover from the jaw breaking punches quickly and painlessly, but she'd try her best to fulfill her orders, her programming.

"This is a specially made electro-magnetic device. It will take out the robots without taking out the drive and camera systems on deck here. Well, I hope it won't. I made it from scratch. So, if these robots come near me or don't turn themselves off I will let this bomb go off and their GEM cell drives will be fried. For all intents and purposes they'll be dead. Even if you left backups of your memories on other GEM cell drives, the EM device could fry those, too."

"You're bluffing, Vinny" Peg said.

"No. That I'm not. If you don't order them to shut off in three seconds, I will detonate this bomb. Three . . . two . . ."

"Shut down. All of you shut down." Peg collapsed.

Jack Cluewitt and the Imbrium Basin Murders   Ruth J. Burroughs

"I'm sending the Jovian water over with nano program to overwrite yours," Maelstrom said, "When they're turned back on they must drink the water."

⚔

The Oort Explore-bot One and all its crew were escorted toward shorter orbit with Cadaver Facility Fullerene colony near Saturn. Then it would take them back toward JoMars in even lower solar orbit. It was difficult to move so large a colony from the longest or tallest orbit Cadaver City had ever traveled out from Earth-Moon, but with the secret fuel it traveled faster.

In the brig, sitting on a cot with her head in her hands, Peg felt the pull of the Oort clouds and the yearning to explore deep space scream from every cell in her body. Most people were afraid of the dark and the cold. She lived for it. Her plan hadn't worked, but at least he wouldn't melt down her robots and rebuild them. The nano-juice had overwritten her Green programs inside the robot brains. Her new jack-ware in her brain sensed the robots moods.

Immaculata was doing EVA; even though she was just a robot, she wore a space suit, so as not to be radioactive on her return to living quarters. They had her restore the Corporation logos and get rid of the fake signs. It was a sad day.

Peg's ships and her robots were programmed for exploring, not shepherding. She had felt their excitement for exploring through her own biochip and now it was filled with sadness, not unlike her own. She stood up and grabbed the bars of her cell and looked out of the smart glass at the receding fields of diamond-like glinting comets of water ice.

⚔

Loon-Earth and Rappel stayed deep near the core of Celestial Raygun Fullerene, far from radiation, too. Sally stayed with Hildy. Vincent didn't have the money to buy her, but Henri was trying to get money from INC to make her an emissary. She wrote her own poetry and was far more creative than Hildy. Hildy was all business. Zero-One was still Zero-One, but he only took orders from Maelstrom,

247

and/or Immaculata. When they got to Saturn space and Cadaver City Henri let Jazmin go back to living with Celia, though she protested. He basically had to arrest her to get her to go back. Ruad and Weather lived nearby.

Jack held Loon-Earth. He traveled back to Saturn space with Rappel, Loon-Earth and Hildy in her luxury yacht, along with Vincent Walskiwhitz and Sally Solilo Queue. It was a touchy situation having his ex-girlfriend and his current girlfriend living together even for a few weeks, but he did his best. Once they drew near Saturn, Maelstrom ordered Jack, Rappel and Loon-Earth back on board his Fullerene. It became clear to them that he was the one who actually owned it and not Henri. He was far more powerful than he'd pretended. Rappel and Jack watched all of Peg's robots be forced to take the Jovian water dosed with the nano reprogramming software that installed Maelstrom's laws, thoughts and feelings. After that, they took orders from Henri and Maelstrom. The robots seemed to walk slower and the glint in their eyes was gone. Vincent and Sally were an item.

It was at least a month before they'd reach JoMars-Space and five more before they'd get back to Earth. Rappel wanted to raise Loon-Earth on the Moon with Organdy or on Mars with her parents. Jack had no problem with either. The judge took their matter in private and kept their records sealed, but was saying they had to get a robot nanny because neither was good parenting material, her, with her undercover work, and him, with his homicide investigations. In the meantime Zero-One was a certified nanny bot, so he had legal custody of the child over Jack and Rappel. That was the law. If anything happened to Zero-One another nanny bot would be found for Jack and Rappel. Rappel named Organdy as the godfather of the child. But Maelstrom had taken a liking to the child and pursued custody since he felt he owned Zero-One already. He was pressuring Rappel and Jack to sign over Zero-One and their child, but they just ignored him. Rappel was still nursing, and she was an organ enforcement agent. They knew he could make them disappear though. So they didn't argue with him. They just said the child needs to be nursed first. At least he wasn't trying to have them sliced and diced for organs because of his insanity, due to what he'd done to his family and his insane vegetarian revenge on meat-eaters.

Loon-Earth was eating a little now and Jack was trying to feed him, but the baby liked getting it all over her-his face, hands, bib and baby chair tray.

A hologram activated, "Jack, I need you and Jane. Where's Rappel?" Maelstrom said.

"She's taking a nap."

"Leave Loon-Earth with a nanny bot and wake Rappel. Meet me at the command core."

He logged out.

A certified nanny bot lived with Rappel and Jack. He was relieved not to have to live with Hildy and Rappel together all the way back to Earth-Moon and was glad to have left her luxury yacht, despite its amenities when they'd finally arrived at Cadaver City. Hildy was very sad when they left. She seemed to want to be the one who'd carried his baby. They had a long private talk. He still felt deeply for her.

He woke Rappel. He regretted having to leave Loon-Earth. She-he was such a joy. Her-his blue eyes smiled and she laughed often, like the world was the funniest place. He-she had curly black hair. The doctor said she-he could have children if he-she wanted, either by impregnating or becoming impregnated. Jack was fascinated by that. He didn't know that was possible. Rappel was just as thrilled. She was far more athletic than Jack and would be taking Loon-Earth to all the ballgames. Jack didn't care much for sports. He liked reading, art and movies. Jane and Rappel were baffled at that. A guy who was not into watching sports. Jack handed the baby to his-her favorite nanny bot and took Rappel's hand. They didn't want to leave Loon-Earth behind, but orders were orders.

Everyone was gathered in the galley of the deck of the command core center of Cadaver City, anyone who mattered to Maelstrom anyway.

From what Jack could gather, the Green Party ships and Corporation troop ships were docked on the hull of

Jack Cluewitt and the Imbrium Basin Murders   Ruth J. Burroughs

VAQ-ORE Fullerene while another Fullerene called First Farm, because it was the first one built, orbited close.

Weather, Ruad, Ken, Peg, Magdalena, Pin, Sunny, Hildy, Sally, Vincent, Rappel, Jane, Henri and Jack were all brought together for some crazy reason of Maelstrom's. Why they were gathered in the Cadaver City's Command Core cafeteria was a question only Maelstrom could answer.

Jack wondered where Zero-One and Immaculata were.

"Well, the time has come," Maelstrom said.

"What's going on?" Henri asked.

"First, we have supper."

It was buffet style. Pin came up to Jack with an empty tray.

"I bet you think you're the hero in all this," Pin said to Jack, angrily. Pin was very short, even for a Vietnamese person. Jack and Jane told him that he and Magdalena should take the case for them, to protect Rappel's identity. Jack knew the JoMars PD had stuck him with the biggest girl they could find for a partner for him as a department-wide joke and to bring out his insecurities, but the two made a great team, and Jack thought they were both competent despite Maddie's black market organ connections. He'd seen their files. They closed more cases than anyone in their department, and he heard through the snitch grapevine that they weren't the framing kind of cops. Not easy to be honest in space. Most cops played judge, jury and executioner if they thought you were a violent felon, not willing to risk a whole colony for one.

"How can I think that, Pin? We can't even arrest Maelstrom for all his crimes. He's a homicidal maniac, and I let him go so he wouldn't hurt Rappel. I failed."

"Yeah, sure. You think because you're so tall and handsome you're the hero in all this." Pin looked up at him, angrily.

"Why would you even say that?"

"Because, I'm the short Vietnamese guy, that's why and you're the tall white, Anglo-Saxon American, hero-looking guy."

"Well, my adopted parents are Anglo-Saxon or maybe Dutch, but apparently I am Jewish and Irish if that makes you feel better, and I have a scar on my face so maybe I'm the bad guy."

Jack Cluewitt and the Imbrium Basin Murders   Ruth J. Burroughs

"Well, you're not, you know."

"Not what?"

"The hero in all this."

"Look, Pin. If you can get us out of this and arrest Maelstrom, you're my hero, okay? I don't care how tall you aren't."

Pin, scowled. He punched Jack in the arm. "You're not so bad, Jack." Pin walked away and got in line for some grub.

Just about everyone ate vegetarian. Jack, Jane and Rappel enjoyed some bugs and some sushi. Henri had a steak and Pin and Magdalena had thinly sliced meat and vegetables in a Vietnamese dish.

"We're guests of the First Farm, which was of course the first agricultural facility built for space citizens. First Farm of Five Hundred. There are only three hundred and eighty farms left today. Many were lost to accidents and disease. Some were disassembled and some are believed to have been stolen. We'll be eating our desserts on First Farm. Anyone who likes may also have after dinner drinks as well," Maelstrom said.

"I don't need to be involved in all this, Maelstrom . . ."

"Oh, no, Henri. You certainly must go." Maelstrom grinned. Henri did not look pleased, but forced himself to smile.

"Can Rappel stay here on Cadaver City? She's still nursing."

"No, Jack," Maelstrom said, pleasantly, "I'm so glad you're concerned about radiation, but I've taken every precaution to ensure all of your safety. You're wearing state of the art space suits with high grade nano-poly-fibers."

"Can we get some of these for the department?" Jane asked.

"Sure, if they consider going vegetarian," Maelstrom replied.

First Farms was a huge place. The tour director was a friendly British chap, by the name of Sten Harrington. They followed behind him as he showed them tank after tank of fishes, each in a different gestation stage being raised for the Erthworlds with oceans. Whales, lobsters, octopuses, bass, carp, swordfish, tuna, yellow tail, mackerel, and many others. Jack wondered where Zero-One had gotten to

251

as they passed the dripping tanks that smelled of seaweed and saltwater.

They stood on a platform overlooking the interior surface of First Farm's Fullerene and what appeared to be grazing animals. Everyone looked on in awe at the enormity of it.

Immaculata and Zero-One joined them with half a dozen First Farm robots, gathered around the director, Sten Harrington.

"What's all this?" Sten asked.

"You're going to show my friends here the real facility. I've reprogrammed your robots with a Green Party priority and you're now all under arrest here. INC and the Green Party Police are taking control of this facility. You can check your suit com. They're on their way now and they will receive no resistance because, while you were giving us the tour, my faithful robots Zero-One and Immaculata have reprogrammed every AI on board."

"Urrr . . . Isn't that illegal?" Sten asked.

"If it is, that can be changed too," Maelstrom said and motioned them onwards. Sten led the way into the dank depths of the real facility. Maelstrom ordered him to turn off the fake pastures.

The first stalls were filled with pink milking hairless cows, stuck with tubes going in one end and out the other. One was filling her with food, another with sperm and other tubes milked what was left of this cycle's mammary glands. She moaned, in the dim light. From out of her teats came millions of gallons of milk and cheese and when she was too old her body would be ripped apart by the meat machines. If she were lucky she'd be dead or unconscious first, but that didn't always happen.

Then the next corridor was full of pigs. Only Jack was surprised to see that most of them were there only for their organs. They were all connected to tubes, like the cows; human-like skin, organs and ears were harvested from these.

Despite the tubes, the stench was horrible. Hildy, Rappel and Sunny were throwing up. Magdalena lit a zeegarette, despite the signs and the dangers. Pin took a swig of whiskey and passed it to Henri.

Maelstrom showed them how the fish were killed. Henri looked thoroughly pissed off. He didn't seem to care. Jack

Jack Cluewitt and the Imbrium Basin Murders   Ruth J. Burroughs

knew he generally thought animals were put in the universe for people to eat and that was that.

They went to the lambs and calves corridor and then the baby pigs and mothers for bacon and ham facility and then it was Jack's turn to vomit.

"Those who know what goes on inside these facilities call them The Meatballs, instead of Buckminster Fullerene farms, as if you cared," Maelstrom said.

The last corridor opened up and Maelstrom led the way in. Sten looked shocked. Maelstrom gleefully explained why there were humans in here, tubes coming from both ends as they hung from their stalls.

"My solution. For all crimes committed against Mother Earth and her creatures I will be placing people here for an undetermined time. Zero-One, Immaculata, INC and the Green Police have been gathering law breakers for me to this facility, secretly. Here they will serve as organ and skin donors. You can see how well it's going. This one here, prisoner number five, he owns this facility and was a great consumer of meat. It took me a lifetime to track him down. He put all that money he was paid by the wealthy elderly in the retirement Fullerene, to buy First Farm from a pirate. Look. He's making amends now. He's growing three healthy livers. Isn't that sweet? He's so generous. Here, everyone, meet Brick Cardigan also known as my brother, Brick Corrigan. I mean Meat Brick, Brick Meat the gang."

Brick struggled in his chains. He moaned for help. His eyes pleaded.

"Don't worry. Brick is treated humanely. We afford him all the things he afforded his animals. We even pipe in news and entertainment. See?" Maelstrom said and pushed on button on a remote device in his hand. The hologram activated and the news played. Maelstrom pushed the volume down.

Sunny was crying. "How could you?"

"I told you I hunted for this greedy man my whole life. How do you think he got the money to buy a meat organ farm? By killing my wife, my children and all the other families on the freighters. He shot at me three times and he's my half-brother. What kind of family does that to family?"

Henri cleared his throat, "He's the one who stole all the organs and food and why you had to feed your wife to your children in Cannibal Alley?"

"That's right, my dear friend. See, I don't kill you, even though you're a meat eater. I'm a good person. I just need justice. This man destroyed many lives. I'm not talking about the ones who died. I'm talking about the ones who survived. Ruad was there. Of all the people, he should understand. He survived too. If he hadn't eaten his family he'd be dead too."

Sunny sobbed.

"That's okay. They were already dead before Ruad ate them, and Brick's sentence is life. We won't execute him. We're very liberal in that regard. I'm going to pardon you, Sunny. You were one of the first on my list for skin grafts because of your lack of Green Quotas and your penchant for eating fish. Since you didn't get dissected in the Cadaver machine I was going to hook you up with Brick, but I'm so happy right now I'm in a very forgiving mood."

Sunny sobbed and leaned onto Hildy. Hildy and Rappel comforted her.

"Now, stop that. You've been pardoned. Okay, who's next? "

No one said anything.

"Well, I think. As a favor to Henri. Peg and Ken will be hooked up next to Brick. That's for not giving us the Oort Explore-bot ships and robots sooner."

Peg cursed at Maelstrom and tried to kick him as the robots chained her down. Ken struggled to try to save her.

"Don't worry, Peg. Your sentence is much, much shorter than Brick's. Now, the rest of you behave. Why don't we retire for some drinks and ice cream, or cake, or cookies? They all come from this facility. The eggs, milk and cream. You should see the chicken facility. They're all treated humanely now, too." Maelstrom smiled.

In the Farm's command core everyone had lost their appetite, but no one refused to drink.

Jack sat at a table playing with his drink. He wanted to eat some of the ice cream, but he'd lost his appetite after hearing what his biological father had done out in Cannibal Alley. Also, having seen where the ice cream came from . . . They were animals, right? So how would they know the dif-

ference between being robotically inseminated or naturally? Apparently natural insemination was once dangerous
to the agriculture so this awful procedure had continued
into space, despite space cows having smaller legs and no
hooves. Jane, Weather and Ruad sat next to Jack. Hildy
and Rappel were comforting Sunny at seats the next table
over. Henri was pleading with Maelstrom in the corner of
the dining area, perhaps for his life, since he'd eaten the
steak. Pin and Magdalena were both getting sloshed and
were eating the cake and ice cream.

Zero-One and Immaculata stood nearby, awaiting orders.

"Zero-One, Immaculata, I just can't believe you'd do
something like this," Jack whispered.

Jane nodded, her hands crossed over her chest.

"It is what we are programmed to do."

"What could possibly make you do that to a human being, Zero-One?"

"It is the Green Law now, Jack," Immaculata said.

"And, I'm just serving my master," Zero-One replied.

Jack sighed; he rubbed the scar on his face. "But it's
cruel."

"If it's cruel to the humans to be subjected to such a
life, why is it not cruel to the animals?" Immaculata asked.

"We didn't know. I didn't know. Well. I try not to think
about it. I always think some authority is telling them to
run these facilities in a humane fashion. I mean . . . it is the
law to treat these animals humanely before they're butch-
ered. So I just thought they were being treated well."

"Me too," Jane said.

Zero-One shook his head. "Jack, I've nagged you about
your Green quotas since you were knee high and now look
at where all this comes from. You're a glutton."

"True, Zero-One. But doesn't our friendship mean anything to you? You've been eating beef stew since you were
a pup."

"Even robots need fuel, and you designed us to enjoy
eating. Maelstrom is going to change all this."

"How? Is he going to make everyone starve?"

"No. He's going to design animals to be free roaming in
Fullerene forests, not unlike the one in Cadaver City, and
their meat will be used after they die a natural death, due to

255

Jack Cluewitt and the Imbrium Basin Murders   Ruth J. Burroughs

sickness or old age. He's experimenting with the meat tree to make it taste better."

"Shouldn't this have been started long ago?" Jack asked.

"It was," Sten Harrington replied. "But the government took spending away from the projects because this way worked, and since no one complained the meat factories wanted to save money. Every penny. Everyone likes to think meat grows on trees. How do you stop a hundred billion hungry mouths from perpetuating the robot-assembly-line food-processing plant?"

Maelstrom interrupted, "You can't. It's like trying to stop a Tsunami flood tide from reaching the shore. One lone vegetarian cannot stop a billion gluttonous mouths. But you understand, Jack, why I have to do this, right? Why all the bad people have to be punished."

"Yes, Maelstrom. They need to pay for what happened to your wife and children."

"Right, Jack. All of them have to pay." Maelstrom took a long serrated knife out of his pocket and stabbed Ruad in the abdomen and then twisted the knife. Ruad screamed, but grabbed Maelstrom and quickly handcuffed him.

"Got you, you little Green vegetarian son of a bitch," Ruad said and pushed Maelstrom at Jack and collapsed, passing out, onto the deck of the dining room.

"There, Jack. Now see what you'll do to save your dad before he loses that organ I just surgically destroyed. See how devout a Natural you are now."

Jack threw the handcuffed Maelstrom at Jane, "Take him to the brig."

Zero-One stood in the way.

"Get out of the way, Zero-One," Jane said.

"I can't."

"I won't let you take him either," Immaculata said.

Jack picked Ruad up off the floor and placed him on a table. "Zero-One, see what's wrong with my father and repair him."

"That, I can do," Zero-One said. He stepped up to the table and examined Ruad. "It's his liver. He'll need a new one. Brick's clone livers are CHARM. Ruad's immune system would be able to adjust."

"Then do it," Jack said.

Jack Cluewitt and the Imbrium Basin Murders   Ruth J. Burroughs

Zero-One hesitated. Maelstrom nodded and Zero-One leapt to obey. He headed directly to the human organ clone facility where Brick was kept, to fetch one of his livers.

Jack felt like he was selling his soul to save his father. First he'd compromised his integrity to save Rappel and now to save his father. But that Brick was a devil. Should he put a devil's liver in his father?

The Meat Factory
Chapter Twenty

Overrun with Maelstrom's Green robots, which all seemed to have gained back that glint in their eyes and in their step, the animals in the Meat factory were freed from their pens and replaced by Green Law-breaking criminals. Jack was forced to unlock the cuffs. First Maelstrom directed his robots to build pasture rooms for the cows to graze naturally along the inner walls of the Fullerene. The cows didn't walk. They crawled, since they didn't have much in the way of legs below the knees. The pasture would be supplemented with grain. Only natural death animals would be killed, according to Maelstrom's orders. And they could procreate naturally as well, which would keep up the meat quota. He'd also grow extra limbs on them in case they didn't die quickly enough. He filled the stalls with humans for organ cloning instead. Screams echoed down the corridor into the dining area as their organs started the cloning process.

Henri fumed. First his wife Celia wanted him to quit smoking, then she wanted him to quit drinking and now Maelstrom wanted him to quit eating meat. He bought her the best fur coats, too. It could get cold out here in deep space; an animal coat was one of the warmest things to snuggle in. Animals were for eating. They were being bred as dumb as possible. At least Maelstrom hadn't hooked him up like Brick to the machines.

Zero-One was queued up to the surgical satellite five hours into surgery with assistance from doctors all over the JoMars-Net and was arm-deep in Ruad's torso, putting in the new liver. He didn't sweat. He wasn't nervous. Jack and Weather paced the dining room. Indigo Jane shadow-boxed in the corner, and Pin and Magdalena were sleeping.

Hildy and Rappel were eating cake and ice cream and Loon-Earth was asleep in a crib. Immaculata cleaned the tables and floors. She couldn't help it.

Maelstrom was off ordering more changes to the Meat farms' structure and overseeing the intake of more prisoners from all over the Ring of Stones.

This wasn't Henri's dream. He needed these robots to police the system and blow up asteroids and comets or shepherd them to a safe area for blowing up. They were being wasted here, but he knew he couldn't push Maelstrom. Not now. This was the happiest he'd ever seen the man. In time he'd get his INC ships back and maybe even some of Peg's ships and robots, now that they were controlled by Maelstrom, even if that meant being another one of Maelstrom's henchmen.

When the surgery was complete, Zero-One looked exhausted. Green robots picked up the table on which Ruad lay to take out of the dining room.

"Where do you think you're going with that?" Jack said.

"Maelstrom's orders. Ruad is to go to the infirmary to recover. It's not clean here."

"Oh, yes it is," Immaculata chimed.

The robots carried Ruad toward the door. Jack stepped in their way.

"Don't worry, Jack. I'll go with him." Weather pulled Jack out of the way and took Ruad's hand, "He'll be okay."

Jack watched Weather take his father out of the room. He wanted to ask him about Cannibal Alley, but that had happened before he was born.

Zero-One brought him a cold Ceres ale. Zero-One drank a hot one.

"Look, Jack. If you have a plan. Now's the time."

Jack was surprised. His jaw fell open.

"Well, are you going to drink with that mouth or use it to catch flies?" Zero-One said.

Jack closed his mouth and took a sip of the ale. He set the mug down on the table, but had to pick it up to let Immaculata clean underneath.

259

Jack Cluewitt and the Imbrium Basin Murders   Ruth J. Burroughs

"Urrr . . . I don't have a plan. If we try to escape he'll catch us and you know what he does with criminals. I'm curious. Why are you helping me now? I thought you were re-programmed to serve him."

Zero-One lapped up the warm ale, "I am kind of, sort of. I'm programmed to care about animals. I hate to tell you this, Jack but, you're an animal."

"Umm . . . no. Humans aren't just animals, humans are spiritual beings."

"You had me fooled."

"Ha, ha, ha, ha, ha . . ."

"Well. Maelstrom made a mistake in his program. We're to follow his orders. His orders are to care about animals. To do whatever it takes to make sure of their well-being. The only way to do that is to take complete control over all your affairs. Government. Transportation. Food. Everything."

Gulp.

"I don't think that's a good plan, Zero-One."

"I don't think Maelstrom is going to like it, either. He is so pleased with his punishments. We'll be removing all the humans from their organ clone stalls, but we're going to allow Maelstrom to believe they're still there. We believe Hildy would make the best president, or General Secretary of the Commonwealth, so we're allowing her to be the representative for humans in space. Otherwise all government decisions will be made by robots from now on."

Maelstrom entered the room with a gun on Vinny the Waltz, and Sally S. Queue, the latter of whom was wearing stiletto heels and a blue dress.

"So, thought you could outsmart me, Jack. I thought you might have had some firewalls set up in these bots."

Jack shook his head. They hadn't worked as far as he could tell. "It's all them, Maelstrom."

"Waltz, get the bomb out of the bag."

"I'm not killing my girlfriend, Mael. You're just going to have to shoot me."

Maelstrom pulled the trigger. A bullet splashed through Vinny's lung, in through the front, out through the back and slammed into the wall echoing as it slammed into another wall in the next room. Vinny collapsed.

260

"Guns are illegal in space," Jack said, thinking the bullet could have hit someone or blown up an oxygen tank. A pressurization alarm rang.

Sally sat down and held the sputtering agent, who had a look of absolute shock and dismay on his face.

"No one, no one, no human or robot is taking over anything or turning off any of my human clone factories. Where do you think those lost and stolen ones are? Hidden in the Kuiper Ring is what. Where do you think I get all my illegal organs from? I'm no beginner. I'm the master of human organ engineering. I created chemistry harmonics organ fuser."

He picked up the bag. "There are more of these. I have the detonator. You robots follow my orders. My scientists are mixing up some Ceres water with a new nano program that excludes care of humans from your orders."

Zero-One bounded over to Vincent. Sally applied pressure to the wound.

"He will die if you don't call the med docs."

Maelstrom shrugged. Zero-One attacked Maelstrom.

"Nooooooooo . . ." Jack yelled. He stood up. Maelstrom pushed a button. The bomb exploded. Hildy and Rappel screamed. Pin and Magdalena woke up.

Zero-One and Sally collapsed. Their cyber brains fried. Immaculata, who was almost out of range, went into convulsions.

Jack ran to Zero-One and picked up the limp body of his German shepherd majordomo. Vinny sputtered blood. He crawled over to where Sally had been writhing and held her limp robot body in his weakening arms.

Jack held Zero-One's head to his chest.

"Wake up old boy." Zero-One's head flopped from side to side. Jack choked back a sob.

Sally S. Queue stirred.

"What's this?" Maelstrom said.

"I wasn't sure my homemade bomb would work. I pray to God it doesn't work. My Sally . . ." Vinny's lung collapsed. Sally came to. She took off her leg and threw it at Hildy, then fell dead.

Hildy quickly made some adjustments and fired the Raygun at Maelstrom. The blast hit him and threw him back, burning a hole in his chest. But not enough to kill.

Jack Cluewitt and the Imbrium Basin Murders   Ruth J. Burroughs

Only enough to burn a hole in his protective smart jacket. He ran.

"Hildy, get Vincent some help before he dies," Jack said.

"I can't. I have to go after Maelstrom. This is my fault."

"Immaculata, get Vinny some help. Jane, go with Hildy. I'll cover your backs."

Jane nodded and without a weapon followed Hildy out into the corridor. Immaculata, still convulsing, picked up Vinny the Waltz and carried him to the med center.

He pulled the old puppy brain GEM cell out of his pocket and placed it in the dead robot butler's brain case. At first nothing happened and then a little shiver ran down Zero-One's spine. His eyes blinked open and his tongue lolled out as he started to pant. He barked like a puppy and then jumped up onto Jack, licking him and punching his shoulders with his prehensile paws—all while wagging his tail.

"Give me the anti-psychotic drugs, Zero-One," Jack said, but his majordomo was gone and the robot dog wagged his tail and barked. Jack told the canid to sit and Zero-One did; Jack opened a compartment in the dog's chest and took out the anti-psychotic drugs Pops T. Van de Woestyne had sold him a lifetime ago on Earth. He stuck them in his pocket.

"C'mon, Zero-One." Jack ran toward the corridor through which Maelstrom made his escape; it was a curving corridor. Zero-One bounded after him on all fours. He saw Hildy and Jane in the distance, blocked by a herd of cows at a four-way crossing. Picking up speed, Jack ran up the wall and over the ceiling and landed on the other side, Zero-One following closely at his heels; they both landed on the other side of the stream of cows.

"Back up and get a running start!" Jack yelled over the mooing. Despite their short legs, the cows were still a good five feet from the ground. He didn't wait for the girls to catch up.

He found Maelstrom pushing buttons on a console until he saw Jack and the dog robot coming and he took off with a look of surprise on his face at seeing Zero-One alive and well.

Space gravity didn't make running easy, even when you were used to it. But Maelstrom was thin and wiry and seemed to have a lot of stamina.

If he hadn't freed all the pigs he would have gotten away. The sows stopped him. Jack caught him tripping over them as the robots herded them down another corridor. He hurled himself, but miscalculated. He knocked Maelstrom down, but went spinning farther down the corridor. Maelstrom grabbed him and strong-armed him toward an airlock. They wrestled with each other and for once Jack was glad Rappel had nagged him to exercise. Neither would let go as they grappled. Jack risked taking his hand away and took out the syringe of Varmygdala- Restore and jabbed Maelstrom's arm with it. He jammed one of the neuro chips into the back of Maelstrom's skull, into the jack outlet in the back of his neck.

Maelstrom pushed and kicked Jack into the airlock. Zero-One came running full tilt at Maelstrom and he barely ducked in time as Zero-One flew over him and into the airlock. He locked the door. Within seconds the air depressurizing alarm blared. Jack looked for a suit. None. He climbed into a container and pulled Zero-One in and closed the lid. He heard the bay doors slide open and then the silence of space crashed down on them as the little container shot out into space.

Cold. Dark. Space.

It wasn't even a good canister. It was thick enough, but it was old and he had to hold onto the lid from the inside, but the air was turning quickly into his own exhales of carbon dioxide and it was cold. Fortunately Zero-One's engine was warm and he breathed carbon dioxide and exhaled oxygen but he was also running out of air to breathe. They tumbled in cold space, having no idea where they were going. Jack felt the gold Chinese coin pop off his chest like a suction cup popping off. It tumbled around inside his shirt. They bumped into something. Or something bumped into him. He almost lost the grip on the lid as the container silently bounced and collided, but he could only sense the movement in mild vibrations through his hands, feet and backside. Hardly any sound came to him and he felt a pain in his joints. Suddenly he felt a wash of warmth and pressure as the container tumbled into something and he could hear sound again, banging, scratching and metal screeching.

Knock. Knock, knock.

"Open up, Jack." It sounded like Weather.

Jack let go of the lid. Weather, dressed in a spacesuit helped Zero-One and Jack step out of the container.

"Where are we?"

"You're in a depressurization chamber, but I'm going to pressurize it so you don't get the bends. Stay here. It will take a few minutes. You're in a trash hauling mining Spider. I saw what was going on. The cameras to the cafeteria and the hallways are in the hospital. I told the robots Maelstrom would kill you otherwise so they let me take Charlotte out and she grabbed the canister with her nano-fiber silk and reeled you two in. Ruad is still inside the Farm. Maelstrom might try to kill again. We have to go back."

She hugged him. Jack winced. He handed her the gold coin. She took it in her gloved hand.

"Yes, of course. We have to go back. You're right I think I have the bends."

Weather wheeled Jack and Zero-One on a Gurney into the infirmary back on the Meatball Fullerene and two human doctors took them to the common hyperbaric room. They helped them onto the beds and then exited the room. Weather and the two doctors, a man and woman, watched from a glass window. One of them increased the pressure in the room.

"How are you feeling, old boy?" Jack asked.

"Good, Jack. You look much older than the last time I saw you. Twenty-five years older I'd guess and much taller."

"You can talk?"

"Yes, it took some time for the brain to crystallize."

"Any memories of the last twenty-five years."

"No, sorry Jack."

"Maelstrom fried them with an EM bomb."

Jack imagined the excess inert gases in his and Zero-One's bodies dissipating. Zero-One's body functioned similarly.

"You had an accident." Jack's voice started to sound squeaky and high-pitched, due to the higher air pressurization in the room. "You've been my butler for the past twenty-five years and my crime busting partner for the past five, but you were just killed by an electromagnetic bomb and I happened to be carrying that memory bar of yours because I just met my birth parents who gave you to me. It's a very high-end brain so you should understand all this quite well."

Weather smiled and waved from the other side of the window. The door inside the cubicle opened and Jane walked in, her indigo dreadlocks bouncing. She sat next to his mother with a concerned look on her face.

"You do have a backup brain bar for me don't you?" Zero-One's voice was high pitched too.

"Yes. But it was too dangerous to travel with and have anyone try to access. And streaming sats cause a lot of download and security problems, since you're a detective's majordomo. I have a backup brain of your memories at home on Earth. We always do that when we leave Near-Earth space. This is the farthest we've ever gone. But you'll have lost all your memories of our case this year."

"I'm sure you can get me up to speed, but I doubt I'll be of any use to you in the criminal case right now. Weather and Ruad kept me in a case and turned me on and told me you were gone. They talked to me now and again to remember, but kept me secret."

"I would be crying, but it's really hard to take anything you say seriously with your voice so high-pitched."

"I concur, Jack. If we weren't talking serious business I would be laughing my tail off."

"Which is the reason why we were chasing Maelstrom?"

"Of course. He's an organ dealer and he's kidnapped nursing homes residents and Green Law criminals and stealing their organs and killing them."

"Where is he?"

Jack heard the clicking and whoosh sound of the com being turned on. The doctors were smiling, but not laughing despite Jack and Zero-One's voices sounding like cartoon characters. Weather picked up the microphone.

"He's gotten away. A portion of this Buckminster Fullerene disengaged from the main Fullerene. Some kind of mini

Jack Cluewitt and the Imbrium Basin Murders   Ruth J. Burroughs

Bucky Ball, and it's headed for the Oort Cloud with INC and Peg's Greepol Explore-bots in hot pursuit. Henri says he'll handle it. The arrest and capture. Hildy's taking Sally back to her yacht to install one copy she had left of Sally's old brain. Vincent left the agency and is going to work for her so he can be near Sally. Sally is too expensive, even for the government to buy. It's one of Hildy's high-end robots she only sells to the very elite and rich. Nothing even the Waltz could afford."

"They leave already?" Jack asked. Weather nodded. "Send Hildy a message thanking her for shooting Maelstrom with her Raygun."

"I'll do that, Jack. You two get some rest. I'll bring Rappel to you when you're in the infirmary.

⚔

Zero-One lay curled at the end of Jack's hospital bed. Ruad sat next to the majordomo, playing chess with Jack on the mobile bed tray. Weather had the Chinese coin mounted on a necklace and gave it to Rappel, who was happy to wear it.

Rappel sat in a seat next to the window, feeding Loon-Earth baby food. "I'm getting so used to this I might apply for motherhood."

"It wouldn't suit you," Ruad and Jack said simultaneously. Rappel laughed. Weather and Ruad liked Rappel and wished the two would stay together, but Rappel told them Jack had abandonment issues and Rappel was already with someone else. It was complicated and she could tell they felt a little responsible.

Rappel wondered how transparent she must be with her dedication to her job. Well. She wouldn't mind a nanny bot real soon. Not because she had work to do, though the case was still pending. She would have chased Maelstrom all over the solar system while carrying her baby, but Henri insisted it was a military issue and that Maelstrom was his to pursue and arrest. She wanted a nanny so she could get a break. Raising a child was no walk in the park, despite her thorough martial arts training. Her first priority was to get back to Mars. Show Loon-Earth to her parents and then see what Organdy would think. Would he raise him-her with her and let Jack raise Loon-Earth too? As far as she was concerned they had solved the case even if they hadn't arrested, tried and punished the perpetrator. And soon Henri, along with Peg, and the Explore-bot ships would be rescuing those poor victims from Maelstrom's evil grasp. The only problem was that Sunny was missing.

✖

Jack and Jane returned with Rappel to Cadaver City and started writing up the case against Maelstrom for the Moon City Green Police murders. They figured he'd slipped Sally S. Queue the vial and controlled her mind while she killed the Green Police, though she was not successful in getting the book. Until they went back to Earth-Moon, they couldn't gather evidence against him. Back on the Moon the crime scene was still taped off indefinitely and no one had been allowed out to that portion of the Imbrium Basin Mine where the murders had occurred. Sydney Atrax had been compromised by Maelstrom's nano virus software and was down for a complete wipe. His ninety-five percent arrest ratio in serious question. Despite feeling like a failure, Jack wouldn't be replaced by a robot cop any time soon.

Hildy returned to her yacht with Vincent and Sally. Vinny had a new lung and was retired from the agency. He now worked for Hildy. Jack apologized to Hildy for his transgression that had led to a baby. She forgave him, but Jack had to make sure that Rappel and the baby returned to Mars and/or Earth-Moon space safely.

✖

Maelstrom took Sunny deep into the labyrinths of Cadaver City. He hooked her up to the clone machine in a huge warehouse of other human captives. Soon she would regain consciousness and visit the hell her meat-eating ways had created for all the poor animals of the solar system. He could still see the puppy fly out of his vegetarian daughter's arms as the bullets riddled her tiny body. He would make sure Jack, Rappel and Indigo Jane joined her there as soon as he had all the robots back under his control. Glad Henri was off on a wild goose chase into the Kuiper belt, Mael-

Jack Cluewitt and the Imbrium Basin Murders Ruth J. Burroughs

strom could now relax a little. Slowly, bits of sanity started to slip into his crazed mind, and he wondered what Jack had injected into his blood and his cyber jack. He couldn't get the chip out. His doctors couldn't either, and were trying to determine what it was. It had powerful antipsychotic properties. His obsession waned, but his heart didn't.

✖

Dr. Rebecca Luna was not a happy grandmother. First of all, Rappel was with two men. One who was not full Japanese and was a mere cook and secondly she'd had a transgendered baby with an atheist American homicide detective while undercover on assignment in deep space. They sat in the kitchen of Rebecca's Martian home, drinking tea.

"But Mom, Organdy is a doctor. He's an organ grower of the highest regard. It's just that he loves sushi. All he ever wanted to be was a cook, his whole life. He's living his dream. He lives for food. And Organdy and I are going to raise Loon-Earth."

"What about Jack?" Rebecca frowned, her arms crossed over her chest. She sat with her daughter and first grandchild in the kitchen of their canyon abode. Smart glass shielded them from dire radiation. But sunshine filtered in, making the room bright and cheerful.

Loon-Earth crawled on the spotless white kitchen floor made from processed Martian sand.

"Jack wants to raise Loon-Earth too. Zero-One is a certified nanny bot, but he has to be re-certified due to the EM bomb that fried his original brain. In the meantime, we're using Immaculata as his legal nanny, since Jack and I are on a case."

"That's a bit dangerous for the child, don't you think?"

"I don't have a choice, Mom."

"You do. You can let him be raised here by regular nanny bots, just like you and your brothers and sisters were."

"No. I want to raise Loon-Earth."

"That's ridiculous. You're not qualified and you'd screw him all up."

"Him-her."

"What?"

"Him-her or her-him. Loon-Earth is both a he and a she."

"Can't you have him assigned a gender?"

"No. She's as much a girl as she is a boy."

"That's confusing."

"Loon-Earth is fine. We're raising him-her as a boy-girl or girl-boy. He-she can choose when she-he's older. It's not for us to decide."

"Darling, how are you going to raise a child and catch criminals at the same time? I didn't approve of the deep cover work you chose to do, and now you want to be a mother?"

"What's wrong with kicking butt and being a good mother at the same time?"

"For one thing, it's illegal; and there are so many certified nanny bots available who are programmed with infinite patience, kindness, and compassion and caring and because of that, it's rare to see mental illness. Tell me. Was this Maelstrom Corrigan raised by robots or people?"

"His parents."

"See. I told you. That's why he's mentally ill."

"A lot of things pushed him over the edge, including a predisposition in his genes."

"And that's another good reason why everyone should be pre-designed. I was. Your father was. You were."

"Yeah, Mom. By Japanese mob! Maybe that's why I'm the way I am. I chose this undercover work because of my designer Yakuza genes. It was either this or the CIA. But I crave being a mother almost as much. I can't change that."

"But you should have designed your baby, like Robert and I did."

"Mom, you adopted me after police officers killed my parents."

"They were Robert's friends. If he'd been part of the force that had been investigating the crime family, he wouldn't have been allowed to adopt you and your older brother. But for the Grace of Earth Mother, you'd have ended up going to your relatives and they were all deeply involved in drugs, prostitution . . . and I think worse, but Robert won't say. But our naturally born children were pre-designed in a dish and given enhancements. You and Jack should have done that."

Jack Cluewitt and the Imbrium Basin Murders   Ruth J. Burroughs

"I'd just almost had my organ stolen. I was on a drug that prevents pregnancy but it didn't work because of the drugs they gave me to change my organs and by the time I knew I was pregnant it was too late."

"Don't even tell me you were thinking of an abortion. We're good friends with the Martian pope. Now we will invite all my friends to the baptism tomorrow and I expect you and Jack to at least be married for that."

"She's not a pope, Mom. She's an abbess."

"Stop splitting nanos. You're tying the knot."

"But Mom, how can I marry Jack? I'm in love with Organdy."

"Well, you should have thought of that before you made a baby. I won't have this baby be born out of wedlock. We're Catholic, child."

"You're not Catholic. Mom. You're an Earth Mother Goddess worshipper. The baby's already been born, Mom, and I can't be married to two people."

"Tell me you're not married to Organdy."

"Not yet. But we are going to be."

"Well, then. You'll just have to settle for a homicide detective instead of your doctor sushi chef. You could have at least told me he was a doctor. I would have been happier if you'd had a child with Organdy, you know. Now. Go get your Jack and get married. We can fix that atheism at some point. And he's loaded, richer than Vasquez and Hofmüller combined. I need to call the Cluewitts to be sure they can make it for both the wedding and the baptismal. Now, should I make out the cards in pink and blue?"

"That, Mother, would be very appropriate and thoughtful of you. But don't forget to invite Rabbi Weather Weiss and detective and firefighter, Ruad Monaghan."

Rebecca smiled. She stood up and kissed her daughter on the head. "Or course. Well, get busy."

Rappel was sure her mother was just thrilled that Jack's family, the Cluewitts, were richer than sin and that Organdy, despite being a doctor wasn't exactly rich. In Rebecca's eyes Organdy was working upper middle class and beneath her daughter's social standing, despite the fact that Robert was a blue collar cop. Robert was also a forensic scientist of the highest caliber and made quite a good

270

living from that as well, but was deeply involved with solving crimes on Mars, of which there were many.

Rappel thought her mother would understand that dual nature, but then how could mothers ever understand their daughters. She looked at Loon-Earth and wondered what kind of gaps might separate her from her daughterson. She couldn't imagine anything that would make them anything but close.

✵

"Hildy would be devastated, not to mention, Organdy." Jack sat next to Rappel on the couch in the bedroom she'd grown up in.

"I don't know what to do. Mom's calling your parents right now and telling them we're getting married today and Loon-Earth's baptism is tomorrow. Jack, I'm Catholic, and my mom is freaking out."

Jack took her hands in his. "I'll get it postponed to next week." Loon-Earth sat in a playpen with his toys next to the princess bed. Rappel tried to get them two separate bedrooms, but Rebecca wouldn't hear of it. In her eyes they were married.

"I'll talk to your father."

"Jack, he's worse. He's going to think you took advantage of me after I almost had an organ ripped from my gut. Plus I was on tranqs. He'll kill you if you don't marry me."

"You could have warned me. You're so independent. I didn't know."

"There's a lot you don't know about me, Jack. It's not like we dated or anything."

"A year is a long time to be away from your boyfriend."

"We may be more than a year and for all I know, he's found someone else. I promised him I would return, but that I might not be able to call. First he finds out I'm an undercover OEA and it hurt him deeply that I didn't tell him. He thought I suspected him. At first I did. When you're in deep cover it's hard not to get involved. Robert. Dad, I mean, told me I would get over him. Dad understands my need to do this line of work. He doesn't approve of it any more than my mom, but he thinks it's because of my Yakuza designer genes that I have a need for dangerous assignments and possibly violent situations—adrenalin junky, you know. Dad's really confused now because of our baby. He doesn't know what to say."

The door chimed.

"Who is it?"

"Immaculata, sir."

"Come in."

Immaculata entered their bedroom. "Time for lunch for the little one."

"Thanks, Immaculata."

"You're welcome. It's my pleasure." Immaculata picked up Loon-Earth and carried the joyful boy-girl out to the kitchen. The door automatically closed behind them.

Jack sat down on the bed. "I have to call Hildy. I'm not sure she'll come to the wedding. I have to tell you I'm not Catholic. I think my parents are Protestants and I think they'll be a little confused. Ruad and Weather will be ok. Weather attends the Catholic Church with him and he goes to Temple with her, so they're both familiar with Catholic concepts. I have no idea how to do this, but I don't want to hurt you or your family."

"Well, by marrying we can keep custody of the child by space law along with Immaculata and Zero-One caring for the child."

"You can keep Immaculata when you go back to Organdy."

Rappel started crying.

"I'm sorry. I didn't mean to make you cry, sweetheart."

"It's just . . . you understand. You're willing to risk your relationship with Hildy, and yet you're willing to marry me and then let me go. You're a really nice guy."

"We needed each other. We need each other. I can only pray Hildy understands. I need you to know I love you too, and if it weren't for Organdy and my promise to take care of you I would have a hard time choosing between you and Hildy. I know you love Organdy more than me. I'm okay with that."

"I loved Organdy, first, not more," Rappel said, crying. Jack took her face in his hands and kissed her. She kissed back.

He pulled off her robe and was immediately hard at the sight of her jumping grasshopper hologram. She smiled.

They enveloped each other and went hard at making another baby.

⚜

Jack called Hildy on the hologram after dinner. She was lounging on a chaise at her father's palatial digs, sipping her requisite one drink per day, a glass of champagne.

"I'm Episcopalian, not Catholic. I'm very spiritual and well. I'm a scientist. That's why I sometimes seem so cold. My dad taught me to be practical. Not to be fooled by love."

"Oh." Jack was flabbergasted.

"Why do you think I own and design all the best sex robots on this side of the Ring of Asteroids? I don't want people losing their place in line to Heaven. And lots of parents buy the sex companions for their hormonal teenagers. Not to mention the company a robot can provide. So how are you planning on having it annulled when Rappel wants to settle down with Organdy on the Moon?"

"Well, first she has to get back to the Moon and talk to Organdy."

"I think she better talk to him sooner. This will be all over the news. You're not an undercover cop, you know."

"She's so independent. I don't understand why, but she insists her parents will think I dishonored her if I don't marry her. It's kind of a shotgun wedding."

"In this day and age?"

"Yes, and her mother told me in no uncertain terms, there will be no prenuptial, so by the time you can have me I may be very poor."

"That's okay, Jack. You saved my robots, and Bane and I are making hand over fist bucks."

Jack coughed. "Aren't you settling for less with me?"

"Love doesn't choose how much you make, Jack. I can't stop loving you, although I've tried. And the fact that you love me back makes it a lot easier. In the meantime, I have my robots."

"Always the practical one, you. How are Vinny and Sally?"

"She's her poetic, artistic self and Vincent is still very much in love with her. He's head of my security now as well. Sally's retired."

"A retired robot?"

"She's half his lifetime's pay. She's worth every penny too."

"So you'll be there? For my wedding?"

"Wouldn't miss it, Jack."

"Okay. I'll see you next week then, my love."

"See you next week."

✖

Loon-Earth was with Immaculata and Rebecca in the nanny bot bedroom. Rebecca thought it best to give Jack and Rappel some privacy and was happy to see Jack looking quite refreshed after their afternoon romp in the sack. Robert had taken Jack up the elevator to watch the Martian sunset. He was very happy to learn Jack was willing to marry his daughter in a Catholic ceremony without a prenuptial and without question. Robert always liked obedience in his children and was very impressed with Jack.

✖

Rappel watched them go up in the glass elevator. Oh, if he only knew what a rebellious and mischievous bad-boy Jack really was. Having sex with her while she was on tranqs. But she'd yearned for Jack for a long time. Since the very first time she'd met him. But then that had been out of the question. As strict as she was, she would never have let that fantasy with him blossom. One side of her was a good girl, and then there were those Yakuza designer genes. At least she had a good excuse for being bad.

She activated the hologram of Organdy. His curly brown hair was not unlike Jack's but everything else was quite French and Japanese.

"Rappel? I thought you might be dead."

"That's no way to greet your future wife," Rappel said.

"Sorry, darling. My strange sense of humor."

"I told you I might be a long time. Did you find someone else?"

"No, of course not. I've been banging French sex robots for a year and they're quite good. I had to buy them though. The renting was getting too expensive."

Rappel knew he wasn't joking, "I'm sorry you had to resort to that, but I'm glad you're waiting."

"Has Jack been taking care of you?"

"Yes, as he promised. But there's a little snag in our plans."

"What's that?"

"Well, I'll be coming back to the Moon a little late."

"Why's that?"

"First . . . Don't hang up, okay?"

"Oh, no. This is bad." Organdy was very sensitive. He was crazy for Rappel and he looked like he was going to be sick.

"It's bad but not that bad. I have to stay in my under-cover identity for a while longer."

"That's not so bad."

"Well. I don't know if you can wait for me. This will be hard for you to hear, but know this, Organdy. I love you. I want to be with you and only you and be a mother to your children forever."

"Why do I hear a *but* in that sentence?"

"Well. Jack and I accidentally had a child. At first I thought it might be yours, but the child looks like Jack. My birth medicine didn't work and by the time I knew I was pregnant it was too late and the child is a Natural. Not a designer like most babies and well, she-he could be not as smart as most people are, but she-he's very beautiful. You'll love her-him."

"Her or him?"

"She-he is a hermaphrodite. It may have been from the Chemistry Harmonics organ fuser that was put in my body when I was kidnapped."

"Kidnapped?"

"I'll tell you when I get back. I'm fine. It was a long time ago and Zero-One saved me. So. Loon-Earth is a little slow and she's a hermaphrodite."

Organdy frowned, squeezing his chin between his thumb and index finger, "Okay. I can deal with that. That's not a problem."

"Okay. Well, the other thing is that I have to get married for a while to Jack. It's part of my OEA deep cover assignment."

"Darling. I'm not stupid. I don't mind raising Jack's challenged child but you don't have to pretend you're undercover as an excuse to be temporarily married. I know your parents would kill you or Jack if you didn't get married. I did a little of my own research after I found out about you. Discreetly I might add. Here I thought I was getting in over my head with a Yakuza girlfriend, but I was in love so I didn't care. It's a relief to know you're a cop, but I don't know if I can live with your desire for danger. Maybe while I'm young."

"I am still supposed to be undercover," Rappel said sheepishly.

"You are so sweet, my darling. I will hump my French bots 'til the cows come home. You do what you need to do and I will wait. But don't be too long, okay? And call me more. I missed you terribly."

"I have a lot of thinking to do, Organdy. I want to raise Loon-Earth with you and have children with you. I can put the OEA career on hold until they're at least in their teens."

"We'll talk about it when you get home. Just tell Jack to bring you back to me safely, or I'll kill him."

"I can do that."

"Okay. I love you. Be careful."

"I love you too, Organdy."

They both air-kissed each other and then Rappel shut the hologram off. Now she had to get ready for a Martian wedding and a baptismal.

<hr/>

Jack and Rappel departed Mars, boarding Cadaver City again to make the journey home to the Moon. Rebecca wanted them to stay, but they told her they had to close the case and if they could arrange work out in Mars space in a few years they would. Robert was pulling some strings to see if he could make that happen.

Weather, who wanted to visit Earth, boarded Cadaver City with Ruad. Her two eldest children, after having met Jack, left planning to see their brother again Near-Earth or on a return trip to Mars.

Jack Cluewitt and the Imbrium Basin Murders Ruth J. Burroughs

⊱✵⊰

Nourishment pumped into Sunny's stomach from a tube. He'd harvested three hearts from her already and had her on rapid organ growth hormone. Tubes went in and out of all the orifices of her body. Next to her was his favorite Brick Cardigan whose skin was stretched as far as it could go and harvested by tiny bots for skin grafts for burn victims.

Slowly her torture forced her to hate meat eaters and want to kill them all. She was glad Brick was being punished. She'd be one of Maelstrom's troops ready to descend upon the masses of space dwellers and force them into vegetarianism or death. She felt her mind slip away.

"Hello, my darling mate. Your Zero-One hero has forgotten you. All of them attended a wedding and forgot to invite you and they're eating meat. All the meat that was hooked up to tubes just like you are now." Maelstrom leaned over and removed the tube from her mouth. She coughed and threw up some of the food. Despite intermittent lucid moments of sanity and feelings of remorse, Maelstrom was still insane, maybe more so for having failed to rule the space worlds just yet, but he wasn't finished. He fought to keep his delusions. He was bringing Cadaver City around to Earth and dumping billions of true Natural dead bodies he'd been saving for the oceans of Earth to feed the billions of fish. Giving back is what he called it, the all Natural Green human food for the fish who'd given billions of their bodies over the millennia to feed humans.

He released the robot controlled ships and sent them to capture billions of meat eaters on Earth. Then he would restore the ecosystems and the oceans back to pre-civilization state. He watched on the hologram as beachgoers on a calm sunny day screamed upon seeing hundreds of human skulls wash up on shore. On another beach a foreign correspondent, wearing a raincoat and gripping an umbrella tightly in the wet wind stood near the shore as a storm raged around him and the waves pounded the concrete barrier. Behind him another storm of human cadavers was being dumped into the Earth's Oceans by Maelstrom's fleet of ancient Chinese robot-guided ships while he narrated.

Jack Cluewitt and the Imbrium Basin Murders   Ruth J. Burroughs

"What are these crazy Americans up to now? The international community is up in arms all across the Orbitals-Grid. The Earth is being invaded by robots and Green Party radicals. Where are International Space Corporation troops now? Aren't they supposed to protect?"

It's about time, Maelstrom thought. *Pay back.* But he needed clones born of his new and holy wife, Vasundhra. Soon she would stand by his side with their children ruling the Commonwealth and protecting the Earth Mother. He would remove almost all the humans from Earth and make it his holy law.

"Maelstrom, is this how the animals feel when they're chained up?"

"Yes, sweetie. Tube fed, tube-impregnated and tube-crapped. All their little babies torn from their breasts before they are properly breast-fed. How are our little veals?"

Then she felt something kicking inside her womb. No. It was more than one kick. Babies. He was cloning babies inside her dormant womb. His babies. This is how the animals felt. He knew she would know how all the little piggies she'd eaten in her fried pork rice dishes had felt. She screamed until she passed out. When she woke, she could hear the click clack of claws on the metal floor of the organ farm. She looked up at the German shepherd robot in the butler suit, smiling.

"Having downloaded some of my memories from a secure feed and some of the latest majordomo programs I'm almost back to myself and I'm at your service mademoiselle."

"Zero-One. I'm hallucinating."

"On the contrary madam, we've found you and we are very pleased. Jack is on his way with Jane."

Moments later, Jack appeared in his burned rain coat, his curly brown hair flopping to the side; Indigo Jane accompanied him, smoking a zeegar; still wearing a space suit. They'd gone around the outside of the Fullerene to get into Maelstrom's secret compartments.

"Zero-One. Get her out of those tubes."

"Yes sir." Zero-One obeyed and delicately helped her out. Jack tore his coat off and wrapped it around Sunny's naked pregnant body.

Jack Cluewitt and the Imbrium Basin Murders   Ruth J. Burroughs

"He'll pay for this," Jack said. The door burst open and Maelstrom, writhing and kicking, burst in, but he was being held by two strange looking Genies. One was very short and had electric blue skin and the other was very tall, with pale skin and hair, and mercurial eyes; both took in impossibly long breaths through what must have been several lungs. They seemed very strong. Sunny shivered and clung to Jack.

"Don't worry. Our genetically engineered skin and nanites aren't contagious." The short blue one's angelic voice vibrated.

The tall yellow one nodded and smiled. Despite being dizzy Sunny noticed he was incredibly handsome when he did that. "Agent Fedorski. He's agent Raynaud. We're arresting one Maelstrom Corrigan for using vials of contagious nanites that have contaminated the Natural antique world. He's broken a dozen federal laws and Title 78 Nanotech Usage, subtitle Nano Software, chapter Chemical Reprogramming, subchapter Controlling or Enslavement through the Use of Nanites, part five, subpart two, section three, subsection eight, paragraph nine, subparagraph one. Thanks go to you and Peg Cardillo for containing this, Jack."

"They don't need space suits," Jane whispered.

Fedorski nodded, "Thanks to you as well, ma'am. We're taking him to the airlock."

"Don't let them take me, Jack. I'm like you. I don't like guns. I'm peaceful. I'm Green. My babies. She's carrying my babies. You can't do this. The medicine you gave me, Jack. I'm better now."

"Speaking of which. You also violated Title 1: The illegal use of a firearm in space, section two of . . ."

"I know, I know, I know the law. My reasons were different. My intent was for the better good of all Earth kind." An explosion tore through the hull and Brick screamed; his bullet that he'd fired twenty-five years ago at Maelstrom ripped through his spinal cord at an impossible speed and then tore through Maelstrom, ripping out all his intestines and blasted through the wall behind them.

Brick died instantly. Jack ran over to Maelstrom and held his head in his lap. "My brother deserved a worse death than that, something slow." Maelstrom coughed blood.

"I know. He was a bad man. But the fates were merciful and space junk took him from your hands."

"And me too. It's not fair."

"No. It's not fair. But you got what you wanted. You'll be feeding the fish. We would have never found you if you hadn't shown your hand."

"You'll take care of my babies, Sunny's babies, Jack. Promise."

"I can't, Maelstrom."

"Name them Jeremy and Geoseffa, after my children, promise."

"Okay. I promise," Jack said, and Maelstrom breathed his last breath and died.

The tall Genie leaned over and closed Maelstrom's eyes, then took the body from Jack's arms.

"We'll place his Natural remains in the Earth Ocean," Raynaud said.

"I think he'd like that," Jack said, standing up.

Sunny cried. She wanted to hug the Genies for saving her, but she hugged Jack instead.

Per aspera ad astra
Chapter Twenty-One

Jack sat at the kitchen table reading aloud, *For Whom the Bell Tolls,* by Ernest Hemmingway, to Loon-Earth. Rappel sat next to him, knitting a sweater. She wasn't sure where the urge to knit came from, but was certain it had nothing to do with her Yakuza genes. *Well, you never know,* she thought. *Perhaps some mobster's grandma liked to knit.*

"Why don't you start him out on *A Farewell to Arms* first, darling? Don't you think that one's a bit advanced?"

"I think he'll like both." Loon-Earth crawled down off Jack's lap and picked up a copy of *The Cat in the Hat,* brought it over to his-her father and dropped it in his hands. Loon-Earth turned and toddled around on the kitchen floor Immaculata had immaculately cleaned. Occasionally Loon-Earth fell on his-her rear end but was soon up and climbing from one piece of furniture to another. He-she looked very much like Jack.

"We'll be coming into near Earth orbit in five hours. Organdy has a shuttle ready for us."

"Does he know Weather and Ruad are coming?"

"Yes."

"I'm going to bring Zero-One to the Moon City Mare Frigoris Robot Hospital for his brain restoration surgery as soon as we land."

"I know. I'll meet you at Organdy's for dinner."

Jack kissed her on the lips. "I'll see you later."

"Daddy. Kiss," Loon-Earth said. Jack bent down and gave Loon-Earth a kiss on the lips.

✄

While Zero-One recovered in Moon City Mare Frigoris Robot Hospital, Jack drove a solar powered Humvee through

Jack Cluewitt and the Imbrium Basin Murders   Ruth J. Burroughs

the regolith of the Imbrium Basin toward the Valles Alpes Rille. Jack found Jane's eighteen month old zeegar butt. He picked it up and had it analyzed for radiation. He threw it back out.

"No good. Though I'm sure it's still fresh, I won't even bother to remove the radiation from it. Too costly."

"That's okay. I don't want glowing lungs. I bought Texan zeegars with my old sapphire teeth back in Moon City," Jane said.

"I like seeing you with regular teeth."

"I thought you would. Maddie liked my teeth jewelry."

"Yeah, she would. I don't suppose you'll be getting tattoos, skin grafts, bone grafts and piercings next."

"Your wife has a tattoo."

"More than one, but she was born with those."

"Well, my designer babies will be born with tatts too."

The Valles Alpes Rille crime scene looked like a ghost town with abandoned machinery strewn haphazardly about.

Jack studied the holographic diagram of the footprints leading in and out of the mine. "These are Apache and Cavity's prints and those footprints belong to Jules. Gretel Roux still believes Jules, not Sally, killed the Green Police."

"Why would Jules kill the Green Police?"

"He wouldn't. But Roux thinks it was because Jules was working for Maelstrom. He must have known about the organ stealing ring, and he had that expensive coffee Henri gave him to keep quiet."

"Jules had to have been paid more than that," Jane said.

"You're right, by Jove. Those mining men love their robot dogs as much as I love Zero-One and I'd do anything to keep him going. Imagine if I weren't wealthy enough to do so. But I think Maelstrom had no idea Jules would get his robot dogs back. That was the canine wrench in the mix that flummoxed the murderous plot. Bane Hofmüller's wrench that is; he was the one who gave Jules money to get the dogs out because he'd figured out it was Maelstrom who'd gotten the robot dogs locked up.

Hildy didn't know Maelstrom had dosed Sally S. Queue with that vial of nano software that reprogrammed Sally to kill the Greepols for the book, and that's why we didn't find

282

a radio frequency controlling her. Hildy didn't do it, just like she said. Maelstrom had pre-programmed the nanites to act just like him. All the robots would have been under his rule if we hadn't stopped him. If Peg hadn't had the forethought to realize he was going to reprogram them our robots would be acting like Maelstrom now. I think Jules is on the run because he was bribed, not because he has any idea who murdered the Green Police. As I said, Bane Hofmüller gave Jules the money to get the dogs out of hock. Bane knew Maelstrom was up to something, and they were both after the book. All Jules cared about was that he'd have enough money for his robot dogs and that Jovian coffee."

"How are we going to prove it, Jack?"

"Maelstrom confessed, and there's proof from the GM humans that he poisoned the robots with nanites in order to control them. Jules didn't do it like Roux thinks. Sally was murdered by Maelstrom with the EM bomb, but I have a feeling Hildy got rid of any memories of Sally murdering the Greepols long before that, so Hildy will get off since she's pretending she had no idea."

"Well, I'm glad you're filing the report. Let's get out of here."

"Will do, Indigo." Jack turned the Humvee around and headed back to Moon City.

<hr>

Jack found Gretel Roux in the coroner's office with the robot, Sydney Atrax, on the gurney his gem-cell-drive brain being cleaned of the Maelstrom nano software and re-evaluated for field work by Cal's crew.

"I've come back for my payment, Gretel."

"What makes you think you won, Jack?"

"I found the perpetrator: Maelstrom Corrigan. I have the evidence that he used the robot Sally S. Queue to kill the Green Police while disguised as several different individuals including me and Niall Heaton. You lose."

"Not really, Jack. We both win when we close a case. But I think you're wrong. I think Hildy did it with her Raygun."

Jack rolled his eyes. "Really, Ms. Roux? Hildy Witter Raygun did it with her Raygun?" Jack smirked.

Jack Cluewitt and the Imbrium Basin Murders   Ruth J. Burroughs

"Don't interrupt. She framed Sally S. Queue and she's in collusion with Jules Helphenstein. I may even prove you had something to do with it to cover your girlfriend's guilt in the crime. I also wonder why your perp is conveniently dead."

"Well, that's what you get for relying on the Grid and robots for your information instead of your mind and old-fashioned gumshoe investigation techniques."

"The case may be closed, Jack, but I'll spend the rest of my life trying to pin it on you and make sure Sydney Atrax or some other robot replaces you."

"Go ahead. Waste your time when there are thousands of cases out there needing our undivided attention. Go plug yourself in."

Jack walked out. He hadn't bet her anything of substance, and for all her cyberware, she wouldn't concede when she'd lost.

Zero-One was so happy to see Jack, even though he wasn't so little any more. When he'd woken after twenty-five years, it had seemed like yesterday when he was playing with five-year-old Jack in Hilda Group Bucky Ball, out in the Ring of Stones near Jupiter. And then the disaster had happened and Weather had taken him out of the puppy body and stored him in a box for over twenty-five years; not that he'd noticed, he'd been asleep. Jack restored him to an adult body in the middle of the fight with Maelstrom, and they'd begun a new adventure. Weather had kept his puppy memories and brain cell intact and now he was going to absorb another personality, one he'd worn in this robot body for twenty-five years, but of whom he knew little, who may as well be a stranger. It was a designer brain, too, though nothing that Weather or Ruad could have ever afforded, and one that was very clever. The doctors thought not knowing much about the other Zero-One would be easier for him. Despite his pleasant puppy demeanor, he was very anxious about the new personality, which he'd heard wasn't so carefree and meant a kind of death for his puppy, loyal-dog persona, which he really didn't want to part with. But he couldn't tell that to Jack. Jack loved this new Zero-One,

284

or rather old Zero-One butler, and Zero-One of the past would do anything to make Jack happy, even if it meant dying again. So he submitted to the operation, but when he woke it was far better than he'd ever thought it would be. His worries had been for naught. It was merely as if his memories of the past twenty-five years had been restored. The puppy memories and the butler memories melded and the two brains became one.

***

Jack had been gone a little over a year, but when he reached the Earth-Moon system he was off by a month. All the Earth time calendars said they'd only been gone fifteen months. So Rappel and Jack had a hard time figuring out when Loon-Earth was born. Even though he was born March 10th, 5030, that was by space ship time leaving Earth, and as the ship moved away from Earth the clocks no longer synchronized. But how could they be off by a whole month? They weren't traveling that fast. Ruad said these types of time discrepancies happened all the time and that's why there were police for different jurisdictions over the whole Grid. But it wasn't unusual to have a moving jurisdiction when you're in pursuit of a criminal.

The other question was, could Jack get his land legs back, and would Weather be able to stand the gravity on Earth? They all had to wear the robot gravity suits. Many people in space and on Earth envied their dual status.

Jack watched as Zero-One played ball with Loon-Earth out on the terrace. All of his robot dog's butler personality had returned, but with the addition of a more friendly, puppy-like attitude, probably because there were two brains inside his majordomo. Immaculata was painting an impressionistic version of Loon-Earth playing with Zero-One on the veranda. She had already made a Caravaggiesque style painting of Weather and Ruad. He was thinking of hiring another maid, since he'd earned quite a few Green credits.

Rappel knitted a pair of booties, one pink and one blue. She was going to return to JoMars space soon and help Peg get her robots and Oort Explore-bot ships back. Loon-Earth and Immaculata were going to stay on the Moon with Organdy for the time-being. Jack and Indigo closed the

Jack Cluewitt and the Imbrium Basin Murders   Ruth J. Burroughs

case on the Greepol murders with an arrest warrant out for Jules, but many people didn't believe he was the true killer of Jara. Some were still trying to pin it on the dead Sally S. Queue, and some even thought Jack was a suspect. For now Hildy got out of it with strings pulled by her rich step-dad, Bane Hofmüller.

Jack noticed the Earth suits had improved tremendously in the fifteen months he'd been gone. He got ready to leave the Octopods to go visit Pops with his new family. John and Marilyn Cluewitt had business in space and would come down the well in a month or two. Zero-One seemed to be limping.

"What's the matter, boy?"

"Gravity stresses my joints, too. Pushed down against this wide Earth, our lives go quickly."

"Yes, I agree. In space life is slower, freed from the gravity of time."

Loon-Earth toddled over in a baby carbon-gravity-suit and gave Zero-One and Jack a clumsy kiss, still not used to his-her own Earth weight. Zero-One picked him-her up and handed him-her to Immaculata.

Like tiny ants, people were rollerblading, skateboarding and biking on the colorful nano-built freeways for pedestrians as Jack looked on from above them. Carefree players who'd grown up with this technology thought nothing of their anti-gravity-like play on the thin interface of magnetic fields, the Thinner Rails.

A post-industrial, pastoral view rolled out beneath the spider-like feet of the nano-built Octopod structures like a rug stitched with bright maples, blue spruce and evergreen trees and dotted with old white, vinyl-sided homes, intersected by warehouses and crisscrossed by old roads, now used only by people allowed down on the earth.

The great Octopod living quarters for millions of Near Earth Citizens, were for those who choose not to live against the ground because they spent so much time in space. A mix of stark technological architecture full of the constant glare of advertising, now it brimmed with trees, gardens, lakes, waterfalls and wildlife because the Green Party laws enforced ubiquitous ecosystems.

He opened the patio door and showed Weather, Ruad and Rappel where to step out on to the Thinner Rail. Indigo

Jane and Zero-One followed behind them. They waited for him to go first and he did. The wind whipped at his lapels in the hot August air as he slid down the tentacle, sliding down around the wind tunnel the kids were screaming in, and over the flower gardens, zipping past the high-risk sports and into the off-traffic flow for pedestrians. The Thinner Rail curved into the flats, and he stepped onto the old concrete sidewalk. He waited for his space family to land, watching them hold on to the handles, as if for dear life, screaming joyfully in the happy sunshine, under a blue sky.

It was hard going as he helped them learn to walk, putting one foot forward, but they all grew impatient and turned on the carbon-gravity-suits' automated features. Faster was better, and they got to the quay of the Hudson River quickly. Otherwise, it would have taken them all day. Everyone wore some kind of cyberware or robotic assistance for fun, not just for need, so they didn't stand out much.

The interior of the used robots and toys store sparkled like the landscape of the moon in a thick silvery dust, like centuries of undisturbed regolith waiting for someone to defy gravity and buy something.

A real fine layer of dust covered an odd assortment of old gadgets, gold and silver toys of every twist and turn. It lay undisturbed, as footprints on the moon, on strangely arrayed piles of paperback books and antique robots scattered about, frozen and lifeless. It even seemed to cover the old man dozing in the corner, his chair tilted against the wall, under a domed skylight.

Jack opened the manual door, jingling the bells, and stepped inside, and Zero-One, Rappel, Weather and Ruad followed, their combined weight making the old hardwood floor boards creak.

Pops sat in a chair near the counter, not unlike the day Jack first met him; dappled sunlight flowed in through the windows and glinted off his gold spectacles.

"Well, what did I do to deserve another visit from you, young fellow? I hope you're not returning anything." Pops lit a cigar and offered him one.

"I don't smoke. Jane and Ruad do though," Jack said, and Pops handed the indigo-haired cop a cigar; she gratefully accepted. Then he handed one to Ruad.

Jack grimaced. "Well, I should give you back your Daisy Zooka Pop gun. I don't deserve it."

"You solved your case didn't you, Jack?" Pops set his cigar down in a sandbag-anchored ashtray and leaned back in his chair, pulled his spectacles off his head and cleaned them with a white silk handkerchief. Rusty emerged from the back, wiping black super conductive robot oil off his hands with an old rag.

"Well, yes, I did—we did. Gretel Roux thinks Jules Helphenstein had a hand in it, but the real mastermind was Maelstrom Corrigan."

"But I thought Hildy did it, with her Raygun?"

Jack smiled. "Ha, ha, ha. No. It was to some extent done by her robot."

"Are you saying Sally S. Queue killed the Green Police?"

"Yes and no. She was re-programmed with Maelstrom's nanites to steal the book at all cost. It was a small push to her original program. Tell me, Pops; are you a robot or a human being?"

"I'm really old, like you guessed. There is very little left of my original brain housed inside, but most of it is uploaded into this robot's genetically engineered molecular cell drive. I was born in 1945. I could live forever."

"Trust me. It's not forever, I was killed. Or I would have been if it weren't for my backup brain. I've lost a year's worth of memories," Zero-One said.

"True. Nothing material is forever, but one of those Cold Fusion coins has kept me going."

"I wanted give you back this coin. It's caused me too much trouble."

"Well, I'm surprised Weather didn't tell you what it was. I'm glad you didn't lose it. C'mon. Follow me."

"He'll know soon enough," Weather said.

Pops hobbled through the curtained back door into the hallway to the robot warehouse. Jack and his retinue followed.

Inside was a giant rocket ship decked out in golden dragons and Chinese symbols.

"After World War I, the Office for Strategic Services suspected the Chinese had space flight and sent spies over there. Officially, the Chinese don't—or didn't realize they

Jack Cluewitt and the Imbrium Basin Murders   Ruth J. Burroughs

did. This is China's first spaceship made during the Qing Dynasty. Its outer shell is gold like the yellow flag of the Qing. The rocket ship design was invented by the Chinese during the Ming dynasty, or about the same time gunpowder was discovered and after cannon or gun manufacture. But their attempts at launching it proved fatal, and for a time they deemed it a waste of resources. But between that time and the 1600s, their chemists worked on improving the rocket fuel and discovered liquid oxygen long before the western civilization did. They were launching manned rocket ships into space long before there was radar to detect them.

"Over time they never revealed it to the world, but kept it from the Nationalists and the Communists when the Qing dynasty came to an end. A secret society of alchemists and scientists kept going into space. To keep it simple, the OSS called this society of advanced space travelers from the Qin Dynasty, Varunas, the Sanskrit Vedic name for *Water God;* they settled near Neptune in the Kuiper belt, mining water from the asteroids for LOX—liquid oxygen—in order to power their golden imperial rocket ships. They developed a liquid plasma shield to reduce radiation and from those studies they invented Cold Fusion, sometimes called Cold Plasma. There is no need for currency in space, but they used ancient Chinese coins in the process of making Cold Fusion to power their ships, as LOX can be very dangerous. Though the golden rocket ships can be fueled by LOX, the newer ones are fueled by the Chinese coins with the dark matter, the Cold Fusion."

"So it's not alien fuel. It was invented by the Chinese?"

"Yes. My dad worked for OSS during and after World War II. There was this little known OSS program called Operation Paperclip, in which German rocket science engineers were brought to the U.S. to develop classified space exploration, without sharing it with the world . . ."

"Wait, wait . . . How can you be that old?" Jack asked.

"There's some brain left, but this is a robot body, Jack. Operation Rocket Ship was so classified that anyone speaking of the fact that we were in space long before the Sputnik and the Soviet Union would have been silenced quickly. My father, along with the OSS, discovered the hidden Varuna base on the moon. Because our space exploration hadn't

289

Jack Cluewitt and the Imbrium Basin Murders Ruth J. Burroughs

been publicized, the Varunas weren't expecting us, and we were able to overpower them and steal their technology. Their moon base had three golden rocket ships, but only one saucer shaped vehicle. My father learned how to pilot all of the vehicles, but they were unable to reverse engineer the Cold Fusion that pulsated inside the Chinese coins. The OSS were able to explore far and wide in space due to the capacity and power of the engines.

Because we couldn't transmit the highly classified information across the radio waves back then, it was nano-coded into paper books for secrecy. My father was with those few OSS agents who discovered the Varuna settlement near Neptune, and he embedded the location of all the ships and outposts in the Kuiper belt into the pages of that edition of *The Worlds in Space,* written by Martin Caidin and published in 1954. On their way back with the information, they were sabotaged by the Varunas remotely manipulating the fuel to jump drive. At the time we didn't know the Cold Fusion was capable of that kind of speed. They sent the ships straight into the Asteroid field. After sabotaging my father and his men so we couldn't find their outpost, they retreated from Near-Earth space so we couldn't detect them. So we lost this technology until Weather found it again.

The Varunas didn't want to be found. With the death of my father and his men and the loss of the Chinese coins, the golden rocket ships and the saucer vehicle, the CIA was only able to secretly colonize moon and Mars space with known materials, metals and LOX. But we knew they were out there somewhere.

We've developed shields around our fuel now to prevent them from manipulating the drives in the saucer ship we recovered and the ones Peg recreated.

Weather found my father's body inside the saucer vehicle stuck into the asteroid 253 Mathilde, along with two of his fellow astronauts. She contacted her friend and well-known roboticist Peg Cardillo and gave her everything she'd discovered. My father had identification on him; Charles P. Van de Woestyne, and Peg contacted me, knowing I was either CIA or the like, and she recognized the OSS shoulder insignia on my father's space suit. Between the two of us, we figured out what the code meant and made paper copies

Jack Cluewitt and the Imbrium Basin Murders Ruth J. Burroughs

of the location of the Varuna Colony in the Kuiper Belt. We gave Weather the book back for safe keeping.

Weather kept the book because it was a map to where the rockets and saucers were hidden in the Kuiper belt. The book *The Worlds in Space,* was partially factual.

When we started publicly colonizing space in the three thousands, we had to send a lot of misinformation back to Earth, especially since everything was already up and running.

Weather sent the book with you, Jack, so it wouldn't get into Corporation hands. Peg and I had been working on the rocket ships, the saucer and the map before and after Jack was born. Peg and I rescued Weather and Ruad. When you brought me the book here in my shop, I realized you were Jack Weiss Monaghan. While you were growing up a Cluewitt, Peg and I took the coin and the saucer vehicle with the information from the coded book and recreated the three golden rocket ships based on the mangled ships. We were able to extrude the three Cold Fusion power coins from the crushed ships and integrate them into the new ones. They've been visiting us for a long time. Peg's robots pilot two of the golden rocket ships, and the saucer that's powered by the Cold Fusion."

"That's some story, Pops," Jack said.

"Well, I have no use for outer space and I don't want to meet the Varunas who killed my father. Know anyone who could use this ship, Jack?"

"I could use it. Jane and I will be getting EMMA JO, Earth-Moon-Mars and Jupiter gold shields."

"Well. Go ahead then, Jack. She's yours. Do you still have the Daisy Zooka Pop gun you coveted?"

"Of course, Pops."

"I know. It's like a nice lady. Can't leave without her, can't afford her. So did Hildy do it with the Raygun?"

"I wish people would stop saying that. No, Maelstrom killed the Green Police using Hildy's robot, Sally S. Queue," Jack said. Pops handed the gold Chinese coin back to him.

"Just hop on board the rocket ship and go inside. You'll see where to place the Cold Fusion coin. Despite everything being in Chinese, I think you can figure it out. Where are you going?"

Jack Cluewitt and the Imbrium Basin Murders   Ruth J. Burroughs

"Someplace with nice weather," Indigo Jane said and hopped aboard. She was glad to be going back out to space and away from Earth's gravity and curious to check out the golden antique Chinese space ship. Weather and Ruad were quick behind, and Rappel and Zero-One waited patiently for Jack.

"I heard you had a kid."

"Yup. He's with Immaculata. You're welcome to visit him in my apartment in the Octopods." Jack activated a hologram of Loon-Earth from his watch.

"Cute baby. I'll do that. Have a good trip, Jack."

"Thanks . . . Pops."

Rappel smiled and waved, and Jack thanked him, then they moved on into the ship. Zero-One was the last to board and closed the ornate dragon door from inside. Jane remotely opened the roof hatch and daylight poured in. The quiet Cold Fusion huffed, trembled and hummed. Slowly the golden dragon ship quietly hovered and then lifted up and out of Pops' Used Robots and Toys Store, its tiny white tail smoking behind it into the glorious blue sky.

"Per aspera ad astra: Through hardships to the stars . . ."

About the Author

Inspired by Dodie Smith's *Starlight Barking,* the sequel to the more famous spotted dog book *Hundred and One Dalmatians,* Ruth has been writing science fiction since the age of 13. She is an award-winning artist and holds a Bachelor of Science degree in Studio Art from the College of St. Rose. She works and lives near Ithaca, New York with her mutts, Grizzly and Rudeebega

WEBSITE:
http://mareimbriumdowns.wordpress.com/about/
TWITTER: https://twitter.com/UrthJeenColvil
FACEBOOK:
https://www.facebook.com/ruth.burroughs.1
BLOG: http://mareimbriumdowns.wordpress.com/
OTHER: http://isleburroughs.livejournal.com

CPSIA information can be obtained
at www.ICGtesting.com
Printed in the USA
BVHW070240050122
625522BV00005B/97